D1711575

ICE

A Chris Matheson
Cold Case Mystery

by
Lauren Carr

ICE

All Rights Reserved © 2018 by Lauren Carr

Published by Acorn Book Services

For information, call: 304-995-1295
or e-mail: writerlaurencarr@gmail.com.

Designed by Acorn Book Services

Publication Managed by Acorn Book Services
www.acornbookservices.com
acornbookservices@gmail.com
304-995-1295

Cover designed by Todd Aune
Spokane, Washington
www.projetoonline.com

ISBN-10: 1983743380
ISBN-13: 978-1983743382

Published in the United States of America

ICE

A CHRIS MATHESON
COLD CASE MYSTERY

CAST OF CHARACTERS

The Geezer Squad

Christopher Matheson (Chris): Single father of three girls. Lost his wife in terrorist attack in France. After his father's sudden death, he retires from FBI and moves to family farm in Harpers Ferry, West Virginia.

Elliott Prescott: Founding member of the Geezer Squad. He could tell you what he did before he retired, but then he'd have to kill you.

Jacqui Guilfoyle: Retired medical examiner from Pennsylvania. Widow with no children. Lives alone in elegant home on a mountaintop overlooking Shenandoah Valley.

Ray Nolan: Established cyberwarfare task force after 9/11. Retired from Homeland Security after he took a bullet in the back from a home-grown terrorist. Lives with his daughter and her family.

Bruce Harris: Retired attorney general from Virginia. He owns a winery in Purcellville, Virginia. His wife is an architect with her own firm in Leesburg. Has son in college.

Francine Duncan: Retired investigative journalist from the Associated Press. Divorced children and grandchildren living with her.

Characters in Order of Appearance

Sandy Lipton: Twenty-four years ago, this eighteen-year-old woman and her unborn child disappeared.

Carson Lipton: Sandy's older brother. Cook at family's diner located across street from racetrack.

Ethel Lipton: Sandy's mother. Owns apartment complex and greasy spoon diner.

Emma (6 yrs old), Nikki (10 yrs old) and Katelyn (13 yrs old): Chris Matheson's daughters.

Traveler: Chris's gray Thoroughbred. Retired race horse.

Sadie (Doberman) and Mocha (golden Labrador): Sadie was a retired law enforcement canine, trained in security. Mocha was a retired search and rescue dog. Doris Matheson's entourage.

Thor: Female fifteen-pound tan and white rabbit with long floppy ears. Usually seen wearing frilly pink clothes.

Doris Matheson: Chris's widowed mother and grandmother to his daughters. Her late husband was Kirk Matheson, captain of the West Virginia State Police's local troop. Director of the Bolivar-Harpers Ferry Public Library.

ICE

Sterling: Two-year old German shepherd. Law enforcement canine. Retired after surviving ambush in which his handler was killed. Elliott and Doris were told that he was goofy. They don't know what that means.

Peyton Davenport: Daughter of Mason Davenport. Vice President of Security at Stardust Casino and Races.

Mason Davenport: CEO of Stardust Casino and Races.

Sierra Clarke: Sixteen-year-old high school student. Part-time employee at the library. Her mother is Helen Clarke.

Helen Clarke: Lieutenant with the West Virginia State Police, in charge of the local homicide division. Divorced. Chris's first love. Sierra's mother.

Mona Tabler: Murder victim. Restaurant manager at the Stardust. Divorced. No children. Lived in big house in Shepherdstown.

Shirley Rice: Murder victim. Member of Berkeley County Commission. Lived in Martinsburg.

Opie Fletcher: Murder Suspect. Confessed to killing Mona Tabler, but never arrested.

Victor Sinclair: Jefferson County Prosecutor. Had a crush on Sandy Lipton in high school. His father is Steve Sinclair.

Steve Sinclair: Powerful business lawyer. Mason Davenport has him on retainer.

Rodney Bell: Jefferson County Deputy Sheriff. Chris's childhood friend.

Felicia Bell: Rodney's estranged wife. Dated Chris in high school. Helen Clarke's childhood friend.

Sheriff Grant Bassett: Jefferson County Sheriff. Rodney's boss.

Tommy Bukowski: Murder victim. Cybercrime expert working with an organized crime family. Body found on Matheson farm.

Regina Patterson: FBI agent leading investigation into Tommy Bukowski's murder. Chris's former boss.

Dr. Frederic Poole: Medical doctor. Treated Sandy Lipton during her pregnancy. Chairman of the local pregnancy center.

Tamara Wilcox: Pregnant woman dropped off at Jefferson Medical Center. Died during childbirth.

Angela Romano: Murder victim in Lancaster, Pennsylvania. Divorced three times.

Carla Pendleton: Murder victim from Mount Airy, Maryland. Widow.

Patricia Handle: Murder victim. Administrative assistant with the federal government. Never married.

Rachel Pine: Director of Cybersecurity at the Stardust Casino and Races.

Seth Greene: Driver at Stardust Casino and Races.

The wise man must remember that while he is a descendant of the past, he is a parent of the future.

Herbert Spencer

PROLOGUE

Charles Town, West Virginia - Twenty-Four Years Ago

"I get it. It's cold," Sandy Lipton told the meteorologist on the news. "That's why I'm inside where it's nice and warm. Like why do I need to watch you shivering outside and telling me that I should be inside because it's freezing?" Snickering at how clever she sounded to herself, she shoved her hand down between the cushions of the threadbare sofa to find the remote to change the television channel.

During the search, the baby inside her stomach kicked as if to object to her waking it up.

"Sorry," she said while rubbing her plump tummy. "I'm sure you'll be much more comfortable next week after you come out and we officially meet." She aimed the remote at the television and changed the channel to a daytime court program.

Across the street, a steady stream of vehicles arrived at the Sure Thing Diner, the most popular lunch spot for jockeys, trainers, and other employees of the Charles Town Races' stables.

Her family owned and operated the greasy spoon and the apartment complex behind their home.

With a cringe, Sandy hoped her mother wouldn't leave the lawyer's office until after the lunch time rush had finished. It was difficult enough for her brother, Carson, to cook meals for a diner full of hungry patrons without Ethel Lipton showing up to push his buttons.

No one put Carson in a bad mood faster than their mother.

The memory of Carson's face, twisted with fury, flashed through Sandy's mind. Her heart flipped and then flopped. She clutched her chest until the pain subsided.

That's been happening a lot lately.

Sandy rubbed her stomach. She was in no condition to be on her feet waiting tables so close to her due date.

She could barely manage the apartment complex. The convenient location, inexpensive rent, and month-to-month leasing made The Sure Thing Apartments the go-to for the transient racetrack crowd that frequented the Charles Town Races, the biggest thing in the West Virginia town.

Named after George Washington's brother, Charles Town fought to cling to its colonial atmosphere. The state's eastern panhandle had become a magnet for escapees from Virginia's and Maryland's metropolitan areas. Train service and highways made commuting easy for families working in and around the nation's capital to take advantage of living in the Shenandoah Valley.

Nestled just outside the Charles Town city limits, the Thoroughbred racetrack hoped to play a role in the area's growth. It had no choice. Dwindling attendance drove the high caliber horses to more popular tracks. Lack of revenue meant fewer employees, which had a direct effect on tenants in the apartment complex and patrons at the diner.

The frigid wind outside and bare trees against the gray sky foretold a future that sent a chill down Sandy's spine. She pushed herself up from the sofa and waddled into the kitchen.

Catching a glimpse of her reflection in the mirror in the back of the china closet, Sandy stopped. Chris Matheson would have made some sort of joke if he could see her long skinny arms and legs and pregnant stomach. She smiled softly.

I miss Chris.

The baby tickled her insides. Lovingly, she rubbed her hands across her stomach and giggled. The baby must have also seen her. He or she must have a sense of humor like Chris.

The sound of a car engine in front of the house prompted her to check the time. Eleven-thirty.

Mom must have finished her meeting with the lawyer. Strange that she would meet with him about the paternity suit without me.

She had enough hope to think that her visitor could have been Chris. The possibility was remote, but it was enough to spur her to run to the door. Just as quickly as the thought crossed her mind, reality set in.

As mad as Chris had been the day before, he'd never come back.

A wave of remorse washed over her when she recalled the fury in his gray eyes.

At least he's alive. That's what counts the most.

Sandy checked her reflection in the foyer mirror. The pregnancy had wreaked havoc with her complexion. It didn't do much good with her hair either. What had once been chestnut had dissolved into the color of dull dark ash. It would all be over in one more week. She wondered how long it would take her body to return to its former slender shape. At eighteen years old, she had youth on her side.

Sandy ran her fingers through her limp hair. The doorbell chimes startled her. She peeked out the window to see a man holding a bouquet so big that the flowers hid his face.

Her heart leapt. Once again, hope washed over her.

It's Chris after all! He's thought things over and will give me a chance to explain.

Sandy yanked open the door. A blast of freezing air hit her in the face. Blinking, she shielded her face with her hand against the icy sleet pelting her. While waiting for the wind to subside, she fantasized that when her vision cleared, Chris with his steely gray eyes would be before her to take her into his arms and declare his undying love.

The wintry blast subsided. Sandy Lipton's vision cleared and her fantasy turned into an icy nightmare.

CHAPTER ONE

Present Day

"Good bye, my dear friend."

The icy winter wind blew across the hilltop to nip at Chris Matheson's nose and cheeks. The bare branches of the oak tree behind him danced as if to take part in the memorial ceremony.

As their aged leader had often done before them, the Doberman and golden Labrador contemplated the farm down below. Even Traveler, Chris's gray dapple Thoroughbred, hung his head in a show of respect for their departed friend.

"Winston, you were such a good, brave, and loyal friend. We all miss you so much. We'll never forget you."

Chris grasped the lid of the urn and pried it off. The wind immediately took hold of some ashes to scatter them like dark snowflakes across the field. With the back of his hand, he wiped away the tears of remorse and cold from his eyes. He sprinkled the ashes of his beloved German shepherd under the tree that had been his favorite spot from which to watch over his domain.

When he had finished, Chris put the lid back on the urn, stuffed it into the saddlebag, and climbed up onto his horse.

The ceremony over, Sadie, the Doberman, and Mocha, the Labrador, headed off to the farmhouse. Retired law enforcement canines, they preferred the warmth and comfort of the indoors.

Chris looked out across the farm, one hundred and fifty acres of hills, forest, and pastures that had been in his family for three generations. A tree lined road ran along the Shenandoah River at the bottom of the hill.

He spotted the yellow roof of a Jefferson County school bus up the road. The icy cold tingling the back of his hands and cheeks forewarned of a snow storm mixed with ice brewing. Many speculated that the schools would be closed the next day. If Chris failed to meet the bus at the end of the lane, the driver would return his daughters to the elementary school. Then, he'd have to go to the school to pick them up.

Chris urged Traveler to gallop down to the bottom of the hill and make a sharp right. As the bus neared the stop at end of their lane, he leaned forward in the saddle to urge Traveler to catch up. The children on board shrieked with delight at the impromptu race.

His ten-year-old daughter Nikki was the loudest. "That's my dad!" she said to the bus driver before hopping down the steps.

Chris dismounted to give her a quick hug and kiss. Anxious to enjoy a horseback ride, Nikki shoved her backpack into her father's hands and climbed up onto Traveler.

His youngest child, Emma took longer to disembark.

A widower, Chris and his three daughters had returned to the family home six months earlier. Already, the pretty blond-haired girl with a wide toothy smile was the most popular second grader at Blue Ridge Elementary.

"You be sure to get home before the ice storm comes, Mrs. Brady," Emma was saying when Chris arrived at the door to hurry her along. "I'd hate for you to have an accident."

"Thank you, Emma," Mrs. Brady said.

"Mrs. Murphy says that the bridges freeze first. Did you know that?"

"Emma," Chris said, "Mrs. Brady knows how to drive a bus. She knows all about the bridges." He held his hand out to the little girl clad in a pink coat with matching boots, hat, and gloves.

"What do you have to do to become a bus driver? What's that?" She reached for a button on the dashboard.

Chris lunged up the steps, threw his arms around his daughter, and carried her off the bus. Laughing, the children waved good-bye to her.

Nikki had input the security code on the keypad to open the metal gate securing the lane leading up to the red-brick farmhouse. By the time Chris carried Emma off the bus, she was leading Traveler into the barn.

Even though Nikki had grown up in the suburbs of northern Virginia, she had been riding horses since she was old enough to walk. Her first words were, "I want a pony." In spite of her slight frame, the ten-year-old had yet to meet a horse she couldn't handle.

"Hey, Daddy," Emma asked her father after he secured the gate, "what's Bastille Day?"

Chris cleared his throat before answering. "That's a French holiday. Pretty much like our Fourth of July. Why do you ask?"

"I overheard one of the parents asking Mrs. Murphy if it was true that Mommy was killed on Bastille Day."

"What did Mrs. Murphy say?"

"I didn't hear. She shushed the lady and looked like this at her." Emma scrunched up her face, narrowed her eyes, and furrowed her brow to make an amusing expression.

In spite of the topic, Chris had to laugh.

"It wasn't a selfie moment." She gave her head such a firm shake that her hat fell off. Chris picked it up from the frozen ground and knelt to put it back on her head. "Is it true that terrorists killed Mommy?"

He gazed into her big blue eyes—so much like her mother's. Emma's bubbly personality was another trait she had inherited from her. "Yes, honey. Mommy was killed in a terrorist attack."

"Why did they decide to take my mommy away, Daddy?"

"Because there are some people who are just plain evil. They do evil things."

"But isn't it your job to catch them? Why don't you arrest them, Daddy?"

"Because…" Chris stopped and sighed. "How do I explain this?" He swallowed. "It was hard after your mommy died for me to take care of all of you."

"But you took care of us before those evil people killed Mommy."

"Yes, I did," Chris said. "She was supposed to come back home after she'd finished her job in Germany. But then, she—" A cold breeze sent a shiver down his spine. "The French authorities caught up with the actual bad guy and his friends who'd killed your mother and a lot of other innocent people. I worked for the FBI. Do you know what that is?"

She nodded her head. "You were a fed."

"Yes, I was a fed. And my job was to investigate crimes and catch bad guys here in the United States."

"Did you catch bad guys like the kind who killed Mommy?"

"Sometimes, yes. But then after Gramps died and Nonni was left here on this big farm by herself, she and I thought that we could help each other. So I retired and moved you girls back here. I help Nonni run the farm and she helps me take care of you and your sisters."

"And Katelyn, Nikki, and I can all have ponies!" Emma said with a grin.

Pleased to see her bright smile again, Chris stood up and took her hand. "Yes, you can."

"And we have a swimming pool! Can I have a pool party, Daddy?" Emma hopped with excitement.

A moment ago, she was sad about losing her mother, and now she's talking about a party. In the back of his mind, Chris suspected he got played by a little girl. "An ice storm is coming."

"They already closed the schools for tomorrow. That means all of my friends will be free to come to my pool party." She ran on ahead. "I'm going to go send out an email to invite them!"

At the farmhouse, the lane snaked along the outer edge of the side yard and back to the barnyard. One outbuilding housed the tractor and other farm vehicles. Beyond that was the barn for the horses and numerous cats.

Somehow, word had spread that the Matheson farm was the place to drop off homeless cats, which were invaluable in keeping the rodent population down. Chris's mother, Doris made a point of having each new cat spayed to reduce unwanted litters. Still, every year there was at least one litter of kittens born in their barn.

A master carpenter, Chris's father had constructed a built-in wooden cabinet that took up the length of one wall in the mud room in which to hang coats, hats, scarves, and other outer gear. It contained hooks, drawers, boxes, and even a space for dog bowls.

The century old farmhouse had recently undergone a renovations. The modernized kitchen included a breakfast nook, formal dining room, and enclosed sun porch, in which Sadie and Mocha liked to sleep on the furniture.

The in-ground pool, closed for winter, rested on the opposite side of the patio. From their beds, Sadie and Mocha watched the happenings among an assortment of bird feeders that Chris's mother had erected in the back yard. They weren't the only ones viewing the birds. Thor spent most of her day bird watching.

Chris's late wife had given their daughters a baby rabbit, a French Lop bunny, as an Easter present before moving overseas for an assignment with the Department of State. The tan and white rabbit with long floppy ears had grown into a fifteen-pound furry bundle.

His daughters had selected three different names for the rabbit and Chris pulled the winning one out of a hat.

Thor was the winner.

It didn't matter that the bunny was a female with a pink rhinestone harness. Nikki's choice had won. So, the cuddly rabbit, who was usually dressed in frilly doggie clothes, was named Thor.

The scent of brownies warmed up in the microwave wafted into the mudroom where Chris removed his riding boots and put on his slippers. After hanging up Emma's discarded coat, hat, and gloves, he went into the kitchen where his thirteen-year-old daughter, Katelyn, was perched on a stool at the kitchen counter. She munched on a brownie with a glass of milk while reading a book on her computer tablet.

Chris greeted her with a kiss on the forehead on his way to the platter of warm brownies. "I didn't see the bus drop you off. Did Alison's mom give you a ride?"

"Yeah." Katelyn glanced in his direction.

Concluding that there had been a development in an ongoing drama, the center of which being a thirteen-year-old boy named Zack Daniels, Chris opted to say nothing.

She watched his back while he poured a glass of milk to go with his brownie.

Katelyn had inherited his fair coloring—from his steel gray eyes to his light auburn hair. Chris had been in his mid-twenties when his hair gradually turned silver at the temples. By the age of forty-six, his hair was an equal mixture of silver and brown curls.

While he drank his glass of milk, Chris saw Katelyn's eyes darting from the tablet to the cupboard behind him and across the room. She couldn't look him in the eye. "What's wrong?"

"Nothing." She bit into her brownie and squinted at the screen on her tablet.

"What happened at school today?"

"Nothing happened."

Chris let out a deep sigh. "How's Zack?"

Katelyn swallowed and set down the tablet.

"What happened with Tara?"

"She's a bitch," Katelyn said. "That's what happened."

Chris tried not to roll his eyes over yet another drama between Katelyn and her arch rival, Tara. The war had been ongoing since October. Both eighth graders were pursuing the same boy. Bouncing between the two of them like a tennis ball, Zack enjoyed the attention of two girls fighting over him way too much. The boy wasn't worthy of either of them.

"What'd Tara do this time?" Chris asked with a heavy sigh before taking another sip of his milk.

"She told everyone that you're a perv."

This got Chris's full attention.

"She said you raped a teenaged girl when you were in college and got her pregnant. Then you killed her and that's why you ran away to join the FBI."

"What the—"

"It was some girl named Sandy."

Chris felt as if his soul had been ripped out of his body to take him back to another time and place—to when the nightmare had begun.

Sensing that something was up, Sadie and Mocha stopped surveilling a family of squirrels invading the bird feeders to turn their attention to the scene brewing in the kitchen. Their eyes were wide like orbs.

Thor was more interested in the carrot that Emma had given her before racing to the study to email her friends.

"It's not true. Right, Dad?"

"What's Tara's last name?" Chris asked in a soft voice.

"Sinclair," Katelyn said. "Her mom is some big wig on the county commission. Her dad is—"

"Victor Sinclair," Chris said.

"He's the county prosecutor."

"I know. I know them all very well."

"You didn't do what they say you did, did you, Dad?" Katelyn stared up at him.

"No!" Chris slammed the glass down so hard onto the counter that the milk inside splashed over the rim. "How can you even ask me that? You know me. You've seen me with your friends. What makes you think I'd take advantage of a young girl like that?"

Katelyn's eyes were wide with fear.

"Do you really think that I'm that warped?" Chris demanded an answer.

She sobbed.

The sight of her tears broke Chris's heart. "I'm sorry." He went around the counter to take her into his arms. Refusing to let him touch her, she raced up the back staircase to her room. The last word in the conversation was the slam of her bedroom door.

Grief, frustration, and anger from the last twenty months built up inside him. If he didn't do something, he would explode. Desperate for some way to release the pressure, he turned around in circles.

With a deep roar, Chris grabbed his glass of milk and hurled it at the wall. The glass shattered. Milk splattered all over the floor, much to Sadie's and Mocha's delight.

Chapter Two

"How is he?" Elliott Prescott dared to take his eyes off the road to glance over his shoulder at the passengers in the back seat of his SUV.

Doris Matheson smiled over at the German shepherd resting his head on top of the seat. The sedative the vet had given him was wearing off. His nose twitched while he took in the many scents of his new surroundings. She rubbed his shoulder. "He's perking up a bit."

"That may not be a good thing." Elliott stopped at the intersection marking the turnoff into Harpers Ferry, nestled in the fork of the Shenandoah and Potomac Rivers. "They drugged him because he tried to eat my face."

"I'm sure you deserved it," Doris said in a chirpy tone. The dog's fur was growing back from surgery he had received only eleven days earlier. The police canine had taken two bullets to the chest. He was lucky. His handler wasn't.

"Why do you assume I deserved it?" Elliott pressed his foot to the accelerator after the light turned green.

"Because no one with a face like Sterling's would do that to someone who didn't."

The crow's feet around Elliott's eyes deepened as he squinted back over his shoulder to where the sable, two-year-old German shepherd was eyeing him. His thick salt and pepper eyebrows furrowed.

"I think you and Christopher are meant to be together," she told the dog. "Winston died on the same day you lost your partner and your home and your job. You need each other to heal."

"Are you sure Chris is ready for another dog?" Elliott asked. "It isn't like you don't have enough critters on that farm for him to bond with. What about Thor?"

"Thor can't go out on trail rides."

"True."

"Christopher had Winston longer than he had Blair." She muttered, "And Winston was more loyal, too."

Elliott's ears perked up. "What did you say?" He peered at her reflection through the rearview mirror.

"Nothing." Her thick blond hair framed her lovely face. At sixty-five, Doris Matheson exuded a timeless beauty. Wrinkles added character, not age. The widow of a West Virginia State Police captain volunteered much of her time to animal welfare causes and her church's mission work. As if having a full time job at the library and volunteer work was not enough, Doris also taught yoga and swam three miles, four times a week.

Damn, she's beautiful when she's cagey. Elliott shot her a wicked grin through the rearview mirror.

"Watch out!"

A red BMW SUV ran the stop light while he was turning left to take Millville Road along the Shenandoah River.

Elliott turned the steering wheel to the right. The rear wheels of his vehicle hit a sheet of ice. The BMW shot past Elliott's SUV while it spun like a top. Doris threw herself on top of Sterling to prevent him from being thrown to the floor. The German shepherd yelped.

The BMW turned left and continued on its way to Charles Town.

Thanking God for his good reflexes, Elliott took a quick note of the BMW's license plate. STARDUST

"What was that?" Doris stroked the top of Sterling's head with trembling hands.

"Peyton Davenport," Elliott said as he eased his vehicle out of the middle of the intersection.

She shook her head. "Someday that girl will end up dead from her reckless behavior. It isn't her I feel sorry for as much as her father."

"Why would you? He created that menace to society."

"Mason Davenport met Peyton's mother when she was his secretary at the racetrack. Everyone says it was love at first sight. They tried for years to have children and Julie became obsessed with having a baby. When she finally got pregnant, she spent the whole pregnancy in bed. After Peyton was born, Julie drove herself mad from fear of losing her and ended up throwing herself off the bedroom balcony."

"Sounds like a Shakespearean tragedy," Elliott said.

"Has all the earmarks. I hate to say it, but Peyton isn't worth killing herself over. That girl is one evil little witch."

"Tell me how you really feel about her." Elliott laughed.

"Do you remember Colin Rodgers, the wide receiver for the WVU Mountaineers?"

Elliott nodded his head. "On his way to the pros until he died of a drug overdose."

"Peyton Davenport and Colin Rodgers were hot and heavy," Doris said. "She was at the Rose Bowl game when he won the team's MVP. The lead detective in charge of the investigation told Kirk that the last phone call Colin had made was to Peyton Davenport and they spoke for quite a long time. The police did question her."

"Was Colin Rodger's death a suicide or accidental?"

"Not suicidal in the least," Doris said. "He had a lot going for him. The suspicious thing is that according to his friends and family, Colin was not a heavy or habitual drug user. So the investigators wanted to talk to Peyton about that phone call, but they didn't get very far before her daddy's lawyer shut them down."

"Steve Sinclair works hard to earn his monthly retainer."

"Kirk used to call him Mr. Potter," she said, "after the villain in *It's a Wonderful Life*. Power hungry, arrogant, and void of human compassion. That's Steve Sinclair."

"His son, Victor is a sniveling worm. The only way he got nominated for county prosecutor was because everyone's afraid of Steve. He's the one pulling the strings behind the scenes in the prosecutor's office." Elliott turned onto the lane to lead them up to the Matheson farmhouse. He lowered his window and punched the security code into the keypad to open the gate.

Sterling sat up in the back seat. His eyes flicked back and forth while he took in everything.

"You're almost home." Doris stroked him down the length of his body.

On the way to the house, Nikki stopped in the middle of the driveway when she saw the SUV roll to a halt in front of the side porch. She let out a shout of delight when the German shepherd's face came into view. "It's a dog! Dad! Come see! He looks just like Winston!" She threw open the door and ran into the house.

"There goes any hope of him getting lost in the pack," Elliott said.

Doris was climbing out when Nikki raced back outside, jumped from the top porch step down onto the ground, and ran up to the SUV.

Chris was close behind her. "Nikki, you don't just grab dogs you don't know. He's probably scared. We know nothing about him. Mom, what have you done?"

"He looks just like Winston, Dad." Nikki squeezed around Doris to touch the German shepherd. "Only his snout is black. Winston's was gray because he was old."

"Don't you think we have enough dogs, Mom?"

"Easy, Nikki." Doris fought to ease the girl's enthusiasm. "He just got stitches removed from his chest."

"What happened to him?" Nikki asked.

"He got shot," Elliott turned to Chris. "Did you hear about that K-9 officer and his dog that got ambushed a little less than two weeks ago?"

"The same day that Winston died," Doris said.

"Officer was sitting in his car at a red light," Chris said. "Didn't stand a chance."

"Sterling was locked in his crate in the back," Elliott said. "Took two bullets to the chest. Miracle he survived. Problem is, he can't be crated anymore. He about ripped me apart when I tried to put him in the crate to bring him here."

"If I took two bullets to the chest while locked up in a crate, I'd rip you apart, too, if you tried to put me back in it," Chris said.

"Like mother, like son," Elliott murmured.

"Vet says he's claustrophobic," Doris said. "They had to drug him to get him in the back seat."

"He got booted from the police due to failing his psyche exam." Nikki sat next to the dog. "We're keeping him, right, Dad? He needs us."

Chris looked through the open door at where the German shepherd was resting his head in Nikki's lap. His expression reminded him of Winston's when he had said good-bye.

In silence, everyone waited for Chris's response.

"Nikki, Winston's bed is in the mud room," Chris said. "Go set it up next to the fireplace."

Announcing the new dog to anyone in hearing distance, Nikki ran into the house. Chris climbed into the back of the SUV and picked up the hundred-pound German shepherd into his arms. He carried him across the yard and inside.

"Told you he'd take him," Doris said in a low voice.

"Sterling is easy. The book club is a whole 'nother thing."

"As soon as I break out my secret weapon, he'll be riding back to the library with you."

In the comfortable living room, Chris's daughters surrounded Sterling, who laid across the worn dog bed. Each girl spoke in soothing tones to him while he took in his new home.

Thor jumped up onto the sofa and stood on the arm. Studying the newcomer, she twitched her nose.

"He's bigger than Winston was," Emma said. "Look at his paws." She stroked one of his front feet.

Their heads cocked, Sadie and Mocha observed the intruder from across the room. Chris sat in the recliner between them and the German shepherd to jump in if need be, which was unlikely. Their extensive canine training had made them sociable to other animals.

He was more concerned with what Sterling would do when he noticed Thor. Surrounded by dogs her entire life, the rabbit was unaware she was a prey animal. She used to sleep curled up against Winston.

"So far, so good," Chris said when Doris and Elliott entered the room after shedding their coats and boots. "Thanks."

"No problem," Elliott said. "Sterling's a good dog—a little goofy—"

"Goofy?" Chris asked. "How is he goofy?"

"I have no idea," Elliott said. "My friend told me he's downright eccentric—but he didn't elaborate. To tell you the truth, I was too busy trying to stop him from eating my face to get all the details."

"What did you do to Sterling to make him try to eat your face?" Nikki asked.

"It's a long story," Elliott said with a sigh.

"I understand the schools are closed tomorrow," Doris said.

With wide grins, the girls confirmed that they were.

"I guess a lot of evening activities are canceled because of the ice storm," Doris said. "Elliott, is your book club still meeting?"

"Yes, it is," Elliott said. "Storm isn't supposed to start until ten o'clock tonight. Our meeting ends at nine. Everyone will be home long before it starts."

"You know, Christopher," — Doris patted her son on the shoulder — "you should join Elliott's book club. You love to read."

Chris tore his attention from the dog to look up at his mother. Her smile of encouragement reminded him of the time she pushed him into joining a group of boys his own age to go fishing along the river. It was fun until they started drinking and smoking pot and hatching a scheme to get some easy money. Chris reported their plans to break into the home of an elderly neighbor to his father and his new friends ended up in jail.

"They read mysteries, thrillers, suspense—all crime books," Doris said. "The same books you read. Not only that, but the members of Elliott's group are retired law enforcement. Your dad was the founding member."

"On account that your mother kicked us out of hers," Elliott said.

"Gramps got kicked out of a book club?" Katelyn asked. "What'd he do?"

"He and Elliott would go on tangents," Doris said. "After your grandpa retired, I thought it would do him good to get out and make friends—not hold himself up here on this farm—"

"Like I'm doing," Chris said in a low tone.

"Exactly." From behind the chair, Doris tapped Chris on the top of his head. "So I talked him into joining my book club."

"Nagged," Chris said.

"And he joined," Doris said. "That's where your grandfather met Elliott."

"And then you kicked them out," Katelyn said.

"Because they would only read the book if it had a dead body in it," Doris said. "If it didn't have a dead body, they weren't interested. Love stories were out of the question. We tried to read more crime fiction to make them happy. But then, they would rip the books apart. They'd go into everything the writer got wrong. Heaven forbid if the plot reminded them of one of their cases. Then they'd go off on tangents rehashing every gory detail. It was a book club, not a cold case detective squad." She sighed. "We had no choice but to vote your grandfather and Elliott out."

"So, we started our own club," Elliott said. "All of our members are retired law enforcement professionals."

"And you read crime fiction?" Chris asked.

"And rip them apart," Elliott said with a grin. "We have lots of fun doing it, too. We meet the first Tuesday of the month. Everyone brings in a snack to eat and Bruce Harris provides the wine."

"I bought a cheese tray for you to take, dear," Doris said.

"Wine?" Chris said. "Sounds awfully fancy."

LAUREN CARR

"Not really," Elliott said. "Bruce Harris is a good guy. Retired attorney general from Virginia. He owns a winery over in Purcellville, right across the state line and brings a few bottles to our meetings."

"You like wine, Christopher," Doris said.

"I didn't read the book. Besides, I won't fit in with their group."

"You're a retired FBI agent," she said.

"I'm only forty-six. I'm sure Elliott's friends are—"

"We're not exactly ready for the home," Elliott said. "Our youngest member is fifty-six. But we're all active."

"I'm sure you read the book. You read everything," Doris said. "What was your book this month, Elliott?"

He picked up a paperback novel resting on the end table next to Chris's chair. "This one."

"You have to pick up my car at the library tonight anyway," Doris said. "I left it there when Elliott took me to get Sterling."

Chris turned to look up at his mother, who was grinning at him.

"As long as you're at the library, you might as well have a glass of wine." Doris arched one of her elegant eyebrows at him.

She turned to her granddaughters who were cooing at how Sterling was allowing Thor to sniff his snout without biting the rabbit's long floppy ears off. "Girls, wash for dinner. We're having tuna casserole."

There was a collective groan throughout the room—with Chris's being the loudest. Their tails between their legs, Sadie and Mocha hurried up the stairs to the second floor.

Chris pushed up from the chair. "Give me twenty minutes, Elliott, to shower and change my clothes." He jogged up the back stairs to his bedroom, which occupied the attic.

Doris winked at Elliott. "Never underestimate the power of my tuna casserole."

CHAPTER THREE

In 1859, John Brown kicked off the Civil War by raiding the federal armory in Harpers Ferry. From then on, the tiny town nestled in between the fork of the Shenandoah and the Potomac Rivers became the prize of the War Between the States. It changed hands no less than fourteen times.

After the war, Harpers Ferry embraced its important role in history by becoming a national park and a popular tourist spot for Civil War buffs. The town's middle school rested next to a field where one of the war's many battles had been fought.

The Bolivar-Harpers Ferry Public Library made its home in a cozy single story building among a grove of tall ancient trees behind the school.

The last thing on anyone's mind was reading books. Locked inside their homes, residents prepared for the ice storm threatening to paralyze the nation's capital and neighboring area for two to three days.

To Chris's surprise, the library appeared to be bustling with activity when Elliott pulled his big old SUV into the main entrance. A Mercedes, a mid-sized SUV, and a pickup truck were lined up next to Doris's dark blue sedan. Elliott parked under the bare branches of an oak tree.

"Considering the bad weather coming in, I expected a thin turnout for your group," Chris said.

"Our members are devoted." Elliott threw open the door to allow an icy burst of wind to cut a knife-like path through the passenger compartment. He hunkered down inside his thick winter coat and slid out of the driver's seat. "Ray Nolan texted that he wasn't going to make it." He ushered Chris up the front steps. "He's in a wheelchair. Had to retire from Homeland Security after he took a bullet in the back. He'd set up their cyberwarfare task force after September eleventh and his name got leaked out to Al-Qaeda." He held the door open for Chris, whose hands were full with the cheese tray his mother had purchased for the meeting. "A homegrown terrorist tried to make a name for himself by shooting Ray in front of his grandson in a Chuck E. Cheese parking lot."

Chris stopped. "Tell me they got the guy."

"Ray's daughter put three bullets through his black heart. She's one soccer mom you'd never want to mess with." Elliott followed him through the entryway. "Ray's got a remote hook up at home—so he'll be joining us—no matter what the weather."

"Using a remote hook up to attend a book club meeting?"

"I told you. Our group is devoted."

"Hey, Chris!" Sierra Clarke, the librarian manning the checkout desk, paused in processing a stack of books to greet him with a wide grin. "Great to see you! Are you joining Elliott and Jacqui's group?" She handed the books to an older woman with long blond hair, who she referred to as Jacqui.

"Our club is by invitation only." Jacqui looked Chris up and down with her blue eyes narrowed to slits. Chris had difficulty judging her age. She had the slender, sensuous build of a young woman, but the lines around her eyes and mouth suggested that she was older.

"Chris is a legacy," Elliott told her. "He's Kirk's boy. Retired FBI."

"Retired?" Jacqui cocked her head at Chris. "I have shoes older than he is."

Chris suppressed a laugh. Never had he heard of a book club being so picky. Usually, they begged for members. He preferred to turn around, jump in his mother's sedan, and leave before the ice storm hit. The scent of Swedish meatballs reminded him that he'd be returning home to tuna casserole.

"He did a stint with the army's special ops to pay for his college before he became an investigator with the FBI," Elliott said. "So, he was able to retire at forty-five."

Eyeing Chris with suspicion, Jacqui took the cheese tray from him and moved into the adult book section where four tables had been arranged to make one big table. Someone had attached a webcam to the side of one of the library's computer monitors and set it at one end of the table.

To change the subject, Chris shifted his attention to the perky high school student manning the check-out desk. "I'm surprised to see you here, Sierra. If you were my daughter, I'd have you off the roads by now."

"You sound like Mom," Sierra said with a roll of her dark eyes. "The storm hasn't even started and she refused to let me drive. She's picking me up—" She pointed behind Chris. "There she is now."

Chris felt a rush of cold air hit him in the back of the neck.

A petite woman bundled up in a dark uniform coat of a West Virginia State Police, including the gold shield pinned to the upper chest drew the door shut behind her. Her short dark hair caught in the wind to blow across her face. Shaking off the chill, she brushed it out of her eyes. When she saw Chris, she let out an audible gasp.

Chris's eyes grew wide with recognition. He had known Sierra for at least four months—since she had moved into the area from southern West Virginia. Since her parents' divorce, Sierra had often spoken about her mother, to whom she was close.

Never, in all those months, had they met.

"Helen," he said in a soft voice.

She swallowed. "Hello, Chris."

"I had no idea Sierra was your daughter."

Helen smiled. "You mean your mother didn't tell you."

"Hey, Chris!" Elliott called to him from where he, Jacqui, and another man surrounded the cheese tray. "If you want any pinot noir, you better get your butt over here."

"I'll be right there."

Jacqui and Elliott exchanged soft smiles.

Helen urged her daughter to pack her school books and put on her coat. "We need to get home before it starts sleeting. I don't feel like walking up the mountain in the dark."

"Sierra told me that you were with the state police," Chris said.

Helen nodded her head. "I'm just sorry that I transferred back here after your father had passed. I would have given anything to have him as a mentor."

"Dad always did like you." He held the door open for them. "I thought you wanted to be a lawyer."

"Changed my mind about that in my second year of law school," she said. "A soon as I got my degree, I signed up for the police academy."

"Where she met my dad," Sierra said, "who dumped us for a twenty-five-year-old personal trainer with size-D implants."

"TMI, Sierra," Helen said in a low voice. "Let's go."

"What department are you working in, by the way?" Chris asked her.

"I'm lieutenant in charge of homicide."

"Dad's old job—before they promoted him to captain."

"So I heard." While her daughter ran to her mother's police cruiser, Helen stopped to gaze up into his face. "It's good to see you again, Chris." She smiled. "You look good."

"So do you, Helen."

He watched her hurry out into the cold. A gust of wind ruffled her hair while she yanked open the door and climbed into the car.

"Why didn't you ask her out?" Jacqui called over to break the memories of adolescent romance flowing through Chris's mind.

"Why is it that every time a man admires a hot woman, people think they should immediately slip between the sheets?" Elliott asked.

Meanwhile, Bruce was pouring red wine into a goblet. His muscular frame and sun kissed face indicated long days working in his vineyard. Peering at Chris with green eyes, he held out the glass. "Taste and tell me what you think, Christopher."

While Chris tested the wine, Jacqui waved her arm to indicate the work room behind Doris's office. "I didn't ask why he didn't take her into the back room and hook up with her here and now. I asked why he didn't ask her out. I was thinking about lunch. Your mind went straight to sex."

Disregarding his colleagues' conversation, Bruce stared at Chris. "Well?"

"It's good." He picked up a cracker which he covered with a slice of cheese from the tray.

"Maybe he didn't want to be pushy." Elliott handed a paper plate to Chris. "It isn't like he doesn't know where to find her. Her daughter works here."

Chris set his copy of the book down on the table to fill his plate with Swedish meatballs, and cheese and crackers.

"Good?" Bruce's expression was similar to that of a man who had just lost his job, home, and family. "He said it was... good?"

Cursing under her breath, Jacqui struggled in setting up the computer and monitor for the remote hook up. Ray snapped instructions to her from a speaker phone.

Sitting down to eat, Chris noticed that he was the only one who had the copy of the book that Elliott had said they were covering that evening. Everyone else had folders and binders.

Must be some heavy duty reading group.

"Screw it, Jacqui!" Ray said. "Where's Francine?"

"I'm right here, Ray." A short woman dressed in a thick winter coat with a furry hat pulled down over her ears ran in from the side entrance. She dumped a book bag thick with folders and notebooks into a chair. "Sorry I'm late!"

With a sigh of relief, Jacqui backed away from the equipment. She moved on to fill a plate with cheese and crackers.

"The internet went out at home just as I was leaving," — Francine checked the settings and pressed buttons on the keyboard — "and my grandson promptly became mildly hysterical. Luckily, all I had to do was reboot the system."

Jacqui took a sip of white wine from a goblet. With a grin, she held up the glass in a toast. "This sauvignon blanc is lovely, Bruce. Delicate but strong. Its sweet taste complements hearty boldness of the cheese. Yet, it's not a wimpy wine either."

"So, you don't think it's *good*?" Bruce shot a glance in Chris's direction.

Elliott took the seat between Chris and the vineyard owner. "Now, Bruce, not all of us are wine enthusiasts."

"I said it was good," Chris said, "which is a compliment."

"Yeah," Jacqui said, "he could have said it was bad."

The face of a man with a gray beard and thick eyeglasses filled the computer monitor.

"Hey, Ray!" the members of the book group called out almost in unison.

"Nice to see you guys, too." Ray saluted them. Abruptly, his smile dropped. "Who's the kid?"

Francine spun around to notice Chris on the other side of the table. A broad grin crossed her wide face. "Well, it's about time we got a touch of class."

"Kind of young if you ask me," Ray said with a grumble.

"This is Kirk's boy, Chris," Elliott said. "He's retired FBI."

"He's forty-five," Jacqui said.

"Forty-six," Chris corrected her.

"Still not even fifty."

"I've got underwear older than he is," Ray said.

"And he doesn't know anything about wine," Bruce said.

"I said it was good. Look, I had no idea this book club was so selective about new members." Chris rose from his chair.

With a hand on his shoulder, Francine, who had rushed to move her seat next to his, shoved him back into his chair. "Elliott says he's retired FBI. That's good enough for me." She leaned over to whisper in his ear. "I'll do the talking, sweet cheeks. You just keep sitting there looking handsome." With a salacious grin, she admired his attractive features and let out a moan of pleasure.

"Doris suggested that I invite him to—"

"That explains everything," Jacqui said with a heavy sigh.

"What explains everything?" Chris asked.

"Doris," Jacqui said. "Elliott can't say no to Doris Matheson."

"I can so say no to her," Elliott said. "As a matter of a fact I said no to her just today."

"In reference to what?" Francine asked.

"She asked if I'd gotten a haircut." Elliott raised his voice to be heard over their laughter. "But that's not important. Point is, Kirk was our founder, which means Chris here has a right to be a member of our group. Our primary rule for membership is retired law enforcement. Chris is retired FBI. If that doesn't allow him in, then what does?"

"His retirement is basically only a technicality," Jacqui said. "He's too young. Some agency or contractor will make him an offer and he'll be back out there talking about the Geezer Squad."

"I've said nothing to him about the Geezer Squad," Elliott said with a crooked grin.

"What's the Geezer Squad?" Chris asked.

"Hey!" Bruce sat up straight in his seat. "What's the number one rule about the Geezer Squad?"

"Never talk about the Geezer Squad," the group, including Ray on the monitor, said in unison.

In silence, Chris peered at each of them. He pushed his paper plate, still half-filled with food, to the center of the table. "Since you aren't interested in any new members—"

Francine shoved him back down into his seat. "Nowhere in our bylaws does it state a minimum age requirement to be eligible for the Geezer Squad."

"When did we write up bylaws," Ray asked, "and why didn't I get a copy of them?"

"We don't have any bylaws," Bruce said. "If we did, we'd insist that our members learn *something* about wine."

"Since we have no bylaws," Francine said, "that means we have no rules saying that this hunk of beefcake here is too young to belong to the Geezer Squad."

"And since his father was our founder, and he is retired," Elliott said, "then I vote that we let him in."

"Don't I have a say in this?" Chris stood up. "Maybe I don't want to belong to a group that calls itself the Geezer

Squad. What is it you guys do anyway?" He held up the book. "I suspect it has nothing to do with reading."

"You better hope we decide to let you stay, Christopher." Bruce poured the last of the pinot noir into a goblet and held it up to the light. "At this point, you've seen too much. So if you don't join our group, then we're gonna have to kill you."

"Are you serious?"

"No, he's not," Jacqui said with a laugh.

"Yes, I am," Bruce said. "It's in our bylaws."

"You don't have any bylaws," Chris said.

"Well, if we did have bylaws then that rule would be in them right before the paragraph about knowing the proper way to drink wine."

"When did we say that group rejects would have to be killed?" Elliott took a sip from the goblet.

"Hey, I've never been a reject in my life," Chris said, "and I'm not about to start now."

"Don't you remember back when we came up with our group name? Kirk said that it was imperative that no one know about us, especially Doris, on account that she'd kill—"

"Shh!" Elliott hissed at Bruce, who, seeing Chris's questioning expression, drained his glass.

Chris looked at each person around the table. "You're all retired law enforcement. You're not reading books. You're working—what? Are you private investigators?"

"Kind of," Jacqui said.

Elliott turned in his seat to face Chris. "Your father never wanted to retire. After he got shot, he was itching to get back to work, but he loved your mother more than anything. She became a nervous wreck worrying about losing him." He shrugged his shoulders. "He retired to make her happy, but he was miserable. He told me that he felt like an old fire horse locked in the barn unable to run when the sirens went off."

"That was when he started adopting retired race horses," Chris recalled.

"I think your mother saw how unhappy he was," Elliott said, "but she didn't want him to be out on the streets."

"The worst thing isn't so much not being out there," Ray said, "as much as it is not being allowed to use your mind."

"Seeing that," Elliott said, "your mother suggested that your dad join her book club. That's where I'd met him."

"The book club that you two got kicked out of," Chris said.

"So, we started our own," Elliott said.

"But it wasn't a *book* club."

"We had every intention of it being a book club, specializing in mysteries and suspense and thriller books. With us all being retired law enforcement folks, we'd be free to go off on our tangents—the type that got us kicked out of your mom's group."

"Man!" Francine said. "We ripped those books to shreds."

"The book club lasted two meetings," Ray said.

"Then what happened?" Chris asked.

"The book we had read that month struck me too close to home," Ray said. "The plot was too similar to—well."

"It was the case that kept Ray up at night," Jacqui said.

"You know the type of case we're talking about, don't you, sweet cheeks?" Francine said.

Thinking about his conversation earlier that day with his daughter, Chris nodded his head.

"So," Elliott said, "we decided to look into Ray's case. Reopen it. Each of us using our own separate area of expertise to investigate it."

"Ray invented cybersecurity at Homeland Security," Jacqui said. "I'm Jacqui Guilfoyle, a retired medical examiner from Pennsylvania."

"And I'm a retired investigative journalist from the Associated Press," Francine said.

"Suddenly, this group of geezers came to life," Elliott said. "We each had something to contribute to thaw out the cold cases that kept us up at night. That's when we became the Geezer Squad."

"Each month, we look into a different cold case," Francine said.

"What case kept my father up at night?" Chris held up his hand to stop her before she could answer. "Let me guess. The Mona Tabler case."

Everyone sitting around the table nodded his or her head.

"And the Shirley Rice murder, too," Jacqui said.

"Dad was convinced the same guy killed both women," Chris said, "even though they'd been raped and murdered five years apart."

"There's no physical evidence to connect the two cases," Bruce said. "Nor does there appear to be any connection between the victims."

"Except the M.O. and the victim profiles are the same," Chris said.

"Generally."

"You must have been a defense attorney at some point," Chris said.

"No, I was a prosecutor, and I was very good at it. Do you know why?" Bruce tapped his temple. "Because I knew how the other side thought. By the time I retired, I could figure out the other side's strategy before they did."

"Bruce became a criminal lawyer after his mother's murderer got off on a technicality," Francine told Chris in a low voice. "He was one of the most ruthless prosecutors east of the Mississippi."

"Which is why they made me attorney general," Bruce said. "They figured I'd be less dangerous behind a desk and out of the courtroom." He chuckled. "They were wrong."

"Both victims were middle-aged women," Elliott said. "Mona, the first victim, lived alone in a big house next to Morgan Park in Shepherdstown."

"Two-fifteen Morgana Drive," Ray said while referring to his notes. "Divorced. No children."

"She was the restaurant manager at the Stardust," Francine said.

"Over thirty years with the racetrack," Ray said.

"Davenport kept her on after Penn National Gaming bought the track and renovated it to add the casino with a fancy hotel and fine dining," Elliott said.

"Mona had quite a reputation for running a tight ship," Chris said. "When I was going to college at Shepherd, a few of my friends got jobs waiting tables at the restaurant. One guy walked out in the middle of his shift. He said she reminded him of a guard in a women's prison. Cold as ice."

"That's why Davenport picked her to manage the casino's restaurants when he became CEO," Ray said. "She only lasted a couple of years before someone killed her."

"It's also why Dad had a suspect list as long as his right arm. She'd made a lot of enemies. There was one guy," — Chris scratched his ear — "What was his name?" — he snapped his fingers — "Opie! Opie Fletcher. He had actually told people that he'd done it. The police department was flooded with calls saying that Opie was bragging about how he'd killed her. Mona had fired him years before when he had been a dish-washer. Dad brought him in for questioning. Turned out he was mentally challenged and he was telling everyone he'd done it for attention."

"He ended up getting more attention than he'd bar-gained for," Francine said. "We actually managed to track down the source of that rumor. After getting fired as a dish-washer, Opie got a job cleaning stables at the track. He was having lunch in the cafeteria when everyone was talking about Mona Tabler's murder."

"One of the guys at the table told Opie, joking of course, that he'd better be careful or the police were going to catch him," Elliott said. "To which Opie announced that he did it. He whacked her. A bunch of folks heard him and there the rumor got started."

"Were you able to prove Opie didn't do it?" Chris asked.

"He's officially off our suspect list," Francine said.

"Then five years later, Shirley Rice was beaten, raped, stabbed, and her home torched," Bruce said.

"Shirley Rice was on the county commission," Chris said. "She was separated from her husband, a plastic surgeon with a wandering eye. She lived in Martinsburg. Just like with Mona, she had been raped and murdered."

"Both assaults were extremely violent," Jacqui said. "Blows to the face. Dozens of stab wounds."

"The murder weapons were taken from the victims' kitchens," Chris said. "Then, the killer set fire to their homes." He held up a finger for each point of similarity. "Both victims were middle-aged women. Beaten. Raped. Stabbed. And then arson. Five points of similarities."

"Killed five years apart and there's no connection between the two victims," Bruce said.

"That's because the killer's other victims were out of Kirk's jurisdiction," Ray said. "Kirk didn't learn about them until after the Geezer Squad got on board."

"Other victims?" Chris asked.

"When your dad told us about Mona and Shirley, I did a search of the federal database to find cases matching theirs," Ray said. "I found three other victims. All middle-aged women—beaten to a pulp—raped, stabbed and their homes torched. One was in Lancaster, Pennsylvania. That was in 1995."

"That's three years before Mona's murder," Chris said.

"Another was in Mount Airy, Maryland, in 2000. Then we had a woman killed in Fairfax, Virginia in 2006."

"Sounds like a serial killer with a long cooling off period," Chris said.

"That's exactly what it is," Jacqui said.

"Two women with similarities in their murders does not a pattern make," Bruce said. "But five? Now that's a pattern that's difficult for a defense attorney to discount."

"So we contacted the investigators of the other cases and we've been comparing notes and evidence," Francine said. "I found where the victim in Lancaster had told a friend of hers that she felt like she was being watched just ten days before her murder. That tells me that the killer stalked his victims and learned their patterns before he attacked. That's why he's so hard to catch. He knows when to strike."

"But we haven't figured out how he picks his victims," Jacqui said. "We need to identify his hunting ground."

"With them living so far apart," Chris said, "the killer must have a job that includes some sort of travel—like a truck driver. As a restaurant manager, Mona would have dealt with delivery drivers on a regular basis."

"But not Shirley, who was on the county commission," Francine said.

"Still, that's progress," Chris said with a grin. "Have you identified a suspect?"

"Unfortunately, not yet," Elliott said.

"But we have given him a name," Francine said.

"A name?"

"All serial killers need a name," Francine said. "Otherwise, how do we know who we're talking about?"

"It's a media thing," Jacqui said. "Notorious psychopaths have to have names."

"We call him the Graduate Slaughterer."

Chris thought about the name for a long moment.

"Too long, huh?" Jacqui turned to Francine. "I told you it's too long."

"It is not too long," Francine said.

Jacqui ticked off on her fingers. "The Zodiac Killer. Jack the Ripper. Son of Sam. They're all names that roll off the tongue. The Graduate Slaughterer is too clunky."

"I don't get it," Chris said. "Graduate of what?"

"Did you ever see the movie *The Graduate*?" When Chris shook his head, Francine let out a deep breath. "Dustin Hoffman and Anne Bancroft? Mrs. Robinson?"

"In *The Graduate,* Dustin Hoffman was a young college graduate who's seduced by his middle-aged neighbor, Mrs. Robinson," Elliott said.

"Is the killer a young man?" Chris asked.

"It's a fair bet that he started out that way," Jacqui said. "I did a psychological profile. I believe he was in his early twenties at the time of the first attack. Definitely has mommy issues. I also believe that the first murder was not his first rape. With each murder that we identified, he has become more and more brutal."

"So, if he was in his early twenties at the time of the first murder in…" Chris searched to recall the date.

"The mid-ninties," Ray said. "He'd be in his late forties or early fifties now."

"But you haven't identified a murder since 2006," Chris said. "Either he's committed other murders that you haven't identified, or he's stopped killing for some reason."

"He's either in jail for another crime or he's dead," Bruce said.

"Or he's worked out his mommy issues," Francine said.

"I doubt it," Jacqui said. "His murders were getting worse not better. The only way the Graduate Slaughterer will stop is if he's made to stop."

"We'll catch him," Elliott said. "We geezers have a lot of time on our hands and we don't give up."

Those around the table bumped fists as a sign of comradery.

Francine turned to Chris. "So, now that you're a member of our team—"

"I never agreed to join your group."

"Oh," Francine said, "are you saying that you sleep well in your bed every night, angel? In all your years of working law enforcement, there is not even one case, one victim, one face that you see when you close your eyes?"

As she leaned toward him, Chris pulled away and looked around the room in silence.

"Give us a name," Jacqui said.

"Sandy," Chris said in a soft voice—barely above a whisper. "Sandy Lipton."

Chapter Four

"Sandy Lipton disappeared twenty-four years ago last month," Ray reported from notes he had found in a law enforcement database. "She was eighteen years old and nine months pregnant."

Chris was afraid to ask where Ray found his information. In the short amount of time he had spent with the Geezer Squad, he saw each one had maintained sources to a wealth of information since retiring.

Pacing around the table, Bruce would pause to pick up a slice of cheese from the tray while reading notes over other squad members' shoulders.

Before launching into their research, Bruce had opened a fresh bottle of white wine and poured glasses for everyone. After tasting it, Chris declared it "tasty," which Bruce found to be as offensive as "good."

In her seat next to Chris, Francine scoured the internet using the library's wi-fi and scribbling notes on a yellow pad. Each discovery caused her to utter a sound of either pleasure or displeasure. She pursed her plump red lips and arched her copper-colored eyebrows during the hunt.

Jacqui searched the internet as well. Occasionally, she would check with Ray on what he was finding on his end.

Elliott used the old-fashioned means, making phone calls to friends. Chris recognized some as being former colleagues of his father.

"If she disappeared twenty-four years ago," Jacqui pointed out, "you would have been only—"

"Twenty-two when all this happened," Chris said.

"Did you—" Bruce started to ask.

"I never touched her." Chris narrowed his eyes to gray slits at what he assumed they suspected. Even Elliott, who had known Chris for years, regarded him with doubt. "Her disappearance was the worst thing that ever happened to me."

"From the looks of it, it was the worst thing to happen to her, too," Bruce said. "After all these years—I assume she has been declared presumed dead."

"Declared dead eighteen years ago," Ray said.

"I'm very aware of that," Chris said. "The sorest point for me—and my family—is that all of this happened because I did a favor for a sweet girl who I considered a friend. What do I get in return? Accused of something disgusting and perverted and my reputation in this town is ruined."

He uttered a deep sigh. "I guess I hoped it would go away and folks would forget about it. Thing is—today my daughter heard about Sandy Lipton at school." He swallowed. "Now people are telling my daughters that their father killed some girl after taking advantage of her."

"Anyone who knows you, knows you'd never do something like that," Elliott said.

"No offense, Elliott," Chris said, "but there are a lot of folks who love to speculate about my dad using his influence to keep me out of jail for murder."

Francine closed her tablet. "Well, now's your chance, sweet cheeks, for us to uncover the truth and clear your name—not just for you, but for your family, too."

"Tell us about this favor that ended up with this young pregnant girl going missing," Jacqui said.

Chris looked around the table. Except for Elliott, they were strangers to him. For the last twenty-four years, he had never told anyone—not even his late wife—about Sandy Lipton and the dark heavy cloud of suspicion that hung over him.

Somehow, never speaking of it—ignoring it—rendered it non-existent.

He was wrong.

He was suspected of murder and would continue to be until he found the real killer.

"There used to be a diner next to the racetrack before it became the Stardust Casino," he said. "The Sure Thing Diner, owned and run by the Liptons, who also owned a low rent apartment complex. A lot of jockeys and horse people lived there. The diner had good bacon cheeseburgers and fries that were really cheap. I used to stop there for lunch a couple of days a week. Back then, I'd work as a courier for the libraries in the area. If a patron made a request here for a book that was at the library in Summit Point, I'd be the one to drive out there to get it and bring it back here. Sometimes, I'd stop at the Sure Thing for lunch during my runs."

Silence fell over the room while they waited for Chris, who had become lost in his thoughts, to resume.

"And you met Sandy at the diner?" Francine asked.

"She worked the lunch counter." Chris shifted in his seat. The discomfort of discussing the painful topic made his body ache until he had to get out of his seat. "Her brother, Carson, was the cook." His voice trailed off. He stared out the window into the darkness. The leafless trees reminded him of eerie skeletons.

Elliott stepped up behind him. "You said you did her a favor."

Chris started at the sound of his voice. Turning around, he studied each of their faces—searching for clues that they believed him.

"Sandy had a crush on me. I knew it. She'd hang out and talk to me while I ate." He sucked in a deep breath. "She was shy and awkward."

"Was she pretty?" Jacqui asked.

Chris shook his head. "She wasn't ugly. She was plain looking. But she was nice. She was a sweet kid. That's how I saw her. A kid."

"A kid who was in love with you." Bruce's wicked tone prompted Chris to step toward him, only to have Elliott stop him with a hand pressed against his chest.

"It's the truth," Elliott said.

Chris shook off the offense. "I did nothing to encourage her. I was a senior in college. My application to the FBI had been accepted, and I was getting ready to graduate when she gave me a Valentine's Day card and a little teddy bear with a heart. I had been so wrapped up in my studies that I hadn't even realized what day it was. She asked me to be her date for senior prom."

"And you accepted." Francine was breathless.

"From what I could see, she didn't date. She had no social life," he said. "She had to work up a lot of guts to invite me." He shrugged his shoulders. "I felt like if I said no she would've been absolutely crushed. So I said yes."

"And then she got pregnant," Jacqui said.

"It wasn't me," Chris said. "I took her to the prom. I took her home afterwards. I didn't even go inside their house. I kissed her good night on the doorstep—that's it. Then six weeks after I moved to Quantico, Dad calls to tell me that I'd been slapped with a paternity suit."

"Did she say you were the baby's father?" Bruce asked.

"I guess that's what she told her mother," Chris said. "Ethel Lipton was leading the charge—suing me for child support and charging me with statutory rape since Sandy was only seventeen at the time. She offered to settle out of court for a bunch of money, but my lawyer shot that down real fast."

"All you had to do was wait for the baby to be born and do a blood test to prove you were telling the truth," Bruce said.

"That's why Sandy's disappearance was the worst thing that could have happened. With her and the baby gone, everyone assumed I got rid of her because the blood test would have proven I had taken advantage of an underage girl. If that happened, the FBI would have canned me like that." He snapped his fingers.

"She could have been raped," Francine said. When Chris opened his mouth to object, she shot up her hand. "By someone who threatened to harm her or her family if she revealed who he was. She loved you, but she feared the rapist more."

"In which case, the rapist wouldn't want the blood test done because it would have brought out the truth," Jacqui said. "When did you take her to prom?"

"April," Chris said.

"And she was nine months pregnant when she went missing in January." Jacqui counted on her fingers. "So she got pregnant the same month you took her to prom."

"And he was in the area when she disappeared," Ray said.

"She went missing on the same day I left to go back to Quantico after coming home for Christmas break."

"Did you see Sandy when you were home?" Francine asked him.

"Sandy's mother alleged he went to their house and threatened Sandy the day before she went missing," Ray said.

All eyes turned to Chris.

"I did not threaten her," Chris said. "Yes, I did go to see her. I tried to talk sense into her to make her tell the truth about nothing happening between us."

"You were angry," Elliott said.

"Yes, I was. This whole thing was tearing the town apart," Chris said. "There were folks who believed that all law enforcement was crooked, who were convinced that I had raped Sandy. Then there were people who considered Ethel Lipton to be trash. She saw her daughter's condition to be on par of winning the lottery. On that day, I had run into a couple of friends of mine at the store. One had been my best friend since grade school. He wouldn't even acknowledge me. When I got home, he called to tell me he was still my friend. He just couldn't be friends with me in public because his wife, who I had dated for close to a year in high school, thought I had done it." He sighed. "I lost it. I went over to Sandy's house and let her have it—but I didn't threaten her. I told her that as soon as the baby was born we were going to do a blood test and the truth would come out. The world would know she and her family were liars."

"That was when Ethel Lipton threw you out of her house," Ray said while referring to his data.

"Her, Carson, and a couple of guys were there, too," Chris said.

"What guys?" Francine asked. "Young or old."

"Middle aged," Chris said. "Well, back then I would have put them at middle aged. One was older—fifties at least. The other was in his mid-thirties or so. Very well dressed, too. I didn't even know they were there when Sandy let me in. Then, when she started crying, her mother came running out of the kitchen and they followed her. The older guy comforted Sandy. The other guy kept hanging back like he didn't want me to see him. Carson escorted me outside. He said Sandy was imagining things. He said at first he thought she had made up the pregnancy—until the doctor had said it was real."

"There's no one else in the statement witnessing you threatening Sandy except Ethel Lipton and her son Carson," Ray said.

"The case against Christopher would have gotten more traction if these two men had come forward to confirm him threatening Sandy," Bruce said.

"You're right," Chris said. "Why didn't they make a statement to the police?"

"Because they didn't want anyone to know they were there," Francine said.

"We need to find out who those two men were," Elliott said. "Do you remember what they looked like, Chris?"

"Let me think about it. I was so focused on Sandy and fighting off her mother that I didn't really pay attention to them. I remember thinking that the younger of the two men, the one hanging back toward the kitchen, looked like a lawyer. As a matter of fact, I kind of assumed he was their lawyer. But I found out later that Ethel had hired that worm Sinclair."

"Let's work on finding out who they were and what role they played in all this," Elliott said.

"What do you remember about the night of the prom?" Francine asked.

"Was there anyone hanging around Sandy who seemed particularly interested in her?" Elliott asked. "Maybe he followed you when you took her home.

Chris shook his head before saying, "Victor Sinclair."

"I know him," Francine said. "Jefferson County Prosecutor. He's also an idiot."

"His daughter goes to school with mine," Chris said. "She's the one who announced to the middle school that I'm a rapist and murderer."

"But he attended that prom," Bruce said, "and showed an interest in Sandy?"

Chris nodded his head. "I realized real soon after we got there that Sandy had let her imagination go a little wild. She introduced me as her boyfriend. Her friends were in awe that quiet little Sandy had a boyfriend in college. She was on cloud nine and I let her stay there."

"You didn't call her out," Francine said with a smile. "You really are a nice guy."

"I was graduating and moving to Virginia. What harm would it do me to let her live her fantasy for just one night? I played Prince Charming to her Cinderella."

"What role did Victor Sinclair play?" Francine asked in a low voice.

"He asked her to dance not long after we got there," Chris said, "and she turned him down—saying emphatically that she had reserved all dances for her boyfriend. He didn't look happy at all. He kept lurking around—so much so that I did suggest to Sandy that she dance with him, but she refused. She told me she didn't want to encourage him." He shook his head. "I can't believe I had forgotten about that."

"That's what your daddy used to say happens with cold cases," Elliott said. "If you let them get cold enough, then they turn into ice. Most folks think that once a case turns ice cold that it'll be impossible to solve it. But all it takes to melt ice is for someone to put a little bit of heat under it."

Chapter Five

*Want pancakes for breakfast tomorrow am? Get pancake mix &
milk after mtg.*

After members of the Geezer Squad had finally called it
an evening, Chris let out a sigh of exhaustion when he read
Doris's text.

Damn!

Ray had managed to get into the police computer system
to download the case files and forwarded digital copies to their
email accounts—including Chris's.

Energized by the details of Sandy Lipton's disappearance,
the group worked until almost ten o'clock when Elliott noticed that it had started to sleet.

The meeting ended with each member volunteering to
use his or her own expertise to tackle the missing person's case.
Jacqui promised to search databases in the neighboring states
for Jane Does who matched Sandy's description.

Francine decided to check into Victor Sinclair's
relationship with Sandy Lipton. "He's obviously got an ax to
grind since he's still pointing the finger at you after all these
years," she said while packing up her tablet and notebooks. "It
wouldn't hurt to find out his agenda."

"He thinks I took advantage of Sandy and then killed her," Chris said.

"Or he raped her himself because she rejected him and he's blaming you to divert suspicion." She blew him a kiss which made Chris smile. "Keep your chin up, handsome. The Geezer Squad's on the case. Before you know it, we'll find out who did what to your friend and clear your name while we're at it."

Bruce slapped Chris on the shoulder on his way out the door. "What's the first rule of the Geezer Squad?"

"Never talk about the Geezer Squad."

"Especially to your mother." Bruce shook his finger at him. "Don't you forget. I'd hate to have to order Elliott to kill you. Your pa and I were really good friends—even if he was a cop."

"And you were a prosecutor." Chris recalled that his father never did like lawyers. The legal system made him jump through too many hoops—only to have perpetrators set free due to a technicality—even when everyone knew they were guilty.

"Well," Bruce said with a shrug of his broad shoulders, "no one's perfect."

Chris took note of Bruce's plaid shirt under his worn winter coat and tattered fedora on his head. He didn't look like any lawyer he'd known in Washington. "How long have you been retired?"

"Twenty-two years," Bruce said. "I retired at forty-five, too—after my wife got pregnant."

Chris's mouth dropped open.

"That was my reaction, too," Bruce said. "I was a stay-at-home dad while my wife pursued her dream of starting her own architect firm. She's got a big office in Leesburg. Does pretty good, too. Our son is in his junior year at Virginia Tech. Your dad invited me to join the squad after we became empty nesters. This group is important to all of us. My wife, Miriam would have a fit if she found out what I really do at these meetings." He poked Chris in the chest. "So keep your mouth shut."

Chris made a gesture of turning a key to lock his mouth. With a pleased nod of his head, Bruce went out into the cold. At first, Chris thought the vibrating phone in his pocket was a shiver from the icy wind whipping around his neck. Instead, it was a message from his mother—instructions to pick up pancake mix and milk for breakfast the next morning.

With a groan, Chris zipped his coat up tight and ran for the blue sedan. The icy particles in the air warned of more coming their way.

The convenience store at the end of the street did not carry pancake mix. That meant he'd have to drive up the road to the all-night department store in Charles Town.

Ok, he replied to her text. *On my way.*

Her response was instantaneous. *Don't forget to use your bonus card!*

K

He made his way onto the main road. As expected, the roads were vacant. Everyone was tucked in for the night— warm and safe in expectation of the storm predicted to dump at least half an inch of ice.

Schools were closed for the next day. Some parents would be lucky enough to have off as well. Families could spend time together. Thus, Doris's insistence that Chris pick up pancake mix so that they could have breakfast as a family.

Chris grinned at the thought of a long leisurely morning with his girls as he liked to call them. If the weather cleared enough, Chris would take them out on a trail ride. Maybe he could even convince his mother to join them.

He had become well aware that he was the only male in the house—even Sadie, Mocha, and Thor were female. He wondered if Sterling figured out what he had gotten himself into.

Winston understood. Chris's beloved shepherd went everywhere with him. He loved to ride in the front passenger seat next to his master.

Sterling could take Winston's place.

Chris doubted it.

There was only one Winston.

Besides, Elliott had said the police declared Sterling goofy—whatever that meant. He'd never heard of a law enforcement K-9 being "goofy."

The department store's parking lot was sparsely filled and dark—much to Chris's disappointment. He hated going to the store late at night—not that he made a habit of doing so.

The odds of being a crime victim increased significantly in all-night store parking lots. The lack of police presence and high risk people who frequented around-the-clock businesses made them magnets for criminal activity.

After locking the car door, Chris shoved his hands deep into his coat pockets. He laid his right hand on the small semi-automatic that he always kept close by. With luck, he'd find the pancake mix, grab a gallon of milk, use the self-checkout, and return home before the roads got too slick.

The road along the river iced up fast. The Mathesons had chains to put on their vehicles to get in and out without relying on the state plow.

The last thing Chris needed was to be stuck on the side of an icy road putting chains on Doris's sedan in the dark in the middle of an ice storm.

He wanted to go home and climb into his warm bed.

When he returned to the front of the store, Chris sighed with relief to see that there was no line for the automated cashiers. He hurried to one of the stations and pressed the button to begin checking out.

"Please scan your frequent shoppers card," the computerized voice instructed.

Chris vacillated between saving time from searching his pockets for his keys with the tag to save a few cents or not to.

He could hear his mother asking him if he remembered to use the bonus card. If he did use it, she'd never ask. So, she wouldn't know. Yet, it was guaranteed that if he didn't use it, she'd find out.

With a groan, he fished through his pockets while the automated voice nagged him to scan the card. Finally, he extracted his keys only to find that the cashier had given up.

"Please scan your first item."

He pressed the plastic tag onto the reader.

The cashier ignored him. "Please scan your first item."

"After you scan my card." Chris moved the plastic tag back and forth across the screen to get the cashier to read the bar code.

"Please scan your first item."

"Come on. Scan it already."

"Please scan your first item."

Muttering under his breath, he dropped his keys into his pocket and slid the pancake mix across the scanner.

"Get your hands off of me, bitch!" a shrill voice demanded a few stations away.

"What you gonna do about it, tramp?"

Chris recognized the voice of one of the women, but was unsure how he knew her. He peered down the row of checkout stations. Kicking and scratching for all they were worth, two women were engaged in a brawl. A male employee and a security guard attempted to pry them apart by wedging their bodies between the fighters.

A ding and instructions from the automated cashier prompted Chris to scan the gallon of milk. It sounded like the men managed to break up the fight.

"I'm pressing charges," one of the women yelled. "I'm pregnant and she assaulted me! Call the police!"

"You! Come back here!" the security guard demanded when the other woman grabbed a suitcase of beer and hurried out the door.

Unfastened, her worn winter coat was askew. Its hood dropped down behind her back. Her long hair was yellow from a bad dye job. She reeked of cigarettes and stale booze.

Chris caught a glimpse of her skeletal face before she darted past him and out into the darkness. It was a mass of wrinkles.

She's kind of old to be getting into fights.

The first woman wailed about being the victim of an assault while demanding that everyone stay to act as witnesses in her lawsuit for pain and suffering.

At once, people scattered.

Chris tucked the box of pancake mix, wrapped in the store's plastic bag, under his arm and picked up the gallon jug to head home.

Outside, he made his way down the aisle toward his mother's sedan. He recognized the woman from the fight several feet ahead of him. The suitcase of beer hung at the end of her arm. Her coat slipped to expose one shoulder.

A dark van approached from the opposite end of the parking lot to catch her in its headlights.

Chris heard the swish of a van's side doors opening. While the vehicle quietly cruised toward them, he recognized the silhouette of an assault rifle's muzzle aimed out of the open door.

Chris's heart leapt up into his throat to gag him so that he had to force out the word. "Gun!"

He dropped the jug. Milk splattered onto his pant leg before Chris dove for the grassy plot of earth between two rows of parking.

The patter of automatic gun fire was drowned out by the woman's anguished screams as a barrage of bullets ripped through her body. The van's driver gunned the engine. At the end of the row, he spun the van around to make a U-turn and raced down the next aisle.

Chris yanked his gun out of his pocket and sprinted toward the far end of the parking lot. By the time the van was gunning for the exit, Chris stepped directly into its headlight beams. He raised the gun and aimed it at the van's windshield.

Amused by Chris's display of bravery, the driver pressed the gas pedal to the floor. It didn't matter to them if he was too foolish to get out of their way. They had proven they weren't shy about taking a life.

With the van firing at him like a four-ton bullet, Chris pulled the trigger of his gun again and again—aiming for the dark figure behind the steering wheel. If he was lucky, he'd hit the shooter in the back as well.

In a matter of seconds, his semi-automatic was out of bullets.

Chris stepped to one side.

The van swerved past him. Hitting a patch of ice, it spun from one side of the lane to the other. At the end of the lot, it mowed down a stop sign and jumped the curb. After plowing through an old jeep, the van rolled over onto its roof and skidded several yards before coming to a halt.

The sparks of the metal ignited gasoline spilling from the van's gas tank, which had been punctured by the pole from the sign. The van exploded—lighting up the dark parking lot with brilliant orange flames.

Stunned, Chris watched the black smoke billowing up into the night sky as a sheriff deputy's police cruiser, with its blue lights flashing, arrived on the scene. Upon seeing a vehicular bonfire and a lone man holding a handgun, the deputy screeched to a halt.

His partner spilled out of the passenger side and crouched behind the open door with her weapon drawn. "Drop the gun! Now!"

There was no point in arguing. What were they to do? They answered a simple assault call and arrived to discover a van engulfed in flames, a bullet riddled body, and a guy with a gun.

Wordlessly, Chris held out his arms with his hands and fingers spread out. He allowed the semi-automatic to dangle from his index finger. Slowly, he eased toward the ground and dropped his weapon onto the pavement. As he got on his knees, he placed his hands on top of his head and laced his fingers together.

While her partner called into dispatch for assistance, the deputy hurried over to pat him down for more weapons.

"I have a backup weapon in a holster on my left ankle," Chris told her.

"You sound like you're no stranger to this drill." She lifted his pant leg to remove the thirty-two caliber semi-automatic.

"Been through this *several* times."

Chapter Six

It wasn't the first time Chris found himself in the back of a police cruiser.

As always, the seat was extremely uncomfortable—especially sitting with his hands cuffed behind his back. The rear seats of cruisers were hard and cramped for a reason. Why should criminals be content?

Chris's retired federal agent identification was insufficient for gaining the deputies' trust. After all, he admitted to shooting at the two people who died in the van.

Unfortunately, there were no witnesses to back up Chris's account of the men in the van gunning down the woman whose bloody body they had found on the other side of the parking lot. He prayed that the store's security cameras were working. He wasn't going to bet on it.

Until they had the facts, the sheriff deputies weren't taking any chances. They called in their supervisor. Until he arrived, they shoved Chris into the back seat of the cruiser with his hands cuffed.

His cell phone vibrated in his pocket. He assumed it was his mother wondering where he was with the milk and pancake mix. Unable to respond to her queries, coming every few minutes, Chris rolled his eyes.

Oh, no! He remembered the milk he had dropped after seeing the muzzle of the rifle. He searched his memory to figure out what had happened to the pancake mix. He had had the box wrapped up in the plastic bag and tucked under his arm. *I must have dropped that when I hit the ground.* He sat up in the seat and craned his neck to see if he could spot the bag where he had dropped it.

The rear door of the cruiser flew open.

"Chris Matheson, I never expected to find you cuffed in the back of one of my cruisers." The sandy-haired deputy chuckled at him while a gust of wind reached in to slap Chris across the face.

"Son of a bitch," Chris muttered before forcing a smile onto his lips. "Rodney Bell. How're you doing?"

"I'm the deputy sheriff." Rodney tapped the gold police shield displayed on the breast of his winter coat. He glanced around the inside of the cruiser. "How do you like it sitting back here?"

In spite of his leg cramps, Chris shrugged his shoulders. "At least I'm not working a crime scene in below-zero wind chill."

"Oh, but I have a feeling things are going to get real hot, real soon." Rodney winked at him.

Rodney's wink annoyed Chris as much as it did when they had been teenagers. "Don't count on it. Did you talk to any of the witnesses?"

"Ain't none. The few who stuck around after bullets started flying say they were inside watching some pregnant girl screaming bloody murder about being assaulted. That's the incident my uniforms had been sent out to take a report on."

"The assault was over by then. I saw it. As a matter of fact, the gunshot victim was one of the women in the cat fight." Chris let out an exasperated breath. "Are the security cameras working?"

"We'll be checking them out." Rodney stuck the end of a toothpick in his mouth—a trait Chris didn't recall from their youth. "Even if everything went down the way you say, there's still a problem."

"What?"

A slim grin crossed Rodney's face. He was enjoying the moment way too much. "The old woman who the two crispy critters in the van allegedly shot?" He paused to squint at him. "You ever seen her before?"

Chris started to say he hadn't but then remembered that her voice was familiar. "I've been gone for twenty-four years, Rod. I may have known her from back when we were kids."

"Oh, yeah, I'm sure you did," Rodney said. "She was Ethel Lipton, Sandy's mom. You remember Sandy, don't you?" He chuckled again. "The underage girl you knocked—"

"I did not knock her up, Rodney, and you know that."

"Not really, Chris. Sure, you were always the one every momma hoped their little girl ended up with. The boy scout. But then, when you wanted something—"

"Do you seriously want to go there, Rodney?" Chris jerked his chin in the direction of the van that the firefighters were still working to put out. "Your deputies took my gun into evidence. Once ballistics compares my spent cartridges from those of their assault rifle, then that will prove I didn't shoot Ethel Lipton."

"You may not have pulled the trigger that killed her, but that doesn't mean you weren't behind the shooting. The van was reported stolen an hour ago from a hang out in Martinsburg. Loco Lucy's. Extremely popular with the drug crowd. We've had two other hits go down the same way in the last six months. Detectives suspect a couple fringe members of this gang have been earning extra bucks by whacking folks for hire."

"So you suspect me of hiring them to kill Ethel Lipton, while I was on the scene, and then took them out so they couldn't talk. Wouldn't my being at the crime scene at the time of the hit defeat the purpose?"

"That's what you want me to think. We go too far back, Chris. I know how your mind works."

"After not seeing Ethel Lipton for over twenty years, why would I risk everything by having her taken out?"

"Because she came to me today saying that she had information on a murder. You being here when she was shut up permanently?" With a chuckle, Rodney winked at him again. "That's just too much of a coincidence to ignore."

The ice storm had begun.

At least it was warmer in the Jefferson County Sheriff's Department interrogation room. By the time the deputies had transported Chris to the station for further questioning, everything was coated in a sheet of ice. Even with his coat on, Chris fought to keep from shivering. He refused to give Rodney the pleasure of seeing him tremble and assume it was out of fear.

He traded the pain in his legs for arm cramps. Not taking any chances, the deputies handcuffed Chris to a hook in the center of the table. For an hour, he waited alone for someone to take his statement.

Rodney Bell was playing with him. The deputy sheriff studied him through the two-way mirror—waiting for Chris to become anxious. It would be easier for Rodney to push his buttons during the interrogation once he was on edge.

Having been former best friends, Rodney knew which buttons to push.

That was a two-way street.

Abruptly, the door flew open and Rodney rushed in with a folder in his hand. The cockiness in his grin annoyed Chris.

After slipping into the chair across from him, Rodney opened the file and slid Chris's identification and concealed carry permit across the table. "Why do you carry multiple concealed weapons, Matheson?"

"I'm a retired federal investigator." It was Chris's turn to grin. "But then you know that, Bell. We put in our application to the FBI together. They selected me, but not you."

Rodney's eyes narrowed to a glare. "That doesn't answer my question."

"I spent over ten years working undercover. Several people would not only like to see me dead, but they'd have no problem trying to make it happen—including a couple of drug cartels." Chris leaned across the table. "So, the last place that I'd go would be a drug dealers' hang out like Loco Lucy's."

Rodney's mouth dropped open slightly.

"As a matter of fact," Chris said, "when I saw the muzzle of that assault rifle, I assumed I was the target. Maybe someone from one of my operations recognized me. Started tailing me. Saw an opportunity in a dark parking lot and decided to take a shot."

"And Ethel Lipton, who just today asked for a deal in exchange for information on a murder, simply got caught in a crossfire?" With a shake of his head, Rod stuck a toothpick in between his teeth. "I'm not buying it."

"If Lipton had information on her daughter's disappearance from twenty-four years ago, why would she be in here today looking for a deal?" Chris asked. "If one of my daughters disappeared, and I got info, I'd be giving it to whoever'd take it—not dealing it." He shook his head. "What did she need a deal for?"

"She got her fifth DUI day before yesterday," Rodney said. "Nine o'clock in the morning, she ran a red light and had a head-on collision with an SUV out by the country club."

"Anyone hurt?"

"Driver of the SUV got six broken ribs, a punctured lung, a fractured arm and leg. Could have been worse. Ethel was on her way home from the casino. She practically lives out there. The Stardust paid her one and a half million dollars for her apartment complex and greasy spoon to build their parking garage. She used the dough to buy a big house out by the country club. But that was over two decades ago. She's been spending all her waking hours drinking and gambling at the Stardust ever since the casino opened."

"Even one and a half million dollars isn't going to last that long if you don't have any money coming in," Chris said.

"Maybe Carson has been supporting her," said Rodney. "He's the head chef at their fancy restaurant."

"*Head* chef? Sounds like Carson has done pretty good for himself."

"Studied up in New York. Went from the culinary institute to the Stardust after graduating."

"That could have been part of the deal to get the Liptons to sell. Nah…" Chris's voice trailed off.

"What?" Rodney's lip curled. The toothpick wiggled in the corner of his mouth.

"Ethel treated him like garbage. He wanted to leave, but every time he'd save up money, she'd manage to get ahold of it and blow it at the track or on drugs." He shook his head. "He'd never support her. As a matter of fact, I'm surprised he came back here. If he was halfway good—"

"He is," Rodney said. "People come from miles away just to eat at the Stardust's restaurant. It's five-stars. Have you eaten there?"

"No, I've been too busy to get dressed up for fine dining." Chris said, "So Ethel Lipton got her fifth DUI and almost killed a guy…"

"The driver of the SUV is talking about suing everybody—especially after he got wind that Ethel was coming home from the Stardust—who's got the deepest pockets in town," Rodney said. "The casino manager swears that he poured her into the back seat of one of their limos and had a driver take her home after he saw that she was trashed. He said that was eleven-thirty in the evening. The driver said she was passed out, and he carried her into her house—even fished the keys out of her bag to unlock the door. He put her on the sofa and she was sleeping it off when he left."

"But where was her car?"

"At the casino," Rodney said. "She woke up and had a friend drive her back to get her car."

"After having a hair of the dog that bit her."

"She blew over the limit after the accident and was arrested on the spot. This being her fifth arrest, the county prosecutor told her lawyer that he was throwing the book at her. They're going for jail time. After her lawyer told her that, she came to see me and wanted to make a deal."

"Immunity on the DUI in exchange for information on a murder." Chris scoffed. "Rodney, think about it. Do you really believe that if I had been involved in Sandy's disappearance, and her mother had any proof to pin it on me, that she would've kept it to herself?"

Rodney responded with silence.

The interrogation room door flew open. The deputy's eyes were wide when she said. "Bad news, Bell."

"Matheson's lawyer's here," the deputy sheriff said with a sigh.

"Worse. His mother."

Rodney's eyes were as wide as the deputy's when he looked across the table at him. "You called your *mother?*"

Chris grinned.

"And she brought Sheriff Bassett with her," the deputy said before running down the hallway to get as far from the imminent battle as possible.

"I'm sure this is all a big misunderstanding, Doris." Sheriff Grant Bassett held the door open for Doris, clad in a black leather coat, gloves, and tall fashion boots, to step into the room. "We'll get everything straightened out and you and Christopher will be on your way ASAP."

While Doris appeared polished, Sheriff Bassett's shirt was wrinkled and haphazardly buttoned. His hair stood straight on end as if he had been in such a hurry that he didn't bother combing it.

Rodney jumped out of his chair as if he were greeting the governor. "Ms. Matheson, what a pleasure to see you."

"Is it really, Rodney?" With the precision of a leader inspecting her troops, she looked him up and down while removing her leather gloves. "A pleasure to be seeing me, I mean."

She shot a glance over to Chris, who was enjoying the beads of sweat forming on Rodney's forehead. Her gray eyes narrowed upon seeing that Chris was handcuffed to the table. "Are you serious? You have Christopher handcuffed?"

"Really, Bell? Seriously?" The sheriff hopped toward the table as if to remove the handcuffs himself. "What were you thinking?"

"Well ..." Rodney swallowed.

"Well what?" Doris demanded an answer.

"Don't just stand there, Bell! Uncuff Matheson!" When Rodney didn't move fast enough, Sheriff Bassett raised his voice. "Now!"

Rodney spun around to remove the cuffs from Chris's wrists. Rodney's fingers trembled so much that he had difficulty getting the key into the lock. Seeing a bead of sweat roll down the side of the deputy sheriff's face, Chris asked, "Is it just you or is it getting hot in here?"

Rodney shot a glare into Chris's eyes before yanking the cuffs from his wrists. "Go home, Matheson."

"I'm not finished with you, Rodney," Doris said. "Would you mind telling me and Sheriff Bassett on what grounds you felt the need to interrogate Christopher?"

"Ethel Lipton, Sandy Lipton's mother, was killed at—"

"And Christopher halted the gunmen's escape, possibly saving other people's lives," Doris said. "So why did your people handcuff him, drag him in here in the back of a police cruiser, and throw him in an interrogation room like a common thug?"

"Yeah, Bell, why are you treating Matheson like a common thug?" the sheriff asked with wide angry eyes.

Rodney shot a glance in Chris's direction, as if he expected help from his former best buddy. In silence, Chris grinned up at him.

"Ethel Lipton told me yesterday that she had information on a murder. Since Chris was a person of interest in her daughter's disappearance—"

"The FBI *cleared* Christopher as a suspect in Sandy's murder decades ago," Doris said with a wave of her hand.

Rodney's mouth dropped open. The toothpick dropped onto the floor.

"Yeah," Sheriff Bassett said, "the FBI cleared Christopher, Bell. So what are you interrogating him for?"

"If you'd quit acting like a moron and take a few minutes to read Sandy Lipton's case file," Doris said, "you'd see that the FBI had a team of investigators confirm Christopher's alibi themselves. If he hadn't been cleared, he would've been fired at the very least."

"I thought he didn't have an alibi," Rodney said. "He was driving back to Quantico when she disappeared."

"Which included toll roads, which have traffic cameras at the gates," Doris said. "They got pictures of his car with him behind the steering wheel, license plate, and time stamps."

"Plus, I had a roommate," Chris said. "He confirmed the time I got home. There was no way I could have abducted Sandy around noon, driven to my apartment in Quantico by one o'clock, and meet friends for a volleyball game at two."

"But-but everyone says—" Rodney stuttered.

"Because they only believe what they want to believe," Doris said. "Kirk's political enemies wanted to believe he used his influence to protect Christopher and cover up a murder. The FBI made a statement to the media about clearing him, but no one publicized that because the truth is never as sexy as the lie." She looked the deputy sheriff up and down. "Even you, Rodney. I know you have issues with accepting responsibilities for your own mistakes—"

"Now with all due respect, Ms. Matheson—"

"Have you talked to Clarence Stengel?"

"Who?" Rodney glanced again in Chris's direction.

"Hey!" Doris snapped her fingers in Rodney's face, causing him to stand at attention as if he were before a law enforcement superior. "Don't look at him. Look at me. I've asked you a question."

"I don't know who Clarence Stengel is." A bead of sweat rolled down Rodney's temple to his cheek. "I swear."

"He's the assistant manager at the department store and witnessed the altercation Ethel Lipton had moments before she was killed by two gang-bangers."

"Did you take Stengel's statement, Bell?" the sheriff asked.

"Well…"

"Clarence knew the young woman that Ethel had gotten into a row with," Doris said. "The police and DEA are very familiar with her. Her name is Precious Hawkins, the baby momma of Jose Martinez. She has a couple of kids by this animal—and takes great pride in having a big drug dealer for her man."

"We know Martinez." The sheriff turned his full attention to Rodney. "His middle name is Bad News."

"Precious cut in line in front of Ethel," Doris said. "That started the fight, which Precious recorded and sent to Jose with a text about what this awful woman had done to her—playing the victim card to the hilt. She then called him while store security was notifying the police. Jose assured her that he would take care of it."

His face red, the sheriff asked through clenched teeth, "Bell, have you even looked at Martinez for being behind this?"

"Um—"

"'Um' is not an answer," Doris said. "I found this out with one phone call to Clarence while putting chains on the truck after Christopher called to tell me about you acting like an idiot."

"Her word, not mine," Chris said. "I used the word 'jackass.'"

"Christopher, come. We're going home."

Sheriff Bassett shoved Rodney out of the way in his rush to open the door for her.

"Yes, ma'am." Chris met his mother in the corridor.

"Did you remember to pick up the milk and pancake mix?"

"Um…"

"'Um' is not an answer."

"I remembered to use our shoppers bonus card."

"Get in the truck, Christopher."

Sheriff Bassett leaned into the corridor to admire Doris's departing figure. Once she was gone, he turned his attention to his second in command. "Did you see that?"

"I saw Chris Matheson kill two men tonight and walk out of here," Rodney said. "You even held the door for him."

"I was talking about Doris." Sheriff Bassett smoothed his hair with his hands. "Did you see the blue sparks that came to her eyes when she was yelling at you?" He sighed. "I wonder if she's still in mourning."

CHAPTER SEVEN

As sleep gently slipped away, Chris became aware of a cold wet triangle pressed against the back of his neck. He opened his eyes only enough to peer out under his heavy eyelids and turned his head to see a huge black dog snout.

During the night, Sterling had migrated from the dog bed in front of the fireplace to Chris's room, which had been converted from the finished attic.

Chris reached out from under the blankets to pat the German shepherd on top of the head and rolled back over onto his side. Equally mixed with snow, the sleet tap-tap-tapped on the roof above his head to lull him back to sleep.

He was grateful he and his mother had made it home before the storm reached full intensity. They had to crawl along the river road and up the lane through one inch of snow, under which was a half an inch of solid ice.

Pulling the thick comforter and blankets around him, Chris drifted into the sleep that comes from gratitude of not having to go outside into such weather.

"Daddy?" said a soft little voice. "Are you asleep?"

Fighting to stay in his sleep filled state, Chris reached out from under the blankets and tapped the little girl standing next to his bed. His fingers caressed the soft fur and long ears that he recognized as belonging to Thor. He walked his fingers up to the neck and small face.

"Nonni wants to know if you want eggs to go with your pancakes," Emma said.

"We don't have pancake mix," Chris said in a whisper, so as to not wake himself up.

"She's making them from scratch."

"But we don't have milk."

"She's using almond milk."

"Oh, Lord, have mercy." Chris rolled over onto his stomach and covered his head with the pillow. Thor jumped onto his back and climbed over him to join Sterling on the other side of the bed.

Emma nudged him in the shoulder. "Do you?"

"Do I what?"

"Want eggs with your pancakes?"

"Tell her I want eggs and no pancakes."

Pressing his eyelids shut, he listened to the pitter patter of her footsteps across the hardwood floor and down to the next floor. With a heavy sigh, he drifted back to sleep. Sterling curled up at the foot of the bed and Thor made a nest between Chris's ankles.

While Chris had been at the book club meeting the night before, Doris had introduced Thor to Sterling. Surprisingly, when they returned home from the police station, they found Thor sleeping with Sterling in the dog bed.

Chris was vaguely aware of two small feet clambering up the steps and across the floor to his side of the bed.

He stretched his arm behind himself and out from under the covers to grasp her arm. This girl was bigger than Emma. He felt a Pandora bracelet on her wrist—the same one that he had given to his late wife for Christmas the year Emma was

LAUREN CARR

born. After his wife's death, he had given it to Katelyn, who never took it off.

"Dad, are you asleep?"

"No, I'm chopping firewood. Don't you see the pile of logs at the foot of the bed?"

Katelyn giggled. "Nonni wants to know if you want bacon or sausage or both."

"Both."

"And how do you want your eggs?"

"Scrambled."

She made it to the top of the stairs before Chris stopped her. "Katelyn honey?"

"Yes, Dad?"

"I'm sorry I yelled at you yesterday," he said while keeping his head under the pillow. Apologizing was easier if he didn't have to look at her. "You didn't do anything wrong. I was just upset about Tara digging up lies from ancient history to hurt you."

"Well I'm sorry for even asking you about it. I don't know what I was thinking. You're right. You'd never do the stuff they were saying you did. Forget it."

"No, I won't," he said. "I'm going to find out what happened to that girl."

"Daddy, you don't have to do that for me."

"Not for you. Not for me either. For her. Sandy was a nice girl. Something happened to her—something awful. She deserves justice."

There was a smile in her voice when she said, "And knowing you, Dad, you will find out what happened. I'd hate to be the bad guy when you catch up with him."

He listened for her to trot down the stairs. Instead, she returned to his bedside. "Dad?"

"Yes, honey?"

80

"Can I have an advance in my allowance?"

Do we have to have this conversation now? He groaned. He could make it easy and say yes. She'd leave happy, and he'd go back to sleep. Or, he could do the right thing and interrogate her, which would teach her a lesson about being responsible with money.

"How much of an advance?" he muttered.

"Thirty dollars."

"For what?"

"Valentine's Day," she said. "It's this Saturday and Zack invited me to go to the movies and dinner."

"And you want to buy a Valentine's Day present for Zack." Chris fought to conceal the abundance of disgust wanting to spill into his voice.

"No, I already got him a Valentine's Day present," she said. "That's what I used my allowance for. I need money for the movie and dinner."

Tossing the pillow aside, Chris rolled over to face her. The daylight caused him to blink several times before she came into view.

Proud of being asked out on her first date, Katelyn had a wide smile on her face.

"This boy asked you out on a date for Valentine's Day, but you have to pay?"

Katelyn nodded her head. "Of course."

"Of course? What do you mean 'of course?'" he said. "You bought him a Valentine's Day present, and he asks you out and expects you to pay. That's not a date."

"You don't understand, Dad."

"Make me understand."

"He can't afford to pay my way because he's taking Tara to lunch and the matinee."

"I thought he was taking you to the matinee."

"After her," she said. "And it isn't fair for us to expect him to pay for both of us, so he's not paying for either of us." She smiled. "I've got him for dinner. Isn't that great?"

Afraid of what he might say, Chris dropped down onto his back and pulled the blankets up over his head.

"Daddy?"

"Not now."

"But—"

"We'll talk about it later."

She hurried downstairs.

Thor burrowed under the comforter and proceeded to chew on his hair. Chris ignored the bunny because mentally he was busy giving Zack Daniels a lecture on being a gentleman. At the climax of his speech, Chris grabbed Zack by the throat and shook sense into him. He was so enthralled with his lesson about gentlemanly manners that he didn't hear his remaining offspring gallop up the stairs and across the floor.

"Hey, Dad," Nikki said in such a loud voice that he jumped under the thick blankets, "do you want me to clean out the stalls and feed the horses so you can sleep in?"

The snow and sleet tapered off by noon. The clouds parted to allow the sun to shine on a four-inch deep snowy blanket trapped between two thick layers of ice.

Except for Emma's chatter, all was still when Chris led his girls on horseback along the trails winding through the thick woods at the opposite end of the farm. The woods ended at a two-lane road that led to the freeway cutting straight across the mountain to connect Virginia with Charles Town. The snow-covered riding trail also acted as a service road to the utility poles located at various points across the countryside.

The riders heard an occasional vehicle whizzing by on the freeway on the other side of the woods. The highway department had continuously salted the road during the night to keep it clear for those unfortunate enough to not get a day off.

At first, Chris feared that Sterling would take off and get lost in his new surroundings. But, Sterling had instantly become attached to his new master—following him around the farm house and darting out the door to tag along when he and Nikki went to saddle up the horses.

On the trail, the German shepherd trotted alongside Traveler while Mocha and Sadie disappeared into the woods in their pursuit of various critters.

Watching the Doberman and lab, Sterling's ears would perk up. He'd gaze up at Chris sitting on top of Traveler, as if to ask permission to follow. Even when Chris consented, Sterling chose to stay with him. Instead, the dog trotted up and down the line of horses, as if to take count to make sure no one was missing.

They rode single-file, Chris at the front of the line and Doris bringing up the rear on her chestnut mare. Off in the distance, a train making its way through Millville blew its whistle. The CSX and metro train tracks ran along the river, past the tiny town, and then snaked through the countryside to Martinsburg in the next county.

Far up along the trail, Mocha's and Sadie's barking took on an urgent tone.

"Sounds like they found something to chase," Doris said.

"I hope they don't go too far." Katelyn sat up in her saddle and leaned over to peer around Chris. "Cat Tail Road is only about a half mile up ahead. If they decide to chase it out into the road—"

"They both know better than to run into the road," Doris assured her.

His ears standing tall, Sterling had moved up ahead of them on the trail and waited. Chris held up his hand in a fist—a signal for them to stop.

There was something about the tone of the dogs' barks that he didn't like. It was more serious. They weren't playfully chasing a squirrel.

After a long moment, the barking stopped. Sadie came into sight—trotting toward them with something in her mouth.

"What did they catch?" Nikki asked.

Equally curious, Sterling moved in for a closer look. The Doberman ran past him to trot up to Chris, who leaned down from his saddle to grab the object.

It was a fedora hat.

"They brought down Indiana Jones!" Katelyn said with a giggle.

While the girls laughed, Chris twisted around to peer at Doris. She was not laughing. Neither was he.

A retired security dog, Sadie had returned without Mocha, whose experience was in search and rescue. The lab had been trained to locate and stay with someone who had been lost or injured.

"Stay with the girls," Chris told his mother while gesturing for Sadie to lead him to Mocha. He galloped up the trail and around the bend to find the Labrador sitting on the side of the path. Mocha peered at a thick leafless briar bush at the bottom of a gully.

"What did you find, girl?" Chris dismounted and petted the dog who led him downhill to the thicket. As he drew closer, he noticed a pair of legs clad in dark trousers and boots sticking out from under the bush.

Off the service road, tucked under the overgrown bush at the bottom of a hillside, the body could have easily gone unnoticed if it hadn't been for the dogs picking up its scent.

Careful to leave as few footprints as possible, Chris approached the figure, clad in a cloth coat, to see if he was still alive. He doubted it. The body was covered in ice and snow. He had been dumped before the storm.

Still, Chris had to check to see if he was still alive. He moved in closer to examine the body.

The side of his head was covered with thick blood from what appeared to have been a blow to the side of the skull. His flesh was blue.

In spite of the body's condition, Chris was able to make out his facial features. As he peered at him, he experienced a sense of recognition. The dead man had been unattractive in life. His nose was oversized with a huge bump at the end. He had a wide square jaw—not unlike the bottom of a jug.

The memory of who he was and under what circumstances they had met sent a shock wave through Chris's body. He fell back onto his rump in the snow. Careful to retrace his steps back to the road, he took out his cell phone and hit the button for Doris.

"What'd they find?"

"A body dump," Chris said. "Take the girls back to the house."

"Do you want me to call the police or should you?"

"I'll call," Chris said before he had a second thought. "Mom, do you know Helen's phone number?"

"Yes, I have it on my phone. Why?"

"Can you call her for me? Tell her to get out here—off the record."

"Off the record? Why?"

"Just ask her for me, please, Mom. It's important."

CHAPTER EIGHT

"Oh, Tommy, what did you get yourself into this time?" Chris asked the dead man in a low voice as if he feared that someone might be listening to their conversation.

After his girls had left, he returned down the hill to examine the body. Carefully, he retraced his footsteps by stepping in the same prints he had previously left and squatted to search the dead man's pockets. He wouldn't leave fingerprints since his hands were encased in winter gloves.

He found nothing. No wallet—no identification—not even a cell phone.

Chris stood. "Two guesses of where you were staying here in town." Careful to not leave any more tracks in the snow, he made his way back up the hillside.

Focused on something across the field, Traveler stood at the bend where Chris had left him and Sterling. Realizing that he had not seen the dog for a while, Chris jogged to the horse and peered across the field.

The sight prompted Chris to cry out.

At first, he assumed someone had been hiding nearby and chose to attack and hang his German shepherd from a tree while he was busy with the body.

Chris charged across the field to where Sterling was swinging from a branch high up above the ground. As he drew nearer, he saw Sterling's hind legs kick up—causing him to sway from side to side and back and forth.

He's alive! There's still a chance to save him. Chris extracted a hunting knife that he kept in a sheath on his belt and picked up his pace. *Why didn't he bark? Why didn't he defend himself?*

Three feet from the ground, Sterling kicked his hind legs again, causing him to sway more. The German shepherd's body jerked. He pawed the air as if to dog paddle.

As he drew closer, Chris discovered that Sterling had jumped to capture the thin but sturdy branch in his teeth and swing high above the ground. When the ride slowed, he would kick and paddle to continue his fun.

"Sterling?"

The dog stopped. He rolled his eyeballs to peer with wide eyes at his master.

"What are you doing?"

Sterling opened his jaws and dropped to the ground. He shook to smooth his fur before jumping up to tag Chris in the chest.

"You scared me to death, you goofball." Chris was so happy to see that he was okay that he gave the dog a hug.

"Did you call me out here to help you with this dead body or to watch you play with one of your dogs?" Helen Clarke called to him from across the field.

After easing Sterling's paws to the ground, Chris tucked the knife back into the sheath and ran to where she was petting Traveler. She had parked her SUV at the opposite end of the road and walked along the trail, past the body, to join them.

Sterling ran up to Helen, tucked back his ears, and circled her to beg for a petting, which she gave him with enthusiasm.

"If you aren't a handsome fellow. What's his name?" After Chris had given it to her, she asked about the healing sutures on his chest.

"He got shot," Chris said. "That's why he's retired."

"Poor thing." She knelt to hug the German shepherd who welcomed her affection with a lick.

"He's luckier than his partner," Chris said. "He was killed in the line of duty."

"All give some, some give all." She stood. Her dark eyes were filled with sympathy. "I'd heard about your wife… getting killed in that terrorist attack—"

"Thanks." Uncomfortable with displays of sympathy, he brushed past her to lead her to the body. "Did you take a look at the victim yet? He's covered in ice and snow, so he had to have been dumped here before the storm."

"Not yet. Why did you have your mother call me off the record? You know what to do. Call emergency or—"

"Because I spent last evening in Rodney Bell's office getting grilled and I don't relish doing the same thing today," Chris said.

"What happened last night?"

"Ethel Lipton got gunned down, and I was a witness to it."

"Ethel Lipton?" Helen cocked her head. "She's got a long list of drunk and disorderlies, and DUIs. She must have said or done the wrong thing to the wrong people."

"One would think," Chris said. "The shooters ended up being on the fringe of a drug gang that hangs out in Martinsburg. They run drugs from Mexico to Baltimore—"

"Right through West Virginia," Helen said. "Our vice squad is very familiar with them. Their leader is a silent partner at Loco Lucy's. What does all this have to do with you? You were a witness. With your background, Rodney should have been thrilled you were there."

Chris kicked at a clump of snow at his feet.

Silence stretched between them.

"What are you not telling me?" she asked.

"You were at WVU and your folks had retired and moved to Florida by then." It took every ounce of courage for him to lift his head to look at her. "What do you know about Ethel Lipton's past?"

"Her son, Carson, is the head chef at the Stardust Casino's five-star restaurant." Helen smoothed a lock of unruly dark hair that blew into her eyes. "She's a regular at the Eastern Regional Jail's drunk tank. I've heard her name, but since I've come back I've been in charge of homicide. Unless she's a murder victim or suspect, I have no reason to know anything about her. Chris, tell me what's going on."

"Ethel Lipton's daughter disappeared twenty-four years ago," Chris said. "I was the prime suspect in her disappearance. The FBI cleared me, but most of the local folks believe Dad used his connections to cover up a murder."

"What motive would you have had to kill her?" Helen asked.

"She was pregnant and claimed I was the father." When he saw her mouth drop open, he grabbed her by both arms. "Helen, I never touched her! My lawyer had a warrant for a blood test as soon as the baby was born. That would have proven I wasn't the father. But she disappeared before that could happen."

"Now everyone thinks you killed her and the baby because you were the father."

"Please tell me that you believe I would never have done anything like that."

Her eyes searched his. She reached out to touch his face. The warmth of her hand on his cheek made his heart race like it had so many years before. The passage of time had not dulled the electricity he felt when he looked into her eyes.

He wanted to lean in to kiss her, but if she rejected him, it would have broken his heart.

Abruptly, she jerked her hand away and went over to look at the body resting at the bottom of the gully. "So, for some reason, Rodney suspected you of having this girl's mother killed? But you didn't. What does that have to do with this guy? I'm telling you right now that if you've asked me here to help you dispose of—"

"I asked you here as a courtesy." As the sound of multiple vehicle engines drew closer, Chris hurried around her to step into the main road. "I promise I'll keep you in the loop."

"The loop?"

She ran after him. Chris flagged down the lead SUV in a caravan of government vehicles. They followed Chris's instructions to park along the side of the main road.

Chris wanted the access road disturbed as little as possible. The killer or killers could have left behind foot or tire prints from their vehicle. If the crime scene investigators were successful in making impressions of that evidence, it could prove crucial in identifying and convicting them.

Helen's mouth dropped open when she saw that the people who spilled out of the vehicles wore coats with FBI emblazoned on the back. Most of them grabbed forensic equipment cases from the back of their vehicles. "You called in the feds! Chris, you have no right!"

Chris turned to her. "The man at the bottom of that ravine was with the Krawford syndicate. Fraud, bribery, Ponzi schemes, insider trading, embezzlement, and identity theft. Cybercrime is a biggie."

He gestured for the agents to follow him down the access road to the body. "Tommy Bukowski was one of the architects for the dark web."

"And you know this how?" Helen became increasingly annoyed.

"I met him when I was working undercover for the feds," Chris said. "It was like almost twenty years ago. Tommy was working his way up the ladder for the Krawfords. I worked that case for a year and a half—saw Tommy all the time. His masters was in business, but his love was computers. He had big dreams of taking the Krawfords to the next level of white collar crime by getting on the ground floor of cybercrime. He thought that would get him into their inner circle. When the justice department decided to arrest a group of the middle men to get them to turn on the upper level guys, I offered Tommy the chance to turn federal witness. He refused. As a matter of fact, he blew the whole operation." He sighed. "He warned Eugene Krawford and his sons, who escaped out of the country. Krawford's people almost killed me. Worse, they tracked down one of my sources inside the company and killed her."

"Were the feds able to pin the murder on the Krawford family?"

"No." Chris bit out his response. "The medical examiner ruled my witness's death a suicide. None of our witnesses would testify against any of the Krawfords, and none of the evidence could connect them to the fraud and embezzlement—thanks to Tommy destroying everything that could. After things cooled off, the Krawfords came back into the country and picked up right where they'd left off. And Tommy Bukowski? Well, he got what he wanted. He got his place in the inner circle."

"Sounds like Tommy caused you a lot of trouble?"

"It took me a long time to regain my reputation as an investigator after blowing it by inviting Tommy to turn federal witness. I trusted him and he played me. I never made that mistake again."

"And now Tommy is dead on your property." Helen tilted her head in the direction of the embankment.

After the forensics team collected what information they needed, they assured Helen that the agent in charge would be in touch with her as soon as she arrived from Washington.

"I'm sure the agent in charge of the investigation will be showing up there to question me," Chris told her while climbing up on Traveler. He invited her to meet him back at the farm.

Sterling nuzzled her hand to urge her to accept the invitation. Chris held his breath.

Helen hesitated. "Okay," she finally said in a soft voice.

"Great," he grinned. "I'll see you in the barn."

"The barn?" Her eyes grew wide.

"I don't want to talk about my years working undercover and a murder in front of the girls."

She let out her breath. "I understand."

Chris opened his mouth as if to say something, but instead, shook his head. He gave her the four-digit code for the security gate to drive up the lane. "Pull your SUV up to the barn and come inside."

Watching him gallop away across the field with his German shepherd racing beside him, Helen wondered what she was getting herself into.

You're making a big mistake, Clarke. You're going to end up getting too close and falling in love with him all over again. Like you think he's not going to ask you about what happened last time? When that happens, what are you going to say?

Helen swallowed—hoping to push down the rising sense of panic. *How do you tell the love of your life that he's fallen in love with a fraud?*

CHAPTER NINE

Chris had plowed and salted the paved lane before taking his family riding, but that did very little. Since the temperatures had refused to move above freezing, it was still a treacherous trip up the long driveway. Helen was afraid that even if she did succeed in making it to the barn, she'd end up sliding downhill when she left. She envisioned crashing through the gate, skating across the main road, and launching her state police cruiser into the Shenandoah River.

Helen was holding her breath while creeping up the driveway when Sierra called on her vehicle's hands-free phone. "Mom, where are you?"

"At Ms. Matheson's farm," Helen said.

Sierra uttered a girlish squeal. "Setting up riding lessons for me?"

Helen wasn't crazy about horseback riding—especially for her daughter. She still cringed when remembering the first and only time she had ridden a horse. Chris had taken her on a trail ride and she had suffered a serious fall—receiving a concussion even though she wore a riding helmet. Her parents never permitted her to ride again. That was one rule they had set that she never broke. In Helen's book, horses were beautiful animals to admire, but not to ride.

It was just Helen's luck that Sierra had gone on a trail ride while at a summer camp. She had been itching for lessons and a horse of her own ever since. After six years, Helen had hoped she'd grow out of it. Not so. Sierra's desire for a horse had only grown stronger, especially since she started working for Doris Matheson and hearing stories about their horses. Helen suspected her daughter had been putting money away from her job to buy a horse with the intention of boarding it at the Matheson farm.

At the end of the lane, Helen turned the steering wheel to cross the barnyard to park next to the barn. "I have to talk to Chris for a case I'm working on," she told Sierra.

She cursed under her breath when the SUV refused to make the turn. Instead, like a stubborn animal deciding it'd had enough, the vehicle slid sideways and stopped.

"Ask him about riding lessons," Sierra said. "His mom said he'd give me lessons if you say it's okay."

"Maybe."

"Plee-eeze," Sierra begged as Helen pressed her foot on the accelerator.

The engine roared but the SUV wouldn't budge. It remained crossways at the top of the lane—blocking access for anyone entering or leaving the farm. Helen bounced in her seat, trying to scoot the SUV forward to no avail.

Helen sighed, "Okay." She put the SUV in park before she realized to what she'd accidentally agreed.

"Yes! Thank you, thank you, thank you! I love you, Mom!"

"Wait!"

"I have to call Danielle and tell her that I'm taking riding lessons!" Sierra disconnected the call.

"Wait!" Helen yelled at the communication device in her SUV.

"Wait what?" Chris asked through the closed passenger window.

Helen slumped in her seat.

"I know it's been a while," Chris said, "but the barn is up there." He pointed at the large red building with a silo. "That's where we keep the horses." He jerked his chin in the direction of the farmhouse. "That's a house. That's where we keep the humans."

"Still a smartass, huh, Matheson?"

"Don't worry. I'll tow you out." In spite of her effort not to join in his laughter, she was smiling when he opened her driver's door. He held out his hand. "It's really slick."

"No kidding."

She grasped his arm to keep from falling when she climbed out of the car. Like a couple of figure skaters, they wrapped their arms around each other's waist to make their way up the hill to the barn.

"Helen!" Doris called from the back door of the house. "Are you staying for dinner?"

"I'm just going to talk to Chris for a bit," Helen replied from over her shoulder. "I need to get home to Sierra."

"You're finally going to ask him about riding lessons," Doris said. "That's good. Christopher, I suggest you teach Sierra on Chewbacca. She's gentle but has enough spirit to give her a good ride."

"Riding lessons?" Chris asked Helen.

With a growl, she hurried ahead without him to get inside the barn where she'd have a more secure footing.

Chris turned around to where his mother was on the side porch. Twitching their snouts to test the temperature, Sadie and Mocha flanked her. "What's this about riding lessons?"

"Sierra wants riding lessons." With a shiver, Doris folded her arms across her chest. "I told you that."

"No, you didn't."

"Yes, I did. Remember? You said you'd do it if it was okay with her mom."

"Oh yeah, I remember now," Chris said with a heavy dose of sarcasm in his tone. "That was the same conversation where you told me that Sierra's mom was Helen."

"Yes, exactly. Now you remember."

"That conversation never happened!" Chris said. "I didn't find out Helen was back until I saw her last night."

"I told you Sierra's mom was Helen."

"You told me her name was Helen but—"

"So you admit it."

"But you didn't tell me that *Sierra's* Helen was *my* Helen!"

With a roll of her eyes and a wave of her hands, Doris and her canine entourage trotted into the house and closed the door.

"Women!" Chris spun around and almost tripped over Sterling, who was sitting at his feet. He had a red rubber ball, filthy with mud and bits of straw, clutched in his jaws. Chris recognized it as a toy that he and Winston used to play fetch with until the ball disappeared.

"Where did you find that?" He took the ball from the German shepherd who stood up and wagged his tail in anticipation of a round of fetch. When he tossed the ball up high into the air, Sterling leapt to catch it—with all four feet leaving the ground. A wave of bittersweet nostalgia washed over Chris. Winston used to catch the same ball in the same way.

Something old is new again.

"You've got company," Helen yelled from the barn to interrupt his thoughts. "Your security monitor in here shows a white SUV at the gate. There's a woman driving it."

With Sterling following in hopes of another throw, Chris went into the barn to a converted tool room where he had two security monitors displaying feeds from multiple security cameras. Upon moving back home the summer before, he had set up a security system, which included motion detected cameras positioned around the farm. He zoomed in on the woman sitting behind the wheel of the SUV waiting at the gate.

"Matheson," she said into the mic located next to the keypad, "it's me, Patterson." She uttered a sigh. "We gotta talk about that body you found."

"Sounds like she knows you," Helen said.

"She does." Chris punched the button to open the gate. "She used to be my boss." He ran back outside to direct the white SUV to park behind Helen's cruiser and help her up to the barn.

Helen braced for meeting the federal agent from Washington DC. She saw a smile cross Chris's face as he made his way across the ice to the driver's door and opened it. "Patterson, what have you been up to?" he asked as he grabbed the door handle and pulled the door open.

"Oh, not much," Agent Regina Patterson replied in a pleasant tone.

Seeing his former boss's bulging stomach, Chris's eyes opened wide and he let out a loud gasp, followed by a laugh. "You've been busy, Chief."

He grasped her arm to help her climb out of the SUV and wrapped an arm around her thick waist to steady her on the ice.

Helen hurried across the ice to take her other arm to keep the pregnant woman from falling. When Chris started to guide her to the barn, Regina asked, "Is there a bathroom in there?"

When Chris answered that there wasn't, she replied, "Then take me to the house. This baby likes to sit on my bladder."

Doris, who had been watching through the kitchen window, met them at the door and ushered the agent to the guest bathroom. By the time Special Agent Regina Patterson returned to the kitchen, Doris had put a tea kettle on and set a platter of cookies on the table. She had also sent her granddaughters to the family room to watch a movie to allow them to discuss the case in private.

"What are you doing out here on an inch of ice eight months pregnant?" Chris asked his former boss while she poured honey into her tea.

"What are you doing with a dead mobster on your farm?"

"What was the cause of death?" Helen asked. "I didn't see any gunshot or knife wound."

"He did have a blow to the side of the head," Regina said. "But even on-scene, the forensics people don't think that was serious enough to kill him."

"I saw bits of manure and straw on his coat and shoes," Chris said.

"And you have a barn and horses," Regina said with an arched eyebrow.

"Yeah, well," Chris said, "just the presence of the manure and straw is significant because Tommy suffered from allergies. He was basically allergic to mammals."

Helen and Regina exchanged glances.

Chris gestured at the dogs lined up along the French doors. They were peering out at the birds gathered around the feeders. Even Thor, perched between Sterling's front paws, was watching the show. "Tommy couldn't come into this room without an inhaler and antihistamine."

"You're saying that he wouldn't willingly go into a horse stable," Helen said.

"Not unless he had a damn good reason."

"When was the last time you saw Tommy?" Regina asked.

Thinking, Chris shrugged his shoulders. "Close to twenty years ago? Back when I knew him, he was with the Krawford organization."

Regina nodded her head. "Still is from what little I was able to find out before running out here. Eugene Krawford passed away six years ago. His eldest son, Boris, is now running things—which we believe will make it easier to pin a RICO charge on him. Morale is at a low point in the organization, and Boris is not one bit afraid of killing any one who threatens his criminal enterprise."

"Chris listed the types of things the Krawfords were into," Helen said. "Mostly white collar. What would one of their people be doing here?"

"Tommy loved to gamble," Chris said.

"He was included in the inner circle of the Krawford Enterprise," Regina said. "Loved to flash money and brag about being a big shot."

"He was brilliant when it came to computers and information technology," Chris said, "but he lacked what my dad used to call horse sense. I'm willing to bet he got mixed up into something he shouldn't have at the casino."

"His credit card indicates that he was gambling at the casino," Regina said. "The last sign of activity on his account was checking out of the Stardust Hotel Monday morning."

"If he liked to gamble, he could have gone to the racetrack, and that's where he got the manure and straw on his shoes," Helen said. "There's a lot of shady characters who hang out at the track. That's an expensive coat he was wearing. Maybe he got mugged."

"That would explain why he had no wallet, identification, or cell phone on him," Regina said. "He could have been gambling at the racetrack and gotten killed during a robbery gone wrong. The perps hid his body in a stall until they could dump it. That would explain the manure and straw. What do you think, Chris?"

Instead of answering, his brows were furrowed in deep thought.

"Chris?" Helen touched his arm.

Startled, he jumped in his seat.

"Are you still with us, Matheson?" Regina asked.

"You said Tommy was gambling at the casino and staying at the hotel," he said. "He checked out Monday morning?"

"Yes, that is pretty much what I said verbatim."

"Last night, a woman was murdered at the department store in town," Chris said. "She'd gotten a DUI the day before, which would be Monday. She offered the police information about a murder in exchange for a deal. She hung out at the casino. She could have seen or heard something in connection with Tommy's murder."

"What exactly did she offer the police?" Regina asked.

"We'll have to ask the deputy sheriff," Helen said. "His name is Rodney Bell." She saw Chris cringe at the prospect of bringing Rodney into the case.

"Let's plan on meeting with him tomorrow." Regina drained her cup of tea. "We should have a positive ID on the body by then." She closed the notepad on which she had been taking notes and stood. "If the facts of the two murders show a connection, then we'll go over to the casino and—Augh!"

Chris and Helen leapt out of their chairs to help the woman clutching her stomach. Doris ran in from the main part of the house.

"Chief! Are you okay?" Chris asked.

Uttering a deep gut wrenching groan, she said, "I think I'm having a baby." She doubled over and let out a scream.

Sadie and Mocha whirled around and retreated from the kitchen with their tails tucked tightly between their legs.

While Chris and Helen stood frozen in shock, Doris ushered Regina toward the breakfast nook while snapping orders like a drill sergeant. "Don't just stand there with your hands in your pockets, Chris. Pull the table out of the booth to make room. Helen, call emergency and order an ambulance."

"But there's an inch of ice outside," Helen said while fumbling with the case to get her cell phone out, "and my car is blocking the driveway."

"Then they'll have to bring the gurney up the hill," Chris said.

"How far along are you?" Doris asked Regina in a surprisingly calm tone.

"I'm not due for three weeks," she said between gasps.

"That makes your baby one of those go-getter types," Doris said. "That's good. Chris was a month late, and I had to push him all through life. I have a friend whose baby was three weeks early, and he ended up being a type A—graduated top of his class a year early and went to West Point." She patted Regina on the shoulder. "Don't you worry. Your baby couldn't be in safer hands. So you just sit back and relax and we'll take care of everything."

She turned to Chris. "What are you standing around for? Go get the truck and tow those cruisers out of the way and put more salt on the lane."

"What do you want me to do, Doris?" Helen hoped Doris would order her outside to help Chris.

"Stay on the phone with dispatch." Doris turned her attention back to Regina. "I'm just going to check on my granddaughters and get a blanket for you. I'll be gone two minutes. If you need anything, Helen will be right here."

As Doris hurried out of the room, Regina uttered a deep sigh of relief. "Wow. If I was going to go into early labor, I guess this was the place to do it. What does Chris's mother do? Is she a nurse?"

"She's a librarian," Helen said.

Regina wrapped both arms around her stomach.
"It's okay. She reads a lot."

CHAPTER TEN

The slimmest sunbeam poked through the curtains of Chris's bedroom window. His cell phone started buzzing and vibrating on the nightstand next to his bed. He lifted his head from the pillow and saw that he needed to stretch across two life forms to reach it—Emma and Sterling.

Forget it. Too early for so much effort.

He dropped back onto the bed and waited for the buzzing to stop—which it eventually did. Closing his eyes, he drifted back to his dream—at which point the phone demanded his attention again.

"Damn it." Chris stretched across the bodies to snatch the phone from the nightstand. He didn't recognize the number listed on the caller ID.

The time was twenty minutes after six in the morning. He had been looking forward to sleeping in since the schools were still closed due to the ice-covered roads.

He punched the screen to connect the call and put the phone to his ear. "What?"

"Why didn't you tell us that someone knocked off Ethel Lipton?"

Still waking up, Chris paused to put a name to the familiar voice. "Elliott?"

"I vouched for you to get you on the team. Keeping pertinent information to yourself makes you look like a lone wolf. There's no place for lone wolves on the Geezer Squad."

A draft across his neck made Chris shiver. "What the—"

"Jacqui thinks she found Sandy Lipton."

"Are you kidding me?" Every bit of sleep left Chris's body. He sat up straight in his bed. In doing so, he pulled the blankets off Emma and Sterling.

"Do you know where Billie's is in Ranson?"

"I'll find it."

"Meet us at Billie's at seven." Elliott ended the call.

Sterling reached over, grabbed a mouthful of the comforter and plopped back with the blanket covering Emma and himself. She wrapped her arms around the German shepherd and buried her face into his fur. Chris noticed then that there were three bodies in bed with him—Emma, Sterling, and Thor. The bunny was tucked in between her friends on top of the blankets.

Chris tossed the phone onto the end table and climbed out of bed. As soon as his bare feet hit the hardwood floor, he jerked them back up. The floor was freezing. There was a chill in the air. A quick glance at the electric clock confirmed his first suspicion.

The power was off.

Ah, man!

Chris found his mother starting a fire in one of the house's three working fireplaces. One fire was already going in the dining room's fireplace. He was thankful that he had filled the firewood bin on the back porch as soon as the weather bureau had predicted the ice storm. Nothing was more miserable than hauling firewood from the wood pile during bad weather.

Billie's Restaurant had been located on a street corner across from Ranson's city hall. Ranson was a tiny town next to Charles Town.

Good on food, short on atmosphere, it was a favorite diner for local folks. Chris had seen the building boarded up and assumed it had closed. Obviously, the diner had moved to another location since the Geezer Squad was meeting there. The best source for finding their new location was Doris Matheson.

After reporting that Billie's had relocated into a shopping center across from the post office, Doris followed her son into the mudroom. "You're going out for breakfast?" she asked when she saw him putting on his coat and boots.

"I'm meeting Elliott and—" Realizing how strange it would sound to be meeting his book club for breakfast on such short notice, Chris stopped. "Elliott. He called and asked if I'd like to meet him for breakfast."

"Elliott?" Doris clasped her chest. Even Sadie and Mocha were cocking their heads at him. Three pairs of eyes narrowed. "Why?"

"Why not?"

His quick response gave her reason to pause, but not long enough for him to make his escape. "You do know the power is out?"

With a nod of his head, Chris responded that he did. "Do we have enough milk, bread, and toilet paper? I can stop in town if we don't."

"Yes, but you know those girls are going to have fits when they realize that we don't have cable or wi-fi."

"Which is why I'm leaving before they wake up," Chris said with a wicked grin.

"And you're leaving me here alone with them?"

He grasped her shoulders. "Mom, no one is better in a crisis than you. I saw you practically deliver a baby yesterday."

"I did not deliver a baby," Doris said. "I only calmed three hysterical law enforcement officers highly trained to handle emergencies until the ambulance got here. And don't think I didn't notice you taking an extremely long time to clear that lane, which you conveniently didn't finish until *just* when the EMTs arrived. Even after the ambulance got here, you hid in the barn until after they took Regina away in the ambulance."

"I was being thorough in salting the driveway."

"And all of that was for what? False labor."

"Do you think Patterson wanted to go into false labor out here? She just landed a big case—one that can make her career if we can prove the Krawford family had something to do with Bukowski's murder. Now she's bedridden until she has the baby."

"You get along with her, don't you?" Doris asked. "Can you trust her to not frame you like Rodney Bell is probably going to try to do for Ethel Lipton's murder? From what you told me about this Tommy Bukowski, someone with a grudge against you could spin it to make it seem like you whacked him. They could say you saw him around town and decided to get even with him for getting one of your witnesses killed."

"And left his body on our property for me to find? That would be just a little bit stupid."

"Or just a little bit genius depending on how you look at it."

"Regina Patterson does respect my experience and skills," Chris said. "Plus, she's fair enough to keep me in the loop during her investigation, which is why I agreed to help her while she's bedridden."

"I knew you'd find some way to worm your way into this case," she said. "Is Regina still at Jefferson Medical? If the power doesn't come on soon, I'll take the girls in for breakfast and we can stop by to visit her."

"No, she'll be gone," Chris said. "Her husband was going to take her home as soon as they released her. He's a nice guy. Helen and I waited around at the hospital last night until he got there. She'll be working remotely from her bed. Speaking of Helen, why didn't you tell me that she'd moved back here?"

"I did."

"Did not."

"Did so." Her hands were on her hips. "It was the Friday after Sierra started working at the library and Helen came in to pick her up." She wagged her finger at him. "I told you at dinner that night."

"Mom, I'd remember if you'd told me that Helen Lawson had moved back here."

"We were eating tuna casserole, and you said, 'Uh-huh.'"

"That explains it." He wrapped his scarf around his neck. "What?"

"We were having your tuna casserole," he said. "I was obviously too traumatized to notice what you'd said."

"Stop being a smart ass. I told you that Helen Clarke has moved back, and you said, 'Uh-huh.'"

"Her name was Helen Lawson."

"Her name is Helen Clarke."

"Now," Chris said. "Back when we were dating, it was Helen Lawson. When you told me that Helen Clarke had moved back here, I had no idea who you were talking about."

"If you didn't know who I was talking about, why didn't you ask me?"

"Because I didn't care." He zipped up his coat.

She folded her arms across her chest. "If you didn't care, why are you upset now?"

"I'm not upset."

"If you're not upset, why are you beating my chops about not telling you that your first love had come home."

With a low growl, he yanked open the door—allowing a sharp breeze through the mudroom that sent Sadie retreating into the kitchen.

"Don't forget your hat! You'll catch your death of cold!"

With a sigh, he reached through the doorway to snatch his knit hat from the coat hook.

Power company service trucks were all over town. With the temperature still in the single digits, the heavy ice had taken its toll on many tree branches—causing them to snap and take down power lines.

Chris found that the power was on in Charles Town and its neighboring town of Ranson, which proved to be a very good thing. Many residents drove into town to get breakfast. The roads were busy with cars, SUVs, and trucks—all filled with folks in search of some place to stay while waiting out the power outage.

Billie's was packed. Chris only counted two servers, who looked exhausted from trying to take care of the unusually large crowd.

It was Chris's first time at the new location, but he quickly saw that the atmosphere hadn't changed. The restaurant had its regular crowd—mostly local residents who knew each other. Patrons would greet each other with handshakes and pats on the back. The servers seemed to know each customer by name and would take time for a friendly conversation while taking orders.

Chris found Elliott, Jacqui, and Francine occupying a table tucked in a corner away from everyone.

"Sit right here, my hunk of beefcake." Francine patted the chair next to her. "Because when you find out what we've uncovered, you're going to want to kiss someone and I want that someone to be me."

As Chris took his seat, he noticed that each of them had a copy of a recently released thriller book resting next to their place setting.

The server, whose nameplate read, "Annette," arrived with a carafe filled to the top with coffee. While she filled each of their cups, Chris searched the breakfast menu to decide what to order.

"Sorry for the wait," Annette said, "but with the power out all over the place, we got a lot of caffeine addicts in here who couldn't get their fix at home. One guy is threatening to lay down with his mouth open under the coffee maker and drink it as it brews."

She flashed Chris a grin while filling his cup. "You look kind of young to be a retiree? Whatcha reading this month?" She leaned over to study the book cover. "Hey, I heard of that. Is it any good?"

"The protagonist's brains are in his pants," Jacqui said, "which is how he ends up in his predicament. As stupid as he is to get himself into that situation, it's totally unbelievable that he's intelligent enough to escape it."

The server's painted eyebrows rose high up on her forehead.

"Hey, did you ever go out with that guy your mother was trying to fix you up with?" Francine asked. "The songwriter?"

"Poet," Annette corrected her with a roll of her eyes. "He was a poet. Has written quite a few books. He teaches at Shepherd University."

"A professor?" Jacqui said with a grin. "Sounds promising. If he's a poet, I'll bet he's a romantic."

"Maybe." With a frown, Annette took out her notepad. "I'm not sticking around long enough to find out."

"What's wrong with him?" Francine asked.

"For one, he lives with his mother."

With a cringe, Chris focused on the menu he had spread out in front of him.

"Snap," Elliott said with a chuckle.

"Did I say something?" Annette asked about Elliott's low laughter.

"I… I live with my mother." Chris closed his menu.

"Well, he's like forty."

"I'm forty-six."

Annette's face turned red. Clearing her throat, she pressed her pen to her notepad. "What will y'all be having this morning?"

"Get the cheese omelet and home fries with a side of bacon," Francine whispered to Chris after giving her order.

Anxious to put in his order so that they could discuss Sandy Lipton, Chris followed her instructions. As soon as Annette was gone, he said, "Out with it. What did you uncover and how did you do it?"

"Why didn't you tell us that Ethel Lipton got gunned down the other night?" Jacqui asked. "We had to find out from Francine."

"Good thing I still maintain my sources from my AP days."

"I was a little busy getting drilled by the deputy sheriff, who's convinced I was behind it," Chris said. "He thinks I hired the thugs who killed her and then killed them in what looked like self-defense to cover my tracks."

"Did you?" Jacqui asked.

"No!"

"That would be a very clever plan if you had," Elliott said.

"Was it a professional hit?" Francine asked.

"I think so," Chris said.

"Who are our suspects?" Elliott asked.

"This isn't your case."

"But it's yours?"

"Yes," Chris said. "My old boss was assigned the case to investigate a body that I found at our farm yesterday—"

"You found a body on your farm?" Francine said. "Why didn't you tell us?"

"Because—"

"So you're investigating two murders and you left us out in the cold?" Jacqui turned to Elliott. "He's not a team player."

Her bottom lip sticking out, Francine folded her arms. "Not at all."

Elliott picked up his coffee. He turned away from Chris while taking a sip from the cup. "If you're not going to share with us, then why should we share with you what we've uncovered?"

They turned their backs to him. Even Francine scooted toward the far corner of the table — away from him.

"Seriously?"

Elliott turned back to him. "You're too young and haven't been retired long enough to know what it's like, Chris. This may seem like a game to you, but it's real for us. We were all extremely good at what we did—just like you." He tapped his temple. "Mentally, we were like athletes. The mind needs to be exercised—wants to exercise—otherwise you lose it, just like with every other muscle in your body."

"You get so bored that you feel like you're going to go crazy," Francine said.

"That's why we work as a team," Elliott said. "We're all in the same boat. Feeling bored and useless."

"While mentally, we still have a lot to offer," Jacqui said.

"When one of us gets a case, we share with the rest of the team," Francine said.

"And you'd be surprised what your team members can offer," Elliott said.

Chris looked around the table.

Annette arrived with a tray laden down with plates. In silence, he studied each member of the squad one by one. He felt like a child who had received a fabulous new toy that he had hidden to keep to himself—only to have it discovered by his friends.

Guilt washed over him.

"I'm sorry," he said after Annette had left. "I didn't realize. You're right, Elliott. I'm still mourning my wife—and now losing Winston. I've been so busy adjusting to coming back home that I haven't really had time to get settled and bored yet. But that's no excuse. You invited me to join the Geezer—"

The three of them shushed him while glancing around to make sure no one heard him.

Grinning, Chris corrected himself. "Your book club. I'm sorry. Please give me another chance."

The three of them looked at each other.

"Okay," Elliott said. "On two conditions."

"What?"

"One, you tell us everything about Ethel Lipton's murder and the body you found at the farm."

"I'll share everything I know," Chris said. "What's the other condition?"

"You pick up the check for breakfast."

Chris saw the corners of each of their mouths turn up while they awaited his response. Slowly, he nodded his head.

Francine let out a laugh and moved in close to him. "Now that that's done, time for you to brief us."

"What about Sandy Lipton?" Chris asked.

"You go first," Jacqui said. "Tell us about this hot federal case that you managed to snag."

"And why haven't any of my sources found out about a body being found yesterday?" Francine asked. "I usually learn about that type of stuff before it hits the media."

"Because the feds want to keep it quiet," Chris said. "They don't want the victim's boss, who is being investigated for organized crime, to realize that the body had been discovered—just in case he's involved. The body was taken to Washington for the autopsy and only one member of local law enforcement knows about it."

"Who?" Elliott asked.

"Lieutenant Helen Clarke."

Letting out an "ooh" Elliott and Jacqui exchanged smirks.

"What?" Francine asked them.

"You were late the other night," Elliott said. "When Chris saw Sierra's mother…" He gave a wicked chuckle at the flush that rose on Chris's cheeks.

"There were actual sparks between them," Jacqui said.

"We're old friends," Chris said.

"Did you date her?" Francine asked.

Chris sighed. "Yes."

"Who broke it off?"

The question made his chest ache at the memory. "To get back to what we were talking about—"

"Who called Helen?" Jacqui asked with an arched eyebrow.

"I-I did." He added, "Out of professional courtesy."

"Yeah, right," Jacqui said.

"Saturday is Valentine's Day," Francine said.

"We're just friends," Chris said.

"Oh, but you want to be so much more," Jacqui said.

"Say it with flowers," Francine said.

Changing the subject, Chris rattled on about the shooting, Rodney Bell's interrogation and revelation of Ethel's claim to know something about a murder, and the discovery of Tommy Bukowski's body on his farm.

He finished up by telling them about Regina Patterson's false labor pains.

"The thing is," Chris explained, "Regina is up for a big promotion. If Tommy's murder is connected to the Krawford family, then she would be a shoo-in for the promotion. So she's still working on the case while bedridden and she asked me to be her leg man."

"Even though you're retired, and the body was found on your farm, which makes you a suspect?" Elliott asked.

"She's keeping as much under wraps as possible," Chris said.

"And what do you get for this?" Jacqui asked.

"To be on the inside of the case."

Elliott grinned. "You're curious. Even if she didn't ask you to help, you'd be all over this case. You're just like your old man."

"Rodney Bell thinks the murder Ethel Lipton was talking about was her daughter's," Chris said. "I think it was Tommy's because Ethel was a regular at the casino and Tommy was a gambler. I'm going to have to prove it because Rodney has his sights on me and he's not going to look at any other suspects."

"If he's any good as a detective, he'd be more interested in evidence than rumors," Elliott said.

"It's not so much rumor as it is a personal grudge," Chris said. "We used to be friends."

"Used to be?" Francine asked. "What happened?"

"Life," Chris said with a shrug of his shoulders. "Childhood rivalries got in the way. I grew up and moved on. Based on how quick he was to put me at the top of his suspect list, he hasn't."

Chris shoved his breakfast aside. He had been so busy reporting on Ethel Lipton and Tommy Bukowski, that he didn't have a chance to eat his omelet before it turned cold. "Okay, I spilled my guts. Now it's your turn. Did you find a murder victim whose description matches Sandy?"

"Not a murder victim." Jacqui opened her tablet and scrolled through the screens. "I got together with Ray yesterday—" She let out a sigh in an exasperated tone. "I hate going to Ray's place when his daughter is home."

"Why?" Elliott asked. "I think Sheena's nice."

"Yes, but…" Her voice trailing off, Jacqui narrowed her eyes. "I go over to see Ray pretty regularly because he's got the whole setup—computers and databases. Well, Sheena noticed me visiting him all the time and got suspicious. She started asking Ray about what was going on—"

"He didn't tell her, did he?" Francine covered her mouth with her hand. She lowered her tone to a whisper. "Why, if Sheena found out about the Geezer Squad, Ray would be toast."

"No," Jacqui said. "But Ray had to tell her something."

"What'd he tell her?"

"That we were having an affair."

Their eyes wide, Elliott and Francine jumped back in their seats. While Chris had only seen Ray on the computer monitor, he could not picture the older, plump man with a scruffy beard with the elegant woman sitting across from him.

"Sheena is thrilled about her father finally having a social life," Jacqui said. "All yesterday, she kept smiling at me and giggling when she saw the two of us together."

Francine covered her mouth and giggled.

"Just like that." Jacqui pointed her finger at the journalist.

"Ray must be getting better at this lying stuff," Elliott said. "Last time he had to cover up what he was doing on the computer, he told Sheena that he was watching porn."

Jacqui uttered a growl before turning her attention back to Chris. "Anyway—Ray and I went through the national database, plus the state records here in West Virginia, and Maryland, Virginia, and Pennsylvania. We searched everywhere for a Jane Doe matching Sandy's description who could have been killed around that timeframe."

"And?"

"Nothing."

Chris slumped.

Francine grabbed his elbow. "Then Jacqui thought of something." She gestured at her. "Tell him."

"I remembered you saying that she was pregnant—only a few days from her due date. So I did a search of hospitals—"

"Been there. Done that." Chris held up his hand. "The police did a search of all the surrounding hospitals during that time period for an unidentified pregnant woman or woman who had just given birth. One of our first theories was that she'd been kidnapped in order to steal the baby. The police found nothing."

"Maybe because they were looking for an unidentified woman."

"What do you mean?"

"I did a search of local hospital records around that time period of all Caucasian women between sixteen and twenty-one years of age who gave birth during the week of Sandy's disappearance."

"It wasn't that big a number," Francine said. "So it was a cakewalk to follow up on each one."

"You've lost me," Chris said.

"If someone had abducted Sandy to steal her baby, then they would have had to have taken her someplace to have the baby delivered," Jacqui said.

"Unless the baby was delivered at home with a doctor or midwife," Chris said.

"Don't rain on my parade until I've finished," Jacqui said. "If Sandy had been taken to a hospital to deliver her baby, her abductors couldn't have used Sandy's name. The authorities would've found her and the baby immediately."

"Assuming they cared enough about Sandy to want her to have medical care," Chris said. "I once investigated the case of a couple wanting to steal a woman's baby. They just slit her throat and then cut her stomach open to take the baby."

"Hear me out," Jacqui said. "Suppose her abductors did care enough about Sandy to want medical care and took her to the hospital to have her baby delivered. They would have had to check her in under a different name."

"In which case, she wouldn't have been a Jane Doe," Elliott said.

"And back when Sandy went missing, hospital security was not so tight about checking identifications and keeping records so secure," Francine said.

"They could have used the name of the mother stealing the baby," Chris said.

"That's a thought," Elliott said.

"During her pregnancy, Sandy was being treated by her own doctor under her own name," Jacqui said. "I was thinking that it's unlikely that the woman stealing Sandy's baby, if that's the motive, had any record of pregnancy before the delivery. That's what I was looking for—records of a young woman who gave birth who had no prior arrangements or connections with the hospital and I found one." She handed the tablet to Chris. "Tamara Wilcox. Eighteen years old. She arrived at Jefferson Medical—"

"That's only one block from Sandy's house," Chris said.

"According to the hospital records," Jacqui said, "Dr. Frederic Poole was walking into the hospital when a car, driven by a young man, pulled up in front of him and the driver begged him to help his wife who was in labor. The doctor found her unconscious in the back seat."

While Jacqui continued, Chris's brow furrowed.

"Dr. Poole grabbed a couple of nurses and they took her straight into the operating room to deliver the baby by caesarian. Tamara never regained consciousness and died on the operating table. After the smoke had cleared, it was discovered that the young man never checked the woman in. He had disappeared. Later on, someone found her purse with her Maryland driver's license. She had a Baltimore address. Both proved to be phony."

"What happened to the baby?" Chris asked in a soft voice.

"A girl," Jacqui said. "But she only lived an hour before she died."

Chris felt as if he had been kicked in the gut. "Doesn't make sense," he murmured.

Francine said, "If the motive for kidnapping Sandy was to steal the baby—"

"I'm thinking the kidnappers didn't plan for Sandy to have a cardiac arrest," Jacqui said. "They abducted her to steal the baby, but she had a heart attack during labor."

"They panicked and took her to the hospital—giving a phony name," Elliott said. "Unfortunately, both Sandy and the baby died." Noticing that Chris was deep in thought, he reached across the table and snapped his fingers in Chris's face. "What are you thinking, Chris?"

"Dr. Frederic Poole was Sandy's doctor," Chris said. "He's the chairman of the board for the pregnancy center here in town. He treated Sandy through her pregnancy." He shook his head. "If it was Sandy who he'd found unconscious in that car, then he'd know who it was immediately."

Jacqui let out a deep breath mixed with a groan of disappointment. "Then Tamara Wilcox couldn't have been Sandy Lipton."

"Unless…" As he pieced it together, Chris sat up in his seat. "Unless Dr. Poole was in on her disappearance."

"Why would Sandy's doctor be in on it?" Francine asked. "What would he have to gain?"

"Steal her baby to sell on the black market," Elliott said.

"But he's a doctor," Francine said.

"I've put more than one doctor away for murder," Elliott said.

Francine uttered a sigh. "What I mean is, if the intention was to steal the baby, and this guy was a doctor, and he treated Sandy through her pregnancy, why bother taking her into the hospital?"

"Tamara Wilcox went into cardiac arrest," Jacqui said. "Let's just suppose Dr. Poole was in on it. He knew that Sandy was a young single girl and the alleged father of the baby wanted nothing to do with it."

"I wasn't the father," Chris said.

"This isn't about you," Jacqui said. "It's about Sandy. Dr. Poole sees that she's pregnant and isn't in the best of situations. Meanwhile, suppose he is contacted by a couple who desperately want a baby—desperate enough to buy one on the black market."

"Or suppose Dr. Poole has been up to his eyeballs in the black market sale of babies all along." Francine turned to Chris. "You say he's on the board of the pregnancy center?"

Chris nodded his head. "He's got a lot of influence in this town."

"The pregnancy center would put him in contact with a lot of young desperate, vulnerable girls with unwanted pregnancies," Elliott said.

"Okay, let's say this Tamara Wilcox was Sandy," Francine said. "He's a doctor. Why not deliver the baby someplace other than a hospital in the very same neighborhood where she lives where someone can identify her?"

"Something went wrong," Chris said.

"He may have given her a drug to induce labor," Jacqui said. "If she had a bad reaction to the medication, that could have caused her to go into cardiac arrest. So he drives Sandy, unconscious, to the hospital and Poole makes up a story about finding her in the parking lot and gives a phony name."

"But if Sandy had survived, she would have given her real name and named Dr. Poole for being one of her abductors," Francine said.

"They may have kept her drugged the entire time so that she wouldn't have known who her abductors were," Elliott said. "Was there an autopsy?"

"Yes," Jacqui said. "The medical examiner determined that death was natural causes. She had an undetected birth defect in her heart."

"That birth defect may have contributed to what killed her," Chris said. "There are poisons and toxins that aren't discoverable unless you look for them."

"No tox screen was done."

"If the motive was to steal the baby, then how were they going to kidnap it from inside the hospital?" Elliott said.

"This was twenty-four years ago," Jacqui said. "Hospital security was not as tight as it is now."

"Even back then, Dr. Poole was a very influential doctor in the area," Chris said. "He would have had the means of getting the baby released to adoptive parents."

"We need to find some way to positively identify this Tamara Wilcox as Sandy Lipton," Elliott said. "What happened to her body?"

"And the body of the baby," Chris said.

"That's another suspect we can't forget," Francine said. "The baby's father. Maybe Dr. Poole was working in cahoots with the father. The father could have been the one who put the baby up for sale."

"Not only will the baby's DNA clear me, but it may identify Sandy's real killer," Chris said. "Jacqui, can you and Ray find out who claimed the bodies of this Tamara Wilcox and her baby?"

"It wasn't until weeks after she'd died and the body had never been claimed that the hospital started asking questions," Jacqui said. "At that point, she still had an ID—Tamara Wilcox. The hospital assumed that the family couldn't afford to make arrangements for her body."

"But the police were looking for a Jane Doe or Sandy Lipton," Chris said. "That's why they never found her."

"The police were looking for Sandy Lipton in a shallow grave someplace when her body was in a morgue all along," Francine said. "Like *The Purloin Letter*. Hide a letter among a bunch of other letters. Our killer poisoned Sandy and delivered her to the ER to die. When she died, she ended up in the morgue to get lost among other dead bodies."

"It wasn't until much later that the hospital's business office discovered that the address and ID were a phony," Jacqui said. "The hospital assumed that they had been given fake information because she and her family couldn't afford the medical care. They had no idea this woman was a missing person."

"I'm sure her body is long gone," Chris said.

"Hey, don't underestimate us," Francine said. "In less than forty-eight hours, Jacqui and Ray found a woman who had been missing for twenty-four years. We'll find her body."

"The morgue doesn't just toss out unclaimed bodies with the trash," Jacqui said. "Wherever Sandy's and her baby's bodies went—there's got to be a paper trail. All we have to do is follow it. And, when we find them, then we'll be able to ask them what happened. Even dead bodies talk—no matter how long they've been dead."

Chapter Eleven

Usually, the morning rush at Billie's would end by mid-morning. However, on this morning, the power was still out in most communities east of Charles Town. After they had finished eating, many customers lingered while debating whether to return to their homes or find another place to hang out.

The Geezer Squad gave their table to a family with three small children. Each member of the squad took an assignment to follow up on Jacqui and Ray's findings. Somehow, Jacqui was going to access the hospital records to find out what had happened to Tamara Wilcox's body, as well as that of her baby. Chris was afraid to ask how she would be able to get into the hospital's secure records.

Francine was going to dig into Dr. Frederic Poole's background for evidence of him using the pregnancy center to deal in black market adoptions. She was also going to check her sources for information about an illegal adoption ring that could have kidnapped Sandy to steal her baby.

Elliott fell in step with Chris as he made his way along the plaza's walkway to where he had parked his truck. "How long has it been since you had any contact with the Krawford family?"

"I wasn't even married then. At least fifteen years. Why?"

"And you were undercover when you worked that case."

Chris stopped and turned to Elliott. "I didn't say—"

"You wouldn't have been able to make any progress in the case against them if you weren't. You need to find out if this dude had gotten himself offed by the Krawfords—if it'd been a professional hit. You could ask them, but they'll say no."

"True." Chris was intrigued.

"The only way to find out for certain is to ask someone on the inside."

"Do you know anyone on the inside?"

"I know a guy."

"You know a guy? Close to the Krawfords?" Chris chuckled. "How close?"

Elliott brought his lips to Chris's ear. "Very close." With a wink, he turned and walked away.

Chris called after him. "How long will it take for you to get in touch with your guy?"

"I'll be in touch," Elliott replied with his back to him.

Chris narrowed his eyes to gray slits. *How does Elliott know the Krawfords? Can he be former FBI, too?* At the club meeting, everyone had revealed their background except Elliott.

His phone vibrated to signal that he'd received a text. Chris extracted it from his pocket while making his way to his truck. It was a text from his daughter Emma. The thought of his youngest daughter texting him a note of affection made him smile—until he saw the picture she was forwarding to him. Horror gripped his heart at the sight of Sterling—his eyes bugging—clad in a pink tutu and a plastic tiara wrapped around the top of his head.

"Oh, no!" Chris said to the image of the stunned canine, "Hang on, Sterling!" He shoved the phone into his pocket and ran for the truck. "I'm coming to save you!"

"How was breakfast with Elliott?" Doris intercepted Chris in the family room after breaking up Emma's tea party.

Even Thor, looking splendid in a blue sequined Cinderella costume, seemed disappointed to see Sterling swept away from the table in the girls' playroom. They had been having so much fun eating real sugar cookies and drinking orange juice in plastic tea cups.

"Fine," Chris said while brushing Sterling to make sure he got every speck of the multi-colored glitter that Emma had sprinkled over him out of his fur.

"What did you two talk about?"

"Mysteries."

"What kind of mysteries?"

"The ones on the list for our book club."

He sensed his mother behind him folding her arms—a sure sign of growing suspicion. "Your book club meeting ran ninety minutes late the other night and now Elliott calls you to meet him for breakfast to continue the discussion? That must have been some book."

"It wasn't just Elliott," Chris said. "A couple members of the club met us, too."

"What members?"

"Francine and Jacqui."

"Jacqui?"

Chris gave up on his search for glitter and rose to his feet. "What's wrong with Jacqui?"

"Nothing."

Chris arched an eyebrow at her.

"Her husband was much older than she was," Doris said. "I'm not one to gossip—"

"Of course not."

"—but Jill told me that he was married when they'd met. She was a med student, and he was her professor. He left his wife and children to marry her. He died a little over five years ago. Of course, he left her a fortune. She retired from the medical examiner's office in Pennsylvania and moved to a big showplace up in Eagle's Nest on the mountain."

"If she married him when she was a student and he died around five years ago, they must have been married for a real long time," he said. "Maybe it wasn't as sordid as you think."

"You mean like Blair and her Australian friend?"

As she followed Chris up the stairs to the living room, Doris wished she could suck the reference to his late wife right back into her mouth. Too late. The unspoken truth about why Blair had left her family to take an overseas assignment was out there. The only option she had left was to change the subject. "Katelyn asked me for money."

Chris came to a halt. He squared his shoulders and turned around to face her. At their feet, the three dogs watched the exchange between their masters like it was a tennis match.

"Did she tell you what she wanted the money for?" Chris asked.

Doris folded her arms. Her displeasure matched his. "A date with Zack."

"I hope you said no." With a shake of his head, he held up his hand. "Even if you didn't, I'm forbidding her to go out with him. The guy's a player. He'll break her heart."

"Christopher, don't you remember anything from when you were a teenager? If you forbid her to see Zack then that's only going to make him more attractive to her. She's going to want him more."

"You never forbade me to see anyone. Probably because I didn't get hooked up with losers like this kid."

"Have you forgotten about Rodney? Or how about Felicia?" Her hands landed on her hips. "I can't tell you how many nights I tossed and turned—worried sick while you were dating that tramp."

"Felicia was not a tramp."

"What else do you call a girlfriend who hooks up with your best friend?"

As if the German shepherd were capable of speaking in his defense, Chris looked at Sterling, who laid down with a moan.

Sadie and Mocha almost seemed to smirk in agreement while Doris continued.

"When I could sleep, I had nightmares of Felicia getting pregnant and then we'd be stuck with her in the family. Thank God it was Rodney whose life she ruined instead of yours."

"Mom, you never told me you felt that way about her."

"Exactly!" She practically stabbed him in the eye with a manicured fingernail. "I saw early on that those two were bad news, but I kept my feelings to myself and prayed that your good sense would kick in—which it did." She sighed. "Oh, when you got together with Helen, it was the answer to a prayer."

"And then she ended up breaking my heart," Chris said.

"I'm sure she had a good reason."

With a groan, Chris led Sterling through the mudroom.

"Leave Katelyn to me."

"I don't want you giving her money to go out with that SOB."

"I'll talk sense into her." Doris followed Chris out onto the porch. "You're taking Sterling with you?" Folding her arms across her chest to keep off the chill, she shivered on the porch while watching them cross the driveway. "He's not going to get in that truck. They had to sedate him the other day for us to bring him home."

"He'll ride with me." Chris opened the passenger door and gestured for Sterling to jump in. "Get in, boy."

Sterling looked up at the seat high above him and then back to Chris. He laid his ears back in fear. His eyes were wide.

"Told you."

Chris knelt in front of the former police canine and petted him. "You have every reason to be scared. Something horrid happened to you when you were with your last partner. I get that. But I'm not going to let you be trapped like that. You're not going to be in a crate. You're not going to be locked in the truck unable to get out. Here's the score. If you want to ride with me, you need to get in the truck—front seat. Otherwise, you're going to be stuck here getting dressed up in Lord knows what." He whispered in his ear. "Emma has a Supergirl costume."

Before Chris had time to stand up, Sterling leapt up into the front seat. With a chuckle, Chris slammed the door and crossed around in front of the truck to the driver's side.

"What did you say to him?" Doris asked.

"Can't tell you. It's only between us guys."

Chris and Helen had agreed to meet with Deputy Sheriff Rodney Bell to brief him on the FBI taking the lead on the Tommy Bukowski murder. Hopefully, the lieutenant in charge of the state police's local homicide division could extract details about Ethel Lipton's statement that Chris didn't have the authority to get. They also hoped that her presence would make Rodney less hostile about Chris's involvement in the investigation.

Sterling proved to be a good passenger. Instead of being closed up in the rear compartment of an SUV, he rode in the front seat. When not peering at the passing landscape, he'd cock his head and perk his ears in response to the classical music playing on the truck's radio.

"Oh, that's right," Chris said when he saw Sterling peering at the computer screen built into the dash. "You're used to radio dispatches during your previous ride-a-longs. Do you like music?" He pressed the station selection icon on the screen to change from a Vivaldi channel to Bach.

As the loud thunderous notes of a horn section erupted from the speakers, Sterling sat up straight. His eyes bugged almost as wide as they did when Emma wrapped the tiara around his head.

"It's an acquired taste. You'll get used to it." He patted the dog on the head before turning the truck into a convenience store along Route 340.

They had plenty of time to kill before meeting Helen at the sheriff's department in Kearneysville so Chris decided to fill up his gas tank. He pulled into the service station and climbed out. While pumping the gas, he watched Sterling, who was staring at the radio console in the dashboard, even though it wasn't playing since the engine was off.

While washing the windows to clean the road salt off, Chris smiled at the handsome German shepherd. His markings were very similar to Winston's, but there were telling differences between their personalities. Sterling was much more playful—as shown by using the low hanging tree branch for a swing.

How was he even able to engineer the concept of using a tree branch for a toy? The thought of doing that would have never entered Winston's mind.

How Sterling was able to tolerate Emma putting him in a tutu, Chris did not know. That and his immediate friendship with Thor was clear evidence of his gentle nature. But, gentle dogs don't become police canines. There had to be a fighter lurking somewhere under his mild-mannered exterior.

After he'd finished at the pumps, Chris pulled the truck around to the front of the convenience store. "You're probably wanting a snack, huh?" he asked the dog, who was still studying the radio. The low brooding notes of Johann Sebastian Bach flowed out of the speakers.

Chris slid out of the front seat to go inside to buy a chew bone to keep Sterling occupied during his meeting with Helen. He left the engine running to keep the dog warm during the couple of minutes it would take to make his purchase.

After paying for the chew bone, he hurried outside. Through the windshield, he saw Sterling watching him. His tongue hung seemingly to his chest from his open mouth. When Chris opened the door, an explosion of fiddles playing a Charlie Daniels's tune about the Devil going down to Georgia knocked him backwards.

Sterling had figured out how to change the radio station.

Before climbing back into the truck, Chris reached across the driver's seat to punch the screen until he managed to find another classical station.

Sterling's ears fell to the side. He uttered a whine.

"No country music." Chris climbed into the driver's seat. "Just because we live on a farm and I drive a pickup truck doesn't mean I like country music." He dug the dog treat out of the bag and fought to unwrap it.

Sterling hung his head. His brown eyes darted from where Chris was fumbling with the wrapper that appeared to be cemented around the oversized dog biscuit to the radio's touch screen.

"I hate country music. As a matter of fact, I hate any song with vocals." He let out an exasperated breath and held the unwrapped biscuit out to the dog. "No more country music. I drive and I control the music in the truck. Got it?"

Sterling looked at Chris, the biscuit in his hand, and then back to the console from which a light bouncy classical tune was playing.

"Don't even think about it."

Sterling's eyes met Chris's. Then, quick as a rabbit, he punched the console with his snout. While Reba McEntire lamented about her broken heart, Sterling snatched the biscuit out of Chris's hand.

"I should have left you home with Emma and her Supergirl costume," Chris said as he checked his buzzing cell phone. Helen invited him to meet her for coffee before their meeting with Rodney. "Can I trust you to not take up chewing tobacco while I'm talking to Helen inside the coffee house?"

With the dog biscuit sticking out of both sides of his mouth, Sterling turned his head to look back over his shoulder at him. His arched eyebrow seemed to say, "We'll just see, won't we?"

Chris didn't notice the sheriff's department cruiser in the Black Dog Café's parking lot until after he had turned off the engine. His stomach turned at the thought of the cruiser belonging to Rodney.

As children growing up together, the two boys had been in many fights with each other. As they grew into young men with the same interests and goals, it was natural for rivalry to push the boundaries of friendship, occasionally ending up in a physical battle. While Rodney possessed a bulky muscular build in contrast to Chris's long lean frame, Chris's father had insisted his son train in martial arts from a young age. By the time they were teenagers, Rodney learned that even though he had several pounds on Chris, that didn't mean he could beat him.

Chris realized that he bore some responsibility for Rodney's bitterness toward him. They had both been too immature at the time to understand the value of lifelong friends. After

Rodney's application to the FBI had been rejected, Chris's father offered his recommendation to the West Virginia State Police Academy. Rodney refused it—saying he didn't want Chris's leftovers.

Years later, Chris wondered if Rodney regretted that. If he had accepted Kirk Matheson's offer, he could have the position Helen currently held. That had to be salt on Rodney's wound—seeing the girl he ditched in high school in his job.

Instead, Rodney had married Felicia, the girl he had dated and gotten pregnant behind Chris's back, and worked his way up in Jefferson County's Sheriff Department.

He recalled Rodney's bitter expression when he saw him handcuffed in the back of that police cruiser. "Not my fault he didn't make the cut for the FBI," Chris told Sterling who was still working on the chew bone.

Not wanting to take any chances on running into Rodney, Chris reached to put the key back in the ignition when a tap on his driver's side window startled him.

"Dogs aren't allowed in the coffee shop." A gust of wind blew locks of Helen's dark hair across her cheek. When she tried to brush it out of her eyes, it blew back.

After lowering the window to allow Sterling air, Chris climbed out of the truck. "Stay." He held up his hand to command that Sterling remain in the truck when the dog hopped over into the driver's seat.

When the dog looked at the silent radio in an order to ask that he turn it on, Chris shook his head. "We'll finish that debate later."

"Is the power out at your house?" Helen waited for him at the café's door. "All of Shannondale is out."

"Everything east of Charles Town," Chris said.

"Not Harpers Ferry," Helen said. "Sierra got a text from a friend who lives in Bolivar. She got power an hour ago, so Sierra went over to her place to hang out."

"That means the library must have power. I'll text Mom. She can take the girls there." Chris opened the door and held it for her.

She trotted up to the service counter.

Once inside, Chris stopped to take in the patrons while taking his phone out of his pocket to send a message to his mother. It was a habit he had learned in the military and the FBI. His sense of survival dictated that he constantly be aware of his surroundings. Every time he entered a public establishment, he would stop to take note of every door, window, and person—whether he or she be patron or employee. He also liked to sit with his back to the wall to have a clear view of all entrances and exits to see everyone and their movements.

Doris had told him that his father did the same. "I guess it's a cop thing," she had said.

Chris was making a visual sweep of the café when his eyes met with another pair boring a hole right through him. Rodney Bell put down his cup of coffee.

In contrast to her husband's displeasure, Felicia Bell let out a squeal of delight and rushed over to hug him and kiss his cheek. "Oh, Chris, I heard you were back! It is so good to see you!" The exceedingly slender blonde stepped back and looked him up and down.

Over Felicia's shoulder, Chris saw Helen holding up the line while staring at the two of them. The clerk captured her attention only by raising her voice to repeat her question about what she would like.

"You hardly changed a bit," Felicia said.

"His hair turned gray," Rodney said.

"Not gray. Silver. He gets it from his dad," Felicia said while keeping her focus on Chris. "I think you look very distinguished. Kind of like George Clooney. Don't you think he looks like George Clooney, Rod?"

Rodney curled his lips upward into a snarl.

"I'll let you two go back to your coffee." Embarrassed by her public display of affection in front of her husband, Chris eased toward Helen at the counter.

To his surprise, Felicia moved along with him. She grasped his elbow—not unlike she had so many years before.

"I heard you were living out at the farm. I remember how we used to go out riding together. We used to have so much fun back then." Suddenly noticing Helen, Felicia greeted her with a nod of her head. "Did Chris take you horseback riding when you two were together?"

"Once." Helen eyed Chris over the top of her cup.

"Oh, that's right!" Felicia laughed. "I totally forgot. You only went riding once for about five minutes. Then you fell off and got a concussion. Man! Your dad almost killed Chris. As a matter of fact, didn't he punch you at the hospital, Chris?"

With a sigh, Chris looked down at his feet.

To his surprise, Helen grasped his hand and squeezed it tight. "It was an accident. Dad was just upset about me getting hurt." She caught his gaze with her eyes. "He apologized to Chris afterwards."

"Well," Felicia said, "I loved those horseback rides." She rubbed his arm. "I still have wonderful memories of riding across those fields… and our afternoons in the hayloft."

"Can I help you, sir?" the clerk asked Chris.

"Yeah," he said as he saw Rodney stand, "beam me out of here."

Rodney stepped into his wife's space. "Felicia, we need to finish our conversation." He was close enough to Chris, who was trapped by her hand on his elbow, for him to smell the coffee on the officer's breath.

"I've said all I have to say." Felicia moved in closer to Chris and tightened her grip on his arm.

Chris and Helen exchanged glances. Obviously, they had entered the café while the couple were in the middle of an intense discussion, which Felicia had chosen to end by latching onto Chris.

Rodney stepped forward to find Chris blocking him. "I don't know what's going on here, Rod, but from what I see, you may want to step outside and cool off a bit."

"You're right, Chris. You don't know what's going on here. This is between me and my wife. So stay out of it." Rodney punctuated his point by jabbing him in the chest.

Helen pushed her way in between the two men. "Seems to me Felicia doesn't want to talk to you right now, and you have a meeting with us in ten minutes. So, Rodney, I'm going to highly recommend that you go back to your office and cool off before Chris and I meet you there. You and Felicia can finish your discussion later."

Rodney remained still. His eyes were narrowed to dark slits as he eyed Felicia who regarded him with a fiery glare. He then turned his attention to Chris, who stood braced for a fight.

There was silence throughout the café. Everyone held his or her breath. What would the deputy sheriff do next? All were very aware of the gun he wore on his belt.

Slowly, Rodney turned and left the cafe.

Once he was gone, everyone let out a sigh of relief. Chris rushed to the door to watch Rodney climb into his cruiser and drive out of the parking lot.

He saw that Sterling, sitting in the driver's seat of the truck, was also watching the police cruiser.

"Felicia, what was that about?" Helen asked her in a low tone. "Rod looked like he was going to have a stroke."

"Rod and I separated last summer after our younger son graduated from college," Felicia said. "He isn't taking it well at all. He's convinced there's someone else and there isn't."

"You could file a complaint with the sheriff," Helen said. "Get a restraining order."

"I don't want him to get into trouble at work," Felicia said. "I do love him. He was a good father to our two boys. He was a good husband, too. It's just that we grew apart."

"I can tell you're frightened," Helen said.

"Forget I said anything." Felicia gave Chris a weak smile. "Do you remember what you used to tell me back when we were dating?"

"I told you a lot of things."

"You said that I was one of those people who never knew a good thing until she let it go," Felicia said. "You were right. I never should have let you go." She reached up to wrap her arms around his shoulders and kissed him on the cheek.

In an attempt to push down raising jealousy, Helen found an empty table and sat down.

With the soft kiss, Felicia pulled away from Chris, who stared into her sad eyes. She flashed a polite smile in Helen's direction and left.

"That was… awkward." Chris turned to the waiting cashier to place his coffee order.

While waiting for the clerk to prepare his coffee, Chris tried to ignore Helen's glare by focusing on the headlines of the local newspapers stacked along the counter. He received his news via a phone application. For local news, he relied on his mother, who kept on top of everything. As he glanced at the various headlines, he was struck by the image of his own face looking back at him from one of the front pages.

Sinclair Orders Reopening Lipton Case

Chris grabbed the newspaper and scanned the opening paragraph of the lengthy article. Based on new evidence given to the Jefferson County sheriff, Prosecutor Victor Sinclair had ordered they reopen the Sandy Lipton missing person's case.

"Your coffee is ready, sir." The cashier tapped on the counter top to capture Chris's attention.

Helen watched him stumble to their table while trying not to collide with one of the merchandise displays scattered around the cafe. "What's so interesting in the news? Ethel's murder? Or Tommy Bukowski's?"

"My impending arrest." He tossed the newspaper onto the table for her to read the headline and see his picture.

"Are you serious?" She picked up the paper to read the article. "What are you going to do?"

Chris opened his mouth to respond but before he could say anything, they heard a scream followed by deep angry barks from outside.

CHAPTER TWELVE

Chris was first out the door. He was followed by Helen and a few of the café's patrons.

Rodney had apparently driven around the café to intercept Felicia and finish their discussion. Her face contorted in fear, Felicia was pressed against the side of her car. The hundred-pound canine was poised between them. Rodney released his grip on his bloody right arm to reach for his service weapon.

"Sterling! Stand down!" Chris ordered as loud as he could for the dog to hear over his barking.

Instantly, Sterling stopped barking and sat—with his eyes focused on Rodney. Chris grabbed the dog by the collar.

"Is this your dog, Matheson?" Rodney held out his arm. The sleeve to his thick winter coat had been shredded to reveal bite marks on his forearm. "He's crazy. He attacked me for no reason at all."

Chris looked over at Felicia, who was hugging herself. He couldn't tell if she was frightened or freezing in the bitter cold or both. "There must have been some reason. Sterling's a trained law enforcement canine. He wouldn't attack someone for no reason."

"Why did you come back, Rodney?" Helen asked.

"None of your damn business, Helen," Rodney said. "All I wanted was to finish talking to my wife in private. I walked up to her as she was getting in the car and the next thing I know I had a German shepherd attached to my arm." He waved his arm in Chris's direction. "Your dog is crazy and I'm going to have him put down."

"You're not putting down my dog." Chris tightened his grip on Sterling's collar.

Rodney stepped up to Chris. "As soon as the sheriff sees these bite marks, he'll get a warrant for animal control to pick him up. We can't have vicious dogs running around here. The next person he attacks could be a kid."

Sterling uttered a low growl.

"And as soon as the sheriff sees this, he'll put you on suspension." Felicia stepped in between Rodney and Chris. She had shed her coat and rolled up the sleeve of her sweater to show deep bruises on her forearm.

"I'll tell you what happened." She held out her arm for Chris to see the dark markings that outlined a man's hand and his fingers where he had grabbed her. "I was getting in the car and Rodney came out of nowhere and grabbed my arm. I told him to let go, that he was hurting me, but he wouldn't let go and started to drag me to his cruiser. So I screamed for help. That was when your dog jumped out of your truck to come help me."

"So the scream we heard was because Rodney was hurting you," Helen said. "Not because you were afraid of Sterling?"

"Sterling was defending me." Felicia patted the German shepherd, whose tongue hung out of his mouth at the touch of her hand.

"So much for trying to have my dog put down," Chris told Rodney.

"Felicia, do you want to make out a police report against Rodney for assaulting you?" Helen asked.

"Depends." Felicia turned her attention to her husband. "Ball's in your court, Rod. Now that your friends know what you're capable of, I suggest you back off."

All eyes turned to Rodney. He gave his answer by crossing over to Chris. In a low voice, he said, "This isn't over, *Buddy*."

At Chris's feet, Sterling uttered a low growl.

Rodney bumped into Chris's shoulder while passing him on the way to his cruiser, climbed inside, and drove away.

"Did Rodney ever get physical when you dated him?"

Their meeting with Rodney was postponed while he made a visit to the emergency room to have the dog bite treated. They were on their second round of coffees before Chris worked up the courage to ask Helen about the time that she had dated Rodney.

Declared a hero, the manager of the café invited Sterling inside to dine on a complimentary dog treat—his second for the day. During their coffee and conversation, Helen petted Sterling, who laid down between their two chairs.

"No," she said with a shake of her head. "He was jealous of you."

"I would have thought he'd outgrown all that by now."

"It wasn't just because you got better assignments than he did with the Army Rangers and ended up at the FBI," Helen said.

"You'd already left for Morgantown when all that happened."

"Felicia and I have kept in touch off and on," she said. "Back in school, Rodney was so jealous of you that he couldn't see straight. I think being your girlfriend was his main attraction to Felicia. The idea of stealing her from you was too much for him to resist."

"Ain't it ironic?" he said while gazing into his coffee cup. "Rodney stole Felicia from me to hurt me—not knowing that you were the one I wanted all along."

He studied her out of the corner of his eye. She peered at him with her dark eyes. He considered asking her the question that had been on his mind for close to three decades. He was still working up the nerve when she interrupted to return to a topic that was decidedly safer.

"Rodney's resentment was deeper than school boy rivalry," she said. "Your dad would take you camping and come to school events. He was a state police captain—which gave you some prestige. Everyone respected your father. Rodney's dad was a plumber with a bad attitude who kept getting fired."

"Probably so he'd have an excuse to not pay child support," Chris said. "Still, Rodney's stepfather—"

"Was *not* his dad. Sure, his stepfather was a good man, treated him and his mom very well—"

"Bought them that big house in Shepherdstown," Chris recalled. "Gave Rodney anything he wanted."

"You don't understand," she said. "You can't because you grew up with two parents who loved each other and loved you. The point is, there are your parents and then there's everyone else. No matter what Rodney's stepfather did—he wasn't his dad. Rodney would look at your dad—coming to every ball game, school event, beaming with pride about everything you'd do. And you looking up at him like he was—"

The feelings of loss inching in to take over his emotions, Chris shifted in his seat.

"You had the life Rodney wanted and he hated you for it." She paused to take a sip of her coffee. "Do you remember one time—Felicia told me about it—they ran into you at SuperMart months after you and Rodney had graduated from Shepherd?"

Recalling the chilly encounter with the couple who he had considered his closest friends, Chris nodded his head. "They couldn't even look at me. Later, Rodney said Felicia believed the rumors about me and Sandy—that I got some underaged girl pregnant."

"Is that what he told you?" Helen shook her head with a laugh. "Acording to Felicia, he told her that you got accepted into the FBI because your commanding officer in the Army Rangers gave you a huge recommendation after you went to bed with him."

Chris felt his blood boil up into his face. He could feel his cheeks turn red with anger. He tightened his grip on the coffee mug.

"Felicia believed Rod because she couldn't imagine him lying about something like that."

"We dated for almost a year," Chris said in a low voice. "We were intimate with each other."

Helen nodded her head in complete agreement.

"How could she—"

"Felicia isn't the sharpest knife in the drawer," she said. "I know that for a fact. I wrote all of her English and history papers from seventh grade through senior year."

Chris chuckled. "And all through high school, I tutored her in both math and science."

"So, what did *she* do?"

"She brought you and me together," he said.

Helen shot him a coy grin. When his eyes met hers, she turned her attention to her coffee.

"I still can't believe Felicia was stupid enough to believe Rodney about me having sex with my CO."

"She figured it out," she said, "after he used the same lie years later to explain why he got turned down in favor of another deputy for a position with the state police."

"That son of a bitch," he said in a low voice.

"I know he used to be your best friend, Chris."

"'Used to be' is right."

"Rodney always did have a devious streak. So did Felicia. Don't forget about how the two of them sneaked around behind our backs."

Chris's cell phone vibrated to signal a text message.

"They were our friends, and I do like Felicia," she said, "but I wouldn't trust her or Rodney as far as I could throw them."

Chris read the text message on the screen. It was from Bruce: *Red Alert. Emergency Club Meeting at Library ASAP. Break in the Graduate Case.*

Chris texted back. *Library closed due to weather.*

That's why we're meeting there, was Bruce's reply.

Three vehicles were parked in the library's back parking lot when Chris and Sterling arrived. To Helen, he explained the urgent need to leave on his daughters getting into a fight and his mother ordering him home to help her keep the peace.

Bruce's text had come at an inopportune time. Chris would have preferred to spend more time with Helen. He felt as if he was gradually chipping away at the wall that she had put up between them. Where that wall came from and why she had put it up, he had no idea.

Since Elliott had a key to the building, the Geezer Squad had let themselves in and were already setting up a portable squad room in the library's adult section. Jacqui had pulled out a white board and was writing names in columns across the top. Elliott had removed a top from a folder box and extracted five folders, which he set in piles across the length of the table. Each pile contained photographs of murder victims and crime scenes.

Bruce had put two bottles of white wine in an ice bucket and was opening two bottles of red wine. He also had a tray of cheese resting in the middle of the table. "Hope you're hungry, Kid. Francine is picking up a deli tray for our lunch. It may be a long afternoon." With the cork screw, he pulled the cork out of the second bottle of red wine.

Bruce stopped when he saw Sterling on his leash. "That's a dog."

"His name is Sterling." Elliott reached over to pat the dog on the head. "How are you doing, Sterl-man." Sterling offered Elliott his paw. Elliott shook it with a grin. "I guess he's fitting in."

Chris detached the leash. "I had to rescue him from Emma this morning. She had dressed him in a pink tutu."

"Pink is not his color." Jacqui stopped in mid-stroke to look at the dog who sat next to her to stare up at what she was writing. She swallowed. "That's one big dog."

Chris grabbed his stomach when he saw the cheese tray. He felt as if he had been eating non-stop since he had woken up that morning. "Didn't I just have breakfast with most of you?"

"Not with me, you didn't," Bruce said. "I was snuggling with my wife who took the morning off." He held out the tray. "Have some gouda. It's to die for."

Hoping he wouldn't make another offensive mistake while tasting the cheese, Chris took a slice. "Did any of you see the newspaper this morning?"

"Do you mean the Martinsburg paper?" Elliott asked. "The one with your picture on the front page—above the fold?"

"Victor Sinclair has asked the sheriff to reopen the Sandy Lipton case," Chris said, "and I have a feeling I know who's leading that investigation. Deputy Sheriff Rodney Bell."

"Well, I wouldn't worry about that," Bruce said.

"Of course you wouldn't," Chris said. "Because I'm the one who's going to land in jail. Not you."

"We're going to find Sandy Lipton," Jacqui said while double checking the spelling of one of the names she was writing on the board. "And when we do, we'll have everything we need to clear you. The evidence doesn't lie."

His ears perked up, Sterling cocked his head to study the names.

"In the meantime, Victor Sinclair is going to take what circumstantial evidence they do have to the grand jury to try to have me indicted."

"The FBI cleared you," Elliott said. "You have an alibi."

"But they could still claim I hired someone to make Sandy disappear," Chris said, "or someone with influence took care of the situation for me."

"Your father," Bruce said while pouring a glass of red wine into a goblet.

"He isn't alive to defend himself," Chris said.

"But you are," Bruce said, "and so are we. You're forgetting that your father was our friend. None of us are going to let Victor Sinclair, or anyone else, drag his name through the mud. Or yours for that matter."

"Or Doris's," Elliott said. "Especially not Doris's."

"Don't worry about Victor Sinclair." Bruce held Chris's gaze. "I will take care of him."

The low tone in Bruce's voice sent a chill through Chris's spine. "How?"

"Trust me."

Jacqui had finished listing the case information on the white board. "When Bruce says 'trust me,' then you can trust him," she told Chris.

"But—"

"Best not to ask any questions," she said in a whisper. "Less you know the better." She raised her voice to announce that they were ready to begin the meeting.

"Ray has been checking through the case files for the other Graduate Slaughterer victims this morning," Bruce said. "He'll be joining us. Only problem is that we don't have the password to the library computer so that we can Skype him in. Otherwise, we'd have to put him on one of our laptops."

Aware of all eyes on him, Chris reached for another slice of cheese. Casually, he bit into the piece. The corners of his lips curled. "And you think I know the password?"

"I know you know the password," Elliott said. "Doris told me that you were her go to guy for the library's IT stuff."

"Why do you think we let you into the club?" Bruce asked.

Jacqui plopped into the chair in front of the desktop computer and powered it on. Elliott hooked up the webcam. Chris and Bruce stood behind Jacqui while they waited for the home screen to appear.

"You may want to write this down to use in case I'm not here when you want to log on," Chris said.

Elliott grabbed a pen and notepad from the table and stood ready to write.

"Username—all lowercase—is 'doris'."

Jacqui rolled her eyes before typing the name.

"Password—all lowercase—p-a-s-s-w-o-r-d-1." Chris looked over at Elliott, who studied the letters he had written on the notepad. "I can give it to you again if I spelled it too fast."

"'Password1' is her password?" Jacqui asked with a scoff as she continued to open Skype to connect to Ray on the other end.

"I had to put my foot down to make her agree to the *1* to make it just a tiny bit harder to crack."

Chris turned back to the table for another slice of cheese, this one with a cracker, to find Sterling sitting in a chair at the table. To his surprise, the dog was not eating any of the food only a foot away from his snout. He appeared to be waiting for them to start the meeting.

Francine breezed through the door carrying a big tray of lunchmeat and cheeses. A plastic grocery bag containing a loaf of whole wheat bread swung from her arm. "I hope you're all hungry." She stopped when she saw the German shepherd sitting at the table. "I see we got another new member in our group. If I had known I would have gotten dog biscuits."

"He just had two big biscuits," Chris said.

"Is that a dog sitting next to the Kid?" Ray asked.

"This is Sterling," Elliott said while patting the dog on the head. "Sterling, this is Ray and Francine."

His ears fell back, and he opened his mouth to allow his tongue to hang out. The German shepherd held up his paw for Francine to shake.

Taking his paw, she bowed her head in a greeting. "Pleased to meet you, Sterling. Welcome to the Geezer Squad. Though I must say you look kind of young to be a retiree." She set out the food among the case files and pictures.

"Welcome to the Geezer Squad." On the monitor, Ray raised his coffee mug in a welcome.

"He's a retired law enforcement K-9. Shot in the line of duty." Elliott took the cover off the deli tray.

"Retired on medical?" Bruce proceeded to pour the wine into glass goblets.

"Psyche," Elliott said. "Claustrophobic. They had to sedate him for me to deliver him to Chris."

"Didn't need any sedation to get him in the truck this morning," Chris said.

"How did you cure him?"

"I told him that Emma had a Supergirl costume."

"I loved Supergirl." Francine distributed paper plates to each one, including setting a plate in front of Sterling.

"I didn't," Jacqui said. "Much too cutesy for me."

"What female super hero did you like?"

"Black Widow," Ray answered with a wicked grin.

"She's a badass," Jacqui said. "More my style."

Everyone had filled their plates. Elliott even made a turkey and cheese sandwich for Sterling, which he ate with as much decorum as he could without hands and thumbs. While they ate, Bruce went to the board on which Jacqui had listed the Graduate Slaughterer's victims.

"Last night, Miriam and I had dinner at a new Japanese restaurant in Purcellville—one of those that has a hibachi grill. You would never believe who was seated next to us." Bruce pointed up at Shirley Rice's photograph. "Dr. Ben Rice, Shirley Rice's husband. He was there with his second wife, Collette."

"They were estranged at the time of Shirley's murder," Chris said.

"Yes, they were," Bruce said.

"He was cleared as a suspect," Elliott said. "Had an alibi for the time of his wife's murder."

"Wife number two," Jacqui said.

"Doesn't matter," Bruce said. "What matters is what he told me. You see, I told him that I was a retired attorney general and all that. Believe it or not, he opened up to me about having once thought he was going to end up on trial for his wife's murder. Well, saying nothing about my being a member of the Geezer Squad, I asked him to tell me more, and he did."

"What did he tell you?" Francine asked before stuffing the last bite of her sandwich into her mouth.

"He said that the state police investigating the case were gunning for him—"

"That's not true," Chris said. "Dad always thought Shirley's murder was connected to Mona's."

"Let me finish." Bruce picked up a marker. "Ben said that if it hadn't been for the police not finding out about the knock out, drag out fight that he had with Shirley three weeks before she'd been killed, he's convinced that he would have been indicted for her murder."

"What's significant about this fight?" Elliott asked.

"It's not so much the details of the fight that's so interesting as it is the location." Bruce wrote "Fought with Husband at Stardust Casino" under Shirley's name on the white board. Then, he turned to them and waited while their expressions changed from confused to realization.

Chris was the first to speak. "Mona Tabler worked at the Stardust Casino."

Bruce touched the tip of his nose with one hand while pointing at Chris with the other.

"That's the common denominator," Francine said.

"We don't know that for sure," Jacqui said. "That's only two out of five victims." She asked Bruce, "What was the fight about?"

"Shirley found out that Ben had another woman. She followed him to the Stardust where he was meeting her for dinner and she confronted him—causing a scene. Security had to escort her out."

"I'm surprised the police didn't find out about that," Chris said.

"The other woman, who is now wife number two, kept her mouth shut," Bruce said. "This incident was three weeks before Shirley's murder."

"And Ben's alibi for the night of the murder was solid," Elliott said.

"As solid as his mistress saying he had been with her the whole night can be," Jacqui said.

"I'll do a search of the digital case files to see if anything pops," Ray said.

Chris went to the white board to study the pictures of the victims. They were all middle-aged women.

From Lancaster, Pennsylvania, Angela Romano was the first victim. She had been divorced three times. Her age was listed as forty-seven, but she appeared to be much older, with wrinkles etched in her face.

The third victim from Mount Airy, Maryland, was Carla Pendleton, the fifty-two-year-old widow of a veteran.

The fifth victim, three years after Shirley Rice's murder, was Patricia Handle, a sixty-three-year-old administrative assistant with the federal government. She had never been married.

"Doesn't Lancaster have a bus that regularly brings people here to the casino?"

"Sure does," Francine said. "The casino is a big draw for people from all over. Not just for the gambling. People commute here on the buses for the shows and the food. The Stardust would be a great hunting ground for a serial killer."

"Hey, team," Ray said, "I didn't turn up anything in a word search of the files."

"We need to find out if any of the other victims had ever been to the Stardust Casino shortly before they were killed," Francine said.

"Didn't you say that the victim in Lancaster," Chris read the name, "Angela Romano, had told friends that she felt like she was being followed and watched?"

"Yes," Francine said. "We think the killer stalks his victims first to find the best time to strike."

"Three weeks is plenty of time for stalking—especially if he's careful," Bruce said.

"He'd have been caught by now if he wasn't," Elliott said.

"Mona was a hard-ass restaurant boss at the Stardust," Chris picked up the marker and underlined the word "manager at Stardust," that Jacqui had written under her picture. "Her domineering personality and boss job had to have drawn attention to her."

Using the marker as a pointer, he tapped Shirley Rice's portrait. "Shirley confronts her husband when she catches him dining at the restaurant with another woman." He circled the line Bruce had just written "Fought with Husband at Stardust Casino."

"The killer targets the victims after they draw attention to themselves," Francine said.

"Or maybe he targets them *because* they draw attention to themselves," Jacqui said. "I think before we draw any conclusions, we need to check with the other victims."

"You do that." Chris put the marker on the shelf on the white board. "I'm going to the casino to find a killer." He grabbed his coat off the back of his chair.

As he headed for the door, Sterling leapt out of his chair to fall in behind him.

"I'm coming with you." Grabbing her coat, Francine rushed after him.

"Think you'll find a bigger story doing leg work than making phone calls, Francine?" Bruce asked.

"Hey, we can't deny that Beefcake has been the one seeing all the action on these cases."

CHAPTER THIRTEEN

"But I like Carrie Underwood." From her seat in the back, Francine leaned between the two front seats.

Sterling hit the radio with his paw to change the radio back to the country music station.

"Whoever's driving picks the music." Chris pressed the touch screen. "I'm driving and I choose Vivaldi." He held out his hand to block Sterling's paw. "If you want to listen to songs about cheating men and their pretty little souped-up four-wheel drives, then you drive next time." He slapped Sterling's paw away from the console. "And take Mr. Itchy Paws with you."

Francine sat back in her seat. "What's your plan? To put out a request across their PA system asking that all serial killers meet you at the front door?"

"Mona was the restaurant manager," Chris said. "Shirley Rice caused a scene after catching her husband having a dinner date. I vote we start with the restaurant staff."

"There's a big employee overturn in food service. That could explain why we didn't find any more murders fitting this guy's MO. He's moved out of the area and taken up killing someplace else."

"Didn't Ray check the national records?"

"Yes, but—"

"Carson Lipton is the head chef and, from what I've heard, he's been with the Stardust since the mid-nineties. Maybe he'll recall someone who seemed suspicious to him."

"He's also Sandy Lipton's brother."

"And Ethel Lipton's son. Remember, Ethel told the deputy sheriff that she had information on a murder at the Stardust. Carson is a very important link in all three cases." He turned right to drive up the long driveway to the casino's main entrance.

"Your friend Tommy Bukowski was staying at the hotel," Francine said. "All roads lead to the Stardust."

After parking in the garage, Chris rolled down his window for Sterling. "You need to stay in the truck, Buddy." He patted the disappointed dog's head.

"But he'll get cold." Francine shivered.

"With all that hair?" Chris chuckled while following her to the casino's garage entrance.

From the driver's seat, Sterling watched them disappear through the ornate double doors. With narrowed eyes, he waited for them to return. After a long moment, that seemed like an hour to the canine, he whimpered.

"Archie, I have a feeling today's gonna be our lucky day," said an elderly woman in a thick down coat and knit cap.

"It better be, Molly." The old man walking with a cane stopped to catch his breath. "What are we gonna tell the kids? I don't want them to know what a fix we've gotten into."

"It ain't our fault that someone stole your identity and wiped out our savings. Damn computers."

"Damn hackers," he said. "I hope you're right about feeling lucky today. No luck today means no electricity come Monday."

Sterling leapt through the open window and trotted after the couple.

Molly looped her arm through Archie's. "I've been praying every night. Last night, I had a dream that God sent us an angel to pay off our bills. Then, we didn't have to depend on your skill at the blackjack table while the authorities straighten out this awful mess."

Archie opened the door and held it for her to step through. "That's a nice dream, Molly. But miracles only happen to other folks." He followed her inside.

Sterling slipped through the open door before it slid shut.

Francine led Chris through the frosted cut-glass doors of the Stardust's elegant restaurant. Only a few stragglers enjoying coffee and dessert remained from the lunch hour rush.

"I guess your warring daughters declared a truce."

Chris jumped at the sound of Helen's voice from behind him.

Francine turned around to face the state police lieutenant. "Is that her?" she whispered to Chris. "She's very pretty."

Helen was sitting in a corner booth with a man in a chef's white jacket. His face had aged considerably in the two decades since Chris had seen him.

"You know Mom," Chris answered Helen with a shrug of his shoulders. "By the time I got home, my three girls were the bestest of friends again."

Helen turned to her companion in the booth. "Carson Lipton, I believe you know, Chris Matheson."

"It's been ages since we've seen each other." With a broad grin that deepened the wrinkles lining his face, he stood to clasp Chris's hand. "How have you been, Chris?"

"Fine. You?"

With a chuckle, Carson spread his arms wide. "Can't complain. Chef of a five-star restaurant with patrons coming from all over for my cooking. I'm living my dream."

"You've certainly come a long way from that diner across the street. As a matter of fact, I parked my truck in what used to be your kitchen."

Carson let out a laugh.

"I'm sorry about your mother."

"That's why you're here. Lieutenant Clarke told me that you blew away those goons who gunned her down."

"Unfortunately, as soon as the local police found out that she was Sandy's mother, they assumed I was involved in her murder."

Carson shook his head. "I never believed you had anything to do with what happened to Sandy, Chris. Besides, that was a long time ago."

Helen invited them to return to their seats in the booth. Chris introduced Francine, saying that she was a member of his book club. Helen cocked an eyebrow at them, wondering why Chris had invited someone from his book club to join their investigation.

"Chris knew me when I was an investigative reporter with the Associated Press," Francine said. "I once did an expose on gambling and organized crime and he asked if I'd be willing to help. With my sources, I might be able to dig up what Ethel Lipton happened onto here at the casino. Of course, I jumped at the chance."

Wordlessly, Helen regarded Chris with disapproval.

"Francine promised not to publish anything until after we give her the go ahead," he said.

Francine turned her attention to Carson. "If you don't mind my saying, you don't seem awfully broken up about your mother's brutal murder."

"I haven't spoken to my mother in twelve years," Carson said. "Best twelve years of my life."

"But she was a regular here at the casino," Chris said.

"Because they gave her VIP treatment," Carson said. "She'd made a killing when she sold the apartments and diner to Stardust. In four short years, my mother had gone through every penny she had. It's a miracle she still had the house. I keep hearing through friends about the scraps she'd gotten herself into. Loans from the wrong people to pay her gambling debts. Legal fees for DUIs, hit and runs, you name it. Someone keeps bailing her out." He caught himself. "Sorry. Kept bailing her out. Past tense now."

"But you didn't cut her off until recently—long after the Stardust had expanded?" Francine noted. "What happened?"

"I got married," Carson said with a smile. "Mabel. She's the restaurant manager here. She saw that Mom was sucking the life out of me and laid down the law. Said it was her or Mom. Not both. I chose Mabel. Cut mom off completely. Best thing I ever did."

"But she was still a regular here," Helen said.

"Practically lived here."

"And you worked under the same roof." Chris was doubtful.

"I worked in the kitchen." Carson turned in his seat to point toward the hallway leading to the restrooms and a door marked for employees only. "My office is back next to the kitchen and I park in the employee lot. I may go into the banquet facilities in the hotel for special events. As for the lounge and casino—" He shook his head. "I have no reason or desire to go in there and that's where Mom hung out."

"On the same day your mother was murdered," Helen said, "she told the deputy sheriff that she had information about a murder here at the casino—"

"I have no idea what she could have been talking about."

155

"If there was a murder here at the casino, people would have been talking," Francine said in a whisper as if she were taking part in a secret plan. "Come on, you can tell us. Did your kitchen help hear any juicy rumors in the last few days about dead bodies found in the laundry?"

"I don't listen to gossip," Carson said with a shake of his head. "That doesn't mean there hasn't been any rumors flying around. The person you should be checking with is the bartender in the lounge. When Mom wasn't gambling, she was drinking. Ask for Tyler. He works the late shift."

"The deputy sheriff has latched onto the idea that your mother could have found some sort of evidence to prove that I killed Sandy," Chris said.

Carson's mouth contorted as he scoffed. "Mom knew you had nothing to do with Sandy disappearing."

"But she swore up and down that I did and accused my dad of covering it up."

"Because she was jealous. How dare you come from a functional family where everyone worked for everything you had? That's one of the things that Sandy loved about you—your family. She had this fantasy of being part of a family like yours—instead of the trash that ours was."

Carson's blunt response dropped a blanket of silence over the table.

Chris cleared his throat before asking, "Did your mother make Sandy say I got her pregnant?"

"No, Sandy came up with that on her own. I mean, who else could. Look. That prom was Sandy's first date. You were the first guy who'd ever kissed her. She lived in this fantasy world where you were the baby's father. In the end, you would come riding by on your white horse and carry her off to live in your castle on top of the hill overlooking the Shenandoah. Then, the two of you would live happily ever after. Kind of sick if you ask me."

"Who do you think got Sandy pregnant?" Helen asked.

"Whoever raped her. You don't have to be a rocket scientist to figure it out. It wasn't Chris, and Sandy never went out with anyone else. That leaves a rapist."

"Why didn't she say so?" Helen asked. "She ruined Chris's reputation by claiming he was the father."

"Then she stood by and said nothing while your mother accused me of statutory rape."

"Did it ever occur to you that maybe Sandy was more afraid of her rapist than she was in love with you?" Carson asked.

"All these years," Chris said, "you've had to have thought about it. Who do you think raped your sister?"

"Back then, there were racetrack people all over the place—staying in our apartments and eating at the diner. They'd come and go. Any one of them could have knocked on the apartment complex's office door, dragged her into the back room, and raped her."

"But if he was a transient, then he wouldn't have been around nine months later to make her disappear," Chris said. "If the same person who raped her abducted her, then he had to be a regular part of the picture."

"Regular enough to know that blood tests may identify him. So he decided to get rid of Sandy and the baby to keep that from happening," Helen said.

"Any ideas?" Chris asked.

"Have you tried looking seriously at Victor Sinclair?" Carson asked.

Helen's mouth dropped open. "Jefferson County's prosecutor?"

"He had it bad for Sandy," Carson said. "Back then, Victor was just a nerd hoping to make it to the top on his Daddy's name. He had a thing for Sandy, who had a thing for you, Chris."

Carson leaned in Chris's direction and lowered his voice. "As a matter of fact, he came in here for breakfast this morning and asked me about you."

"What did he want to know?"

"He was asking me if I'd remembered anything from back when Sandy disappeared. Wanted to know if I'd seen you since you came back. I told him I hadn't. I also told him the same thing I told him back then. You weren't the baby's father and had nothing to do with Sandy disappearing."

"Thanks, Carson," Chris said. "But I doubt if it did any good."

"Me, too. Victor is out to pin a murder charge on you."

"Why the vendetta?" Helen asked.

"Victor had asked Sandy to prom first," Carson said, "but she turned him down because she wanted to go with Chris. Victor was crazy with jealousy."

"Jealous enough to rape her and then threaten to kill Chris if she said anything?" Francine asked.

Carson tapped his finger against his lips. "I did see Victor's car that night—the night of the prom. When you pulled into the driveway to drop Sandy off, Chris, your headlights shone in through my bedroom window. It woke me up. I checked the time, and it was around midnight. I heard Sandy come in—alone. I don't remember what made me do it, but I looked out my window and saw you drive away. Then, I saw that there was a car in the parking lot at the diner across the street. It was Victor's old blue Camaro."

"Are you sure?" Chris asked.

"Positive," Carson said. "He had no reason to be there. He lived in Shepherdstown. The guy was nuts. A few weeks later, we found out Sandy was pregnant. I think he followed you guys, and then after you left, he broke into the house and raped Sandy."

"Why didn't you say anything?" Chris asked with an edge in his voice.

Carson shrugged his shoulders. "I didn't put it all together until much later."

"When Victor was running for prosecutor, didn't you think the public had a right to know that you suspected him of raping and possibly murdering your sister?" Helen asked.

"I have no proof that he did that," Carson said. "Even back then Steve Sinclair ruled the eastern panhandle with an iron fist. If I had accused his son of rape and murder without any proof, I would have ended up missing like Sandy."

"She was your sister," Helen said. "Your younger sister. It was your job to protect her."

"In case you haven't figured it out yet, my whole family was dysfunctional."

"Did Victor visit Sandy during her pregnancy?" Chris asked.

Carson nodded his head. "Yeah. Sometimes. He'd bring her flowers and stupid gifts. If she saw him pulling up, she'd go to her room and refuse to see him."

Cocking an eyebrow, Helen turned her head. Her eyes met Chris's.

"Speaking of visitors," Chris said in a casual tone, "do you remember the last time I'd stopped by? It was the day before Sandy disappeared."

"When you told us that your lawyer had a warrant for blood tests to be done on the baby as soon as it was born."

"Exactly," Chris said. "There were two men in the kitchen with your mother."

Carson narrowed his eyes and cocked his head.

"When Sandy got upset, your mom and one of the men came out. The other one stayed in the kitchen—like he didn't want to be seen."

"I'm not sure I remember—"

"Don't lie to me, Carson. You were there. I remember very clearly—"

"Now I remember." A grin filled Carson's face. "They were Mason Davenport and Victor's father, Steve Sinclair. He was—is—Davenport's lawyer."

Chris blinked. He was uncertain if he should believe him or not. "That was Victor's father?" He shrugged. "I'd never met him."

"Why would Steve Sinclair and Stardust's CEO have been visiting your mother?" Helen asked.

"To make plans for buying our property," Carson said. "They couldn't have expanded unless Mom sold them the apartments and diner for the parking garage. They needed to know that she'd be willing to sell before they went to the trouble of getting the zoning approved." He nodded his head. "When you came over, they hid in the kitchen because this was real early in the planning stage. They didn't want word to get out about what they were up to because they knew there'd be folks opposed to the expansion and casino."

"And your mother said yes," Francine said.

"Dad used to say that greedy bitch would've sold her own mother if the price was right." Carson looked across the dining room at an exceedingly thin woman with straight white hair approaching their booth.

"The sea bass has just been delivered for tomorrow night's dinner dance. You need to check it before allowing them to unload it." She regarded them with curiosity—not unlike a boss wondering if she'd caught her employees goofing off.

"Time to get back to work." Carson slid out of his seat and gave her a quick kiss on the lips. "This is the love of my life, Mabel," he told them. "Mabel, this is the state police and some of her associates investigating my mother's murder."

"Good luck with that," Mabel said while shaking Helen's hand. "She was nothing but trouble. There're probably half a dozen people in the casino alone who had reason to kill her."

"We only need to find one," Chris said.

"Well, it wasn't Carson," she said in a tone that dared him to say otherwise. "He hasn't seen her since the week before we got married. Do you want to know why?" She went on to answer in the next breath. "Because I told him that if he so much as said one word to her, then I'd be gone." She jerked a thumb over her shoulder. "Out of here and no looking back. I meant it, too."

Chris noted that Mabel was a severe looking woman, whose demeanor lacked warmth. Maybe that was a job requirement to allow the restaurant to keep its five-star rating.

"And that's what he told us," Helen said. "Even so, we do have to question everyone because they may know something without even being aware that they know it."

"Carson doesn't know anything." Mabel folded her arms across her thin chest.

"They were just leaving." Carson gestured in the direction of the restaurant's exit.

While Helen and Francine obediently headed for the doorway, Chris halted. "Actually, there's one more thing."

Francine smirked at Chris's spunk in the face of the cold-hearted woman.

"What?" Mabel snapped.

Ignoring her, Chris kept his attention on Carson. "Would you be willing to submit a sample of your DNA to the police?"

Mabel's face turned red—immediately. Her lips pursed together in a tight line.

His eyes wide, Carson stood up tall.

Mabel opened her mouth to respond, but Chris plunged on as if she wasn't there. "Sandy has been missing for twenty-four years. That was in the early days of DNA being used for identification. Now, I assume her doctor has no DNA samples. But if we can upload your profile into the national database, then we can run a search for all the Jane Does with enough common markers to show a familial match. It could help us find Sandy."

Not offering any response, Carson looked from each one of them to the other—landing his gaze on his wife's.

A smug grin crossed her lips. "You have Ethel's DNA. Can't you run hers through your database?"

"Sandy and I didn't have the same father," Carson said. "I called Sandy's father 'Dad' but he was my stepfather—until he went missing. Mom had a couple of her bar buddies kill him and bury him under a horse stall in the stables at the track."

Thinking he couldn't possibly be serious, Francine let out a nervous laugh.

"The police laughed just like that when I told them," Carson said without humor. "Of course, I was only six years old at the time and I didn't know which stall she had his body buried under. I assume his body's still there."

"Who was your birth father?" Helen asked. "Is he still around? Maybe he'd know something about your mother's murder."

"Doubt it," Carson said. "He was a rapist. Picked my mother up one night when she was hitchhiking home from a bar. Drove her off into some field, raped her, strangled her, and left her for dead." He grinned at their shocked expressions. "That's right. When you heard my mother saying that my pappy was a good for nothin' psychopath, she was tellin' the truth."

"Which is why we cut her out of our lives." Mabel spun on her heels and headed for the kitchen.

With a slight grin, Carson shrugged his shoulders. "Wish I could help you, but like Mabel says, you have Mom's DNA to put into your database. Personally, I don't relish the idea of

Big Brother having my DNA. There's no telling what they'd end up doing with it."

"Carson," Mabel called to him upon realizing he wasn't directly behind her.

"Coming, dear."

Chris waited until they had exited the restaurant before saying, "I wonder if Carson knows he married his mother."

"He wants you to hit him again," Molly told the blackjack dealer, whose hand Sterling was patting with his paw.

"I know." The dealer slipped a card from the top of the deck and tossed it on top of the three that rested in front of Sterling who was perched at the table on a tall stool. "The German has nineteen."

Sterling placed his two front paws on top of his cards.

"He's staying," Molly said.

"We know, Molly," Archie said with a grumble. "He's obviously got a system."

"I think he's counting cards." With his eyes narrowed to slits, the dealer tossed a nine of diamonds on top of his hand. "House has twenty-five. The German wins again."

Molly and a crowd of spectators clapped their hands and chattered with excitement while the dealer added several chips to the impressive pile in front of Sterling.

"Isn't it exciting, Archie? A dog playing blackjack."

"I wish you hadn't given him that chip to get him started, Molly." Archie cursed when the dealer tossed a five of clubs onto his hand, pushing him one over twenty-one. With a look of sympathy, the dealer took the chips he had used to place his bet. "We're probably going to need it."

A low bark drew their attention to Sterling, who slid his paw in their direction. When he lifted it, they found several chips. When Archie looked into his face, he swore the dog winked at him.

"Look, Archie," — Molly giggled while Sterling licked her ear — "he's paying you back. What a nice dog." She patted Sterling on the head as he lapped up his complimentary soda. "Good dog."

"Place your bets!" The dealer used a towel to mop the soda that splashed out of Sterling's glass.

Leaving the chips where the dealer had placed them to let the bet ride, Sterling tapped the dealer's hand with his paw to request a card.

CHAPTER FOURTEEN

A cheer erupted from the casino as Francine led Chris and Helen to the elevators. The crowd was so enthusiastic that they craned their necks to peer inside, but couldn't see through the throng of spectators cheering on one of the gamblers.

"Looks like someone is having a big winning streak at the blackjack table." Francine added in a mutter, "Lucky dog."

Chris grabbed the phone vibrating in his pocket. The caller ID read Regina Patterson. He pressed the button to accept the call and ducked into what he hoped to be a quiet corner.

"Any progress?" she asked him.

"As much as we can without giving away that we know Tommy Bukowski is dead."

"Well, we may have caught a break. His girlfriend has reported him missing. According to her, Bukowski was going on a business trip for his boss—"

"Krawford?" Chris asked.

"That's who Bukowski worked for," Regina said. "And he was supposed to return home last night. But our records show that he checked out of the Stardust Monday morning."

"Two days before his body was found," Chris said.

"And he was killed thirty-six to forty-eight hours before that," Regina said. "Oh, and we have a cause of death. Poison. Xylazine, horse tranquilizer—massive dose. Enough to knock out a horse—kill a human. He had a hairline fracture to the skull. If Tommy hadn't been knocked out at the time of the murder, he was certainly dazed and confused."

"After hitting him in the head, the murderer stuck him with a syringe full of horse tranquilizer," Chris said.

"Our crime scene is a stable," Regina said. "They found traces of horse manure on his clothes."

"If we can get a DNA profile of the manure, then we can identify the horse which will tell us in which stall Tommy was killed."

She laughed. "DNA analysis of horse manure? Do you have any idea how much that'll cost?"

"If it will help solve Tommy's murder to bring down the Krawfords and get you that promotion you want, it'll be worth every penny." Chris told her that he would call with a report after meeting with the casino's security before hanging up.

"Was that your boss?" Helen asked when he rejoined them.

Chris waited for another round of cheers from inside the table games to quiet down before reporting that Tommy's girlfriend had reported him missing and he'd been poisoned with a horse tranquilizer.

"Did this Tommy guy play the ponies?" Francine asked.

"No, he was into table games."

Francine led them to the alcove which contained two sets of elevators. A huge sign announced a black-tie Valentine's Day dinner dance to be held the next night, Friday the thirteenth. At a cost of five hundred dollars per person, the formal event benefited the local animal welfare league.

Silently, Francine nudged Chris and jerked her head in the direction of the sign. Upon getting his attention, she then rolled her eyes toward Helen. "A black-tie dinner dance for Valentine's Day? Sounds romantic, doesn't it?"

"This was Mom's big idea," Chris said. "She's the chairperson for the welfare league."

"Then you can get tickets," Francine rolled her eyes and tossed her head in Helen's direction. "Take your valentine to the dance and make her feel like Cinderella."

Chris glanced at Helen, who was peering at Francine's bobbing head and rolling eyes with curiosity. He was thankful that an elevator arrived behind them and the doors opened.

"No, we don't want that one," Francine told him when he stepped over to hold the door open for them to step on. "Those elevators," –she gestured at the bank of three elevators against the wall— "only go to the guest floors." She nodded at the elevators in front of her. "We want to go to the business and executive offices on the fourth and fifth floor. So we have to take one of these elevators."

An elevator arrived and Chris held the door open for Francine and Helen to step onto the car.

"The killer must have some connection to the racetrack," he told them. "They're going to work up a DNA profile of the horse. If we find the horse, then that could lead us to the killer."

"Who's going to have the fun job of collecting DNA samples from all the horses at the track?" Francine pressed the fifth-floor button.

Chris and Helen exchanged glances followed by smiles.

"I have people who do that sort of thing," Helen said as the doors opened. "Since the victim was found on your property, Chris, we'll also need to collect DNA samples from your horses to eliminate your farm as the murder scene."

"Send your folks out anytime."

Chris held the doors open for them to step off into the business reception area. Helen unclipped her police shield from her belt and stepped up to the reception desk.

Upon seeing the police shield, the receptionist snatched the phone receiver, punched the intercom button, and cut off Helen's introduction. "Judy, a lieutenant from the state police is here."

After hanging up the phone, she said, "Ms. Davenport's assistant will be here in just a minute."

"Ms. Davenport?" Francine asked. "Is she any relation—"

"Mason Davenport's daughter," she said. "Peyton is the vice president in charge of security for both the casino and racetrack. All police inquiries must go through her."

Before they had a chance to sit, a woman with curly artificially red hair arrived to lead them down a long corridor and through a pair of double doors to a suite of offices and cubicles. Everyone seemed to be hurrying from one computer terminal to another. As they passed one pair of glass doors, Chris saw numerous banks of surveillance monitors being scrutinized by a team of uniformed security agents.

Upon rounding a corner, they entered a different world. The outer office was notably more quiet and feminine. Next to the door, there was a table with a display made up of sand and pebbles and what appeared to be a small cactus plant.

"That's a zen garden," Francine told Chris when he stopped to puzzle over the circular designs in the sand.

"What's zen?" Chris asked. "I've heard the word but what is it?"

"It's Buddhism," Helen said.

"Zen is the power of meditation," a sultry voice announced behind him. "It creates an atmosphere of peace and harmony."

Chris turned around to see a young slender woman with a headful of thick dark hair and alabaster skin. Her dark eyes zeroed in on him as she stuck out her hand to shake his.

"Lieutenant Clarke, I'm Peyton Davenport, Stardust's vice president in charge of security."

Helen reached in front of Chris to grasp her hand. "I'm Lieutenant Helen Clarke, Ms. Davenport. This is Chris Matheson. He's with the FBI. Thank you very much for seeing us." She then introduced Francine while neglecting to specify her role in being there.

Peyton grinned—displaying a mouthful of straight white teeth. She kept her eyes locked on Chris's. "I apologize, Mr. Matheson. You just have such an air of authority about you."

Helen's lip curled with disgust while Francine suppressed a giggle as Peyton led them into her office and closed the door.

A woman with long frizzy dishwater blond hair, approximately the same age as Peyton, quietly sat at a conference table in the corner of the office. Peyton's only acknowledgement of her was an occasionally sidelong glance.

"How may I help you?" Peyton asked while taking a seat behind her enormous glass topped desk.

"We're investigating the disappearance of—" Helen paused to make a show of referring to her notes — "Thomas Buk—" she struggled over the pronunciation until Chris interjected.

"Bukowski."

"Whatever," Helen said with an air of boredom. "His girlfriend reported him missing." She flashed a grin. "You know how it is. We have to cover all the bases. According to his credit card statement, he stayed here through the weekend."

"His girlfriend said it was a business trip." Chris said.

"What interest does the FBI have in what sounds like a routine missing person's case?" Peyton asked.

"Mr. Bukowski was from New Jersey," Chris said. "Since this case is crossing state lines, the New Jersey state police requested that our office assist in the investigation." Years of reciting the same explanation repeatedly in many such

169

cases, made the words roll off his tongue as if it had been the truth.

With a glance at the blonde out of the corner of her eyes, Peyton paused before nodding her head to indicate that she understood.

Helen held out her phone with a portrait picture of Tommy Bukowski on the screen. "Do you recall seeing Mr. Bukowski when he was staying here?"

Peyton held out the picture to the blonde. "Yes, as a matter of fact, I do remember him. We met with him on Friday." She finally introduced her subordinate. "This is Rachel Pine, our director of cybersecurity here at the Stardust."

They each shook hands with Rachel between her taking glances at Tommy's picture.

"What was the meeting about?" Chris asked.

"Mr. Bukowski was investigating a ransomware attack," Peyton said. "It seems his boss, Mr...."

"Krawford. Boris Krawford." Rachel handed the phone to Helen. "His system had been hit by a ransomware virus."

"Do you know what that is?" Peyton asked.

"Yes," Chris said. "It's a virus that locks up your computer system so you can't access anything, including your bank accounts. The hacker basically holds your system hostage until you pay a ransom for the key code to unlock it."

"Mr. Krawford paid the ransom and got access to his accounts," Peyton said. "Then he sent Mr. Bukowski to track down the hacker."

"And he tracked the hacker to the Stardust?" Chris asked. "You have a very impressive online casino, don't you?"

"Yes," Peyton said, "and Boris Krawford is one of our regular players."

"Whoever hacked him is not connected to the Stardust," Rachel said. "Our cybersecurity is state-of-the-art."

ICE

"I directed Rachel and her staff to cooperate with Mr. Bukowski's investigation," Peyton said. "We certainly can't have our customers, especially those as powerful and influential as Boris Krawford, accusing the Stardust's online casino of being a doorway for hackers."

"I spent most of Saturday morning and afternoon with Mr. Bukowski," Rachel said. "Gave him full access to our records from all of Mr. Krawford's digital activities with the casino. He found nothing."

"Mr. Bukowski emailed me on Monday morning stating that he'd found no evidence of the hacker accessing Mr. Krawford's computer through our casino," Peyton said. "He thanked me for assisting him on his investigation and that was the last contact we had with him."

"Our information indicates that Mr. Bukowski checked out two days early," Helen said.

Peyton shrugged her shoulders. "I'm assuming that's because he was through with his investigation and he needed to get back to New Jersey to report to his boss." She lifted the lid to her laptop. "Would you like to see the email he'd sent to me?"

"That would be helpful," Helen said.

"It's not very long."

Francine and Chris studied Rachel, who chewed on a thumbnail while watching her boss.

Helen read the message on the screen of the laptop while Peyton sent it to print.

Peyton's eyes lit up. "I just remembered something. I saw Mr. Bukowski down in the lounge on Sunday night. He was with a young woman. Short red hair. Very pretty."

"Have you ever seen her before?" Chris asked.

Peyton paused to smile at him before answering. "We get so many people here at the Stardust. We get busloads of people from Washington, Pennsylvania, Ohio, and down in southern West Virginia. There's no telling who she is or where she came from. She looked awfully friendly, and he wasn't fighting her off," — she shot a grin, with the corners of her mouth curling, in Chris's direction — "if you know what I mean."

Chris returned the smile. "I know exactly what you mean, Ms. Davenport."

"Peyton." She handed the printed copy of the email to Helen. "Could I do anything else for you?"

Helen tore her frosty gaze from Chris to respond, "Can we get a printout of Mr. Bukowski's invoice and accounting for his stay while he was here?"

"Of course." Peyton turned to Rachel. "Can you ask Judy to print up Mr. Bukowski's records for Detective Clarke please?"

"It's lieutenant," Helen corrected her.

"Lieutenant." Peyton licked her lips while casting a glance in Chris's direction.

"Did Mr. Bukowski say anything to you about where he was going to look next in his search for the ransomware hacker?" Chris asked Rachel.

Her eyes grew wide while she gazed at Chris in silence.

"Didn't you tell me, Rachel, that Bukowski had said something to you about a Russian import company that Mr. Krawford had been doing business with?" Peyton said.

"Yes," Rachel said. "Russians. He told me that Mr. Krawford had been doing some business with Russians and since he'd cleared us, that it had to be them. The Russians."

"Those Russians are so sneaky," Peyton said.

"Can't trust them for a minute," Chris said with a wicked grin in her direction.

Helen gave her business card to Rachel and asked that she call her if she could think of anything that could prove helpful in their case.

"Please feel free to call me if you can think of anything that could helpful… or just to talk." Chris handed his business card to Peyton. When she took it, he clasped her hand in a firm shake. "Thank you very much for your time, Peyton." Aware of Helen watching them with a frown on her face, he kept a firm grasp on her hand.

"You can call me anytime, Chris."

"How about tomorrow?" He shot back. "I noticed a poster advertising a benefit dinner dance."

"It's black tie and they have a band. There will be dancing. Do you dance, Chris?"

"I'm a tremendous dancer, Peyton."

"It's five hundred dollars a plate and you have to have tickets to get in."

He winked at her. "I can get tickets—no problem."

"Here's my home address and private number." She wrote a number on the back of a business card and held it out to him. "Pick me up at six o'clock tomorrow and we'll see how good of a dancer you really are, Chris."

At the library, Jacqui was filling up the white board with additional information that they had been discovering from the detectives investigating the three additional Graduate Slaughterer victims.

With a wide grin filling his face, Elliott thanked the homicide detective from the sheriff's office in Lancaster, Pennsylvania. "That's good information, Stan. I'll let you know if it leads to something on our end." After saying goodbye, he disconnected the call.

Across the table, Bruce was smirking in his direction.

"Well?" Ray snapped from the computer monitor. "Sounds like you actually talked to someone who knew something."

"Everyone that we've been talking to has to go back to check with victims' friends and family to find any connection with the Stardust Casino," Jacqui said.

"Well," Elliott said, "it just so happened that Angela Romano's connection was already in the case files. She was a regular at the Stardust. She'd come out on one of those tourist buses filled with gamblers and spend the whole day playing the slot machines and filling up on the all-you-can-eat buffet. She did that at least once a month up to three weeks before her murder—when she got banned from the casino."

"Why'd she get banned?" Bruce asked.

"She stole another guy's winnings. The detective is not really sure what happened. This guy had hit the jackpot— fifteen thousand dollars. Angela was nearby. When he went to cash in his chips, he forgot some sort of ticket that the machine spits out. That was what they would use to cash in the winnings—not the chips. Angela had grabbed the slip and cashed it in. There were witnesses, and the casino did get her on the security recording stealing the slip. But, by the time security caught up to her while she was chowing down at the buffet, she already had the cash and refused to return it. She was screaming about finders keepers and it was the guy's loss for not knowing the rules. The police were called, and they hauled her out. There was a police report filed. She was charged with theft and the casino banned her for life." Elliott held up his finger. "But she never gave the guy his winnings. The local police said they had no grounds to take it from her since the guy had left the slip of paper behind. She kept the money."

"That's why it was in the case file," Ray said. "The guy she stole the money from had a good motive for killing her."

"He was out fifteen thousand dollars," Elliott said. "He was furious and did threaten her—right there at the buffet in front of witnesses."

"Wasn't Angela the victim who had told someone that she felt like she was being watched shortly before she was killed?" Jacqui said. "That could have been her guilt working."

"The guy had a solid alibi," Elliott said. "Not only that, but their crime scene people found skin under the victim's fingernails—enough to get a DNA profile. It doesn't match his."

"He could have hired someone to kill her for him," Bruce said.

"They found no money trail to prove it." Elliott shook his head. "Besides, the guy really didn't have a real motive. Our local prosecutor did charge Angela with theft and they'd already set up a trial date. He had filed a civil lawsuit against her for theft and had a strong case against her between the security video and witnesses. When she got killed, he ended up having to sue her estate and to this day still hasn't gotten his money."

"The important thing is that Angela Romano does have a definite connection to the Stardust," Bruce said, "just like Mona Tabler and Shirley Rice."

"You said she was confronted at the buffet," Jacqui said. "That's three out of five victims not only connected to the casino, but the restaurant." She checked off each name as she reviewed the list of victims on the white board. "Mona Tabler was the restaurant's hard-as-nails manager. Shirley Rice confronted her estranged husband in the restaurant. Angela Romano was a thief caught red-handed in the buffet."

"All we need to make our theory complete is to connect Carla Pendelton and Patricia Handle to the Stardust." Hearing a gust of wind and the door slam behind him, Bruce turned around in his seat. "Three out of five is a good start."

Before his vision cleared, Bruce suspected who was standing behind him. He could tell by the wide-eyed expressions on the rest of the squad.

Bundled up in her black leather coat, gloves, and high-heeled ankle boots over her blue jeans, Doris Matheson stood before them. "What's going on here?"

Behind her, Katelyn, Emma, and Nikki carried their bookbags to the children's section of the library, where they could amuse themselves with laptops, books, and snacks.

Ray disconnected their satellite connection. Casually, Elliott turned off the monitor while rushing to Doris to distract her while Bruce and Jacqui got rid of the evidence.

"Doris, you managed to get out," Elliott said. "You look lovely, today."

"You're full of it, Elliott. What are you doing here?" Doris leaned to one side to see what Bruce and Jacqui were doing.

Jacqui swung the white board around so that its back was to Doris and snapped a picture with her cell phone of the data they had collected. Bruce stacked the case files and stuffed them into the folder box.

"What are you doing here?" Elliott asked. "I thought the library followed the county school board's schedule as far as closing in bad weather."

"Our power's out," she said. "The girls were going bonkers without wi-fi, so I took them to lunch. Christopher had texted that the power was on here and suggested I bring the girls down." She peered around him. "Speaking of Christopher, have you seen him? Do you know where he's taken off to?"

Elliott shook his head. "I haven't seen him since the book club meeting the other night?"

"He told me he had breakfast with you just this morning." She placed her hands on her hips.

"Oh!" Elliott smacked his hand flat against his forehead. "Did I say the other night? I meant this morning! Yes! I had breakfast with Chris this morning. I forgot. I needed to talk to him."

"About what?" She glared at him.

"I had to ask his permission."

"Permission for what?"

Elliott grabbed her hand. "To ask you to be my date for the Valentine's Day dinner dance."

Jacqui and Bruce froze.

"I mean, Kirk had passed away only eight months ago, and traditionally, a woman is supposed to mourn for a year. But it is Valentine's Day, and the benefit is for such a good cause. I didn't want Chris to think that I was disrespecting his father. So I asked him to breakfast to make sure he'd be okay with it."

"Oh, Elliott." Doris's hand flew to her chest. "What did Christopher say?"

"Oh, he's fine with it," Elliott said. "He even offered to pay for the tickets."

"That's my Christopher."

"So you'll go to the dance with me?" Elliott asked.

"Well," she demurred, "it is a good cause."

"Great."

"Now, that we have that out of the way..." Her smile fell. "What are you doing here, Elliott?"

"Doing here?" Elliott glanced behind him to see that Jacqui and Bruce were rushing to clean up the remnants of their lunch. "What are we doing here?"

"That's my question."

"Well, you're going to think we're crazy," Elliott said.

"Everyone knows you're crazy, Elliott. Now answer my question. What are all of you doing here in the library when it's closed?"

"We're going over the Black Dahlia murder case," Elliott said.

"What?" Doris's face screwed up.

"The Black Dahlia. I'm sure you heard of it. Elizabeth Short, known posthumously as 'the Black Dahlia', was found murdered in Leimert Park in Los Angeles in 1947. The murder was never solved." Elliott extracted a hard-backed book from his book bag. "This book came out last month. The author claims she cracked the case. We're fact checking to see if she got it right."

Doris cleared her throat. "Let me get this straight. All of you came out here to the library to fact-check the clues for this seventy-year-old cold case to prove whether this writer got it right or wrong?"

Jacqui joined in on the lie. "She got it wrong."

"And now we're on the track to the real killer," Bruce said.

"Are you going to notify this author that she got the killer wrong in her book and that you're hot on the trail of the real killer?" Doris asked.

"Of course not," Elliott said. "She'll think we were a bunch of weird old folks with too much time on our hands."

"Why would anyone think that?"

CHAPTER FIFTEEN

Chris recognized the hard glare in Helen's eyes.

The elevator was filled with frosty silence while it made its way to the main floor. Seemingly in slow motion, the numbers above the door lit and dimmed to indicate their descent.

In his head, Chris knew the ride was not taking any longer than usual—it only seemed that way.

"Anybody else chilly?" Francine asked with sarcasm from her spot between the two of them.

"I asked Peyton to the benefit for a reason." Chris directed his statement over Francine's head to Helen.

The elevator doors opened and Helen shot out like a race horse making for the finish line. Chris chased after her.

"We all know why you asked her, Studmuffin." Francine dug her buzzing phone out of her handbag. "She's hot and you're horny."

While running through the gaming room after Helen, Chris caught sight of what looked like a German shepherd tucked between an elderly couple dancing with glee at the blackjack table.

That dog looks just like Sterling. Remembering the German shepherd he had left in the truck, Chris stopped. *Sterling!* He whirled around. The elderly couple were dancing behind a tall pile of chips. The stool where he thought he had seen Sterling was empty. *Must have been my imagination.* He chuckled. *Dogs playing blackjack? Have you lost your mind, Matheson?*

Chris refocused on catching Helen and spotted her at the top of the stairs leading into the lounge. He caught up with her at the end of the bar. "Helen, you need to listen to me."

"About what? You can ask whoever you want to your mother's fancy dinner dance. It isn't like we love each other."

"Is everything okay here?" A broad-shouldered bartender with dark hair and an ultra-short beard and mustache strode from the opposite end of the bar where he was chatting with the lounge's only other customer. Dressed in a maroon suit jacket with the Stardust Casino emblem on the breast pocket, the man was texting on his phone between bites of a cheese-burger and fries.

Both of them eyed Chris as if they were ready to do battle in Helen's defense.

"We're fine," Helen said in a low voice while shooting a steely glare over her shoulder at Chris. "Are you Tyler?" She took her police shield off her belt.

"Depends on who's asking," he answered with a broad grin.

She showed her badge to him. His grin fell, and he shot a glance to the man at the end of the bar.

"Do you remember having this gentleman as a customer within the last week?" Helen showed him a picture of Tommy Bukowski on her phone.

Tyler paused. "We get a lot of customers in here. What's this about?"

Once again, the bartender shot a glance in the direction of the other customer who appeared to be sending a text while glancing in their direction.

"His girlfriend reported him missing," Helen said. "He checked out of the hotel on Monday morning and hasn't been seen since."

"I waited on him the other night," Tyler said. "I'm not sure if I remember which night it was. But I do remember that he was with a gorgeous redhead who was all over him." He lowered his voice to whisper to them. "I think she was a professional, if you know what I mean."

"Had you ever seen her in here before?" Helen asked.

"Once in a blue moon. Her name is Josie." Tyler turned to the customer at the end of the bar. "Seth, I think you saw her. It was that night that Ethel Lipton got so wasted that you had to drive her home."

Chris had to restrain himself to control his excitement. Ethel Lipton had been in the lounge at the same time that Tommy Bukowski had been seen with a mysterious redhead. Tommy ended up murdered, and Ethel told the police she had information about a murder at the Stardust.

It had to be Tommy's murder that Ethel was talking about.

The customer who Tyler had called Seth eyed all of them in silence. "Yeah, I remember her vaguely. I didn't get a clear look at her." He added, "I certainly couldn't identify her in court or anything."

"Right now this is just a missing person's case," Chris said to play down their professional interest. "We just want to find out what happened to him. His girlfriend is worried."

"His girlfriend reported him missing?" Tyler asked with a wicked grin. "The way that babe was all over him, my guess is that he got lucky and decided to ditch the girlfriend. That's not unheard of around here."

"But you just said she was a professional," Helen said. "Does this bar frequently have hookers working here?"

"We try to discourage that," he said, "but we can't really help it if our customers bring them in here for a drink before going up to their rooms. As long as they pay their bill and give me a nice tip," — he shrugged his shoulders — "who am I to complain? As for this redhead—she certainly wasn't one of my regulars."

"I understand Ethel Lipton was a regular customer of yours," Chris said.

"Yeah, she was in here all the time." Tyler frowned. "Haven't seen her lately though." He turned to Seth. "Not since that night that you drove her home."

Seth lifted up his hands and shoulders in a broad shrug. "Maybe she's still sleeping it off. She got so wasted that the man himself—"

"What man himself?" Helen asked.

"Mason Davenport," Seth said. "Mr. Davenport didn't want another DUI connected with the Stardust."

Tyler jumped in. "Ethel had a history of getting drunk here and then having accidents on the way home."

"Even though she only lived five miles away," Seth said.

"Why don't you ban her from the lounge?" Helen asked. "It is okay for bars to refuse service to habitually troublesome customers."

"Ethel is protected for some reason," Tyler said. "Don't ask me why. Davenport lets her get away with whatever she wants."

"Must be part of the land deal," Helen said. "If she hadn't sold him their property, the casino never would have happened."

"So the other night, Mason Davenport ordered you to take Ethel Lipton home," Chris said. "Did anything happen while you were taking her home?"

"No," Seth said with a scoff. "She was passed out as soon as I poured her into the back of my limo. I had to actually carry her into the house. She couldn't even get her keys out of her purse. I had to fish them out to unlock the door." He grumbled. "What a lush."

"What's this about?" Tyler asked.

"That lush was gunned down Tuesday night," Chris said.

Tyler's mouth dropped open. He turned around to Seth, who was wiping his plate with the last of his fries to get every last grain of salt.

"The gunmen were killers for hire," Helen said. "Do you have any idea why someone would have wanted her dead?"

Tyler turned back to Seth, who ignored his gaze. "None. But…" his voice trailed off.

"But what?" Chris held up two fingers. "Two customers in the same bar at the same time. One killed in a professional hit. The other goes missing."

Tyler turned back to Seth, who lifted his eyes to give a silent warning. In response, he shook his head. "I didn't see anything to give me the impression they knew each other. Ethel was drinking here at the bar. This other guy was in the booth over there," —he pointed at a dark corner in the lounge — "with Josie all over him."

Helen fished her business card out of her purse and slid it across the bar in Tyler's direction. "If you remember anything…" she was saying as Francine rushed in and grabbed Chris by the arm.

"We've got some exciting new developments in the Graduate Slaughterer murders," she said in a harsh whisper.

Hearing her, Helen turned around. "The Graduate Slaughterer?"

"I know. It's a mouthful." Chris followed Francine out of the lounge to a bench in the common area.

"Bruce was right," Francine said.

"Who's Bruce?" Helen took a seat across from them.

"A member of our book club," Chris said.

"What does your book club have to do with someone called the Graduate Slaughterer and who is the Graduate Slaughterer?" Helen sighed. "You're right, Chris. That is a mouthful. Who came up with that name?"

"I did," Francine said with a frown. "Isn't my fault all the good serial killer names are already taken."

"Serial killer?" Helen let out a gasp. "What serial killer? We were working on the suspicion that the mob killed Tommy Bukowski. A couple of thugs for hire assassinated Ethel Lipton." She shot a glare at Chris. "What the hell is all this about?"

"We're talking about a couple of Dad's cold cases," Chris said. "Now they're yours. Mona Tabler was murdered in Shepherdstown in 1998, and Shirley Rice killed in Martinsburg in 2003."

"Five years—"

"Plus three other women from the surrounding states," Francine said. "All of them have the same MO. Not only that, but both Tabler and Rice, plus another one of the other three were all connected not just to this casino, but the restaurant." She arched an eyebrow in Chris's direction. "Three out of five. Since we're in a casino, care to place a bet that the other two have some sort of connection?"

"Who do you think you are that you can go looking into my cold cases?" Helen asked.

"They were Dad's."

"Your father is dead. I'm in charge of the homicide division and those cases are mine." Helen headed for the exit.

"Helen—"

"Don't you have a tux to rent?" She shot over her shoulder before disappearing into the crowd.

"Man," Francine muttered under her breath. "Talk about sexual tension so thick you can cut it with a knife."

Chris dropped back onto the bench. "I didn't ask Peyton to the benefit because I was interested in her. Couldn't you see that?"

"Do I look like I was born yesterday?"

Chris sucked in a deep breath. "I asked her out because she knows a hell of a lot more about Tommy Bukowski's murder than she's letting on. Did you see how fast she found that email? Have you ever found a particular email so fast? She had it all ready to show us and print up. Plus, she had an answer for everything. She knew we were coming, and she had rehearsed her responses."

"She had it all figured out," Francine said.

"Did you see how smoothly she directed us toward the redhead? Enough to make me wonder who paid for her services."

"But that was the night before he checked out," Francine said.

"Bukowski checked out online," Chris said. "It was in the accounting that Davenport's secretary gave us. He didn't check out at the front desk. That means anyone who had access to his room and the online service on the television could have done it—"

"And as vice president in charge of security—Peyton and her whole staff—"

"Not to mention most of the hotel employees—"

"Could have checked out for him hours after he had already been murdered," Francine said.

"Exactly," he said. "That's why he checked out two days early. He was dead."

"He must have found the ransomware hacker," she said. "Could he have?"

"Peyton said she gave orders to Rachel Pine, the director of cybersecurity, to give him access to their system," he said. "Bukowski was on the ground floor of computer hacking." He nodded his head. "He would've known exactly what to look for in their system. If it was there, he would have found it."

"And told them?"

"Honor among thieves." Chris looked around at the dozens of slot machines and the wide array of gaming tables—thousands upon thousands of dollars pouring through the casino. "Think about all the millions of dollars this casino makes—here at this brick and mortar location. Can you imagine how much they make through their online casino?"

"More than you or I will ever see."

"Think about it," Chris said. "This hacker that Bukowski was looking for—and maybe found here—slips through the digital door that the online gamblers open to enter the online casino."

"Many of those viruses, once they get into your system, they can look at everything," she said. "A lot of different types of folks do online gambling. High rollers, like Boris Krawford—"

"People who have secret accounts they don't want spouses, business partners, or the government to know about."

"A smart enough hacker could even gain access to secret accounts and drain them," she said.

"We're talking about millions of dollars available to be stolen," Chris said. "And if this ill-gotten or hidden money is stolen, then do you really think the victims are going to report it? That's why Boris Krawford sent Tommy Bukowski to find the hacker—so that he could get his money back and issue his own form of justice." As the pieces came together to form the scenario in his mind, he nodded his head. "The ransomware hacker killed Bukowski. Somehow, Ethel Lipton found out about it and tried to use it as a get out of jail free card. So that hacker hired those goons to kill her."

"Imagine that," Francine said. "A hacker, a murderer, and a serial killer all in one casino. Knowing that, I don't feel safe just being here. Do you think it's something in the water?"

Reminded of the Graduate Slaughterer, Chris was jerked out of his thoughts about Tommy Bukowski's murder. "I thought we had concluded that the Graduate Slaughterer had moved on since there hadn't been any murders matching his MO since 2005."

"Well, according to Jacqui, the victim in Lancaster got banned from the Stardust for stealing another gambler's winnings in 1995, three weeks before her murder," Francine said. "Not only that, but security caught up with her at the buffet. So we're not just talking about the casino, but the restaurant."

"Then the murders stopped twelve years ago," Chris stared at the wall across from them—deep in thought. "And they started in 1995."

"That chef," Francine said, "Sandy's brother. Didn't he start working here right out of culinary school? Maybe he'll have some idea who our killer is. The guy had to work in the restaurant. Remember how he said that the restaurant is, like, separate from the casino—he hardly ever went into the casino."

Chris checked the time on his cell phone. "I need to talk to my mother."

"Your mother?"

Chris stood. "Sterling has been in the truck all this time. I need to get him home."

"But the Graduate—"

"I have a suspect." Chris gently took her by the arm. "But I need to talk to my mother before I put his name on our suspect list officially."

They found Sterling sitting patiently in the front passenger seat of the truck—much to Chris's relief. The glimpse of a dog sitting at the blackjack table had made him suspect that Sterling had decided to go for a stroll.

"What a good dog," Francine said while climbing into the truck's back seat. "I'm surprised that he was good enough to not budge after all the time that we had left him here alone."

"He's a highly intelligent police canine." It was with a sigh of relief that Chris patted the dog on the head and fastened his seatbelt. Though, he couldn't help but notice that Sterling's breath smelled like champagne and there was a hundred-dollar chip resting on the seat under his paw.

Helen wanted to kick herself. *You're in your mid-forties, you idiot. If you caught Sierra behaving like this, you'd give her a stern talking to about behaving more her age.* Still, Helen couldn't help herself. When Chris poured on the charm and asked Peyton Davenport to the Valentine's Day dinner dance, she felt the green-eyed monster brewing inside her.

In her head, she knew that Chris was using Peyton's attraction to get close to her so he could find out the truth. It was obvious that Peyton had prepared for a visit from the police asking about Tommy Bukowski.

Helen hoped that she succeeded in giving Peyton and Rachel a false sense of security by playing down their interest and seeming to go through the motions of the investigation to appease a worried girlfriend. Helen was pleased with how she had purposely flubbed up Tommy Bukowski's name. That false sense of security could make Peyton drop her defenses enough for Chris to pick up something useful during their date.

Turning her cruiser into a parking space in front of the sheriff's department, Helen groaned at the thought of Chris taking Peyton Davenport out on a date. Imagining Peyton's privileged family, upbringing, and luxurious life made Helen's stomach ache.

She felt like damaged goods.

Seriously? At your age? After all these years? You went to college on an academic scholarship. Raised an outstanding family. Graduated from law school, the police academy, worked your way up in the state police. You've raised a good kid who's always on honor roll. She sighed. *Guess that feeling never goes away.*

Memories of her time with Chris flooded her thoughts— long talks while holding hands, passionate afternoons in the hayloft, and tender declarations of first love. She felt flush when she recalled how the touch of his hands on her flesh made her heart race with excitement. Never did any man make her feel that way before or since—not even Sierra's father.

If only — Helen pushed the thought from her mind. *No, I had to end it. I'd made a promise and there was no way I could have kept it if I hadn't ended it with Chris.*

She shoved the cruiser door open and marched into the sheriff's department. Accustomed to the state police lieutenant's visits, the deputy allowed her beyond the security check point to go to Deputy Sheriff Rodney Bell's office.

The door open, Helen went inside to find the office empty. Concluding that he had stepped down the hall, she set her briefcase in a chair and took off her coat. After draping it across the back of her chair, she turned to sit when a name on a case file in the center of Rodney's desk caught her eye.

It was not an unusual name. Normally, she wouldn't have noticed it—if she had not heard the name uttered less than thirty minutes earlier.

Tabler, Mona.

Chris's journalist friend Francine had just mentioned it. Chris said the murder had been one of his father's cold cases.

If this is a state police case, then what is Rodney Bell, the county's deputy sheriff, doing with a copy of the case file?

Curious, Helen leaned over to peer at the old brown folder. Chris and Francine suspected Mona's murder was connected to a second case—that both women had been murdered by a serial killer.

"Where's your friend?" Rodney snapped at her as he stepped through the door.

Startled, Helen spun around to face him. Rodney's hand was bandaged where Sterling had bitten him.

"Chris had some interviews to conduct," she said. "How's your hand and arm?"

"Sore. But I'm a man. I can take it." He frowned. "What interviews are you talking about? Chris is retired."

"The FBI hired him on contract to investigate what appears to be a mob hit," Helen said. "The victim was connected to an organized crime boss in New Jersey. I'm the liaison between the FBI and local law enforcement."

"How cozy for you two." Rodney moved around behind his desk. As he plopped down in his chair, he picked up a newspaper that had been resting on the corner and draped it across the case file. "Why'd they pick Chris?"

"Because he's already got the local connections. Everyone trusts him—"

"Not everyone." He held up the newspaper for her to read the headline. "You did hear about his dad covering up for him after he knocked up that girl back—"

"Chris would never do that, and you know it, Rodney. I could believe it of you—especially after seeing Felicia's arm."

Rodney was out of his seat. "I am not a wife beater. Yes, I grabbed Felicia's arm. She pushed me over the edge. You remember how she used to be. She was the one who seduced me to steal me away from you—"

"Ancient history, Rodney! There's nothing any of us can do to change the past." She took her tablet from her case. "According to our information, the murder victim was staying at the Stardust. Witnesses put him in the lounge at the same time, Sunday night, as Ethel Lipton, who told you that she had information about a murder at the Stardust. I want to know exactly what she told you."

"She told me nothing." When Helen scoffed, he said, "She wanted to make a deal to get out of a DUI. She refused to give me any details until Victor Sinclair, the county prosecutor, signed, sealed, and delivered a free pass. She was dead before I had time to even talk to Sinclair."

"Well, she must have talked to someone in order to have gotten herself killed," Helen said.

"Doris Matheson swears her sources indicate Lipton got killed because she got into a cat fight in the department store with Precious Hawkins, the baby momma of Jose Martinez—"

"Who's a major dealer running drugs from Mexico through West Virginia to Baltimore."

"And those two thugs who killed Lipton worked for Jose," Rodney said. "Problem is that the altercation happened only minutes before Lipton got herself gunned down—not enough time for them to have driven out from Martinsburg to teach her a lesson." He sucked in a deep breath and let it out with a snarl. "Chris stated the guys were waiting in the parking lot when he followed Ethel out of the store. He thought they were waiting for him on account of him having put away some heavy operators who had worked for the same drug cartel that Jose belongs to."

"Were these guys sloppy enough to have missed Chris completely?"

"They weren't the sharpest knives in the drawer, but they weren't completely incompetent either. They did some freelance work on the side separate from the cartel."

"Which brings us back to the original question," she said. "Who did Ethel tell what she knew." She narrowed her eyes in thought. "The killer? She may have been foolish and stupid enough to think the killer would pay her a lot of money to keep quiet."

"She was going to go to jail for her umpteenth DUI," Rodney said. "Having a lot of money doesn't do you a lot of good in jail."

Thinking about Peyton Davenport and her influential family, a slow grin came to Helen's lips. "Unless, the killer had the connections to keep her out of jail."

CHAPTER SIXTEEN

"That was when I told Katelyn that she was dating the wrong man." Doris took the stack of dirty plates from Chris to load into the dishwasher. "At which point she told me that I was old and couldn't possibly understand."

The Mathesons had returned home to find that the power had been restored. In case the electricity was out, Chris had picked up oriental takeout. After everyone finished eating, his daughters went their separate ways. Nikki went to the barn to feed the horses and cats. Emma turned on *Supergirl* in the family room. Katelyn sought advice from her friends on getting enough money to pay for her Valentine's Day date with Zack.

"I can imagine your response when Katelyn called you old," Chris said to his mother.

"I said nothing. You would have been so proud of me."

"Nothing?"

The corner of her lips curled. "When it comes to teenagers who think they have it all figured out, you can't bulldoze them with common sense. Their natural instinct is to resist. You have to slip it in gradually in a non-confrontational manner so that they will not only accept your wisdom, but welcome it. And, if you do it just right, you may even dupe them into believing it was all their idea."

"In other words, be sneaky." Chris took the moist sponge from the sink and stepped over Sterling and Thor to clean the table.

Sterling was exhausted. As soon as he had finished eating, he curled up in a dog bed and fell asleep watching the birds and squirrels at the feeders in the back yard. Thor nestled against him with her head resting across the dog's neck.

For once, the kitchen was quiet. Even Mocha and Sadie, strategically positioned under Doris's feet in case something edible fell, were peaceable.

"I made a mistake mixing you up with Elliott's book club," Doris said.

"I thought you wanted me to make friends and get out more."

"Normal friends," she said. "Do you know we went to the library this afternoon and found most of that group there? They had names of suspects written across the white board and reports and crime scene pictures scattered across the table."

Chris froze. "Really?"

"They were dissecting a new book about the Black Dahlia murder to see if the author got it right," she said while rearranging the dishes in the dishwasher. "Your father used to do the same thing after he retired. He was a nut, and it turns out he's not the only one. It looks like he'd collected this group of mixed nuts to analyze crime books."

"Isn't that what book groups do?"

"Don't be a smartass." Grumbling, she shook her head before pouring detergent into the dishwasher.

"They really aren't that weird." Chris cleaned the kitchen counter. "Speaking of strange, tell me what you know about Carson Lipton."

"Excellent chef." Doris turned on the dishwasher. "The Stardust's five-star restaurant brings in a lot of folks just to eat there—and it's all because of Carson. They have original recipes that he created himself. Back when that mess happened between you and Sandy, I never would have dreamed that Carson would have turned out as well as he did. That proves that if one sets their minds to it—they can beat their genes."

"I talked to him today," he said. "He cut off all communication with Ethel. I'm sure that helped. I remember back when I'd eat at the diner," —he shook his head at the memory — "the things she'd say to him."

"Ethel was evil." Doris rinsed out the carafe to prepare coffee for the next morning. "Carson's wife, Mabel, saw that his mother was toxic and loved Carson enough to cut that poison out of their life."

"I met Mabel, too," Chris said. "She's kind of…" His voice trailed off.

"An ice queen?" She smiled.

"Definitely not warm and fuzzy—like you."

"There's no one like me. Your father used to say they broke the mold after making me."

"He was right."

"Even if she isn't Ms. Congeniality, the Stardust can credit Mabel as much as Carson for the restaurant being the success that it is." She held the scooper up in preparation for filling the coffee filter. "Why were you talking to Carson Lipton? Did you go to the casino? When did you start gambling?"

Chris leaned against the counter and folded his arms across his chest. "If you must know, I went to see him. I want to find out what happened to Sandy."

With a heavy sigh, she rested her hand on her hip. "Chris, let it go. That happened a long time ago. Most people have forgotten it. If you go dredging it all up again—"

"I'm not the one dredging it up. Did you see the newspaper today?"

"Nobody reads the newspaper."

"Victor Sinclair has asked the sheriff to reopen the Sandy Lipton case," he said. "My shooting those two thugs brought me to the forefront of the news again. Right there. The whole Sandy Lipton case rehashed with both her picture and mine on the front page. Even before that, Katelyn had heard about it at school and asked me if I took advantage of some young girl. I need to find out the truth for my daughters. Plus, I owe it to Sandy to find out the truth."

"Don't you think that if Carson knew what had happened to Sandy that he would've said something before now?"

"Not if his mother had something to do with it. Carson told me that he thinks Victor Sinclair raped her. He claims he saw Victor's car parked at the diner across the street when I dropped Sandy off the night of the prom."

"Victor Sinclair is no dummy." She peered out the window over the sink. In the moonlight, the trees in the back yard resembled skeletons. "He's a worm, but he's not stupid. If he'd raped Sandy, he certainly got away with it. The last thing he'd want to do is press his luck by ordering Grant to reopen the case. Did you see anything that night that makes you think Carson could be right?"

"No," Chris said with a firm shake of his head. "And if I had seen Victor, I wouldn't have left. Sandy was adamant about not wanting anything to do with him. If I had seen him following her home, I would've confronted him."

"Maybe you didn't notice him following you."

"Mom, I had already served with the Army Rangers. If I was being tailed, I would have noticed."

"Do you think Carson lied?"

"I'm not sure." Chris's eyes met Doris's. "I asked for his DNA to put into the national database to see if we could get a familial match with any Jane Does to help us find Sandy. He refused."

"Did he say why?"

"Mabel said we had Ethel's DNA, so we didn't need his."

"That's true."

"Mom, I saw the look in his eyes. He was scrambling for a good excuse to decline before Mabel mentioned Ethel's DNA. Afterwards, he said it was because he didn't want Big Brother tracking him."

"There are a lot of people who feel that way, Christopher." She picked up the dogs' water bowl to refill with fresh water.

Chris stepped around the counter to join her at the sink. "Do you remember the Mona Tabler and Shirley Rice murders?"

"I've heard all about them. Your father worked on those cases up to the day he died."

"Mona Tabler was the restaurant manager at the Stardust," Chris said. "She was hard hearted, just like Mabel. Some of my friends in college worked there. One guy said she made prison wardens look like pussy cats. I found out today that Shirley Rice had caused a big scene in that same restaurant just a couple of weeks before she was killed. The MO in both murders is the same. Not only that, but a woman from Lancaster had been murdered a couple years before Mona. She'd been banned from the casino after stealing another gambler's winnings. Security caught up with her at the buffet in the restaurant."

"Are you thinking they were all murdered by a serial killer?" She set the bowl down in the corner of the kitchen.

"A profiler I talked to says the perp would have had serious mommy issues, which Carson has."

"Lots of people have mommy issues, Christopher, but that doesn't necessarily make them all psychopathic murderers."

"He even burns down the victims' home. That indicates a hell of a lot of rage."

"How many women do you think this guy murdered?"

"I've identified five," Chris said. "The murders stopped twelve years ago. Well, that happens to be when Carson married Mabel, who ordered him to cut off all relations from Ethel."

"That's totally circumstantial, Christopher. Do you have any actual proof that Carson Lipton is a homicidal maniac?"

"They'd found DNA at the scene of the first murder," Chris said. "I just need someone to help me get a sample of Carson's DNA to have compared to it."

"And how do you intend to get that?"

"I assume he'll be the chef for tomorrow night's dinner dance," Chris said with a sly grin. "I'm hoping you have two tickets left."

"Two tickets for whom? You and a certain police lieutenant?"

"No," Chris said with a heavy sigh. "Helen's mad. She's not even speaking to me."

"What did you do to Helen?"

"Why do you assume I did something to her? Why don't you assume she did something to me?"

"Because Helen is a nice girl."

"Well, some people seem to think I'm a nice guy."

"Christopher, those people don't know you like I do." Doris spun around to head out of the kitchen. Mocha and Sadie scrambled to their feet to escort her.

"Aren't you even going to ask who I'm taking?"

With a heavy sigh, Doris turned to him. "What tramp are you taking to the dinner dance?"

"Peyton Davenport."

To his surprise, Doris's frown deepened. "Over my dead body."

He had not heard that tone of voice from her in years—since he had been a child under her command. "Excuse me."

"You are not taking Peyton Davenport anywhere. I forbid it."

"Forbid me?" Chris laughed. "What are you going to do next? Send me to my room?"

Realizing the ridiculous nature of her order, Doris circled the kitchen in search of a suitable response to her dilemma. "I didn't even know you knew the Davenports personally."

"I'd just met Peyton today at the casino."

She stopped circling. "Well, if those are the type of people you're socializing with—then you can go live elsewhere."

"What are you talking about 'those type of people'?"

"Peyton Davenport is trouble with a capital 'T'. Anyone who gets mixed up with her ends up dead. Did you hear about the sex scandal at the high school about ten years ago?"

"A group of high school girls were seducing teachers, recording it, and then blackmailing them."

"It was genius on Peyton's part," Doris said. "Of course, the victims didn't say anything. They had too much to lose. The only way it came out was that one of those girls ended up dead. When your father investigated the case, he found a hornets nest and Peyton Davenport was in it up to her pretty eyeballs."

"If we're talking about the murder I'm thinking of, wasn't a teacher arrested for it?" Chris asked.

"Oscar Newton," Doris said. "Very nice man. Married and had two children."

"He got a sixteen-year-old girl pregnant," Chris said, "and then killed her to keep her quiet."

"It was an accident," Doris said. "They got into a fight. He gave her money to get an abortion. Here Peyton had set up a hidden camera and recorded the whole thing. Jocelyn was bleeding him dry. They got into a fight and Jocelyn slapped him. He snapped and strangled her. He still has no memory of actually killing her and dumping her body in the river."

"Did they ever find her body?"

Doris shook her head. "Her poor parents. They think it must have washed up in a remote part of the river and gotten eaten by scavengers. It was a tragedy all the way around."

"None of it would've happened if Mr. Newton hadn't had sex with a sixteen-year-old girl."

"It wouldn't have happened if Jocelyn hadn't gotten mixed up with Peyton Davenport," she said. "Jocelyn was a nice girl. She had a lot going for her. Then, she became friends with Peyton. You should have seen her at Jocelyn's memorial service. Crocodile tears flowing like a river. People like Peyton are incapable of having friends."

"Whoever would've guessed that a pregnant teenaged girl getting strangled would turn out to be part of a whole sex ring operating in little old Jefferson County?"

"With Peyton as their ringleader," Doris said. "Your father wanted to arrest her for extortion. But her father's lawyer, Steve Sinclair was going to put her in a white dress with pearls and paint her as the victim of all these men. Your dad convinced the prosecutor to take the case to the grand jury but before he could do that, he was conveniently killed in a car accident. His replacement dropped the case."

"I hate to say this, because I did have a lot of respect for Mr. Newton, but he was the one who decided to have sex with Jocelyn," Chris said. "He knew the law."

"He was set up!" Doris said. "Jocelyn seduced him with the sole motive of blackmailing him. Your dad interviewed a lot of people. Peyton and her friends had a whole scam— organized—going on. They targeted older men in power- ful positions, seduced them, recorded it, and then would hang the evidence over their heads. They wanted grades, letters of recommendation for scholarships and colleges, or sometimes just plain cash in exchange for their silence. And Peyton Davenport was the brains behind the whole thing."

"Sounds like Peyton is quite an ambitious girl. How long ago was that?" Chris's mind swirled to the current scheme that Tommy Bukowski had been investigating at the Stardust.

She wagged a finger at Chris. "Peyton Davenport ruins the lives of every man she touches—which is why I'm forbidding you to go out with her."

"Well that is very good information to know."

"So you'll take Helen instead," Doris said with a nod of her head. "We can make it a double date."

"Double? Who are you going with?"

"Elliott, of course. You said he could ask me. By the way, you owe me a thousand dollars for our tickets."

"A thousand dollars? When did all this go down? Where was I?"

"Christopher, that's why Elliott invited you to breakfast this morning—to ask your permission for him to take me to the dance." She cocked her head at him. "Don't you remember?"

"Oh, yes!" He let out a loud laugh. "Of course, I remember giving Elliott permission to ask you to the dinner dance. How could I forget? It's just that I was so busy today—breakfast seems so long ago now."

"I don't know about you, Christopher." Doris shook her head. "I wanted you to join Elliott's book club because I was worried about you not going out or having any friends. But now, you're stranger than you were before you had friends." She let out a deep sigh. "I'll reserve a table for four at the dance. Me and Elliott, and you and Helen."

"Mother, I'm taking Peyton."

"Have you lost your mind?"

"According to you, yes."

"Peyton's young enough to be your daughter."

"No, she's not," Chris said. "Maybe young enough to be my much younger sister, but not my daughter."

"Yes, she is." Doris blinked her eyes several times while she struggled to comprehend a fact that she knew was somewhere in her memory bank. "I remember when she was born. LeAnn Reaves—one of our parish nurses at the church—"

"I know LeAnn—known her most of my life." Impatient for her to continue with her story, Chris uttered a deep sigh. "Go ahead. Tell me about LeAnn." He spun his finger in a circular motion in a gesture for her to continue.

"LeAnn was a maternity nurse and sent out a prayer request to everyone at the church when Julie Davenport was brought in. She was in really bad shape—physically and emotionally. Julie wanted a baby so badly, but from what LeAnn saw, she was certain it was going to be stillborn. Well, Peyton was born alive, but she couldn't breathe on her own."

Doris snapped her finger at the memory. "You were visiting us—it was the first Christmas after you'd gone to live in Washington."

"Are you sure about that?"

"I remember when everything happened based on what you were doing at the time."

Chris had to chuckle. "I do the same thing, too, based on what the girls are doing."

"The day after you went home, I went to church and LeAnn and everyone was praising God for such a miracle. They didn't think Peyton was going to make it a full day, but when LeAnn went in to work for the night shift, Peyton was breathing on her own. She truly was a miracle baby—which is why her parents spoiled her rotten."

"And that happened that first Christmas after I graduated from Shepherd?"

Doris nodded her head. "You were twenty-two years old then—which means that you are old enough to be her father."

"Mom, get—"

He was about to tell her to get her mind out of the gutter when their discussion was cut off by a high-pitched scream. The terror from the noise was punctuated by the impact of its owner seemingly bouncing down the front stairs to land with a climactic crash at the bottom.

In Shepherdstown, Steve Sinclair turned his luxurious Cadillac SUV off the cobblestone street and pulled around the circular driveway to park in the garage.

The thought of going into the house to face his wife and hear the latest gossip and social positioning was exhausting. Still, he had to go inside sometime.

Appearances are everything. That was why Steve Sinclair lived in the largest colonial mansion in Jefferson County. It had once been home to some of the area's most distinguished figures in the county's history. There had been rumors that Charles Washington, George's brother, had at one point lived in the Sinclair home.

Steve climbed out of the SUV, turned out the light, and stepped outside to hurry up the icy walk to go inside.

"You look tired, Steve," a voice said from out of the darkness.

Steve froze. "Who's out there?"

"Greed weighs heavy on the soul." Bruce stepped out of the shadows.

Steve whipped out his cell phone. "Whoever you are, leave now, because in two minutes the police will be here and you won't be seeing the light of day until hell freezes over."

Amused, Bruce smirked at Steve's bravado. "Are you sure about that?"

To Steve's surprise, his phone did nothing. He peered at the screen. No bars.

"No one can hear you, Steve." Bruce held up a small contraption for him to see.

His wife threw open the house's side door. "Steve! Are you out there? What's taking you so long?"

"Unless you want her to find out about the prostitute you just paid two hundred and fifty dollars for consulting, you'll tell her that you're taking out the garbage."

"I'm okay, dear!" Steve called out. "I'm taking out the garbage."

She closed the door.

"We have to talk." Bruce went into the garage and held the door open for Steve to follow him.

Steve refused to move. "Not until you tell me what is this about."

"Your son and why it would be in your best interest to convince him to let the Sandy Lipton case go cold again."

CHAPTER SEVENTEEN

Each one of Emma's pain-filled screams felt like a stab wound delivered to Chris's heart.

The emergency room doctor and nurse at Jefferson Medical Center had to examine her broken arm, but the panic-stricken child was determined to not let that happen.

Desperate, Chris told her, "Honey, Supergirl would be brave and let the doctor help her if she broke her arm."

"Supergirl wouldn't break her arm." Emma wiped her runny nose and tear-stained face with her red cape from the Supergirl costume she was wearing when she jumped from the top of the front staircase.

Upon finding Emma sprawled at the bottom of the stairs with her badly broken arm beneath her, Chris had told Doris to stay home with Katelyn and Nikki while he rushed her to the emergency room.

Chris alternated between pleading and ordering his daughter to cooperate with the doctor, but neither technique worked. He sensed that Doris, with her maternal strength, would have been more successful.

"Emma, what have you done now?"

The gravelly voice of the elderly woman broke through the wailing. The doctor, who looked barely old enough to shave, backed away to allow the woman clad in a pink hospital uniform to step up to Emma.

"I fell down the stairs, Grandma Patty." Sobbing, Emma held out her injured arm for her to see.

"She was trying to fly like Supergirl," Chris said.

"Could have been worse," Grandma Patty said with a maternal grin. "She could have tried taking off from the roof like you tried to do."

Chris felt his cheeks flush.

Emma stopped crying to ask, "Daddy tried to fly off the roof?"

"No—"

"Yes, you did." Grandma Patty leaned over to tell Emma, "He wanted to test out a parachute that he had made himself out of an old bedsheet. Lucky thing his father caught him before he jumped." She grinned up at Chris. "If I recall correctly, he was the same age you are now."

Emma's sobs turned to giggles.

The children at their church called the motherly woman "Grandma Patty." Every child's favorite babysitter, Patty often spent her days off with a handful of children playing games, making crafts, watching movies, and baking sugary treats.

Even the stressed out young doctor seemed calmer upon Grandma Patty's entrance, which made Chris wonder if he had once been one of her charges.

"Do you now understand why you can't fly?" Grandma Patty asked while examining Emma's arm. The doctor moved next to Patty to examine the bruised and swollen limb.

"Because I'm not from Krypton?" Emma sniffed. "Is Nonni here?" She looked around for her grandmother.

"No, she's home with your sisters. She texted to give me a head's up." She smiled. "Bet you didn't know that I worked here at the hospital, did you?"

"Are you a doctor?"

"No." Grandma Patty shook her head. "I'm too smart to be a doctor. I'm a photographer. I have this really big special camera that takes magical pictures of the inside of your body. It's really cool. Would you like to see it?"

Emma's eyes were wide with wonder.

Grandma Patty turned to the doctor. "Can I take Emma to my office to show her my camera?"

The doctor nodded his head. "You can even take a picture of her arm."

"Would you like that, Emma?"

Minutes later, Emma was enjoying a ride in a wheel chair down the hallway with Grandma Patty to get her arm X-rayed.

Finally alone, Chris plopped into a chair and rested his head back against the wall. He closed his eyes and listened to the quiet, which gave way to the conversation he had been having with his mother right before they heard Emma's flight fail.

It had something to do with Peyton Davenport and the circumstances behind her birth.

"Where's Emma?"

Chris hadn't realized he had fallen asleep until the sound of LeAnn's voice made him jump in his seat and bang the back of his head against the wall behind him.

A maternity nurse, LeAnn laughed while checking the back of his head for any injuries. "I didn't mean to wake you. I assume Grandma Patty took Emma to X-ray."

"And I assume you got a text from Mom. What did she do? Send out a BOLO for the two of us?"

"She worries, like all good grandmothers." Standing over him, LeAnn squeezed his shoulder. "How's single parenthood treating you?"

"Takes a lot of getting used to." He rubbed the back of his neck.

"You and Doris are very lucky to have each other. We were all worried when your dad passed so suddenly."

"Ah, I don't think anyone has to worry about Mom," he said. "She's the strongest woman I know."

"It's been my experience that people who come across as being the strongest are not," LeAnn said. "Your mom was only eighteen years old when she married your father. She'd never been alone before. You coming home has been the answer to our prayers." She headed to the doorway to return to the maternity ward. "She loves having you and the girls home—and relishes being a grandma."

Instantly, Chris remembered what they had been talking about when Emma's scream interrupted them. "LeAnn, do you have a minute?"

"I'm on break." She glanced at her watch. "I have a few minutes."

Chris stood. "Mom was telling me about a prayer request you had sent out years ago when Peyton Davenport was born. Something about her almost dying…"

"Oh, yes," she said. "I remember that all right. I'm not sure if you remember, but back in the early nineties, before texting, our church's prayer network was very old school. Everyone on the list had designated prayer partners. To send out a prayer request, you'd call two people and then they would call two people. Now, you send out one text—"

"I know how it works," Chris said. "I'm on the network. What I want to know is about Peyton Davenport. Mom said something about a miracle—"

LeAnn's eyes lit up at the memory. "It was a miracle. I've seen a lot of miracles in the maternity ward, but Peyton Davenport's takes the cake." She held up her hand. "I honestly thought she was dead—stillborn. It was an extremely difficult birth for her mother. Poor woman. You know she ended up committing suicide?"

"No, I didn't."

"Threw herself off the second-floor verandah of their mansion. So sad. Mason Davenport is an extremely nice man. He adored Julie, who was really sweet—even if she was a little touched. He gives a ton of money to the pregnancy center to help at risk women. That's just one of the charities he helps in the community."

Conscious of the time, Chris eased LeAnn back onto topic before her break ended. "You said you thought Peyton Davenport was stillborn. Obviously, she wasn't."

"Dr. Poole insisted on putting her on the respirator and life support himself," LeAnn said. "He must have picked up some tiny sign of life."

"Dr. Frederic Poole?" Chris recalled that the same doctor who had delivered Tamara Wilcox's baby had also delivered Peyton Davenport.

Tamara Wilcox was the woman who Jacqui had found in the hospital records whose husband had abandoned her and her baby after they had died. The hospital's business office discovered much later that Tamara's identification was a fake.

Dr. Frederic Poole had also been Sandy Lipton's doctor.

Possible scenarios flashed through Chris's mind.

"Dr. Poole was Julie Davenport's doctor," LeAnn said with a nod of her head. "Now, I never touched Peyton. But I saw her, and she was blue. Dr. Poole took her straight to the life support system. I sent out a prayer request right away. When I came back on shift that night—" Tears filled her eyes.

"It was a miracle. Peyton looked like a different baby. She was off life support and breathing on her own."

"She looked like a different baby," Chris muttered. "Speaking of Dr. Poole, do you remember a woman whose husband dropped her off here in the parking lot."

"We get quite a few people dropped off in our hospital parking lot, I'm sorry to say."

"Her name was Tamara Wilcox," Chris said. "She was in labor and unconscious. She died of cardiac arrest and the baby died soon after delivery. It was a baby girl. Turns out the husband never checked her in and her identification was a phony."

"I remember Tamara Wilcox," LeAnn said. "I was off duty when she was brought in. So I only know what I had been told. Both the mother and her baby had been abandoned in our morgue. What made you think about that? That happened years ago."

"Cold cases are a hobby of mine."

"The church finally took up a collection and gave her and her baby a proper burial."

She checked the time on her watch while Chris asked, "So she did get a proper burial?"

"Oh, yeah," LeAnn said. "Doris organized the whole thing."

"Doris? As in my mother Doris?"

"Your mother is such a great lady," LeAnn said. "As soon as I told her about this poor mother and child abandoned in our morgue, she went right to work. Took up a collection to buy a casket and a little headstone. Got Old Man Drake to donate his burial plot at Edge Hill Cemetery on account that he and his wife had decided to get themselves cremated and divided up among their six kids. She guilted Reverend Ruth into officiating for the little funeral in the spring. It was lovely. Your mother is such a generous woman. To think that she did all that for a young woman and child who she had never known."

"That's my mom."

She gave Chris a hug. "I've got to get back to work. Give Emma a hug for me. Nice talking to you."

As she hurried down the hall, Chris took out his cell phone and sent a text to Elliott: *I located Sandy Lipton's body.*

"Nonni!" Emma's voice was heard from down the hallway.

Chris stepped into the doorway to find Emma hopping up and down in the wheelchair which Grandma Patty was pushing. Doris hurried from the opposite end of the hall to meet her.

"My arm is broken," Emma announced as if she had just received a wonderful gift. "Grandma Patty says they're gonna put a cast on it and everything."

"Oh, you poor baby," Doris said.

"She did a real number taking that flying leap down those stairs," Grandma Patty said.

"Could have been worse," Doris said. "She could have jumped off the roof like Christopher tried to do."

"Mother, why did you have to tell everyone about that?" Chris asked. "Everyone's going to think I'm foolhardy and reckless."

"Christopher, everybody already knows you're foolhardy and reckless."

Behind Doris, Grandma Patty nodded her head in complete agreement.

Their discussion faded away into the background as Chris took note of his mother's companion.

In silence, Helen waited by the security doors through which they had entered the emergency room. Aware of his gaze on her, she raised her eyes to meet his. Hesitantly, she closed up the space between them. "Doris called to ask—"

"Sierra is babysitting Katelyn and Nikki," Doris finished while wheeling Emma into the examination room. "We couldn't leave you alone here while Emma was hurt."

"I haven't been alone since Katelyn was born."

"And you never will be," Grandma Patty said. "Take my advice. Be thankful and embrace it."

The touch of Helen's hand on his arm caught his attention. Turning his head from the two older women fussing over Emma, he saw her lovely face only inches from his. She squeezed his arm. He felt the heat of her touch all the way through the padding of his winter coat to warm his heart.

"I thought you were mad at me," he said in a low voice.

"As hard as I try I can't—"

The automatic doors flew open. Doctors, nurses, and medical technicians appeared from seemingly nowhere to rush to their stations. Even Grandma Patty practically knocked Chris over in her flight down the hallway to radiology. The nurse and doctor who had been attending to Emma followed the gurney surrounded by EMTs, nurses, and doctors down the hallway to another examination room.

"We have a burn victim coding!" a nurse yelled. "Chopper from Fairfax's burn unit is four minutes out!"

Chris could smell gasoline and smoke as they whizzed by to wheel the gurney into the examination room.

"She went out a second-floor window," one of the EMTs said to a medical technician holding a clipboard. "Broken bones—"

"She's got a knife in her upper chest!" another nurse said in a loud voice to be heard over the long loud beep of the machine indicating cardiac arrest.

Snapping orders, the doctor went to work trying to save the woman's life.

Helen broke away from Chris to wander to the doorway of the examination room. With the eye of a detective, she watched the doctor attempt to restart the heart of the woman suffering from burns, stab wounds, and broken bones.

Chris stepped over to one of the EMTs. "What happened to her?"

The emergency technician shrugged his shoulders. "Answered a call for a house fire on Morgana Drive in Shepherdstown. We could smell the gasoline. We actually saw her—on fire—jump out the second story window. Someone stabbed her and set her house on fire. Whoever did it must have really been mad at her."

"Morgana Drive?" Chris asked. "In Shepherdstown?"

"Chris!" Helen covered her mouth with her hand.

When he reached her, she buried her face in his chest. "What is it?" He peered into the examination room where the doctor was calling the time of death for their records. While Helen sobbed in his arms, he saw the reason for her despair.

On the gurney, under all the soot and ash, Chris recognized the lovely face of Felicia Bell.

"You're getting old, old man," Chris murmured to the blurry reflection in his bathroom mirror. He dried his freshly washed face with a towel, rehung it on the rack, turned off the light, and padded across the hardwood floor to his bed.

Chris took in a deep breath and let it out. In the dark, he wondered if Helen, in the guest bedroom, was as exhausted as he was or if sorrow made sleep impossible.

It was close to midnight before the hospital released Emma. Helen was distraught over Felicia's death. So Doris had insisted that she and Sierra spend the night in the guest room on the ground floor. Sterling had chosen to sleep with Emma and Thor, who had become the dog's best friend.

For once, Chris was sleeping alone—alone with his thoughts and memories.

Felicia was more than just "an old friend." She had been one of the four musketeers. Through high school, the four of them were inseparable. Even after Rodney and Felicia had betrayed Chris and Helen with their affair, the four of them remained close.

Chris chuckled at the memory of how their friends joked about Chris and Rodney "swapping girlfriends" in their senior year.

The thought of calling Rodney to offer his condolences crossed his mind. *No, those days are gone.*

Chris and Rodney's friendship had managed to withstand adolescent competition, lies, and even betrayal, but it couldn't weather envy. Chris's selection for the FBI over Rodney's was the straw that broke the camel's back.

"I'm sorry they didn't select you for the investigator training program," Chris told Rodney on the first day of their last semester at Shepherd College.

At that point, the two of them had been together through six years of school, served in the same unit of the Army Rangers, and attended college. Chris was at a loss in understanding why Rodney had never called him back after Chris received his letter of acceptance from the FBI. After Doris had learned from Rodney's mother that he had been declined, he realized why.

"I know how much it meant to you," Chris said after finding Rodney in the student union on the first day of their last semester.

Rodney looked up from his egg sandwich.

Chris was startled by the glare of intense hatred in his friend's eyes—directed at him.

How could Rodney switch from his best friend, his bud, his brother in arms, to an enemy so quickly over a job? It takes a long time for jealousy to brew to become strong enough to dissolve such a strong friendship—to create that much hatred.

"Dad said that the state police would be honored to sponsor you for the police academy."

Rodney rose to his feet so fast that he knocked over his chair. Chris fell back from the table.

"I don't need your leftovers, Matheson."

With that, Rodney picked up his backpack and walked away from Chris… and their friendship.

"Are you asleep?"

Helen's soft voice made Chris jump. He had been so absorbed in his thoughts that he hadn't heard her open the door at the bottom of the stairs and make her way to the top floor.

Squinting at her silhouette in the moonlight shining through the window and skylight, Chris wondered if he was dreaming. She was dressed in one of his mother's long nightshirts, which happened to be sheer enough that he could see the outline of her body. It was as slender as he remembered.

"Chris?" she whispered.

Afraid that she was going to leave, he said, "I'm awake." He grimaced when he heard a boyish squawk in his voice. "Where's Sierra?"

"Sound asleep." She stepped closer to the bed. "I can't sleep. I can't get Felicia out of my mind."

"Me, too."

"You're going to think I'm…" Her voice trailed off.

Chris pulled back the covers. "Do you want me to hold you, Helen?"

She slipped in between the sheets and wrapped her arms around him. Pulling her close, Chris held her. She buried her face into his neck.

Her breath sent a wave of excitement through his body. Instantly, he yearned for her.

He tried to push away his desire. It would be unfair to take advantage of her grief just because he wanted her back in his life—wanted things to be the way they used to be.

That's not possible. Things have changed. You have changed. She's changed. Circumstances have changed.

He told himself that they were just two friends comforting each other, but flashes of memories—along with all the intensity of their former passion—sent shock waves throughout his body.

"Helen," he whispered into her hair while trying to shift over to the other side of the bed to conceal his rising desire.

Helen tightened her hold on him. Her fingers brushed down his spine to his hip, slipping beneath the waistband to his lounging pants. "I've missed you, Chris." She planted a kiss on his jaw.

Chris let out his breath. "I'm not going to have a one nightstand with you, Helen."

"I'm not asking you to."

He searched her face. In the moonlight, he was able to see into her eyes—pleading with him—for what, he was unsure.

Pressing her body against his, she kissed him softly on the lips.

He caressed her face. "You've always been the one, Helen." He kissed her softly. "Not a day has passed that I haven't thought about you and when we were together."

Returning his kiss, she wrapped one of her legs around his. "I've never stopped loving, Chris."

"Keep this up,"–he kissed her again— "and I'm going to lose control."

"I think we're already there."

Chapter Eighteen

Helen woke up to the faint warmth from the morning sun shining through the skylight onto her face. She rolled over and buried her face in the pillow to pick up Chris's musky scent. Memories of the early morning hours rushed to the forefront of her mind. She reached for him. Upon finding the other side of the bed empty, she opened her eyes and searched the dimly lit room.

A sliver of light sliced through the crack of the bathroom door. The water was running in the sink.

As usual, Chris had woken early to clean the stalls and feed the horses before breakfast. She recalled that even as a teenager, Chris would be up hours before school to finish his chores.

She slid out of bed and reached for the nightshirt that she had tossed to the floor.

The bathroom door opened.

"You're awake." Fully dressed in his faded jeans and a thermal shirt, he stepped out of the bathroom. "There's no need to rush. Schools are on a two-hour delay." He walked over to the bed.

"I should get back downstairs before Sierra wakes up and finds me gone." She tilted her head back for him to kiss her on the lips.

He knelt before her as she sat on the edge of the bed. "What are you going to tell her if she asks where you went last night?" He placed his hands on either side of her.

Hesitating, she took in his scent. He smelled like the fresh outdoors. His breath brushed her jaw and feathered across her breast. That was when she realized that she had picked up the nightshirt, but forgotten to put it on.

"Ah," he said in response to her silence, "you don't want to tell Sierra about us. Does she know about our past?"

"Sierra and I don't have secrets from each other."

"All teenagers have secrets," he whispered.

"Sierra is different."

"So was I, and I kept a lot of secrets from my parents and you did, too."

"I did n—"

"Homecoming night," he breathed into her ear.

Helen blushed.

With a chuckle, Chris started to stand. She grabbed his arms to pull him back onto his knees.

"I don't want to hurt you again. I just—I haven't dated at all since Sierra's father." She rubbed his chest with her hands. "I didn't date much at all after you. Sierra's dad came along and he asked me to marry him and—" She shrugged.

"What happened to us?" Chris asked. "Why'd—"

Her mouth opened. Tears filled her eyes.

Seeing the tears, Chris shook his head. "No, don't tell me. I don't want to know." He clasped her face in his hands and kissed her. "I love you, Helen, and whatever you decide to tell Sierra—"

"She'll be fine with us," she said. "I just don't want her to know how fast all this happened. From me not having any life to suddenly—" She gestured at the nightshirt that she had allowed to fall to the floor. "this."

"I get your point." Chris kissed her on the cheek and rose to his feet. "You don't want your sixteen-year-old daughter to know that you're sexually active. You want her to think you're a virgin." He picked up his fitness monitor from the nightstand and buckled it around his wrist. "You have about as much chance of pulling that off as I have of convincing my mother that I'm still a virgin."

With a laugh at his quip, she pointed at the monitor. "I imagine you register a lot of steps on that pedometer with all the farm chores you do."

"I average twenty-thousand steps a day." He picked up the nightshirt.

Her mouth dropped open. "Twenty-thousand?"

"My health insurance plan pays me money when I reach certain thresholds," he said. "So, theoretically, I'm getting paid for doing my chores."

"The state police have the same deal with our health insurance," she said. "We're all required to wear them. Not only do they register our steps, but our heart rate, too. Some officers who are really into conspiracy theories are afraid the insurance company is sharing data with human resources to give them a heads up of any health issues."

"Some guys I'd worked with were afraid that they had GPS chips to track us." He bent over to kiss her on the lips while handing the nightshirt to her. Enjoying the taste, he kissed her again and then once more.

"I need to go downstairs before Sierra wakes up," she whispered while holding onto his wrist. She pulled him down to kiss him again—deeply. She leaned back across the bed.

"You should go," he said in a soft voice while climbing on top of her.

"I know." She slipped her hands under his shirt. She could feel his heart thrumping. "I want to see exactly how much activity your monitor can take."

"You look happy." There was a smile in Doris's voice.

She bent over the back of his chair to kiss Chris on top of his head on her way to the coffeemaker. "Did you get a good night's sleep?"

"Like a log, Mom." He released his hold on the mug with which he was warming his hands to pat her hand on his shoulder.

Dressed in multiple layers of clothes and his boots, he was drinking a hot cup of coffee to work up the motivation to go outside in the zero degree temperature. Helen had sneaked downstairs ahead of him to slip back into the guest room. Chris assumed by the silence she had been successful in climbing back into bed without Sierra realizing she had spent the night with him.

"Logs sleep alone and in silence." Doris continued her way to the coffeemaker. The full skirt of her robe billowed behind her while Sadie and Mocha followed on either side like a couple of attendants. At the counter, she prepared her cup of coffee—extra cream and two sugars.

Chris set the mug down on the table. "How did you know?"

"Nothing happens in this house that I'm not aware of," she said. "It's an old creaky house—especially the stairs going up to your room. I heard Helen go up—"

"Could have been one of the girls," Chris said. "Emma comes up to my room half the time."

"And climbs into bed with you and goes straight to sleep." A sly grin crossed her face. "Helen's footsteps were softer—like someone making an effort to be very quiet. Then, once she got up there, based on the noise coming from your bed, you were much busier than usual."

Chris buried his face in his hands.

"Hey, I'm not complaining." She sat across from him. "It'll be nice to have a daughter-in-law who I can actually have a healthy relationship with." She raised one elegant brow at him while taking a cautious sip of the coffee.

"Mom, Helen and I have just gotten back together," he said. "Don't go sending out wedding invitations yet. A lot of time has passed. We're not two teenagers sneaking around anymore. We're two middle-aged single parents sneaking around."

"Did she tell you why she dumped you?"

"No and I don't want to know."

"Why not? I'd want to know. What if you did it again?"

"It's in the past," Chris said. "If I did something to tick her off, then—"

"Not only did she break your heart, she broke mine. Your father and I loved Helen. She became like a daughter to me. I truly expected the two of you to get married and give us beautiful grandchildren."

Chris set down his coffee mug. "You never did approve of Blair."

"Christopher, it wasn't Blair I disapproved of," she said, "but how she treated you. She didn't appreciate you and all the sacrifices you made for her."

"Maybe." He looked at her out of the corner of his eye. "Mom, can I ask you a question?"

She touched his hand. "Of course."

"Suppose a genie or angel or whatever told you that he could turn back time to when Helen and I had graduated from high school. Only this time, we'd get married. Helen and I would have spent the last thirty years happily married.

We'd have those lovely grandchildren that you imagined—" He stopped when he saw Doris grinning.

He laid his hand on hers. "But, there would be a price in exchange for that wish."

Her smile fell.

"You'd have to give up the grandchildren you already have. Katelyn, Nikki, and Emma." He leaned toward her. "If Helen had not broken my heart, I would not have married Blair. And as much as you disapproved of her, Blair gave me three daughters who are my reason for getting up in the morning."

Doris blinked away the tears that started to well up in her eyes. "Mine too."

"Helen feels the same way about Sierra."

Doris smiled with pride at her son. "When did you become so wise?"

He chuckled. "I got it from my momma."

They exchanged good-natured grins while sipping their coffee. Sterling and Thor sat side by side, peering out the window at the bird feeders in hope of spying the first squirrel of the day violating their territory.

Waiting for the caffeine to kick in, everyone, human and fur-covered mammals, drifted off into each one's own thoughts.

Finally, Chris broke the silence. "Tell me about the mother and baby that the women's fellowship group buried out at Edge Hill Cemetery."

"Wh-what mother and baby?" Doris stammered while Chris sipped his coffee in silence. "What are you talking about?"

"How many mothers and babies have you and your friends buried?"

"Oh!" Doris waved a hand in the air. "Tamara and her little angel. Nobody knew her name. The hospital had been given a phony driver's license when she got dumped there. She was in full cardiac arrest. Fred took her straight into OR and delivered the baby by caesarian. They had no idea how long Tamara's heart had been stopped—"

"During which the baby would have been without oxygen," Chris said.

"The baby only lived a little bit." Doris blinked. "Her husband, boyfriend—nobody knows what he was—abandoned them. No one ever claimed them from the morgue."

"Were the police ever called in?" Chris asked.

"No," she said with a shake of her head. "She died of natural causes. The medical examiner said Tamara—that's what everyone called her because it was the name on the phony driver's license—had died of heart failure."

"Did you ever see her body?"

"No," Doris said. "She'd been dead in the morgue at least two months before LeAnn told our women's group about her at one of our fellowship breakfasts. That was after the hospital had discovered that her identification was a fake."

"As far as the hospital was concerned, no crime had been committed," Chris said. "That's why no one ever called the police."

"She and the baby had been abandoned by their family, probably because they couldn't afford to bury them," she said.

"The hospital wrote off the bill."

"The two of them were going to be separated and donated as cadavers to a medical school," Doris said. "We took up a collection for a casket to bury the two of them together. I got a plot donated at Edge's Hill. Oh, it was such a nice plot, right under a tree with a pleasant view of a pond. Reverend Ruth did such a sweet eulogy for them. It was a pleasant spring day. You couldn't have asked for nicer weather. As a matter of fact, a sweet breeze blew cherry blossoms across the cemetery at just the perfect time during the blessing."

She looked across the table at him to see that Chris was cocking his head at her. "Why are we even talking about Tamara and her baby? You were in Washington when all that happened. How do you even know about it?"

Chris leaned across the table and took her hand. "Mom." He flashed a grin at her. "Mother. Tamara got dumped at Jefferson Medical Center on the same day that Sandy Lipton, who was nine months pregnant, disappeared."

Doris's mouth dropped open in a loud gasp. Her mouth hung open while she blinked at her son, who sat back in his seat to sip his coffee.

When he received no response, he sat up to tell her, "Sandy Lipton is the girl whose murder everyone thinks Dad covered up for me by the way." He drained his cup and set it on the table.

Doris was still gathering her thoughts when he leaned over to whisper into her ear on his way to the mudroom to get his coat. "Of course, no one is going to think anything when they find out it was my mother who buried her and her baby."

He called to her while shrugging into his coat, "When you're ready, we'll have a long talk."

He opened the door to a howling wind. When he slammed the door shut behind him, silence fell over the kitchen.

"This isn't good." After taking a sip of her coffee, she looked down at Sadie and Mocha, who cocked their heads at her. "This isn't good at all."

"Sterling, I wouldn't get too close to them if I were you," Chris warned the German shepherd inching toward the cats eating breakfast at a row of foil pie plates.

Judging by the curiosity on the dog's face, Chris wondered if he had much experience with cats. Since the dog had been trained strictly for law enforcement, Chris doubted he had many encounters with cats, especially barn cats. He had easily adapted to his new environment. His curiosity proved to be a problem—evidenced by the yelp Chris heard before Sterling scurried into the room where he was trying in vain to bring the security monitors back to life.

Neither would power on. They had worked before the power outage. *Must have been a power surge.* With a curse, he yanked the surge protector from the outlet.

Keeping a close eye on an orange tabby, Sterling pressed against Chris's leg while his master slid the paddock door open and whistled to call in the horses.

"Well, if this doesn't feel like déjà vu."

Chris heard Helen enter the barn just as the herd of horses raced in from the paddock. She was standing in the center of the aisle between the two rows of horse stalls—directly in the path of the horses galloping in for their morning meal.

"Stand back!" He grabbed her by the waist and body slammed her up against the far wall as the horses split up to go into each one's stall.

Helen's knees buckled when she realized she had almost stepped into the middle of a small stampede. When he felt her slump, Chris picked her up and pinned her against the wall with his body.

"Another instance of déjà vu," she murmured looking into his gray eyes. "I keep forgetting how dangerous this barn is."

Her hair smelled like the winter breeze. "The loft is pretty safe."

The heat of his body against hers made her heartbeat quicken. "Oh, I do have fond memories of that loft."

"I got a new pulley up there. I don't suppose you want to see it."

Her heart said yes, but her mind reminded her that their children were in the farmhouse preparing for school—any of whom could walk in at any moment. She swallowed. "The girls are up," she said in a low voice. "Can I have a raincheck?" She winked at him.

He brushed her cheek with his lips, slowly making his way down to her neck, then back to her ear. "Anytime for you."

She tried not to melt to the floor when he stepped away to close each of the stall doors. She counted a dozen horses and two ponies. Spotting the gray Thoroughbred she had petted before, she let out a soft gasp. "He's beautiful." She took a step toward the horse. When he tossed his head, she stopped.

Chris reached into the stall to stroke his head. "His name's Traveler." He urged her forward to stroke his muzzle.

"Like Robert E. Lee's horse."

"I don't know if he was named after Lee's horse or not. Dad bought him from a horse trainer who wanted to race his own horses. Only the guy had a big gambling problem. He bought Traveler with the winnings from a lucky long shot. Then he got unlucky with a series of long shots and owed money to the wrong people. They wanted Traveler to pay off his bets."

Traveler warmed up to Helen enough to hang his head over the stall door to allow her to scratch his ears.

"How did your Dad end up with him?"

"These people he owed money to were into drugging horses and he didn't want that to happen to Traveler. So he went to Dad. The guy agreed to wear a wire and helped the police to bring them down."

He fished a carrot out of his pocket and broke it in half—handing half to her. "That was Dad's last case. He got shot when they went in after the suspects discovered the guy's wire. Dad took a bullet to save the trainer's life, and he gave Traveler to Dad to thank him."

"Then, both your dad and Traveler retired."

Traveler rubbed his head against Chris's chest. "Dad rode him every day. I try to take him out as much as possible." He fed his half of the carrot to the horse. "You'd like that, huh, boy?" He told Helen. "He didn't really like racing. His thing is jumping."

Chris picked up the handles on a wheelbarrow filled with horse manure and wheeled it to the other end of the barn to deposit outside.

Helen stuffed her hands in the pockets of her winter coat and shivered. The temperature was so low that it was freezing even in the barn.

Pressure against her leg informed her of Sterling's presence. Sitting, the German shepherd leaned against her with all of his weight. He gazed imploringly at her with his brown eyes as if to request that she scratch his ears like she had done for Traveler. She complied.

"I see you made a friend," Chris said when he returned with the empty wheelbarrow.

"Can never have too many friends." Reminded of Felicia's death only hours before, she swallowed and blinked her eyes to fight the tears yearning to return. "I'm sorry. You must be thinking I'm such an emotional wreck—breaking down last night the way I did."

"You had a natural reaction to the brutal death of a friend who we saw only twenty-four hours ago. I'd think less of you if you didn't react."

She flashed him a reassuring grin.

"Did you contact your superiors about you being on the scene at the hospital?"

"Yes," she said. "It's my case. Sheriff Bassett went over to Rod's house last night to give him the news—the rental where he's been staying since him and Felicia separated. The arson investigator will meet us at the house at ten."

Lost in their thoughts of the past—the days of their youth, they strolled out of the barn. Sterling galloped on ahead to where Sierra and Chris's daughters were climbing into Doris's blue sedan.

"Sierra, what are you doing?" Helen broke into a run to stop her daughter from driving off in a car that did not belong to her.

"We're going to breakfast at iHop," Katelyn said. "Wanna come?"

"I thought Nonni was making pancakes and sausage," Chris said.

The girls broke into a storm of giggles.

"Did a dog get them?" Chris asked.

"The dogs won't even touch them," Nikki said. "Nonni mixed up the sugar and salt *again*."

"So she gave us a credit card and told us to go get something nutritious for breakfast before school." Katelyn extracted the credit card from her pocket and waved it for them to see.

"I'll drop the car off at the library when I go in after school," Sierra said. "You can pick me up after I get off, or," — she flashed Chris a grin — "Doris can bring me home with her, and Chris can give me a horseback riding lesson."

"I have plans for tonight," Chris said. "I can give you a lesson tomorrow morning if it's okay with your mother."

All eyes turned to Helen, who sucked in a deep breath and nodded her head. Sierra threw her arms around her in a grateful hug before moving on to Chris to hug him as well. She was still squealing with glee when she drove off with Katelyn, Nikki, and Emma—who was waving her casted arm like a prize.

"Were we ever that young and brave?" Helen asked.

"We still are," Chris said. "Look at what we do for our living."

"I don't feel brave most days. When I saw Felicia on that gurney—I felt fury. She didn't deserve what happened to her." She looped her arm through his and they made their way to the porch. "Do you remember when Felicia and you were partners in chemistry and she came down with laryngitis like the day of your project presentation—"

"And I had to do the whole presentation, including her part."

"For her part, she played Vanna White, posing and pointing while you did all the work. Even Mr. Shatner was laughing."

"Which meant it had to be funny because Mr. Shatner had no sense of humor," Chris said.

"Felicia could make anyone smile," Helen said. "That's why she was the most popular girl in school. But she wasn't snobby about it." She sniffed. "I remember my first day of school, in junior high, she walked right up to me and introduced herself. We were best friends ever since."

"Remember when she went behind your back and stole your boyfriend?"

Helen shot a quick glance over at him. She pulled her arm out from his. "We were all young then, Chris. Self-absorbed. We all made mistakes. I forgave Felicia for that. After I moved back here, we reconnected. We'd have lunch and text and talk."

"Did she tell you that she was divorcing Rod?"

Helen nodded her head. "She didn't love him anymore. I wonder if she ever did love him. Not too long ago, she told me that she made a big mistake dumping you for Rod."

"Like you said, that was all a long time ago—ancient history. We've all grown up—moved on—"

"Rod does have a temper. You saw the bruises on Felicia's arm. And he can hold a grudge. Didn't he jump at the chance to pin Ethel Lipton's murder on you? He's also working with Victor Sinclair on the Sandy Lipton case."

"Do you think Rodney is capable of murdering Felicia so that no one else could have her?"

"I'm praying that he isn't."

Chris opened the door to the mudroom just as Doris was on her way out with her coat on and briefcase in hand. She stumbled across the threshold. "Oh, Christopher, can't you watch where you're going?" She hugged Helen. "I take it you saw that the girls left for breakfast."

"Because you mixed up the salt and sugar *again*," Chris said.

"Accidents happen. I'm meeting Reverend Ruth for breakfast at Panera. I'm getting a mocha latte and a chocolate croissant for free. Do you know why?"

Chris rolled his eyes. "Because you use your Panera card."

"Because I use my Panera card. Every time I use my card, I get points and those points add up. Then, when you get enough points you get free stuff."

"Like chocolate croissants," Helen said. "Last week, I got a free latte."

"Christopher doesn't get anything for free because he doesn't use his shoppers cards," Doris said.

"Because I only have a dozen or so on my keychain," Chris said. "I make sure I use the one for the pet store. Their discount is worth my time digging my keys out of my pocket."

"How are you getting to Panera since the girls took your car?" Helen asked.

Doris dangled the key to Chris's truck. "I assume you're spending the day with Helen, Christopher."

"What if I wasn't?"

"But you are." With a merry wave, she trotted down the steps and across the driveway to the truck. "Oh!" She turned around to shout over the wind to him. "I called Reverend Ruth about Tamara. That's how we ended up deciding to go to Panera. She had a really good laugh after I told her about it. She says the church owns Tamara's grave. So if you need to dig her and her baby up, all you need is the permission of the church's board of trustees."

"And you're the trustee's chair," Chris said.

"Exactly," Doris said. "So go ahead and make arrangement to exhume the bodies."

"Bodies?" Helen asked with a gasp.

"Reverend Ruth only asks that she be there to make sure they're treated with respect." Doris blew a kiss in Chris's direction before climbing into the driver's seat and driving away.

"What bodies?" Helen asked. "Chris, what's this about? Who's Tamara?"

"I suspect Tamara is a missing person," he said while opening the door and holding it open for her. "To prove it, we're going to need to exhume a couple of bodies."

"I guess I'm going to have to make a few phone calls."

"Looks like we have the house to ourselves." After hanging her coat on a hook, he took off his and hung it up.

"Just you, me, and an assortment of critters." Helen jerked a thumb over her shoulder at where Sadie and Mocha were blocking the mudroom doorway into the kitchen. Beyond them, Sterling was sitting on a barstool at the counter eating what looked like a platter of toast.

"There's something you don't see every day," Chris said in reference to Sterling sitting at the counter like a diner waiting for his breakfast. After ordering Sterling out of the chair, he asked Helen, "Would you like an omelet for breakfast?" He opened the refrigerator door and removed a carton of eggs.

"That's right." She climbed onto the barstool that Sterling had vacated. "You used to say you were a better cook than your mother."

"Because Mom never liked to cook." Chris placed two plates on the counter. "When Dad asked her to marry him, she said yes, but had one condition. She didn't know how to cook and had no interest in learning. Dad said that would be fine. He was a very good cook." He proceeded to break one egg after another and plop them into a bowl. "So Dad did all the cooking—until I was ten months old. Then he told her that if they were going to eat, she'd have to learn how to cook." He arched an eyebrow at her with a crooked grin. "She knows just enough to be dangerous."

With a giggle, she answered her cell phone, buzzing in its case on her hip. She checked the caller ID. "It's the medical examiner. He must have already started his autopsy on Felicia." Bracing herself for the news, she put the phone to her ear.

Chris continued his work on their two omelets while casting glances in her direction. He found his thoughts bouncing back and forth between the horrid topic that Helen was talking to the medical examiner about and the past—when all they had to think about was their future and being in love.

Chris's relationship with Felicia had taught him a valuable lesson about life at a young age.

They dated for their whole junior year of high school. Chris was the varsity football's quarterback. Rodney was their captain. Felicia was head cheerleader and Helen was her brainy, but pretty, best friend.

The foursome double-dated every weekend. They went everywhere together. By Valentine's Day, Chris realized that he looked forward to their dates not so much to be with Felicia, as to see Helen.

He had fun with Felicia. She was his first serious—sexually intimate—relationship.

But Helen was different. While he had light, fun conversations with Felicia—he found that he could relate to Helen in a way that made him want her at an entirely different level. With Helen, he learned the difference between being in lust and being in love.

"Hey!" Helen snapped her fingers in front of his face to get his attention. "How long are you going to stir those eggs?" She jerked her chin in the direction of the bowl in which Chris had been whisking the eggs for the omelets.

Chris tossed the whisk into the sink. "Only until you tell me what the medical examiner told you." He took out the omelet pan and set it on the stovetop.

"She died of massive internal hemorrhaging. She had received a brutal beating—"

"Was she raped?"

Helen nodded her head. "Vaginal tearing indicates rape." She choked. "Sodomy, too. No semen, though. Spermicide indicates that whoever it was wore a condom. Medical examiner counted seventeen stab wounds."

Chris stared down at the omelet pan in silence. Beaten. Raped. Stabbed. House torched.

"Felicia didn't deserve to die like that," Helen said with a catch in her voice.

"Did Felicia ever go to the Stardust?" Chris lifted his eyes to the wall across from him.

"If you're asking if she was a gambler, no."

"How about the restaurant?"

"Never with me. Why?"

Chris turned away from the stove. "Remember yesterday when Francine and I were telling you about Mona Tabler and Shirley Rice?"

"The two women who you decided had to be victims of a serial killer?" Helen's eyes grew big.

"They were all beaten, raped, stabbed, and their homes burnt down. Locally, Mona Tabler and Shirley Rice. Both had the same MO, and I suspect I know who the serial killer is."

"Not Rodney," she said with a gasp.

"Why would you think it was Rodney?"

"Because…" she stammered. "Mona Tabler's case file was on Rodney's desk when I went to see him yesterday afternoon."

Chris's eyes met hers. "That doesn't mean he killed her." He grasped her hand. "He's the deputy sheriff. Tabler is a cold case. He had a good reason to have her case file."

She nodded her head.

He read the silent message in her eyes. *We can hope.*

CHAPTER NINETEEN

After they had eaten breakfast, Chris showered and dressed while Helen cleaned up the kitchen.

The forensics team planned to arrive at the Bell home at the same time as the arson investigator. While Helen wanted to see the crime scene as soon as possible, Chris wanted to check on Carson Lipton's whereabouts during the time of Felicia's murder. He had held off on giving his name to Helen, or even anyone on the Geezer Squad. Having been wrongfully accused of murder himself, he didn't want to accuse Carson of being a serial killer until he had proof.

After he had finished shaving, he noticed the bottle of expensive men's cologne that his mother had given him for Christmas in the cabinet. The cologne was so expensive that he refrained from wearing it. After all, the horses and dogs didn't care how he smelled.

Helen might. He grabbed the bottle and broke the seal.

As he caught his reflection in the mirror, he saw himself in a different light. He had allowed his hair, silver with only a touch of his former auburn locks, to grow to where it touched the top of his collar. *When was the last time you got a haircut?*

He leaned across the sink to observe the crow's feet at the corner of his gray eyes when his cell phone blasted. He almost dropped the open bottle of cologne down the sink. While fumbling to catch the bottle, he spilt it down his chest and stomach.

"Damn!"

In the bedroom, he slammed the bottle onto the dresser and picked up the phone. The caller ID read *Elliott*.

"Elliott, I want to talk to you."

"If it's about me going out with your mother, I have nothing but the utmost respect for Doris," Elliott said.

"If you respect her so much, why did you tell her that I'd pay for the tickets for your date?"

"To convince her that you were okay with it. You are okay with it, aren't you, Chris?"

"I'm not okay with paying for other men's dates with my girls."

"Do you want me to pay you back for the tickets?"

"Yes," Chris said with a hiss.

"Boy that was fast. You don't even want to think about it. I mean, if I play my cards right I could end up being your stepfather."

"And I could put in either a good word or a bad word for you with Mom," Chris said with a chuckle.

"I'll give you a check today."

"Good idea."

"Now that we've got that taken care of," Elliott said, "Have you ever been to Loco Lucy's?"

"Not even with a SWAT team for back up."

"Yeah," Elliott said with a chuckle. "I'd figure someone as pretty as you'd get eaten alive in a place like that."

"Hey, I can hold my own," Chris said with a good-natured tone. "Isn't that where the thugs who killed Ethel Lipton hung out?"

"Yep. A lot of drugs go in and out of there," Elliott said. "DEA has been watching it for years. Those two goons who gunned down Ethel Lipton worked for the gang that runs that place. Lucy has a silent partner who runs everything that enters West Virginia on its way to Baltimore."

"Jose Martinez," Chris said. "I've heard of him."

"Well, our case has nothing to do with drugs," Elliott said. "We're talking murder and you would never guess what Lucy's brother does."

"Since you're asking me, I'm assuming he is connected with the Stardust Casino."

"Driver."

"Driver?" Chris's mind went to the driver he had seen the day before sitting at the end of the bar. Seth. "Ethel was driven home a couple of nights before her murder. I met her driver."

"Francine told me," Elliott said. "That driver was the one who hired those goons to take out Ethel. My source tells me that Seth's girlfriend works in the offices at the casino—something to do with computers."

"Cybersecurity?"

"Considering why he hired those goons, most likely."

"Rachel Pine is the director of cybersecurity," Chris said. "She was extremely nervous when we were there yesterday."

"Sounds like Seth's girlfriend," Elliott said. "Anyway, Krawford had sent Tommy Bukowski to track down the people who'd made the fatal mistake in locking up his system with ransomware. Well, whoever it is at Stardust's online casino that uploaded that ransomware didn't know how sharp Tommy was."

"Tommy probably invented ransomware," Chris said.

"Stardust's head of security—"

"Vice president. Peyton Davenport?"

"Seth's girlfriend's boss gave Tommy free rein to check them out, and he found the virus's coding in their program."

"Did he offer them a deal in exchange for his silence?"

"Tommy wasn't suicidal," Elliott said. "If he withheld that information and Krawford found out, he'd be a dead man. Seth's girl—"

"Rachel."

"Whatever. She had to have been the one who uploaded the ransomware into the online casino and she realized Tommy found it. According to Wanda at Loco Lucy's, the girlfriend—"

"Rachel."

"—went running to Seth, who had Ethel passed out in the backseat of his car, and freaked out—"

"With Ethel in the car?"

"They thought she was passed out," Elliott said. "Only she wasn't. She heard them talking about Tommy's murder, which according to what Wanda told me, was going down right then. The girlfriend's partner—"

"Seth?"

"No, her partner in the ransomware scheme?"

"Peyton?"

"No, Peyton is the vice president in charge of security at the casino," Elliott said. "Rachel did the coding and monitored the operations. Her partner in crime selected their targets. According to what Wanda told me, they didn't just hit anyone who entered the online casino. Rachel would send in a spyware that would gather information off the gambler's system. She'd then give that data to her partner who would examine the data. She wasn't just looking for big bucks, but she would also look for off-shore accounts—embezzlement—"

"Activity that would make the target unlikely to report the ransomware to the authorities," Chris said.

"Exactly."

"Sounds to me like Rachel's partner was the brains behind the operation."

"And she was the one who lured Tommy out to the stables—"

"That's where he got the manure on his clothes," Chris said.

"That time of night, races were over and the stables were basically deserted. Wanda said that Seth's girlfriend—what's her name again?"

"Rachel."

"Whatever. I guess she could stomach extorting money from faceless victims across the internet, but murder made her freak out. She unloaded on Seth about it."

"The bartender told us about a redhead named Josie who was all over Tommy that night," Chris said.

"Wanda said Rachel's partner had red hair," Elliott said. "She hadn't met her, but Seth had made the comment about redheads being crazy, and he was talking about Rachel's crime partner when he'd said it."

"So, after the racetrack was closed, Josie lured Tommy to the stables and injected him with a horse tranquilizer to kill him."

"What's her name's partner then ordered Seth to get rid of the body," Elliott said.

"Josie," Chris said. "Sounds like they had it very well planned out."

"Except for a passed out drunk who wasn't passed out who overheard everything."

"When Ethel got a DUI the next morning," Chris said, "she decided to hold that information over the killers' heads."

"So Seth went to his sister Loco Lucy to arrange for a couple of goons to do a drive-by for him," Elliott said.

"Josie sounds like a real piece of work," Chris said. "Does Wanda know how Rachel knows Josie? I don't think she works at the casino because the bartender said she wasn't a regular. As a matter of fact, he told me he thought she was a prostitute."

"No, she's not a prostitute," Elliott said. "You're right. She doesn't work at the casino."

"But she does have access to the stables," Chris said. "You need a security pass to get through the gates after hours. That means Josie has to be connected to Stardust in some way. If she has a security pass and used it to enter the stables on the night of the murder, there'll be a record of it."

"You'll still need Rachel to make a statement about Josie's role in Tommy's murder."

"As nervous as Rachel was yesterday, I don't think it would take much pressure to flip her on her partner."

"Sounds like a plan to me."

Chris was impressed. "For a bunch of geezers, Elliott, your squad really has a way of making cold cases hot again."

"But wait, there's more."

"More?"

"We're five for five."

"Huh?"

"Patricia Handle and Carla Pendleton both have connections to the Stardust," Elliott said. "Both investigators had to go back to the families of the victims and do some digging, but it paid off. Carla Pendleton had a daughter who had her rehearsal dinner at the Stardust four weeks before the murder. While the daughter recalled it as a wonderfully elegant event, her husband told the detective that Carla was the mother of the bride from hell. Nothing made her happy. She complained to the restaurant manager about *everything*."

"That's four out of five who were difficult middle-aged women at the Stardust's restaurant," Chris said. "That makes a pattern. What about Patricia Handle?"

"She's a sad case," Elliot said. "The investigator on the case had to do some hunting to find her connection. Patricia had never been married. She tried online dating and had a blind date set up to meet at the Stardust. This was only a couple of weeks before her death. She got stood up. She waited at that table alone for over two hours. Finally, she ordered dinner. Plus, she had a bottle of wine all by herself. The bill came and wouldn't you know it? Her credit card was declined. Of course, she was embarrassed. Between being stood up and un-able to pay the bill, she broke down into a sobbing mess—caused quite a scene. Patricia told no one—except her best friend who told the detective after he asked her directly about the Stardust. Otherwise, no one knew that she had ever been there."

"Five for five," Chris said.

"That's his hunting ground," Elliott said.

"Can Ray and Jacqui do something for me?"

"Depends. What?"

"Can Ray do that thing he does and access the state police forensics files to get a copy of Ethel Lipton's DNA profile?"

"To run through the national database to see if any Jane Doe's DNA is a familial match?" Elliott asked. "They're al-ready doing that."

"Not just that. I want them to compare Ethel's DNA to that found at the first victim's crime scene for a familial match."

"Are you thinking Carson Lipton, Sandy's brother, is the Graduate Slaughterer?"

"Elliott, he fits the profile. He's the chef at the Stardust, has been there since the first murder, and he's got huge mom-my issues."

"I'll call Ray and tell him to get on it."

"There was another murder last night," Chris said. "Felicia Bell, the deputy sheriff's wife. Beaten, raped, stabbed, and house burnt down."

"Felicia lives locally, I assume."

"Morgana Drive in Shepherdstown. Problem is—Helen says Felicia has never been to the Stardust that she knows of. That breaks the pattern."

Elliott let out a gasp. "Morgana Drive was where Mona Tabler lived. Since she's local, Carson may have spotted her someplace else. Maybe he has a friend who lives on Morgana Drive and happened to see Felicia running in the park or something."

"Rodney has been looking at the cold cases himself, but as far as I know, he only knows about Mona and Shirley. Maybe he got too close."

"If that's the case, then you need to be careful," Elliott said. "I should come over to guard your mother."

"Mom can take care of herself, Elliott. If anyone comes after her, all she has to do is feed them her tuna casserole to kill them."

"The Pennsylvania state police are sending the DNA profile from Angela Romano's murder to our crime lab to compare with Ethel Lipton to see if there's a familial match," Helen said after Chris revealed his suspicions of Carson Lipton being the Graduate Slaughterer. "I also sent a couple of my detectives to go to the Stardust to nose around." She tucked her phone into its case on her belt.

"They have that big dinner dance tonight." Chris took Helen's coat from the hook in the mudroom and held it for her to slip on. "He'll be too busy cooking today to kill anyone for the time being. Most of the area's movers and shakers will be at the Stardust tonight—so he'll have to behave himself."

"Including us." She winked at him while he fastened her coat for her.

"You're going tonight?" Chris fought the grin working its way to his lips.

"I'm not leaving you alone with Peyton Davenport."

Looking into her pretty face, he marveled at how little she had aged.

"You smell really sexy. Did you put on that cologne for me or Peyton?"

He laughed. "Who do you think?"

"What are you looking at?" She moved in close to him and gazed up into his eyes.

"Just thinking," he said in a low voice.

"About what?" Her fingertips brushed the back of his hand. He turned it to lace his fingers with hers.

"In two years, I lost three people—well, three people and a dog—who I cared very much about. Neither Dad nor I were much for talking about feelings, but I know he knew how I felt about him."

"You worshipped him," she said.

"Blair and I had problems."

"Every married couple does."

"I could have taken a leave of absence from the FBI and taken the girls and followed her to Europe, but my pride wouldn't let me."

"Then you and the girls would have been there with her in Nice during the terrorist attack," she said.

"My point is…" His voice trailed off. He started again. "I kept hoping things would work out. So much between us was left unsaid." He squeezed her hand. "Lesson learned. Don't let an opportunity to let someone know how much you care slip by, because there may not be a next time."

She lifted her face—raising her lips to meet his.

He leaned forward.

The ring of her phone made them part as if they had received an electrical shock from their lips.

"Hold that thought." She dug her phone from the case and brought it to her ear. "Clarke here."

Chris snatched his coat from the hook and shrugged into it. He noticed then that Sterling was waiting at the door for Chris to open it. He expected to go with them. "What's the matter? You don't like hanging out with the girls?"

His tall ears falling to the side of his head, Sterling gazed up at him—pleading.

"I know how you feel, big guy," Chris said in a low voice.

Helen disconnected the call. "Children."

"Is there a problem?"

"Sierra forgot she has gym today and left her clothes at home. She wants me to go pick them up and bring them out to the school."

"Mom's got a ton of workout clothes. She does yoga three times a week. Sierra's about the same size as Mom, isn't she?"

Helen smiled. "Let's say she is."

He pointed to the back staircase. "Help yourself."

CHAPTER TWENTY

Smoke permeated the air when Helen turned her cruiser into Morgana Estates in Shepherdstown.

"I didn't realize Rodney and Felicia did so well for themselves." Chris observed the upper middle class homes that lined the street winding through the development.

"Do you know what house poor means?" Helen asked. "Felicia told me that they got the biggest mortgage they could to buy this house. For some reason Rodney was fixated on living here. He put so much pressure on himself to succeed to impress his dad—who didn't care one bit."

"That had everything to do with it." Chris counted the numbers on each mailbox.

One-fifteen. One-forty-five. One-seventy-five.

As the cruiser followed the curve in the road, Chris sat up in his seat in anticipation of the next house number.

Two-fifteen Morgana Drive. Mona Tabler's home.

He pressed his finger against the cold window and counted the houses until Helen brought the cruiser to a halt at the end of the block. *Four houses.*

Two state police SUVs and a red sedan were parked in the street. A team of firefighters cleaned the front yard of a smoldering French country brick home. The steam and smoke billowed up into the sky.

"When did Rodney and Felicia move here?" Chris asked.

Helen thought a long moment. "I was in law school. Rodney had been with the sheriff's department one year. Felicia was pregnant with their second son."

Chris counted the years from when they had graduated from Shepherd together. "Rodney went to work for the sheriff's department after he graduated from the police academy. 1995. Mid-nineties."

He turned in his seat to look back at the colonial-style home at the opposite end of the block. "Not only is the MO the same, but they lived only four doors down from Mona Tabler when she was killed."

"Maybe Rod saw something back then that struck him as peculiar," Helen said. "He put it together recently, and that's why he broke out the case file."

"What kind of thing?"

"I don't know." She opened the door and slid out. "Hasn't that happened to you? Something in a case strikes you as odd, but you don't know what it means until much later." She opened her coat and reached for the cell phone on her hip.

"Happens to me every day," Chris grumbled before getting out of the cruiser. When Sterling moved to the rear door with anticipation on his face, Chris shook his head. "Sorry, this is a crime scene. We can't have you contaminating it, big guy. We'll be back for you when we're finished."

Sterling uttered a series of barks.

"Listen to the radio. Since I'm not driving, you can listen to whatever you want." Chris ducked under the crime scene tape to join Helen, who was still talking on the phone.

"Are you kidding me?" The phone still to her ear, Helen turned to him with her face screwed up in an expression of disgust.

"What—"

Before Chris could finish his question, the cruiser's horn sounded—followed by a bark. He turned around to find that Sterling had jumped into the driver's seat and was repeatedly hitting the horn with his paw.

"Stop that!" When he stepped over to the cruiser, Sterling stopped and cocked his head at him.

Two uniformed state police officers tasked with making sure no one interfered with the crime scene and an older man in a fire fighter's uniform watched the debate from the top of the driveway.

"Don't be rude," Chris told the dog.

Sterling responded with a bark.

"Yes, I'm talking to you. Lay down and be quiet."

Sterling uttered a whine that turned into a pitiful bark.

"I don't care if you are bored. You wanted to come with us, but you can't go into the crime scene."

With a harrumph, the dog laid down and rested his head on the door rest.

"All right. Let me know what you find when you get there." She disconnected the call and placed her hand with the phone on her hip. "You were right."

"I'm always right." He ducked back under the crime scene tape to rejoin her. "What am I right about this time?"

"Lipton didn't show up at the Stardust this morning. Neither did his wife. The detectives found the kitchen and restaurant staff in a panic because of the dinner dance tonight. The Liptons are nowhere to be found. Neither of them are answering their cell phones. My detectives and a couple of uniforms are going to their house to check it out."

The arson investigator, Brad Miller, met them at the door leading into the attached garage. Chris recognized him as the father of one of his childhood friends.

Brad recognized Chris as well. "Matheson? Right? Your mother is the librarian." He clasped Chris's hand. "I'd heard through the grapevine that you came back. Sorry about your father. How's your mother doing?"

"Fine," Chris said. "She keeps herself very busy."

"That's Doris all right. Is she seeing anyone?"

Stunned, Chris glanced at Helen who suppressed a smile. "My dad only died eight months ago."

"I know," Brad said, "but classy ladies like Doris don't stay in circulation very long—"

"Aren't you—"

"Oh, my wife divorced me for a FedEx delivery guy over seven years ago." Brad fished a business card out of his pocket and shoved it into Chris's hand. "Can you do me a favor? When your mom is ready to start dating, can you…" There was a plea in his voice when he added, "Put in a good word for me?"

Disbelief struck Chris speechless.

Helen changed the subject by shaking his hand and introducing herself.

Seeing that they had returned to business, Brad reported the cause of the fire was "pretty obvious. You can smell the gasoline."

"What time did 9-1-1 receive the call?" Helen asked while she and Chris slipped on paper booties to prevent them from leaving footprints that would contaminate the crime scene. They also put on hard hats for their own protection from any falling debris.

"Eight-twenty-one," Brad said while referring to his notes. "The call was made by the owner's security and fire alarm system. The trucks arrived at eight-twenty-seven. According to the captain's report, the victim jumped out the bedroom window." He pointed in the direction of the front of the house. "They didn't even have the hoses out yet. But that's not the interesting part."

Crooking his finger at them, he led them through the garage door leading down a hall that opened into a smoke and water damaged country kitchen.

They crossed the kitchen to a set of glass patio doors that opened to a wooden deck. There was an in-ground pool in the back yard. The spacious yard ended at thick woods. Morgan Park was located on the other side of the woods.

Two crime scene investigators were lifting footprints from the tile floor on which a liberal amount of soot had fallen.

"Any luck?" Helen asked them.

Both of the investigators shook their head. "The fire fighters were more focused on getting the fire out than securing the crime scene," one said.

"No sign of anyone other than the fire fighters forcing their way inside," the other one said. "The home security system was on."

"Almost sounds like she had let him in, or he found a way to bypass the system," Helen said. "I wonder if he had gotten inside earlier in the day and waited for her."

Brad led Helen and Chris up the carpeted staircase. The upstairs was only a charred shell of what it had once been.

"Oh, dear," Helen said in a soft voice.

Brad pointed out a black trail that snaked down the hallway and into every bedroom and bath along the floor. Even though everything was black from the fire, with burnt out holes in the wall, the arson investigator had picked up the fire's path. "He splashed gasoline into every room and over to the top of the stairs. I'm sure the arsonist assumed that the second floor would collapse and destroy all the evidence. Either the fire company got here too fast, or the house was built more securely than he thought."

He led them into the master bedroom which was as black as a cavern. "This is where it started." He pointed at the wall behind the skeleton of what had once been a four-poster king-sized bed. The charcoal remains of an end table lay crumbled on the far side of the bed. With his arms, Brad illustrated a dark, smoky V-shape going up both walls in the corner. "Right there is where the fire started."

He picked up a lamp from the floor and showed them a part of the melted electrical cord. "To most people, this would look like a lamp that had been destroyed in an arson fire. See these exposed wires." He held up the bare ends of the cords that had been twisted around and bent to form a circle. "The fire did not twist these cords around like that. The arsonist did that. He cut off the insulation to expose the bare wires and twisted these cords around something to start the fire. Most likely a match. Then he set the cord with the match down in a pool of gasoline. When the lamp was turned on, the current caused a spark to light the match, which ignited the gasoline that he had spread throughout this upper floor."

"Does the wall switch next to the door turn on the lamp over here?" Helen asked.

"Probably," Brad said, "but if he'd done that, we'd have two bodies up here because the gasoline was spread throughout the second floor. I found an empty gasoline can next to the lawn mower in the garage. Bet you that's where he got it."

"Then how did he turn on the lamp to start the fire without getting caught in it himself?" Helen asked.

Brad turned the lamp over to show them the broken light bulb. "See this bulb? It's a wi-fi light bulb and lamp."

"The killer turned it on remotely," Chris said.

"All he'd have to do is gain access to the house's secure wireless network," Brad said. "He could have turned it on with a phone all the way across the country."

"But he would have had to have access to the house's secure wireless network," Helen said.

"He could have hacked into that," Chris said. "But he would have had to have gotten access inside the house to have killed Felicia and so far your forensics team says there was no forced entry. He could have been someone she trusted enough to give her network's password and let inside the house."

"That limits our pool of suspects considerably," Helen said as shouting out in the street drifted up to them.

"Halt! Police!" They looked out of the window to see one of the uniformed officers chasing a man across the front yard. Abruptly, the passenger side door of Helen's cruiser flew open and Sterling scrambled out to give chase—bringing the man down in the middle of the street.

"How did that dog open my car door?" Helen ran from the bedroom and down the stairs.

"He's goofy. That's how."

By the time they reached the street, the uniformed officer was handcuffing the man wearing a worn army fatigue jacket and gray overalls underneath.

"I didn't do nothing," he shouted over and over again while being hauled to his feet.

Sterling galloped across the yard to jump up and plant his front paws on Chris's chest as if to ask, "Did you see what I did? Did you see what I did? Did I do good?"

"You did good. Now get back in the cruiser."

Instead of obeying, Sterling opted to trot next to him.

"We caught him trying to sneak into the garage," one of the uniformed officers told Helen.

"I was only trying to get my tools before you cops stole them from me. They're my tools. I need them."

"What's your name and what are your tools doing in Felicia Bell's garage?" Helen asked.

"Opie Fletcher. I worked for Ms. Bell. She hired me to do odd jobs after her husband left. Mowing the lawn. Trimming trees. Cleaning the gutters."

"The awn doesn't need mowed right now." One officer took Opie's wallet out of his jacket pocket and handed it to Helen, who removed his driver's license to read the name.

"I came today to trim that big oak tree next to the house. Its branches are hanging over the roof. I was supposed to do it yesterday, but I couldn't make it on account that I got called into my regular job at the racetrack—"

"Racetrack?" Chris asked. "Do you work at the Stardust?"

"Stable hand for over thirty years," he said. "I told Ms. Bell 'bout my gettin' called into work and she said I could come out today. But then when I saw all the police cars, I was 'fraid that you'd all jump to the same nasty conclusion that you did before."

"You're talking about Mrs. Tabler," Chris said.

Opie stomped both of his feet. "I didn't do nothing to that lady, I swear."

Chris led Helen aside. "You're not going to believe this."

"I just saw your dog open the door to my car from the inside by himself. I'll believe anything."

"Opie Fletcher was a person of interest in Mona Tabler's murder."

"Seriously?" she asked. "What was his motive?"

"Folks heard him say that he did it," Chris said. "He was a suspect for years before Dad cleared him. It's in the case file."

"We need to get back to the office and take a good long look at those case files."

In response to the car horn blowing, they turned around to find Sterling sitting in the driver's seat of her car—pressing his paws to the horn.

"Chris, what—"

"Don't worry. He's not driving."

CHAPTER TWENTY-ONE

"Is that him? Is that the dirty bastard who killed my wife?"

Rodney Bell rushed out of the sheriff's office to intercept the two uniformed officers escorting Opie Fletcher, in handcuffs, to an interrogation room. One of the officers pulled Opie away while his partner blocked Rodney's access to the suspect.

"I'm going to kill you, you son of a bitch!"

Chris attempted to settle Rodney down with reason. "We don't know that he did it. They just caught him trying to break into the garage. He claims he worked for Felicia. Helen is going to question him."

"Worked for her? What do you mean worked for Felicia? Doing what?"

Chris glanced over his shoulder and saw that the officers had escorted Opie into the room and closed the door. "Yard work. Odd jobs."

"Where the hell did she find him? What the—" Grasping Chris's arms, Rodney collapsed against his chest. "This is all my fault. I never should've left her. If I'd stayed, then she would've never met that animal."

Chris ushered Rodney, covering his face with his hands, back into the sheriff's office and closed the door.

"Have you told your sons yet?" Chris took a seat in the chair across from him.

With a heavy sigh, Rodney lifted his face from his hands. "They're coming out as soon as they can. I want to be able to tell them that we got the guy by the time they get here." He jerked his chin in the direction of the interrogation room. "What do you know about him?"

"His name is Opie Fletcher."

"Where'd Felicia find him?"

"We don't know yet," Chris said. "It's still early. When was the last time you talked to Felicia?"

"Of course." He rose to his feet. "The spouse is always the first one you suspect."

"Rodney, we have to ask these questions. You were fighting with Felicia yesterday. She showed us bruises on her arm that she claimed you gave her."

"No, I completely understand. You have to clear me first." Rodney fished a toothpick from his shirt pocket. "If the situation was reverse—"

"It has been reversed. Just the other day you accused me of arranging Ethel Lipton's murder."

"And just like you, I was only trying to get to the truth." Rodney stuck the end of the toothpick between his teeth.

"Did you kill Felicia, Rod?"

"I have an alibi. I went to the gym after work. I got there a few minutes before seven."

"Did you talk to anyone? Can anyone confirm you were there?"

"I doubt it. I went straight to the cardio cinema and used the treadmill. It was dark, and I stayed in the theater through the whole movie. Then I went home—alone."

"Cardio cinema?"

"It's a movie theater in the gym. You do your cardio—rowing machine, elliptical, cycle, or treadmill—while watching a movie. It started just as I walked in. I left after it had ended."

"How long was that?" Chris asked.

"Around ninety minutes. Maybe a little less. From seven to around eight-thirty? What time did the fire start?"

"9-1-1 got the call at twenty-one after eight."

"At which time, I was in a dark movie theater." Rodney held up his hand, winked, and pointed at him. "Wait a minute. Just remembered. My membership card has a barcode. I used that when I checked in. They also have security cameras at the front entrance. That'll prove I was there and the security footage will show you exactly what time I left." With a chuckle, he bit down on the toothpick.

"I don't suppose the gym had any other doors that you could've left and come back through during the movie?" Chris asked.

"Fire exits of course," Rodney said. "You can go out, but you'll set off an alarm loud enough to wake the dead. Then after you get out, the doors lock behind you—forcing you to come back through the front door where the security camera picks you up."

"Sounds to me like you checked that out already."

Rodney winked at him. "I make it my business to pay attention to details—just like you."

After his interview with Rodney, Chris found Sterling in the break room. The dog sat in a chair at the table with a newspaper laid out before him. Someone had put a K-9 law enforcement vest on the German shepherd.

"Anything interesting in the news?" Chris asked with a laugh.

The dog put a paw on the paper and uttered a low bark. Chris gave into his curiosity and bent over to peer at the page. The paw rested on an advertisement for heated dog beds at the local pet supply store. The two-hundred-dollar electric bed was on sale for twenty percent off.

"If I get you one of those, then I'll have to get them for everyone."

With a whine, Sterling slumped.

"I have a meeting at noon," Helen said as she entered the break room with her phone on her ear. "Can we meet at one thirty?" Seeing Chris, she let out a quiet sigh and rolled her eyes while listening to the person at the other end of the line. "I do understand the casino's concern for its reputation, Ms. Davenport, but you have to understand ours. This is an active murder investigation. Mr. Bukowski being a Stardust guest does not give the casino the right to demand everything that we uncover in our investigation."

Listening to Peyton Davenport's response, Helen clenched her teeth so hard that her jaw muscles rippled.

"If Mr. Sinclair wants to call my supervisor, then he can do that." Her mouth formed a snarl which she shot in Chris's direction. Abruptly, her eyebrows furrowed, and her eyes narrowed to slits.

"Yes, he's right here." She thrust the phone at Chris. "Your girlfriend wants to talk to you."

With a whine, Sterling slithered out of the chair and hid under the table.

Chris swallowed and took the phone which he put to his ear. "Hello."

"Hey, handsome," Peyton said in a seductive tone, "are we still on tonight?"

"Is the dinner dance still on? Rumor has it your chef and the restaurant manager are MIA?"

"I've heard something about that," she said, "but the Stardust can handle losing one chef and his cold-hearted wife. As our board of directors say, no one is indispensable at the Stardust. Everyone can be replaced."

"That's pretty harsh."

"Reality is harsh."

"You don't beat around the bush, do you?"

"How's this for not beating around the bush?" she said. "I have plans for you and me to get busy this evening. Do you want to do it before dinner, as an appetizer, or afterwards for dessert?"

Chris felt his face flush. He saw by the expression on Helen's face that she had concluded what Peyton was saying to him.

"I like dessert."

"So do I," she replied. "Since I have to work, I'll meet you at the dinner."

"I'd rather come to your office to meet you," he said. "I can zip up your dress."

Helen rolled her eyes.

"Or unzip it," Peyton said. "See you at six."

Before she could disconnect the call, Chris asked, "Do you know a Josie?"

There was such a long silence at the other end of the line that he thought she had hung up. Finally, she asked, "Josie? Josie who?"

"A witness told us that Tommy Bukowski was having drinks in the lounge with a redhead named Josie. Someone suggested that she worked at the Stardust?"

"What's her last name?" Peyton asked.

"Don't have it? Could Bukowski have met her while doing his research in cybersecurity? Maybe Rachel knows who she could be."

"I know every employee in cybersecurity," Peyton said. "I'll ask Rachel and do some nosing around. I'll try to have answers for you by this evening." Her voice took on a husky tone. "I can slip it to you between the sheets."

"I'm looking forward to it."

Helen's dark eyes narrowed to slits. "Can you believe this?" she asked Sterling, who was looking from one of them to the other from under the table.

Disconnecting the call, Chris said, "I'm not going to sleep with her."

"You bet you're not going to sleep with her."

"It's because she's a murder suspect that I'm going out with her. If she lets me get close to her, then she'll let her guard down and I can find out what she's hiding. She's hiding something—that's why she's sicking her Daddy's lawyer on your boss. She wants to find out if we're on to her."

With a pout, Helen had to agree with him. "I don't trust her."

"Neither do I," Chris said while laying his hand onto hers. "But I know what I'm doing. I'd worked undercover for over ten years—going up against every type of psychopath. I can handle Peyton."

"That's what I'm afraid of." She squeezed his hand. "You handling her." She turned back to business. "Does she know who this Josie is?"

"She says she doesn't."

"Do you believe her?"

Uncertain, he shook his head while shrugging his shoulders. "According to Elliott's source at Loco Lucy's—"

"Which isn't just second hand, but third-fourth hand."

"Exactly," he said. "Peyton Davenport gave Tommy Bukowski permission to go through Stardust's records to look for the ransomware."

"Which he found."

"If Peyton knew that the ransomware was in their system, she wouldn't have done that," Chris said.

"She would have had a dozen legal avenues to have kept Tommy Bukowski out," she said. "It's right out of White Collar 101. Peyton delays Bukowski with legal hurdles while Rachel is removing the ransomware and scrubbing the system."

"But that's not what Peyton did," Chris said. "She immediately gave Bukowski access to the system."

"And he found the coding for the ransomware," Helen said. "Now he's dead."

"Either Peyton didn't know about the ransomware because she wasn't in on it," Chris said, "or she did know about it and was in on it—"

"If so, why would she have given Bukowski access to the system to find it? She had every legal right to refuse him."

Chris narrowed his eyes. "Last night, Mom told me that around ten years ago there was a sex scandal at the high school. A group of teenaged girls was seducing teachers and then blackmailing them. One of the girls ended up dead. Turned out to be an organized sex and extortion ring." He looked at Helen. "Peyton Davenport was the ring leader."

"Was she—"

"Never prosecuted." Chris shook his head. "There was also another scandal when she was in college involving a dead football player." He rubbed his chin. "It's been my experience that psychopaths, who generally have no conscience, only become bolder—"

"More arrogant."

"—with each success."

"Part of the turn on is getting away with it," Helen said.

"If Peyton was in on the ransomware, she may not have been able to resist when Tommy Bukowski asked to look at her system—just to see if she could get away with it."

"She is the vice-president of security," Helen said.

"Which gives her the keys to the kingdom."

"Yes, but she was taking a huge risk by letting Bukowski examine their system. The discovery of a hacking ring operating inside the online casino would not look good for the Stardust at all."

"Which is why he had to die," Chris said.

"But she'd have to be smart enough to know that when Bukowski was reported missing—or his body found—that he'd be traced back to the casino."

"She did think about that," Chris said. "Their records show that he'd checked out. They can argue that whatever happened to him happened after he left the Stardust and they have the paper trail to prove it."

"Even if Peyton is not a murderer," Helen said, "I don't want you sleeping with her."

He picked up her hand and kissed her fingers. "There's only one woman I want to sleep with."

With a coy grin, she wrapped her fingers through his and pressed their hands to her heart. "And who might that be?"

His answer was a soft kiss on her lips.

With a deep sigh, she returned to business. "Where's Rodney?"

"Lawyering up," Chris said.

"Your conversation went that well?" She took two bottles of water from the fridge and handed one to him.

"He's been around long enough to know how it goes," Chris said while opening his bottle. "Homicide detectives always start with the inner circle and work their way out. Yesterday, we saw Rodney threaten Felicia. She had bruises on her arm that she attributed to him—"

"Nothing screams guilty like lawyering up."

"I'd lawyer up if I was in his shoes." He focused on the seam of the label wrapped around the bottle. "What is this thing with the toothpick? He's always got a toothpick stuck in his teeth."

"Cause he's got to do something with his hands since he quit smoking."

Chris let out a breath. "Of course. I forgot all about that. He used to smoke." He nodded his head. "That's another reason Mom hated his guts."

"Rodney was in danger of not passing his physical because his blood pressure was so high," Helen said. "So he quit smoking and joined the gym a couple of years ago. Felicia told me that was when things turned ugly between them—when Rodney gave up his cigarettes." She took a drink of water. "Do you think he had anything to do with Felicia's murder?"

"I don't know," Chris said with a sigh. "We all grieve differently. When Blair was killed, I had a million questions. What was she doing? Did she see that truck coming at her? Did that terrorist see her and target her? Did she die immediately or did she suffer? Did she have any last words? Did she think about our girls? Did she think of me? Was there someone there to offer her comfort, ease her pain, her fears, pray for her. I called every source I knew who could answer at least a few of my questions." He looked at her. "Still, to this day, I have questions."

She reached across the table for his hand.

Chris cleared his throat. "Rod didn't ask any of those questions."

"We know he has a motive, but does he have an alibi for the time of the murder?"

"He was at the gym," Chris said. "He didn't talk to anyone, but the gym's keycard system confirmed that he had checked into the gym at six-fifty-six. The gym has agreed to let us view their security footage to see if it was Rodney who used his keycard. Just because his keycard was used to check in, doesn't mean he used it."

She frowned. "Don't you trust Rodney?"

With a dramatic air, he clutched his chest and uttered a gasp. "Helen, why would I not trust Rodney? I've known the guy since kindergarten."

"Which isn't necessarily a good thing," she said. "Unfortunately, Opie doesn't have an alibi. He was watching television in the room that he rents in Inwood. He didn't see or talk to any of his roommates."

"I don't believe in coincidences," Chris said. "I find it odd that Felicia hired him to do odd jobs around her house, which is only four doors down from where Mona Tabler was killed in her home."

"I also find it odd that Felicia hired a guy who was a person of interest in a murder so close to home," Helen said. "That doesn't sound like Felicia." She paused to take a sip of water. "About this pattern in these five murders…"

"What about them?"

She ticked off on her fingers. "Beaten and violently raped. Stabbed. Arson."

"We have more than an MO," he said. "We also have a victim profile. Middle-aged women, all who have had a connection with the Stardust restaurant."

"While there is a pattern," she said, "it's rather general. Don't you think? Isn't it possible that Mona Tabler, this middle-aged woman who worked at the Stardust, was murdered in the same way as the others by coincidence?"

"Dad tracked down the rumor about Opie killing Mona. It started as a joke between a bunch of exercise riders and stable workers in the racetrack's lunchroom."

"According to what I read in the case file, several people had heard Opie saying he killed Mona on more than one occasion. He even gave himself a name. Opie Kreuger. Get it? Freddie Kreuger? Opie Krueger?"

"Opie's not very bright," Chris said, "but that doesn't make him a killer. I really think Carson killed Mona Tabler. She was a ruthless restaurant manager. It's entirely possible that she threatened Carson's dream of being a chef. He had mommy issues, so he took out his rage against his mother by killing her."

"Carson isn't the only person to have had mommy issues," she said. "Opie's mother was a heroin addict. She gave Opie up to the system. His mother wasn't the only woman Opie had issues with. His first job at the track was washing dishes in the restaurant. Do you know who fired him?"

"Mona Tabler," Chris said.

"Opie Fletcher knew her and had a motive," she said. "Then, he went to work for Felicia and she chewed him out for not showing up when he was supposed to—"

"Opie stated that Felicia said she was okay with him coming the next day."

"So he says," Helen said. "Unfortunately, the only one who could confirm that is Felicia, and she's in the morgue."

"Do you think Opie is smart enough to have set up the lamp in her bedroom to start the arson fire without getting caught in it?"

She firmly shook her head.

"Carson Lipton was smart enough to have set up that lamp," Chris said.

"But Felicia never went to the casino."

"Not even for a realtors' cocktail party?"

"I'll keep checking with her friends and co-workers, but I'm not having any luck. Did you ask Rodney—"

"No," Chris said, "and I don't want to. I want to keep the serial killer's hunting ground close to the vest until I have something more solid. Have your people had any luck locating Carson, by the way?"

"You would never believe what my officers found or rather didn't find at the Lipton place."

"He's in the wind."

She nodded her head. "They found Mabel Lipton's vehicle in the garage. There's no sign of them leaving involuntarily. Yet, it's totally out of character for them to not show up for work. Unfortunately, we don't have any evidence that either of them have done anything wrong."

Chris agreed. "Without a familial match between Ethel Lipton's DNA, and the DNA found at the Lancaster murder, all we have is a couple ditching work for a mental health day."

"Until we have evidence that Carson is connected to these murders, or we have reason to believe that one or both of them are in danger, all we can do is simply ask our officers to keep an eye out for them."

Feeling a sense of helplessness, Chris took a long drink of water.

CHAPTER TWENTY-TWO

"Your mother buried the girl who you've been accused of murdering?" Francine's eyes were wide when Chris delivered the news to them over a late lunch at Billie's.

Helen was needed at a staff luncheon meeting. Unable to explain Chris's presence, she opted to drop him and Sterling off at Billie's, where he discovered his book club was meeting.

The group, minus Ray, who Chris had yet to meet in person, occupied the same table they had the day before. Chris suspected Billie's was the Geezer Squad's version of the neighborhood cop bar. Only instead of chugging beers, they swilled coffee and ate fries slathered in catsup.

Clad in a state police K-9 service vest, Sterling laid down under their table where he received a regular supply of fries from each squad member.

"Mom didn't actually dig the grave," Chris said, "though she did pay for the grave digger. But the church reimbursed her out of the mission's fund, and Dad donated a hundred dollars toward the coffin."

"Let's hope it isn't Sandy Lipton," Francine said. "Victor Sinclair will have a field day with all this."

"Victor Sinclair isn't going to be a problem," Bruce said with a wink that everyone around the table understood—except Chris.

"Bruce," Chris said, "why is Victor Sinclair not going to be a problem?"

"How should I know?" Bruce held up his hands in a broad shrug. "It would be wrong for me to use information that I have collected from some of my many sources to coerce someone to do something that they otherwise wouldn't want to do."

"That would be extortion."

"'Extortion' is such a negative word," Bruce said. "I prefer the word 'persuasion'."

"What do you have on the Sinclairs?" Chris asked.

Everyone around the table sat at the edge of their seats with their gaze focused on Bruce, who let out a deep breath. "Let's just say that Victor Sinclair isn't as knowledgeable about law as one would think."

Elliott and Francine exchanged puzzled glances. Chris pondered the statement before he asked, "Are you saying Victor Sinclair cheated on his bar exam?"

"Technically, you have to *take* an exam to *cheat* on it," Bruce said.

"But—"

"Steve Sinclair has a lot of influence. But then, so do I," Bruce said. "You didn't hear it from me."

"Do you have proof of this?" Chris asked.

"As long as the Sinclairs maintain their distance," Bruce said, "I've got nothing to say."

There were chuckles around the table.

"Okay, let's get to work." Elliott rubbed his hands together. "Where were we? Oh, yes. Doris buried the victims' bodies."

"Mom says she never saw the bodies, and she never put the dates together," Chris said. "So much time had passed since

Sandy disappeared and Tamara's COD was natural causes. Anyway, if we had anything to hide, then we wouldn't be exhuming the bodies. If it does turn out to be Sandy, then Dr. Frederic Poole will be at the top of our suspect list."

"I've been searching high and low," Francine said, "and can't find any evidence to suggest that Dr. Poole was dealing in black market adoptions. Why the elaborate cover-up?"

"We still don't know who the baby's father is." Elliott turned to Chris. "Any progress on that front?"

"Carson says it's Victor Sinclair, but I don't think so."

"Well, we'll get answers to all of those questions once we get the bodies exhumed," Jacqui said, "assuming Tamara Wilcox and the baby are Sandy Lipton and her baby."

"I'm assuming since Tamara Wilcox is really a Jane Doe and has no family, that getting her body exhumed isn't going to be difficult," Bruce said.

"Since our church, Oakland Community, technically owns the plot, all we need is the pastor and church's permission," Chris said. "Mom is the chair of the church's board of trustees. When she explained the situation to Reverend Ruth, she agreed—after she stopped laughing. Helen scheduled the exhumation for Monday."

"It'll take a while to process the DNA and compare it to Ethel Lipton's to see if there's a familial match," Francine said.

"There is a faster way," Jacqui said. "I know DNA is the sexiest game in forensics, but it isn't the only game in town. We have Sandy Lipton's picture, and she is smiling."

"Our prom picture," Chris said with a somber tone. "She couldn't stop smiling that night."

"Blow up the prom picture and we can compare the teeth to Tamara's. We can have the results in a matter of hours, if not faster," Jacqui said with a wave of her hand.

"If it is Sandy Lipton," Francine asked, "then who do you think dumped her at the hospital?"

"Could it have been Carson?" Bruce asked.

"Do you mean Carson Lipton, who's in the wind?" Chris asked.

"Are you serious?" Elliott asked.

"Yesterday, I asked if he would voluntarily allow us to put his DNA in the system to see if we could get a familial match with any Jane Does. He said he didn't want Big Brother to track him like a wild animal." Chris looked across at Jacqui. "He definitely has mommy issues and last night, a middle-aged woman living four doors down from Mona Tabler was murdered—with the same MO as the other women."

"You asking for his DNA could have put enough pressure on him to make him snap," Jacqui said.

"We can't find any connection between this victim and the Stardust," Chris said.

"But she lives locally," Jacqui said. "I assume she wasn't a recluse. He could have seen her in the grocery store. She could have cut him off in traffic. He could have had a fight with his wife that made him snap and fall back into his old pattern all over again. This victim may have simply been in the wrong place at the wrong time for him to select to use as a substitute for his mommy."

"His wife is missing, too," Chris said while extracting his vibrating cell phone from his pocket.

"Pray he's not on a killing spree," Jacqui said, "or last night's victim may be the first in a long list of victims."

Seeing that the caller ID read an unfamiliar phone number from Morgantown, West Virginia, Chris hesitated before connecting the call. "Chris Matheson speaking."

"Mr. Matheson, this is Rachel." Her voice shook with emotion.

In the background, Chris heard what sounded like a fight. "Rachel, are you okay?"

"No," she sobbed. "It's Peyton. She's crazy!"

"Die, you bitch!" A man bellowed in the background, followed by a crash.

"Rachel, where are you?" Chris snatched his coat from where he had draped it across the back of his chair. Elliott ushered Sterling out from under the table.

"Home. Prospect Hills!"

A man's agonizing cry drowned out the rest of Rachel's answer.

"She stabbed Seth! Help me! Please!"

Their connection was cut off.

"We don't know where Rachel lives," Chris told Elliott, who pressed his SUV's accelerator pedal to the floor to race out of Billie's parking lot. "Prospect Hills is a big subdivision. You're driving blind."

In the backseat, Sterling lost his footing. He bounced off the backrest to the floor.

As if on cue, Ray's voice came out of the on-board device in the SUV. "Elliott, I plugged Rachel Pine's home address into your GPS. ETA nine minutes. The way you drive, six. Bruce is on the phone with emergency services."

"Bruce had already reported it to emergency," Chris told Helen who he had gotten on his phone.

"Who's Bruce?" Helen asked in a breathless voice.

"He belongs to my book club."

Ray's estimation was correct. Five minutes later, Chris grabbed the edge of his seat when Elliott spun the wheel to turn into a neat neighborhood on the outskirts of town. Sterling hit the side window. The dome of Washington High School rose above the rooftops.

"In a half mile, your destination will be on the left," the GPS lady said.

At that point, they didn't need her. Two police cruisers, one county and one state, were parked in front of a two-story colonial home. A town car with a Stardust logo stuck on the side doors filled the driveway.

They heard the wail of police sirens in the distance.

After Chris and Elliott jumped out of the SUV, Sterling climbed over the front seats to gallop ahead of them to the open front door. At the top of the stoop, the German shepherd stopped with a yelp. He spun around, leapt down into the yard, and let out a commanding bark. Intent on helping the young woman pleading for her life, Chris barged into the house with the four uniformed officers and Elliott.

Their search ended in the living room.

Rachel Pine and Seth sat side by side on the sofa. Rachel was dressed in a pair of shorty pajamas. Bare chested, Seth donned a pair of lounging pants. An ice bucket held an open bottle of white wine. One wine glass rested on the end table. Another rested on its side at Seth's bare feet.

The wide-screen television on the mantle was blasting a daytime drama. The volume competed with Sterling's barking for attention.

"I thought there was an assault in progress." One of the state officers, an older man with a beer belly, shot a glare out the window in the direction of Sterling's barking.

"I heard screaming," Chris said while checking Seth's neck for a pulse. His purple skin felt cold.

The other sheriff deputy was searching for Rachel's pulse on her wrist. When he lifted her arm, it was stiff. Chris nodded his head to the deputy to confirm that he was unable to find a pulse.

Rachel Pine and her boyfriend were both dead.

The state police officer tapped the button on his radio, but before he could speak, Sterling body slammed the window. "Will someone lock up that dog?"

"Someone just came in and took these two out," Elliott said.

"Rigor mortis has already set in," Chris said. "They died last night."

"It couldn't have been Rachel who called you ten minutes ago."

"Looks like someone wanted you to come here to find their bodies." The state officer pounded on the window. "Shut up, you mangy mutt! What's wrong with that dog?"

Chris's eyes met Elliott's.

"It's a trap," Chris said in a low voice.

"That's why Sterling is freaking out. He smells explosives." Elliott grabbed one of the officers by the arm and dragged him toward the door. "It's a bomb! Get out!"

The six men ran for the door. Sterling's barking took on a frantic tone.

At the door, Chris saw that there were only three of the four uniformed officers ahead of him. He turned around to discover that the older officer had slipped on the polished hardwood floor in the hallway. He struggled to climb to his feet.

"My knee!" he groaned. "I broke it."

Chris wrapped the man's arm around his shoulders and lifted him to his feet. Together, they rushed out the door where the other officers helped them into the street.

They cleared the yard as Helen pulled up in her cruiser with Sheriff Bassett's car behind her.

"What's going on?" The sheriff demanded to know the reason for the mass exodus from the crime scene.

"It's a trap," one of the deputies said before answering a question from the dispatch operator in his request to send the bomb squad.

"We have two dead bodies inside," his partner said. "They appear to have died last night."

"But you said there was an assault in progress," Helen said to Chris.

"It couldn't have been Rachel who called me," Chris said. "She's been dead for hours. The call had to be a set up."

"Set up for what?" the sheriff asked.

"A bomb," Elliott said who was examining the older officer's wounded leg. "Someone wanted to lure Chris here to blow him and anyone who was with him up."

"Where's the bomb?"

"Inside the house," Chris said.

"Where in the house?"

"I don't know," Chris said. "Somewhere inside."

"But you didn't actually see any bomb," the sheriff said. "What makes you so sure there's a bomb?"

"Sterling told us."

"Sterling?" Sheriff Bassett turned to Helen. "I don't recall an Officer Sterling. Must be new." He turned back to the deputy calling for the bomb squad. "Did Officer Sterling see the bomb?"

"He smelled it," Chris said.

"Smelled it? Must be some sort of prank." Sheriff Bassett stuck his thumbs into his belt. "Where is this Officer Sterling? I don't like officers pranking my deputies—especially at a crime scene."

Chris gestured in the direction of Sterling only to find that he was not there. Helen spotted Sterling in a driveway two houses away playing tag with a tea cup chihuahua.

The sheriff's face turned red. "You're calling out the bomb squad based on the word of that… dog?" He spun around to the deputy who was already issuing an order to cancel the bomb squad. With an order to the deputies to contain the crime scene, the sheriff marched up the driveway.

"You should allow the bomb squad to check it out first," Chris called to the sheriff. "What if he's right? You're putting your deputies in danger. Sterling is a trained law enforcement K-9. He sensed something dangerous inside that house and became hysterical trying to keep us out."

With a shake of her head, Helen went to her cruiser and opened the door. Chris followed her.

"Animals have very acute senses," he said. "Mom refused to agree to marry Dad until Tipsy, her family's English Bulldog, gave his blessing."

Helen extracted her computer tablet out of her bag. "Maybe he smelled death."

Abruptly, they saw a brown and tan streak cross the yard and launched himself several feet from the stoop to tackle Sheriff Bassett as he was about to enter the house. The hundred pounds of fur and claws hit the sheriff in his barrel chest. Both man and dog tumbled over the metal railing and into the bushes lining the front of the neat home.

Stunned by the attack, the sheriff deputies drew their guns, but before anyone could fire a shot, a blast sent the roof straight up into the air and outward.

The explosion knocked the officers off their feet. Elliott shielded the injured officer with his body.

Wood, glass, nails, and plaster rained down on the entire block.

Chris caught Helen when she lost her footing. Shaken, she allowed him to set her back in the driver's seat of her SUV. Her voice shook when she said, "Or maybe Sterling smelled explosives."

Chapter Twenty-Three

Her heart racing, Doris hurried through the electronic doors to where Chris, Elliott, and Helen were waiting for word on Sheriff Grant Bassett. Upon seeing her, Sterling sat up from where he had taken up the full length of a sofa and wagged his tail. His law enforcement jacket and the fur on his rump and tail had been singed by the blast.

"Christopher, are you okay?" She took Chris into her arms. "I came as fast as I could." She moved on to embrace Helen and kiss her on the cheek. "Thank God all of you are all right." She hugged Elliott. "To think that you almost got blown up."

"It was frightening," Elliott said. "As a matter of fact, I'm still shaking." He held out his hand to show his trembling fingers.

"You poor dear." She wrapped her arms around him again. Over her shoulder, Elliott shot Chris a wide grin and rolled his eyes with pleasure.

With a sigh, Chris folded his arms. When Doris tried to pull away, Elliott pulled her back for another hug.

"I think Elliott's okay now, Mom."

"I can't believe what's been happening in this town." Doris wagged a finger at them. "None of this would be happening if your father was still here."

"We're getting close, Mom," Chris said. "The fact that someone tried to blow me up means we're making progress."

"Are you trying to tell me that someone trying to kill you is a good thing?"

"Not exactly in those terms."

"In which case are you getting close?" Doris's eyes were wide. "Sandy? The murdered mobster? Or the serial killer?"

"Or Felicia Bell's murder?" Helen nudged Chris and cocked her head to grab his attention.

Tall in his uniform of deputy sheriff, Rodney Bell strode across the waiting room. The muscles in his mouth fought the smile wanting to cross his face. "Well, well, well. I see the gang's all here."

Flexing the muscles in his injured arm, Rodney glared at Sterling. The dog's eyes seemed to bore a hole through the deputy sheriff. "I understand the sheriff had a run-in with a certain dog." His lips curled up in a snarl.

"If he hadn't, he'd be dead," Elliott said. "Sterling warned all of us that there was a bomb in that house. Sheriff Bassett refused to take him seriously—putting himself and his deputies in danger. If Sterling hadn't stopped Sheriff Bassett, they all would've gone up with the house."

"You should be thanking Sterling, Rodney," Doris said.

Instead, Rodney turned his attention to Helen. "Sinclair wants a status report on your team's investigation into Felicia's murder. So do I."

"You?" Chris said.

"Sheriff Bassett is going to be out of commission for a few days, at least," Rodney said. "That means I'm in charge. I briefed Victor Sinclair on Opie Fletcher having the means, the motive—"

"What motive?" Chris asked.

"He's unstable," Rodney said. "He's been saying for years that he killed Mona Tabler—even gave himself a maniac's name."

"He didn't—" Afraid of saying too much, Chris stopped.

"Opie also doesn't have an alibi," Rodney said. "He killed Felicia the same way he killed Mona Tabler." He stepped forward to glare into Chris's eyes. "Kirk Matheson dropped the ball when he didn't arrest Opie for Mona's murder. Because of his incompetence, my wife is now dead."

"Kirk was not incompetent!" Doris stepped forward only to have Elliott hold her back.

Rodney held Chris's gaze. "Victor Sinclair and I want Opie Fletcher locked up before he kills someone else's wife." He cast a glance in Helen's direction. "Who knows? Maybe Helen will be next."

"My forensics people have to finish processing the evidence," Helen said.

"Then lean on them to get it done," Rodney said. "Once you get the paperwork together, Victor will issue an arrest warrant."

"The *state* police does not take orders from the *county* sheriff department."

"But we do have to watch out for each other." Rodney lowered his voice. "If the state police won't watch my back, then my deputies may decide not to watch yours."

"Is that a threat?" Helen asked.

"It's reality." A slim smile crossed Rodney's lips. He dragged his gaze to Chris. "Victor Sinclair and I also had a conversation about you."

"I'm sure you did."

"I have a feeling that the sheriff's department is going to close two murder cases that fell through the cracks during Kirk Matheson's watch."

"And I feel your mother turning over in her grave," Doris said. "Her prayer was that you'd be nothing like your father. There is a theory that evil can be hereditary. You're proof of that, Rodney."

With a hiss, Rodney turned in her direction only to find himself face to face with Elliott. "You want a piece of the lady, you're going to have to go through me." Not only did he struggle to keep Rodney away from Doris, but Elliott also had to hold Doris back.

Abruptly, Sterling jumped off the sofa and wedged himself in between Rodney and Elliott, his lips pulled back in a snarl. His fur was straight on end.

"You'll have to go through Sterling, too," Helen said. "Care for a rematch?"

Chris stepped in front of Sterling. His face was inches from Rodney's. Their eyes locked in a glare. The silent message between them was loud and clear.

Everyone held their breath—wondering who would throw the first punch and when.

Rodney stepped back. He raised his arm to check the time on the black rectangular monitor he had strapped around his wrist. "As much as I'd like to go a few rounds with you for old time's sake, Chris, I have a meeting with my deputies—rally the troops—you know." He winked at them. "Maybe next time."

With that, he stuck a toothpick between his teeth, turned on his heel, and sauntered away. Together, they watched Rodney exit the medical center and cross the parking lot.

He had driven away in his cruiser before Helen broke the silence. "He totally did it. He killed Felicia. That's why he had Mona Tabler's case file. He saw that Opie was a suspect and set him up to take the fall."

"He won't get away with it," Chris said.

"He's got Victor Sinclair on his side," Helen said. "I bet Rod called him as soon as he got word that Bassett was in the hospital."

"And in exchange for Sinclair pressing charges against Opie Fletcher, Rodney is going to railroad Christopher into jail for Sandy Lipton's murder," Doris said.

Chris ushered Elliott aside. "I thought Bruce had Sinclair under control."

"He talked to the old man. Maybe Victor didn't get the text telling him to back off if he knew what was good for him."

"Does Rodney know about us exhuming Tamara Wilcox's body on Monday?" Chris asked Helen.

"Only one I talked to about that is the state's forensics pathologist to arrange for her receiving the body and doing the examination," Helen said. "Once she does the identification, she'll send the report back to me. Since the church is exhuming the bodies voluntarily, there's no need to have the county sheriff's department involved."

"How about the county prosecutor? Victor Sinclair?" Elliott asked.

Helen shook her head. "I contact him after I get the pathologist's report."

"Which leaves both Rodney and Victor out of the loop," Chris said.

"Good," Doris said. "Let's leave it that way."

"Peyton Davenport is in a meeting!" The secretary jumped from her desk and tried to block Helen and Chris's path to the vice president's office.

"She most certainly is. She's meeting with us." Chris dodged her to throw open the door and charged inside.

They stopped when they discovered two men sitting in the lounging area with Peyton. The shorter of the two men rose to his feet—ready to do verbal battle.

Seeing the two well-dressed men, exuding wealth and power from their pores, Chris was struck with a sense of déjà vu. During his career as a federal agent, he had tangled with many well-heeled adversaries.

But these two were different. He had encountered them twenty-four years earlier on the day he had confronted Sandy Lipton.

"Chris, I thought our date wasn't until later." Peyton looped her arm through his.

"Date?" The man with the slicked-back hair shot a glance at his client seated in the wing-backed chair at the head of the sitting area.

"Unlike you, Steve, I do have a life." Peyton gazed up at Chris as if he were a prized possession that she couldn't wait to show off.

"Steve Sinclair," Helen whispered to Chris. "Victor's father."

Peyton turned to the man in the wing-backed chair, who had locked eyes with Chris. "Daddy, this is—"

"Chris Matheson," Steve Sinclair finished with displeasure. "Kirk's son. You remember Kirk Matheson, don't you, Peyton? State police captain." He chuckled. "You really know how to pick them."

"Steve Sinclair." Chris held out his hand to the attorney. "We finally get to meet formally. I've heard so much about you."

Steve clasped Chris's hand. "I'm sure your father had a lot to say about me."

"Not just him. We have another mutual acquaintance." Chris allowed a broad grin to cross his face. "Bruce Harris. Retired attorney general from Virginia."

The drop of Bruce's name had the desired effect. Steve's face grew pale. With a glare, he yanked his hand away from Chris's.

The man Chris remembered hiding in the Lipton kitchen, Mason Davenport rose from the chair and crossed the room to clasp hands with him. "Are you still with the FBI, son?" In contrast to his lawyer, he gave Chris a pleasant smile.

"Retired, sir." Helen's hand on his arm reminding him of her presence, Chris introduced the lieutenant from the homicide division of the state police.

"I sense this is not a social visit," Mason said, "even if you do have a date with my daughter."

"It's business," Helen said. "Rachel Pine and Seth Greene, two Stardust employees, have been murdered."

Peyton covered her mouth with a gasp.

Mason Davenport turned around and stared out the window.

"Murdered?" Steve Sinclair asked. "Surely, you don't think anyone here at the Stardust has anything to do with that. They must have gotten mixed up with something outside the casino."

Careful to not divulge too much information about their investigation, Helen said, "They were persons of interest in a murder case."

Chris realized Peyton was no longer at his side. He turned around to see that she had gone to her father and placed her hand on his shoulder. He pulled away from her touch and fired off a glare before moving around the desk to rejoin them.

"Do you have any suspects?" Steve Sinclair was asking Helen.

"A witness told us that a woman going by the name of Josie was seen with the victim of the case we were investigating," Chris told Mason. "A redhead."

Chris saw a flicker of recognition in the executive's eyes. They flicked in Peyton's direction.

"Are you aware of anyone named Josie?" Helen asked.

"Possibly an employee here at the casino."

"We have no employees that I'm aware of named Josie," Peyton said. "I had my assistant check with HR when you asked me about that earlier, Chris."

"Sir?" Chris asked Mason. "We believe she may have been friends with Rachel Pine, your director of cybersecurity."

"I knew Rachel," Mason said. "She and Peyton went to school in Morgantown together."

"Yes, she was a very good friend." Peyton sniffed.

"Peyton has lost many good friends throughout the years," Mason said in a low voice.

Wrapping her arms around her father, Peyton buried her face into his chest. Mason stiffened at her touch. When he noticed Chris watching them, Mason returned the hug.

"Well," Steve said, "we thank you for coming to give us this information. If we come up with anything to help you in your investigation, we will be sure to contact you."

As Steve ushered them out, Peyton pulled away from her father to catch up to Chris before he left. "I'll see you at six. You won't forget, will you, Chris?"

"No, of course not. How could I?"

CHAPTER TWENTY-FOUR

"That's two." Chris tossed the broken security camera from its perch in an apple tree to Nikki below.

Seated on her roan mare named KitKat, she caught the camera and stuffed it in her saddlebag with another broken camera. "That must have been some power outage to have fried our security system."

Chris pointed at a new utility pole further up the service road. "We're lucky it's only two cameras and a couple of monitors. When I was in school, that transformer blew and the power surge took out our well pump. We didn't have electricity for a week and we had to get a new pump."

Chris began to climb down from the tree only to stop when Nikki broke into giggles. He peered through the branches and found Sterling balancing on a thick branch beneath him. "How did you get up here?" He asked Nikki, "Did you help him?"

"Dad, I haven't gotten down from KitKat. He climbed up there himself."

Sterling barked at Chris as if to order him to hurry.

"Hold your horses. I'm coming down." Chris muttered.

Sterling leapt to the ground and circled the trunk while watching Chris's descent.

"What are we going to do for a security system until you replace the cameras?" Nikki asked.

"Same thing as regular folks." Chris jumped down to the ground. "Trust that no one's going to come after us." He picked up Traveler's reins. "We've got our no trespassing signs telling folks that we have recorded surveillance. That's enough to deter most people. If no one knows the cameras are broken, we should be fine."

He climbed up into the saddle. Once he was settled in his seat, he flashed a broad smile at his middle daughter. "Race you back to the barn."

"You're on!" Nikki urged KitKat into a full gallop.

"Are you really going to give Sierra horseback riding lessons, Dad?" Nikki asked while the two of them brushed the two horses after they had finished their ride.

Chris had forgotten about his promise to give riding lessons to Sierra. So much had happened that day, that morning seemed like days ago. After confirming that he was, Chris led Traveler into his stall. "She's coming back out tonight to hang out with you while we all go to Nonni's dinner dance."

Nikki stopped brushing her horse and placed her hand on her hip. The pose combined with the arch of her eyebrow and the tilt of her head was strikingly like that of her grandmother. "Are you dating Sierra's mom?"

"We're working on a case together." He closed the stall door. "Actually, several cases."

"Aren't you supposed to be retired?" She led her horse into the stall and closed the door.

Chris escaped the need to answer her question when he heard a car engine. As he had expected, it was Helen and Sierra. "Sierra's here."

Nikki joined him at the open barn door. "And so's her mom." She looked up at him. "You didn't answer my question."

"Yes, I did. I'm going to start giving Sierra horseback riding lessons tomorrow. You can help if you want."

"I mean about you and her mom dating. We took a vote."

"A vote? About what?"

"About you dating Sierra's mom, and we decided that we're okay with it. We like Sierra."

"How about her mom?"

"Thor loves her, but she loves anyone who'll give her a carrot. Mocha's on board. Sadie hasn't made up her mind yet. She's tough. Sadie, not Ms. Clarke. Sadie has to do a little more research before she makes up her mind."

"As chief of farm security, it's Sadie's job to carefully vet everyone," Chris said. "After all, we can't let just anyone into the clan."

Sierra stepped out of the cruiser and threw her backpack over her shoulder. "Hey, Nikki, I brought that game I was telling you about."

With a squeal, Nikki raced down the driveway to join her.

Dressed in a long coat over her cocktail dress, Helen trotted gingerly across the icy barnyard in her high heels. Chris made sure the two girls were inside the house before he greeted her with a soft kiss on the lips.

"You look pretty," he whispered to her.

"And you look…" She noted his worn jeans and heavy coat, stained with dirt from working in the barn. "Rugged."

"Don't worry." He winked at her before closing the barn door. "I clean up real good."

"Why should I care? You're not my date." She turned serious. "I'm worried about you being alone with Peyton Davenport. I've got a bad feeling about her—especially after you told me about her leading a sex ring and blackmailing teachers when she was only sixteen."

"Don't you trust me?" He draped his arm across her shoulder and they made their way down the hill toward the house.

"Of course. It's Peyton I don't trust. According to your statement, Rachel said that Peyton was crazy."

"Rachel was already dead when I received that phone call. Rigor mortis had set in by the time we found the victims. That means somebody besides Rachel lured me to their house."

"Peyton is the only other suspect we have in the Tommy Bukowski murder," Helen said.

"You're forgetting about Josie," Chris said. "The redhead who Tommy was actually seen with the night of the murder."

"Peyton claims there isn't any Josie who works at the Stardust." Helen trotted to the rear of the cruiser. "Whoever killed Tommy took him to the racetrack to kill him with the horse tranquilizer. The murder occurred after hours. So our killer has to have access to the stables. Peyton has access."

"Would Peyton have implicated herself by using her name in Rachel's cry for help?"

Helen opened the SUV's rear compartment. "If things had gone according to plans, you wouldn't be around now to state that whoever it was that called you used Peyton's name." She extracted a thick case file from her bag. "Or maybe Peyton used her name so that you would assume it wasn't her because who in their right mind would implicate herself?"

She held out the folder to him. "Your father's old case file about his investigation into Peyton's sex ring. Makes for a very disturbing read."

Chris read the name printed on the folder. Jocelyn Davis.

"Did you know that Mr. Newton committed suicide six months after he went to jail for killing Jocelyn Davis?"

Chris felt as if he had been punched in the chest.

Helen tapped the folder with her index finger, its long nail painted a deep shade of red. "Peyton may not have snapped Jocelyn's neck and dumped her body in the river, but she certainly set things in motion to make it happen. Jocelyn was supposedly her best friend. They had gone all through school together."

"I know," Chris said. "Peyton is trouble with a capital 'T' which rhymes with 'P' which stands for Peyton."

"Your dad went so far as to have a psychological profile done," Helen said. "Peyton Davenport is a dangerous psychopath. Brilliantly manipulative. Incapable of remorse. I want you to read this before you go out with her tonight."

"I don't have time to read a whole report."

"Then I'll read it to you while you get ready." She took the folder from him. "It's either that or I'm going to follow you two all evening to make sure nothing happens to you."

"Now you sound like my mother."

Girlish laughter floated into the mudroom while Chris hung up their coats. They dismissed it as girlish hijinks until the laughter gave way to an "ah."

"Doris broke out the photo albums!" Helen shrieked when she looked into the kitchen.

At the kitchen table, Doris and the four girls leafed through a picture book. With every turn of the page, the girls would swoon or giggle while Doris recounted the story behind the pictures with much animation.

"Mom, you never told me that you were homecoming queen!" Sierra said with awe.

"And, Dad, you never told us that you were king," Katelyn said.

"You also never told me that Chris was your high school sweetheart," Sierra said. "If I'd known that I would have figured out some way to take advantage of working for his mother." She winked at Doris.

"Here they are kissing! Ewwwww!" Emma and Nikki screwed up their noses.

"That's Valentine's Day," Doris said. "Your father did extra chores for two months to save up enough money to take Helen to the Bavarian Inn for dinner."

"You should take her to the Bavarian Inn tomorrow night," Katelyn said. "It is Valentine's Day."

Before Chris could respond, Helen said, "I doubt if we can get reservations now."

"There sure are a lot of pictures of the two of you," Sierra said. "That was some hot romance. Mom, why didn't you ever tell me? Homecoming queen. Studly boyfriend. Here, I was thinking you were the invisible woman."

"As long as we're going down memory lane, why don't we go back to 1970?" Chris removed a photo album from the bookshelf and took it to the table.

"Christopher," Doris said with a warning in her voice.

"What goes around comes around, Mom."

Chris flipped open the book and dropped it in the center of the table. The girls uttered a shout in unison at the picture of a seventeen-year-old Doris. In a royal blue evening gown, she posed for the camera with a jeweled crown on her head and a sash declaring her Miss West Virginia.

"Nonni, is that real?" Katelyn jumped out of her seat. "Were you really a beauty queen?"

Her face bright pink, Doris looked up at Chris. "I wasn't going to show them the picture of you naked on the bearskin rug."

"Were you really crowned Miss West Virginia, Nonni?" Nikki asked.

"It was a long time ago."

"Did you get to keep the crown?" Emma asked.

"Yes, it's around here somewhere," Doris said.

"The last time I saw it," Chris said, "it was in a crate with Nonni's old moonshiner's still out in the garage."

"Moonshiner's still?" Sierra asked.

"During the Prohibition, my grandparents made the best moonshine in southern West Virginia," Doris said.

"Why are you embarrassed, Doris?" Sierra asked. "You were crowned the most beautiful, intelligent, and sophisticated woman in the state. That's something to be very proud of."

"It was how she met Dad," Chris said. "He was at the police academy down in Charleston and earned extra money providing security for the pageant's contestants. Mom was Miss Boone County."

"I entered because the main prize was a college scholarship," Doris said, "and a car. A Ford convertible. The day I saw Kirk, I set my sights on him. Of course, so did every other red-blooded girl in the pageant. Tall, broad shoulders, and piercing blue eyes. He was beating them off with a stick."

"How did you beat out the other contestants to win Gramps, Nonni?" Katelyn asked.

Her gray eyes narrowed. Doris paused before she replied, "Beat them? What do you mean by beating them?"

"All these other beauty contestants were chasing Gramps," Katelyn said. "So what did you do to win him away from them?"

"I didn't *win* Gramps, darling," Doris said. "Love, real love, isn't a competition with winners and losers. Either you love someone or you don't. And if someone you love loves someone else and not you—then there really isn't anything you can do to change that."

Katelyn sat up straight. Her eyes narrowed with doubt. "You're kidding me, right?"

"I wouldn't kid you about this, sweetie."

"You mean back then, if Gramps was interested in Miss Jefferson County, you wouldn't have wanted to tear her hair out so that you could have him for yourself?"

"If Gramps was stepping out with Miss Jefferson County, why would I tear *her* hair out? He'd be the dreadful scoundrel cheating on me—not her. Why is it that when a man cheats, the two women tear each other's hair out? They should get together and tear the man's hair out."

"Good point, Doris," Helen said.

"When I was a young girl and had my heart broken for the first time, my grandma sat me down and told me this," Doris said.

"Is this the same grandma who made the moonshine?" Nikki asked.

"Yes, as a matter of fact, she was," Doris said. "To get back to my point, she told me, 'Doris, anyone who'll risk breaking your heart by playing games with it isn't worthy of it. Only give your heart to someone who sees your love for the precious treasure that it is.'"

"That is so true," Sierra said with a dreamy sigh.

Katelyn fell into silence.

Doris's eyes grew misty as she brushed her fingers across her pageant picture. "Gramps was so proud of me when I won Miss West Virginia." She frowned. "I couldn't believe my rotten luck."

"Why was it rotten luck?" Helen asked.

"Because Miss West Virginia couldn't be married," Doris said. "That meant Kirk and I had to sneak around for a full year. There was no way I was going to let myself get saddled with Miss America. I was bound and determined to marry that man. As soon as I unloaded that Miss West Virginia crown, Kirk and I ran down to the justice of the peace and got married. Christopher came along six months later."

"You mean nine," Helen said.

"No, six," Doris said.

"I was twelve before I did the math," Chris said.

"Thank God for girdles or West Virginia would have rocked with scandal."

"What was your talent, Nonni?" Nikki asked.

"I think she just told you her talent," Chris said.

"In the pageant," Nikki said.

"Let me guess," Sierra said. "Dance."

"You're never going to guess," Doris said with a shake of her head.

"Singing," Sierra said. "You have a low sexy voice. I bet it was singing. You wooed the judges with a throaty ballad."

Shaking her head with a smile, Doris packed up the photo albums.

"Dad, what's Nonni's talent?" Katelyn asked.

Chuckling, Chris said, "You'll never guess." He took Helen by the hand and led her to the back staircase. "I'm going to go get dressed for the dinner."

"And you need Helen to help you get dressed, Christopher?"

Chris held up the case file. "We have studying to do before I go on my date."

"Trust me, it'll all come back to you, Christopher," Doris said. "It's like riding a bike."

Chris closed his door at the bottom of the stairs leading to his "apartment" in the attic–a sign that his daughters and mother understood. He was to be left alone.

Resting against a pile of pillows at the head of the bed, Helen removed a report from the case file she had found among Kirk Matheson's records. "Did you know that Julie Davenport, Mason's late wife, committed suicide?"

"Everyone knows that." Chris sat next to her. "She threw herself off the bedroom balcony of their two-hundred-year-old colonial mansion."

"Did you know Peyton was the only one in the room when her mother took that swan dive?" She showed the portion of the report to him. "Steve Sinclair ran interference for the Davenports—not allowing anyone to interview Peyton to find out what had happened in that room. The medical examiner declared it a suicide. But notes in the autopsy indicate that Julie had bruises and abrasions across the back that are consistent with being pushed backwards over the railing."

"What would be Peyton's motive?"

"She's evil," Helen said. "Your mother mentioned a very good point earlier. Experts have identified genetic evidence to support the notion that some people are born with a tendency toward evil? I once read about a case where a man was arrested for raping his son's girlfriend. The irony was that this same man's father, was already serving a life sentence for being a serial rapist. Two out of three generations were rapists."

"Couldn't that be environment?" Chris said. "I don't know about the case, but wouldn't you think that a family like that would believe women were meant to be abused?"

There was a loud knock on the door followed by Doris's voice from the bottom of the stairs. "Christopher, are you decent?"

A wicked grin crossed his face before he replied, "I've never been decent."

"Then how about Helen?"

"Come on up, Doris. Chris and I were just talking." Helen shoved the report into her bag. "You better get ready. You don't want to be late for your date."

Her cell phone clutched in her hand, Doris held it up for them to see when she reached the top of the stairs. "I was just talking to Sylvia, Felicia's mom. I had called to give her my condolences."

Reminded of their good friend's death, Chris's and Helen's eyes dropped to the floor.

""I've known Sylvia for years," Doris said. "We met when you started dating Felicia, Christopher. Sylvia and I went to lunch to get to know each other better. Well, she asked me if the library carried any erotica books. Of course, I told her that we did and she asked for recommendations. When we got back from lunch, Sylvia checked three books out of the library. Well, the next week she came back and just went on and on. She and her husband had used the sex scenes in the books for a guide. Ever since, she comes in every Friday and checks out three hot books to use for sex manuals. She credits me with saving their marriage."

"Mom," Chris asked, "what did Sylvia tell you when you called just now?"

"You know that Opie Fletcher that you're holding for Felicia's murder?"

"I'm very aware of Opie Fletcher," Helen said.

"Do you know how Felicia came about hiring him to work for her?"

"How?" Chris asked.

"*Rodney* recommended him to Felicia."

"No," Helen said with a gasp.

"Yes," Doris said.

"But Opie didn't seem to know anything about Rodney when I questioned him," Helen said. "He told me that Felicia called him out of the blue to come out to do yard work and odd jobs."

"After Felicia kicked Rodney out, she found that she needed a man around to do the yard work and fix things," Doris said. "She didn't want Rodney coming around to do it. Yet, she didn't want to hire a man she didn't know anything about. One day, Rodney gave her Opie's phone number. He told her that a friend of his recommended him for odd jobs. Sylvia thought Opie seemed kind of strange and asked

Felicia about him. Felicia claimed that Rodney had run a background check on him and he was clean."

"If Rodney had run a background check on him, he would have seen that he was a suspect in Mona Tabler's murder," Chris said. "He had to know because Mona lived only four doors down from them when she was murdered."

"Sylvia says the exact same thing," Doris said.

"Rodney totally killed her," Helen said.

"He must have been planning this for months," Chris said.

"That's why he had Mona Tabler's case file—because he wanted to set up the key suspect in her unsolved murder," Helen said.

"Two murders in the same neighborhood with similar MOs," Chris said. "The suspect in the first case just so happens to work for the second victim. Victor Sinclair would easily buy that."

"But Rodney has an ironclad alibi," Helen said.

"Are you sure about that?" Doris asked.

"Positive," Helen said. "He was seventeen minutes away at the athletic club. I saw the security recording myself. He arrived at the club a few minutes before seven o'clock and walked out close to eight-thirty."

"There has to be another door that he left through to sneak home to kill Felicia and get back in without anyone noticing," Doris said.

"Emergency exit. Opening the door sets off an alarm. No way he went out that door without alerting everyone in the place," Helen said. "Besides that, the gasoline fire would've engulfed the whole second floor within seconds. There's not enough time for him to have set it, get back to the gym, and walk out just as the fire department pulled up to the scene."

"Unless he set the fire remotely," Chris said. "Remember the cord on the lamp was cut to expose the wires, and they were wrapped around a match, which rested on the carpet drenched in gasoline."

"Even if the lamp is voice activated, Rodney would've had to have been in the house—"

"Not necessarily." Chris picked up his cell phone. "There's a cell phone app for everything nowadays."

"Yes, Brad did tell us something about that," Helen said. "But Felicia threw Rodney out last year. Wouldn't she have removed him from the home network?"

"Not necessarily," Doris said. "Kirk died last year and he's still listed in our computer network."

"If Felicia didn't set up their home network, she may not have even given Rodney's access to it any thought," Chris said.

"Not only did he have home owner's insurance, but he had a hundred-thousand-dollar life insurance policy on Felicia," Doris said. "He's got a whole lot of reason to kill her and burn down their house."

"And he's got the means to do it." Chris held up his phone. "I have an app that syncs my phone with our home security system. Not only does the system send notices to my phone, but I can send commands to the system."

"He can even turn on the outside spotlight with his phone," Doris said. "When he first installed it, I was unloading the groceries from the car and all of a sudden the spotlight turned on. I heard Christopher asking in this big booming voice, 'Need any help?'"

Chris laughed. "I was at the barber in town."

"Scared the daylights out of me," Doris told Helen. "I dropped a bag of groceries in the driveway. Broke a whole dozen eggs."

"That's your house," Helen said. "Would the Bell home set up be that sophisticated? Even so, the security system would keep record if Rodney used his phone to activate the lights, and he'd have to know that."

"That's why he used a burner phone," Chris said. "After killing Felicia and setting up the lamp and a match, he went back to the gym, got on the treadmill in the cardio cinema where it was dark. Then, just before he finished, he took out the burner phone, which he had synced with Felicia's smart home network, and sent the command to turn on the lamp. The lamp ignited the match which started the fire—all while he was seventeen minutes away. Then he calmly walked out the front door in full view of the gym's security cameras to record his alibi."

"And tossed the burner phone in a dumpster someplace," Doris said.

"After deleting it from the house's network," Chris said.

"Prove it," Helen said. "Rodney is the deputy sheriff. He knows that the only way we can nail him for killing Felicia is to not only prove that he could have done it, but to prove that he did do it."

"And we will prove it. We have to for Felicia."

Chapter Twenty-Five

Friday evening at the Stardust was a beehive of activity even when they didn't have a special event scheduled. The glamour of the Stardust casino made it the place to hold special events.

Chris arrived at the bank of elevators as a group of men and women laden down with musical instruments were crowding into one of the cars. When they squeezed together to make room for one more person, he declined their invitation. After the elevator began its climb, he pressed the call button.

The third elevator was already on the sixth floor where the dinner dance was taking place in the grand ballroom. The second car was on the fifth floor where he needed to go to meet Peyton. With the hour nearing six o'clock on Friday, he assumed most of the business office employees had already left to start the Valentine's Day weekend.

The array of hearts and roses reminded him that the next day was indeed Valentine's Day. While Helen had demurred the idea of going to the Bavarian Inn for dinner, memories of their first Valentine's date made him yearn to return there with her. It didn't seem right to take Helen to a romantic dinner and leave the rest of his girls at home. They couldn't exclude Sierra, either. They were all "his girls."

I wonder if I can get a table for seven. Probably impossible, but there's no harm in trying.

Realizing that he had been waiting a while, Chris glanced up at the lights over the elevator doors. The two cars were on the sixth floor and showing no sign of moving. The car that had been on the fifth floor paused at the third floor before descending. When the doors opened, an elegantly dressed couple got off and headed in the direction of the lounge.

Chris stepped onto the car and pressed the button for the fifth floor with one hand while thumbing the screen of his phone with the other. While the elevator ascended, he opened an app to make dinner reservations. Unfortunately, the Bavarian Inn wasn't one of the restaurants listed in the app.

Guess I'll have to go old school and call them.

The elevator doors opened and Chris stepped off just in time to see Mason Davenport crossing the common area toward the hallway leading to his daughter's office.

With a start, the CEO turned to face him. "Matheson. Good to see you again. I was on my way to see Peyton about appointing an acting director for cybersecurity." He fell into step with Chris. "I hate to sound insensitive. Peyton's devastated about Rachel's murder. But cybercrime is such a huge thing nowadays and we can't risk leaving the casino vulnerable to a breach."

"Did Peyton tell you that there has possibly already been a breach?" Chris asked as they crossed Peyton's outer office. The double doors to her office were closed. "Last weekend, an investigator was here to examine your system because one of your online guests had been the victim of a ransomware attack."

"Peyton did brief me about that today." Mason Davenport rapped on the door. "She was concerned about Rachel being vulnerable to the wrong type of men."

"What about the wrong type of women?"

Mason peered at the door. "Women?"

"Josie," Chris said. "With all due respect, sir, I suspect you know who Josie is."

"Josie won't be causing anymore trouble. She's gone." Mason laid his hand on the doorknob and turned it. "Peyton must be in the bathroom getting ready for your date." He threw open the door and gestured for Chris to follow him into the office. The familiar scent of gun powder permeated his senses.

"Peyton, it's me." Mason strode across the length of the office to the door that led into the executive bathroom. "I know it's a bad time, but before you leave, you need to appoint an acting director for cybersecurity." He threw open the door and stepped inside. "Oh, my God! Peyton! No!"

Chris ran across the office and stepped into the bathroom.

The full skirt of her red evening gown was splayed out around her like the petals of a flower in full bloom. Peyton Davenport lay on her side in the middle of the bathroom floor. The only blemish to her lovely face was a bullet hole in the temple.

CHAPTER TWENTY-SIX

"I certainly didn't see this coming," Helen shook her head while looking down at the woman lying in a pool of blood in the bathroom. A small thirty-two caliber semi-automatic rested on the floor next to her hand.

As a vice president, Peyton Davenport's private bath consisted of a steam shower and sink with brass fixtures. She also had a cosmetics vanity and closet.

"It's suicide." Mason Davenport stepped in behind Helen and Chris to say in a firm tone—not unlike that of a boss directing one of his subordinates. "Her mother suffered from severe depression. Committed suicide. Unfortunately, Peyton inherited it from her."

With a slight shake of his head, Chris said, "Sir, Peyton didn't seem—"

"She hid it very well."

"Was she on medication?" Helen asked.

"She refused to get treated."

"Then you're saying that she was never diagnosed with depression?"

"Not officially," Mason said, "but you can talk to her medical doctor. Dr. Frederic Poole. I'll give him permission to discuss Peyton with you." He cleared his throat. "Such a tragedy. I had so hoped to keep all of this from being made public." He sucked in a deep breath. "How long do you think this is going to take?"

"We will have to do a complete investigation of the scene," Helen said. "Do you know where the gun came from?"

"It's Peyton's. She carried it in her purse."

Helen glanced in Chris's direction. It was all just too neat.

"Mason!" Steve Sinclair called to his client from the outer office. "You better not be talking to the police without me."

When they stepped into the office, they found Steve Sinclair and his son, Victor, both dressed in tuxedos. A pair of uniformed police officers waited for Helen's orders about whether to usher them out or not. With a wave of her hand, she dismissed the officers to return to their posts.

As expected, Steve Sinclair took command. "Whatever Mason said cannot be used in evidence."

"Right now, he's only a witness," Helen said.

"What's he doing here?" Victor sneered while gesturing in Chris's direction.

"He's also a witness," Helen said. "He was with Mr. Davenport when they found the body."

"I came to talk to Peyton about appointing someone to take Rachel Pine's place directing the cybersecurity division," Mason said. "I had just gotten off the elevator and started down the hall when Chris arrived in the next car right after I did. We walked in together. Peyton didn't answer the door. I assumed she was getting dressed for her date. I knocked on the bathroom door and when she didn't answer, I figured something had to be wrong. So I opened the door…" His voice broke.

Helen saw Chris shoot a questioning glance in Mason's direction.

Demanding that he say nothing else, Steve Sinclair grabbed his client by the arm and marched him out of the office.

With his eyes narrowed, Victor stepped toward Chris. A full head shorter than Chris, Victor had to lift his chin to look up at him. Still, he pursed his lips to appear as intimidating as possible.

Undaunted, Chris went back to the bathroom doorway to study the scene.

"I will expect this case to be closed quickly," Victor told Helen. "Mason Davenport is a powerful and generous man to the community. For that reason, we don't want to put him through any more grief than necessary."

"Certainly," Helen said.

As soon as Victor left, Helen joined Chris in the bathroom. Squatting on the floor, he stared at Peyton's dead body. "The forensics team and medical examiner will be here any minute. You noticed something out there when Mason was telling Sinclair how you two found the body. Care to share what it is?"

"He didn't knock on the door," Chris said in a soft voice.

"What?"

He gestured toward the outer office. "He knocked on the office door, but not the bathroom door. He walked right in."

"Are you sure?"

"I have been living with four women long enough to learn three things. Always put the seat down. Never go into a woman's purse without asking first. And never ever walk into a bathroom when the door is shut without knocking first. That door was shut, and he walked in without knocking. Either he has a death wish, or he knew she was already dead."

Helen gazed down at the elegantly dressed woman before them. "What woman gets all dressed up, does her hair and makeup, only to blow her brains out?"

"Why would he kill her?"

"His own daughter."

"I don't think she was his daughter. Still—why did he kill her?"

It was hard not to miss Doris Matheson in her fuschia, strapless gown. The mermaid design fit her body like a glove from the sequined bodice to her slender waist and hips down to where it flared out with a train.

At sixty-five, Doris Matheson put women half her age to shame.

As the chairperson of the committee, she felt obligated to accept the numerous dance invitations from gentlemen vying for her attention during the cocktail party. She was dancing with an arson investigator, the father of one of Chris's childhood friends, when a long stemmed red rose was thrust over her shoulder.

"Your prince has arrived, my lady."

Doris's dance partner frowned.

She turned to find Elliott on one knee. She refused to let him see how impressed she was. "You're late."

He remained on the floor. "I learned something new today."

"At your age?"

"You're never too old to learn something new."

"What did you learn today, Elliott?"

"You can't just walk into a tux place and rent a tuxedo off the rack." Elliott fingered the silk lapels of his formal suit. "Lucky for me, Bruce is just about my size."

She usually saw Elliott dressed in jeans, work shirts, and boots. Half the time, he didn't shave. Even if the tuxedo wasn't a perfect fit, he looked dashing. As he took her into his arms, she changed that. He looked downright handsome.

"I was surprised when you asked me to be your date," she said as they danced to an updated version of *Unforgettable.*

"Too soon?"

"I just didn't think—"

"Doris, I told you that I loved your tuna casserole," he said. "Only a man head over heels in love with you would eat that tuna casserole and proclaim it love worthy."

"I see your point, Elliott," she said. "I guess I'm a little out of practice."

"If you need someone to help you get back up to speed, I'm here for you, Doris."

She kissed him on the jaw.

A broad grin crossed his lips. He leaned in to kiss her lips, only to have her spin around and drag him across the dance floor to where a short balding man danced with an even shorter woman in a bad wig.

"Elliott, wouldn't you like to dance with Carla? Dr. Poole's wife is a huge fan of traveling to exotic places. Carla, Elliott here used to be with the State Department and he's traveled all over the world—absolutely everywhere." With that Doris shoved Elliott toward Carla, who gushed to be dancing with the tall muscular man.

The expression on Dr. Frederic Poole's face was an even mixture of fear and wonderment to suddenly find himself with the desirable Doris Matheson in his arms.

"Uh," Frederic wet his lips, "to what do I owe the pleasure, Doris?"

"I'm doing you a favor, Fred. I'm giving you seventy-two hours' notice."

"Notice of what?"

"January 1994. Do you remember that?"

"That was a long time ago."

"Twenty-four years ago to be exact," she said. "I've been told that you just so happened to be in the hospital parking lot when a young woman in labor was dumped there. She was unconscious and in cardiac arrest. You took her straight into the OR and delivered her baby by caesarian. Supposedly, the baby died."

Frederic's face fell. "I do remember that. Heartbreaking."

"Do you know the rest of the story?"

"What rest of the story?"

"That woman and her baby were abandoned in the morgue," Doris said. "The name on record was Tamara Wilcox, which proved to be a phony name. Our church gave them a proper burial."

"That's very kind of you, Doris. You are one of the most generous, charitable women our community has."

"Now, here's the heads up," she said. "It's been brought to my attention that Sandy Lipton, who was nine months pregnant, disappeared on the same day that Tamara Wilcox showed up at the hospital. Sandy Lipton was your patient."

"What are you saying?"

"I'm saying that we are having Tamara's and her baby's bodies exhumed," Doris said. "Monday morning. If Tamara is Sandy, we will find out. And the first person people are going to come to for answers will be you since you were both Sandy's and Tamara's doctor."

His face clouded over.

The music stopped.

Frederic dropped his hands from her waist and stepped back. "Doris, do you have any idea the damage you've done?"

"My son has been accused of horrible perverted things. People in this town still look at him like he's a monster, which he is not. I don't care what it takes or who it hurts—I'm going to clear his name. Now you have a choice. You can keep a shred of your dignity by telling the truth or let me drag your name through the mud. You've known me for almost fifty years, Fred. You know I'll do it."

Frederic tugged at his collar.

Carla hurried up to them. "Oh, Fred, have you talked to Elliott? He's been to China—though he couldn't really tell me much about his trip. He said if he did he'd have to kill me. Still—he is a fascinating man—just fascinating!"

When she touched his arm, Frederic pulled away. "I need to go find Sinclair."

"You do that, Fred," Doris said as Elliott stepped up to her with two glasses of champagne. "You have seventy-two hours to cough up the truth and clear Christopher's name." She accepted a glass of champagne and held it up in a toast. "After that, it's high noon."

"I'm not saying that I don't believe you," Helen said as she and Chris made their way down the corridor to the elevators.

The police had commandeered one of the cars for the medical examiner and crime scene investigators. They could hear the music from the band on the top floor drifting down the elevator shaft.

"Victor Sinclair is a jerk, but he does have a point," Helen told Chris. "Mason Davenport is one of the most powerful men in the Shenandoah Valley. Without any physical evidence, we can't accuse him of murder based on—"

"My eyewitness testimony?"

"Did he knock on the bathroom door, or didn't he? It's a tiny detail—"

"That means a hell of a lot," Chris said while watching the numbers over the two elevators that were free. One was at the lobby. The other was on the sixth floor. "If he didn't knock, then he knew that she wasn't alive to invite him in."

The elevator in the lobby began its ascent—illuminating the lights above the door.

LAUREN CARR

"And if you're wrong, then we could be accusing a very powerful man of killing his own daughter for no reason."

Chris watched the elevator make its way up to their floor. Meanwhile, the elevator on the sixth floor wasn't moving.

The familiar ding indicated the arrival of the first elevator which was going up. As the doors opened, a couple stepped out. The woman gasped upon seeing the police. "I'm sorry, I thought we were on the top floor. I didn't expect anyone to be around the business offices at this time of night." They scurried back onto the elevator and pressed the button.

"They didn't expect anyone to be around at this time of night." Chris turned to Helen. "Where's Mason Davenport's office?"

She tossed her head in the direction of the corridor on the other side of the common area. Chris turned down the hallway and through the double doors to the spacious outer office of the CEO, whose office occupied the entire corner of the floor. The muffled voices of Mason Davenport and both Sinclair men behind the closed office doors drifted into the outer office.

Chris stepped through a second set of double doors on the other side of the outer office. He turned to smile at Helen.

"What are you so happy about?"

Chris pointed at the end of the hall. The corridor provided a straight shot to Peyton Davenport's office. "I got him."

He brushed past Helen to step back into the executive's outer office. At the same time, Elliott was holding the other pair of doors open for Doris. A sheepish looking man accompanied them.

"Well, I finally found you two," Doris said. "You're missing a wonderful party upstairs. Thrilling dinner conversation. Helen, have you met Dr. Frederic Poole?"

"No."

"Fred, this is Lieutenant Helen Clarke with the West Virginia State Police. She's head of the homicide division in the area. Helen, Fred would like to make a confession."

CHAPTER TWENTY-SEVEN

"Fred, have you lost your mind?" Steve Sinclair's words bounced off Mason Davenport's walls. He gestured at the police lieutenant, Chris, Doris, and Elliott, who had invaded the executive's inner office. "They have nothing on you."

"Maybe not now," Doris said, "but as soon as the police lab gets hold of Tamara Wilcox's body, everything you've done is going to come out."

"Everyone's going to find out what you've done," Chris said.

"Who the hell is Tamara Wilcox?" Victor Sinclair asked.

"The woman whose baby Dr. Poole switched for Julie Davenport's stillborn infant," Chris said.

"What the hell…" Victor Sinclair chuckled. "Good try, Matheson. Like you can entice the public into believing that cockeyed conspiracy theory to stay out of jail for killing Sandy Lipton and her unborn baby."

"Cockeyed?" Chris said. "Let's see how cockeyed my theory is. Peyton Davenport's body is right down the hall. Her blood is all over the bathroom floor. All we have to do is compare that to Mason Davenport's. If it's a match, I'm wrong. If it isn't, then I'm right. Then, to be really sure, we'll just compare Peyton's DNA to Ethel Lipton's—"

"Whose DNA is already in the system," Helen said. "If it comes back showing a familial match, that will prove that Peyton Davenport was Sandy Lipton's baby."

"Sandy Lipton died during childbirth," Doris said, "and Dr. Poole knew it." She leveled her gaze on Steve Sinclair and Mason Davenport. "The three of you let the whole valley believe Christopher arranged for Sandy's disappearance and that my husband covered it up. You should be ashamed of yourselves."

"And Sandy's mother played the role of the victim," Chris said.

"Ethel knew?" Doris cursed and then quickly covered her mouth. "Excuse me but—" She cursed again. "That evil little bitch—excuse me." She sucked in a deep breath. "Okay, I'm through. Continue."

"The day before Sandy disappeared I confronted her at the Lipton home." Chris pointed a finger at Steve Sinclair. "I'm sure you remember that day, Mr. Sinclair. You threatened to have me arrested." He turned to Mason. "You hid in the kitchen, Mr. Davenport, but I still saw you. The other day, Carson told me that you were there to make a deal with Ethel for selling her property to the Stardust so that you could build the casino."

"That's exactly what we were doing there," Steve said.

"You were there to make a deal, but not for real estate," Chris said. "Dr. Poole must have known by then that your wife's baby would be stillborn. Isn't that right, Mr. Davenport? You were afraid she'd have a complete breakdown. She was emotionally fragile. Dr. Poole was Sandy's doctor, too. She had no husband and, as Carson said just the other day, Ethel Lipton would sell her mother for a buck. So you asked Ethel to sell her grandchild to you."

Her eyes tearing up, Doris covered her mouth with her hand. "Oh, dear Lord. She sold her grandchild?"

Steve Sinclair grumbled.

Mason Davenport looked down at his hands in his lap. "Ethel knew damn well that as soon as the baby was born that her suit against you would be dead in the water. She hoped that if she made enough noise, accusing your father of using his influence to tamper with the blood tests, that she'd get something to go away."

"Shut up, Mason!" Steve said.

"Can't you see it's over?" Mason's voice seemed to shake the walls.

"Steve, they're exhuming Sandy's body," Frederic said. "They'll know what happened by close of business Monday. Better to confess and make a deal."

"Are you saying that Chris didn't father Sandy's baby?" Victor asked. "All these years—"

"Sandy had been raped," Chris said. "The trauma of the rape and her own fantasy made her imagine that I was the father because she couldn't handle the truth emotionally."

"Who was the father?" Victor asked.

"Carson told me it was you."

Victor's eyes bulged. "I resent—"

"He was lying," Chris said.

Victor uttered a sigh of relief. "Then who?"

Steve, Mason, and Frederic exchanged glances filled with guilt.

"Out with it," Doris said. "You'd never have made an offer for a baby without knowing who the father was or at least something about him. Ethel knew Chris wasn't the father. She had to have known who was."

"It was Carson," Chris said. "Wasn't it?"

"Her brother?" Helen asked.

ICE

"Half-brother," Chris said. "Remember when you told me that scientists believe there might be a genetic tendency for violent crime? Carson told us his father was a rapist—something Ethel never let him forget. When I took Sandy home that night, she was on cloud nine. Maybe Carson had another fight with his mother. For whatever reason, he decided to take his rage out on Sandy."

"Ethel told me that she walked in on it," Frederic said. "Sandy was in shock for days. By the time we found out she was pregnant, she'd created this fantasy about you making love to her and the baby being your love child. As soon as Ethel heard that, she saw dollar signs. She thought that if her starry-eyed girl said that you'd made love to her that everyone would believe her. Even if it wasn't true, your family might be willing to pay her big bucks to go away."

"But that didn't happen," Doris said. "So Ethel put her grandchild up for sale. Did Sandy know about you buying her baby?"

"We were going to tell her that her baby died," Frederic said. "After Julie's baby was born, I put her baby on life support."

"The maternity nurse said that you personally hooked her up to life support," Chris said, "which is not how it is usually done. You wanted the nurse to think that you had detected life. Once, she was hooked up to the life support system, it started breathing for her, which bought you time to deliver Sandy's baby."

"I'd made arrangements for Sandy's baby to be delivered at my home," Mason said. "All the servants had the day off and we set up the guest room for the delivery."

"But something went wrong," Chris said.

Frederic swallowed. "Minutes after I gave Sandy an injection to induce labor, she went into full cardiac arrest. We threw her in the back of Mason's car and drove her to the hospital. Luckily, no one was around in the parking lot when we put her on a gurney and I wheeled her in saying that someone had dumped her off."

"What about the phony identification that you gave to the hospital?"

"Steve arranged that," Mason said. "I pretended to find it later."

"You leave me out of this," Steve said.

"The whole story about a man in the parking lot and me talking to him after she had passed," Frederic said, "it was all a lie. You'll notice in the records that no one saw Tamara Wilcox's husband, except me."

"Sandy's baby was born alive, and you switched them," Chris said. "The maternity nurse had said that Julie's baby looked like a totally different baby when she went back on duty that night. That's because she was."

"It was the early nineties," Frederic said. "Being her doctor, no one questioned me when I took Sandy's baby for a walk and returned with Julie's. No one thought a thing when I called a code blue because the baby that they thought was Sandy's had gone into respiratory arrest."

"And that's why Ethel Lipton had free rein here at the Stardust all these years," Chris said. "I'll bet the Stardust sponsored Carson's culinary education—"

"That was part of the deal we made with Ethel," Mason said.

"And you hired him as head chef," Chris said.

"Even though he was a rapist," Helen said.

"He never gave us any trouble," Mason said.

"Really? What about Mona Tabler?" Chris asked.

"Mona had trouble with everyone. But she was a damn good restaurant manager."

"How did she get along with Carson Lipton?"

Mason fell silent.

"What is this about?" Steve Sinclair asked.

"Mona Tabler was murdered," Chris said. "Raped, stabbed to death, and her house burnt down. Did she have trouble with Carson, Mr. Davenport?"

"She thought he was unstable—like his mother. Two days before she was killed, she came into my office and gave me an ultimatum. Her or him. I was going to tell him that Friday."

"And you didn't suspect that he'd killed her because of that?" Doris asked.

"People were telling me that some guy named Opie had said he'd done it."

"Unfortunately, Mona's not the only victim connected to the Stardust to have been killed that way," Chris said.

"Carson Lipton and his wife did not show up at the restaurant today," Helen said. "No one knows where they are."

"Yesterday, I asked Carson for a sample of his DNA and he refused," Chris said. "You knew before you hired him that he raped his own sister."

"Usually, violent sexual predators get worse, not better," Elliott said.

"So, let me get this straight," Chris said, "your wife who you loved very much, was on the verge of a nervous breakdown. Your doctor informs you that the baby she was carrying had died. So you buy a baby—"

"It was a private adoption," Steve said.

"Privately adopt," Chris said, "a baby whose father was a second generation rapist, who goes on to become a suspected serial killer—"

"I did not know Carson was a serial killer," Mason said.

"This baby's grandmother had the moral compass of Satan," Doris said. "Don't tell me that you didn't know *that*."

Steve Sinclair stood. "I think we're done here. We'll meet in Victor's office on Monday."

"We're not done by a long shot!" Chris said.

Taken aback by Chris's outburst, Steve Sinclair opened his mouth to respond but found no words.

"Sit down, Father," Victor said. "I want to hear what Chris has to say."

"You can't talk—"

"I am the county prosecutor!" Victor yelled. "All these years you've known the truth about what had happened to Sandy Lipton." He beat his chest. "I loved her. I vowed to get justice for her by making sure this man rotted in jail!" He pointed at Chris. "That's why I ran for prosecutor! Now, tonight, after all these years, I find out that you've known all along that he had nothing to do with any of it!"

"I never told you that Matheson did it," Steve said with a cocky smirk.

"Sit down!" Victor shoved his father into the chair. "Zip it," he ordered with a hiss.

A stunned silence filled the room. Victor stood to his full height and turned to Chris. "Please continue."

"Mr. Davenport, don't tell me that Peyton's genealogy hasn't been running through your mind. When was the first time you wondered about it? When your wife's body was found on the patio and Peyton was the only one in the room when she went over the railing? When the medical examiner noted the bruises on your wife's back—indicating that she'd been pushed?"

"Peyton never connected with her mother," Mason said in a soft voice. "Never."

"Or was it a couple of years later when my father came to you about your darling daughter's high school sex ring seducing and blackmailing teachers?"

"Her best friend Josie was murdered," Mason said.

"Jocelyn Davis," Doris said.

"Peyton called her Josie," Mason said. "Peyton wasn't so much saddened by her murder as she was angry about Josie's murder exposing and shutting down her enterprise."

Chris went around the desk to force him to look up at him. "You'd risked everything to adopt this baby—only to have this child destroy everyone who got close to her."

"Josie was the closest Peyton had ever come to loving someone," Mason said. "That's why she adopted her name."

"Adopted her name?" Helen asked.

"Peyton liked to get dressed up—put on a red wig—and go down to the lounge to seduce men," Mason said. "Successful, married men. She'd take them to a specially reserved room here in the hotel in which she had a hidden camera set up. Then she would blackmail them. She used the name Josie. One of my friends had fallen victim to her. He never knew it was Peyton. She was that good." He uttered a deep sigh. "So good, that I came to realize that Josie was like a separate personality."

"This evening," Chris said, "when we were going to Peyton's office, you told me that Josie was gone. That's because you killed her when you shot Peyton."

"Peyton was insane," Frederic said.

"Most definitely."

"In college," Elliott asked, "she'd organized an illegal on-line gambling ring—betting on college sports."

"Rachel set it up on the dark web," Mason said. "Peyton ran the show."

"They operated under the radar until one of the university's star players caught the fed's attention after throwing a big game," Elliott said.

"He was going to testify against Peyton," Mason said. "Somehow, Peyton got wind of it and suddenly he was dead of a drug overdose."

"Things got too hot in Morgantown," Elliott said, "so Peyton pulled up stakes and moved on to the Stardust."

"And the ransomware?" Helen asked. "Peyton managed that, too."

"She found out that Rachel had developed the ransomware virus," Mason said. "But Rachel lacked the initiative to take full advantage of it—something Peyton had coming out of her ears. She hired Rachel to run the cybersecurity division of the casino purely to target potential victims who would pay up without going to the police."

"Only they made the mistake of targeting Boris Krawford," Chris said, "who was just as ruthless as Peyton. He sent one of his people to investigate and he found the virus in the Stardust's system."

"Peyton killed him herself."

"Pretending to be Josie," Chris said. "Peyton lured him to the stables—using her security pass—"

"When we get the security records, it will confirm that," Helen said.

"Rachel had known Peyton for years," Mason said, "but she never knew Peyton was capable of murder. Peyton ordered Seth, Rachel's boyfriend, to get rid of the body."

"He went to the stables and dumped the body on my farm," Chris said. "Rachel got so nervous that Peyton saw her as a liability. So, Peyton took care of both her and Seth. Then, to make real sure her tracks were covered, she lured me to their house to blow me up and end the investigation."

"She intended to pin everything on Josie," Mason said. "The last one to be seen with this Bukowski guy was Josie. The bartender had no idea Josie was really Peyton."

"But you knew it," Chris said. "You saw something was really, seriously, wrong. So you decided to take care of her yourself before she killed anyone else."

Mason raised his moist eyes to meet Chris's.

"When I arrived here at the casino tonight, two of the three elevators were held up on the sixth floor. One by the band, the other by the catering staff. The third elevator came down to the lobby, and I rode it straight up to the fifth floor," Chris said. "When I got off, I saw you turn the corner—you told me you were heading to Peyton's office."

"That's right," Steve said. "Mason had just gotten off the elevator—seconds ahead of you."

"He couldn't have," Chris said. "because I came up on the only elevator that was available. Since it was near six o'clock on Valentine's Day weekend, the office staff was gone. Mason was leaving after having killed Peyton."

"What the hell!" Steve said.

"Rachel was a good kid," Mason said. "I truly hoped that she would be a good influence on Peyton. Instead, Peyton got Rachel mixed up in this whole ransomware thing. If the authorities found out about what she was doing, it would have ruined everything that I had sacrificed so much to build. So many people depend on the Stardust for their livelihood."

"You knew about the gun in her purse," Chris said.

"Since everyone thought Julie had committed suicide, then I figured it'd be easy to convince everyone that Peyton had been hiding her depression and killed herself."

"She was in the bathroom getting dressed for our date," Chris said.

"I went into her office. Her purse was right there on the desk. I took the gun out and then went into the bathroom. I had the gun behind my back. She didn't notice it until I pressed it to her temple and pulled the trigger. Then, I closed the bathroom door behind me and left."

"You were going to take the elevator on up to the dinner dance. The ding signaled someone coming," Chris said. "So, you turned around and walked away, acting like you had just gotten there on another elevator ahead of me. You must have thought that would be perfect. You and I would find Peyton's body together."

"You have to admit, it was a good plan," Mason said.

"It was," Chris said. "But then you messed up."

"How?"

"You knocked on Peyton's office door, but you didn't knock on the bathroom door. That's because there was no point in knocking since she couldn't answer."

"Because I'd already killed her."

Silence fell over the room.

Helen's voice was barely above a whisper when she said, "Mason Davenport, I'm arresting you for the murder of Peyton Davenport."

CHAPTER TWENTY-EIGHT

The buzzing of the phone on the nightstand dragged Chris out of a deep sleep. With effort, he opened his eyes and rolled them up under his upper lids in a vain effort to break loose from his REM state.

Still, the phone persisted.

He rolled over in his bed and reached out from under the covers. A blast of cold air sent a shiver up his arm and down his spine.

The phone was far away on the other side of Emma, Thor, and Sterling.

"Aw, man!"

Seeing that it would be impossible to reach the phone while remaining in the comfort of his warm bed, Chris sat up and stretched over the sleeping bodies. As his hand made contact with the phone, it stopped ringing.

"Damn!"

He dropped back onto the bed and checked the call list. *Helen.*

There was no picture attached to her caller ID. *I'm going to need to fix that.*

Chris slipped out of the bed. The cold hardwood floor sent an icy shock up his legs and back and across his shoulders. Shrugging into his bathrobe, he hurried to shove his feet into his slippers.

He waited until he made it downstairs to the kitchen and had punched the button to start the coffee brewing before he called Helen back.

"You're up early," he told her after making a note of the time. It was only a few minutes after seven o'clock.

"We have a serial killer out there," Helen said. "Forensics ran that comparison of Ethel Lipton's DNA to the DNA found at Angela Romano's crime scene."

"The woman who was murdered in Lancaster, Pennsylvania, in 1995," Chris said.

"Who we believe to have been Carson's first victim. It's a familial match, Chris. Close enough to be a child of Ethel Lipton and it's male."

"Which, means unless Ethel Lipton has another son we don't know about, Carson killed Romano," Chris said.

"That's not all," Helen said. "Mabel Lipton's body was found in a motel room outside Frederick. She'd been stabbed multiple times. They put the time of death to be sometime yesterday afternoon."

"He killed his wife? Mabel was an aggressive woman. She reminded me of Ethel. She must have done something to make him snap. I hope he's not on a killing spree."

"Well," Helen said, "he got at least a twelve-hour head start. He could have jumped on a bus, stolen a car. There's no telling where he is. I'm heading up to Frederick."

"Do you want me to go with you?" Chris asked.

There was a long moment of silence before she answered, "I'd like for you to go. You know Carson better than any of us, but…" Her voice trailed off.

"But what?"

"You promised Sierra a riding lesson today," she said. "She'd be heartbroken if you canceled."

"We can't have that." Chris smiled. "Send her down and fill me in later."

She was about to disconnect the call when he stopped her. "Happy Valentine's Day."

"Happy Valentine's Day to you, too," she said with a smile in her voice.

"Have you got any plans?" The coffee had finished brewing. Chris took a mug out of the cabinet and filled it.

"Well, I was planning to go out with my guy," she said, "but he didn't dance with me at all last night—"

"Because you were too busy arresting a killer," Chris said.

"You were the one who decided to break the case open before dinner," she said. "By the way, I put in a really good word for you this morning with your old boss Regina."

"Are we talking bonus?" he asked.

"I don't think so," Helen said. "She had her sights set on the Krawford family. She was very disappointed that all she got was a dead changeling."

"Well," Chris said with a sigh, "you can't win them all."

"I'll say. I shaved my legs and all I got was mac and cheese for dinner."

"How about if I make it up to you?" Chris asked.

"What do you have in mind?"

"I've got reservations for seven at the Bavarian Inn."

"Seven? Sounds cozy."

Dressed in several layers of clothes, Nikki galloped down the back stairs and across the kitchen to give Chris a hug.

"My girls won't allow me to go out without them," he said before kissing Nikki on the tip of her nose. "Valentine's Day is a big deal in this house."

"Yeah," Nikki yelled in the direction of the phone. "It's a big deal here!"

"Are you and Sierra game to join us for dinner?"

"Sierra will be," she said. "Me? It depends on what you have planned for dessert."

"What do you want?"

"I was hoping you'd show me the new pulleys you got up in the hay loft," she said. "Sierra is getting dressed. She'll be there in about half an hour."

Chris chuckled. "I'll see what I can do about dessert."

After disconnecting the call, he took a sip of his coffee. He could hear Nikki putting on her riding boots, coat, and gloves in the mudroom.

"What horse are you going to teach Sierra on?" Nikki asked.

"Chewbacca," Chris said.

The chestnut mare was Katelyn's quarter horse. She was both gentle and frisky enough to give an inexperienced rider a good ride without fear of being thrown.

"Do you want me to saddle up Traveler for you, too?"

"No, you're going to be my sample rider," Chris said. "Saddle up Chewbacca and KitKat. Break out Nonni's riding equipment. Sierra can use that until she gets her own." He started up the stairs to his room to get dressed.

"Do I have to wear a dress for dinner tonight?" Nikki called upstairs.

"No, but you do have to dress up."

"No fair! I have to get dressed up to impress *your* girl-friend." The door slammed behind her.

On the second floor, Chris encountered Doris in the hall-way. For the Valentine's Day holiday, she donned her ruby red dressing gown with a faux fur collar and fancy high-heeled open-toed red slippers. As always, Sadie and Mocha flanked her on either side.

"I'm sorry to say, Christopher, I will not be joining you and the girls for dinner at the Bavarian tonight." With a coy smile, she smoothed her hair. "I lie. I'm not sorry."

"Mother, do you have a Valentine's date with a certain book club leader? I did notice the rose he gave you."

She flashed him a demure smile while sashaying past him.

"Should I count on Katelyn to join us for dinner tonight?"

"Never rush a woman to make up her mind." Doris made her way down the stairs.

"My mother," he sighed before continuing up to the top floor to get dressed in his riding clothes.

Emma was still asleep with both arms wrapped around Sterling. She had her face buried in his mane. Thor was curled up against the dog's stomach.

My family. With a shake of his head, Chris marveled at how quickly things change. The year before he was a relatively new widower living in the suburbs of northern Virginia and commuting to the city every morning.

One year later, he was living a life he loved with his girls—all of them—including his first love.

He opened his dresser drawer to take out his riding pants. By habit, he reached into his closet for his gun box to remove the handgun he always wore in a holster on his belt. He paused.

What would Sierra think? She shows up for a horseback riding lesson and I step out looking like John Wayne with a gun on my hip?

His daughters were used to seeing him wearing a weapon on his belt, under his coat, or in an ankle holster for in case he encountered someone from his undercover past. They probably assumed all dads packed concealed weapons at all times.

Granted, Sierra's mom was a state police officer but still, he didn't want to frighten her into thinking he was a big scary thug.

Chris put the case back on the shelf. *It's just in the field next to the barn. We'll be safe for a few hours.*

In the kitchen, Doris stopped at the counter to sniff the rose that she had put in a bud vase. With a soft smile, she remembered how Elliott had doted on her the entire night.

Kirk liked Elliott. He was a good friend. She reassured herself. *Kirk would be pleased.*

With a wistful sigh, she stepped to the coffeemaker.

Katelyn skipped down the stairs, hit the hardwood floors in her stocking feet and slid across the floor to collide into Doris. "Happy Valentine's Day, Nonni!" She hugged her.

"Happy Valentine's Day to you, sweetheart." Doris kissed her.

Katelyn slid to the refrigerator and pulled it open. "Cool rose. Is it from Dad?"

"No," Doris said with a coy grin.

"Who then?" Katelyn took a carton of orange juice out of the fridge. When she saw Doris's smile, she giggled. "Nonni, have you got yourself a boyfriend?"

"He's just a friend."

"Does he have a grandson my age?" Katelyn took a glass out of the cupboard. "Maybe we can double for Valentine's Day."

"What happened to Zack?"

"I kicked him to the curb," she said. "My heart is too precious to waste on someone so unworthy."

"That's my girl."

They bumped fists before hugging each other.

"Hey, Nonni, I figured out your talent."

"Oh, what?"

"Baton twirling."

Doris let out a loud laugh that startled Sadie and Mocha. "Dear, child! Have you ever seen me twirl a baton?"

The horses were skiddish that morning. Traveler, in particular, paced, threw back his head, and whinnied. Nikki dismissed their high spirits to nervousness from the roar of the wind. After wheeling the wheelbarrow over to the first stall, she stopped when she felt the trickle of hayseeds drop onto her head from the loft. She peered up and heard the rustle of something move across the floor. It was bigger than a barn cat.

Bobcats again!

She took her grandfather's old bull whip from the hook next to the door and slung it across her shoulder to use in case the cat was brave enough to show itself. Experience had taught her that wild animals, like bobcats and coyotes, were more afraid of humans than people were of them. She made a mental note to tell her father. He'd take care of it by capturing the bobcat and then turning it loose at a nearby wild nature preserve.

Nikki took Chewbacca out of her stall and went into the tack room to get the grooming box.

When she heard heavy footsteps across the barn floor, she assumed it was her father. Then, several of the horses whinnied and stomped inside their stalls. She heard Chewbacca wail and rear up.

Nikki ran to the doorway and came face to face with a man who she had never seen in her life.

His face and clothes were covered in dried blood. But even that was not as terrifying to the girl as the wild look in his eyes. They reminded her of a desperate predator lusting for prey to kill.

"You must be one of Chris's girls." He took a step toward her.

She backed into the room.

Blocking the doorway, he had her trapped.

Nikki's heart raced. Her first thought was of the horses. *If he kills me, what's he going to do to the horses—to her beloved KitKat?*

With one hand, she snatched the whip off her shoulder and lashed out with it as her grandfather had taught her. She had gotten so good with it that she was able to take aim and pick off one can of soda in the middle of a long row.

Her first lash left a gash across his face. With a wail, he grabbed the stinging wound with both hands while she escaped from the tack room. Once she was out, she turned around and continued her assault in hopes of trapping him inside the room until her father got there.

Insanity pushed through the pain of the attack. Carson advanced toward the doorway. Even as the whip slashed his flesh, he was determined to extract his revenge.

Mabel was dead. It was all Christopher Matheson's fault.

Carson reached out to her. As he expected, she snapped the whip which wrapped around his arm. Then, he grasped it and yanked her toward him to grab her.

"Let me go!" she screamed.

The roaring wind almost drowned out her call when the door flew open.

The gust of icy air slapped Carson across the face.

"Let go of her!" Chris's voice bounced off the rafters and walls.

Wrapping his arm around Nikki to hold her tight, Carson let out a laugh brimming with malice—only to have it turn into a cry of agony. Refusing to give up, Nikki bit down hard on his forearm with such force that her teeth tore through his flesh.

Chris had seen a lot of women fall victim to violence—many unnecessarily because they had been taught to always play by the rules. He made it a point to teach each of his girls that there are no rules when it comes to fighting for your life. Fight hard and fight dirty.

Nikki clamped down on Carson's forearm and held on while he shoved her away. Once she was free, Chris thrusted her toward the open barn door.

"Go get Nonni!" Chris tackled Carson in the midsection and the two men tumbled backward into the tack room.

Nikki ran for the door. As she sped past Chewbacca, she saw that the frightened horse was still tethered to the hitching post. Gasping for her breath, she quickly untied the lead with trembling fingers, and ran out the door with the horse galloping behind her.

Never had the barn yard felt as big as it did that morning. It was far enough for the reality of the situation to hit home.

Her father was doing battle with a mad man in the barn—like the mad man who'd taken her mother away from her—forever.

"Nonni!"

By the time Nikki burst into the house, tears were streaming down her face. Doris turned around in her seat at the kitchen table. Sensing the threat in the barn, Sadie and Mocha ran for the door only to find it shut. Their commands to get into the fight were ignored.

Her face wet with tears, Nikki rushed into Doris's arms and buried her face in the red fur of her collar.

"Nikki, dear, what's wrong?"

"D-dad-dy! B—bad—" Her voice shaking, Nikki found it hard to form the words.

Hearing a car pulling into the driveway, Katelyn got up from the table and looked out through the window. Sierra got out of her car and trotted up the path to the barn.

"Sierra's here," Katelyn said. "She's going into the barn."

"Crazy man in the barn trying to kill Dad!" Nikki screamed.

Katelyn ran for the door to let Mocha and Sadie out only for Doris to yell, "No!"

"No?" Katelyn swore she heard wrong.

Eerily calm, Doris strode into the mudroom and yanked open a drawer at the very top of the cabinet. "Sadie. Mocha." Both dogs sat at attention. "You stay and protect the girls. Sterling will protect Emma and Thor."

Doris extracted a forty-four Magnum, Smith & Wesson revolver from the drawer. Katelyn and Nikki swore it was the biggest gun they had ever seen.

"Don't just stand there, child." Doris checked the chambers. "Call the police to tell them we have a mad man in the barn." She threw open the door. "And we're going to need the medical examiner."

Chris didn't realize there was a whip in the fight until he had pinned Carson to the floor in the tack room, only to have him loop the whip around his neck. As Chris tried to pull away, Carson yanked him back and head butted him.

Fighting the white stars in his eyes, Chris delivered a one-two punch to Cason's head and scrambled off him. He rushed out of the tack room and slammed the door to lock Carson inside—only to have Carson block the door with his leg.

"I'm gonna take everyone you love, Matheson! Just like you did to me!"

Chris fought to untangle himself from the whip while slamming against the door to latch it. Rage out-powered his sense of pain so that Carson showed no reaction to the door continually hitting his thigh.

Freed from the whip, Chris tossed it aside. In the split second that he moved to throw it aside, Carson charged against the door. With a crash, Chris hit the floor—knocking the wind out of him.

Chris rolled over onto his back in the same instant that Carson rammed the blade of a shovel into the floor where his neck had been. Pulling his legs up, Chris planted his feet against Carson's chest and propelled him back. He then rolled over and scrambled to his feet to reach the gun chest that his father had stored near the door. Before he could get up onto his feet, Carson grabbed him from behind, pulled him up and rammed Chris's head into a stall door.

Chris heard a roar in his ears. His head seemed to explode inside his skull. He dropped to all fours.

Chris felt a tightening around his throat as Carson looped the reins of a bridle around his neck and yanked back to pull him up onto his knees. "Gotcha!" Carson breathed into his ear.

Cursing, Chris pulled at the reins to get air into his lungs while Carson dug his hand into his bloodied coat pocket. He loosened them enough for Chris to breathe while keeping them tight enough to control him.

"What are you going to do?" Chris asked with a raspy breath.

He knew the answer when he saw the black knife handle in Carson's hand. He pressed the button with his thumb and the bloody switchblade popped into view.

Carson pressed the cold blade against Chris's throat.

"Hey, Chris—" Sierra sang out as she walked through the barn door. Seeing Chris on his knees with Carson behind him and a bloody knife to his throat, she screamed. She turned to run only to collide with Doris, clad in her floor length red robe and her high-heeled slippers.

"Carson," Doris said, "I can see you've lost your mind. Did you think you would find it here?"

Carson pressed the blade of the knife against Chris's throat. "Tell her not to mess with me."

"Mom." Chris fought for enough air to talk. The lack of oxygen made him dizzy. The white blotches in front of his eyes made it difficult to concentrate. With every breath, the blade of the knife nipped against his skin.

"Don't worry, son," Doris said in a calm tone. "He's not going to hurt you.

Using the reins, Carson pulled Chris back against him. "He killed my Mabel."

"You killed her," Chris said.

"You killed her!" Carson pressed the knife against his throat.

Chris tried not to jump when he felt the sting of the blade slicing his neck and the trickle of blood drip down his throat.

"Everything was fine. I had everything under control. Mom was out of my life. Mabel and I were happy. And then you—you had to come along and start asking questions— wanting my DNA. Like you didn't think I'd figure it out. Suddenly, Mabel was asking questions. She was looking at me. Then, she saw it."

"Saw what?" Fighting to stay conscious, Chris shook his head.

"She saw under the mask," Carson said with a growl that seemed to come from his gut. "She saw the face under my mask. When she saw what I really was—all the love was gone! And all that other stuff was there. Shame! Disgust! Horror! Hatred! I told her to stop! She wouldn't stop looking at me like that!"

Carson screamed into Chris's ear. "You made me kill her! The only woman I ever loved, and you did that to me!"

"I'm so sorry, Carson," Chris said in a soft voice.

"No, you're not. But you will be. You took Mabel from me, and now I'm going to take everyone you love from you —and you're going to watch. You're going to see everyone die in front of your very eyes. Then, you'll know what it's like to lose everything."

"Carson," Doris said in the same maternal tone she used when reading a children's book during story hour at the library, "you're going to put down that knife and release Christopher now."

"Or what?"

"Or I'm going to put a bullet through your right eye, which will continue through your brain and out the back. It's going to make a big mess, and the noise will upset the horses."

"I'm giving the orders!" Carson tightened his grip on the reins. "Not you! I am!"

Chris struggled to loosen the leather straps cutting off his breathing.

"Christopher," Doris said in a strong voice. "Listen to me. Do you hear me, Christopher?"

The tone of her voice commanded his attention. Shaking his head, he blinked to clear the white spots dancing in front of his eyes. He strained to hear her through the roar in his ears. Across from him, he saw her raise her right hand to aim a Smith and Wesson revolver at them.

"Tell her to drop it." Carson pressed the knife against his throat. "Tell her to drop the gun now!"

"Mom, do as he says."

Doris peered at Chris, who nodded his head to her.

Slowly, Doris took her finger off the trigger and knelt to the floor. Keeping her eyes on Chris's, she placed the forty-four Magnum on the floor with her right hand.

As the gun touched the floor, Chris jerked to the side.

Doris's left hand shot out of her pocket and she fired off one shot from a pearl handled thirty-eight caliber Smith and Wesson revolver.

Chris felt the bullet whiz past his temple to hit Carson in the right eye, through his twisted brain, and out the back of his head. He dropped to the floor like a bag of feed.

As his senses cleared, Chris heard the wail of the police sirens and the horses shriek at the violence. Doris unwrapped the reins from around his throat and ordered Nikki, who had been lurking outside with Sierra, to get a rag to press against the cut on his neck.

"Christopher," Doris said in a soothing tone while cradling his head in her lap, "stay with us. Everything is okay. The girls are safe."

Tears in her eyes, Helen took Chris's hands into both of hers. "Chris, I'm here! Sierra called me."

"Mom, you should have seen Doris!" Sierra knelt next to them. "She dropped that guy with one shot—in high-heels, too!"

"The uniforms already told me, dear." Helen waved to the EMTs hurrying into the barn.

"Doris, how did you learn to shoot like that?" Sierra asked.

"Sharpshooting is my talent, dear."

CHAPTER TWENTY-NINE

You took Mabel from me, and now I'm going to take everyone you love from you—and you're going to watch. You're going to see everyone die in front of your very eyes.

The leather straps squeezed around his neck to shut off his oxygen.

Then, you'll know what it's like to lose everything.

With a gasp, Chris sat straight up in the bed.

"Chris, you're home." Helen jumped from his desk where she had been working on her laptop to sit next to him on the bed and take his hand. "Everything is fine. Everyone's okay."

"Carson?" Surprised by how raspy his voice was, he touched his neck and found that a bandage had been wrapped around it. He remembered the knife that Carson had pressed against it.

"He's dead," Helen said. "Doris took him out."

"He blamed me for killing Mabel. Was going to kill… everyone."

Helen slid in closer to him. "It's over. Everyone is safe." Her shuddering breath revealed the fear that had gripped her when Sierra had called with the news. "You're safe."

"Safe." Murmuring, he dropped back onto the bed.

She stretched out next to him and rested her head on his chest. "Do you remember the ambulance taking you to the hospital?"

Between Carson ramming his head into the stall door, and then almost being strangled, the events leading up to waking in his bed were in a fog. "What day is it?"

"Saturday."

"Valentine's Day." Chris threw back the blankets. "I've got reservations."

Helen eased him back down onto the bed. "We're taking care of everything. You got a serious blow to the head. You need to rest."

"Mom isn't making her tuna casserole, is she?" He lay his head back on the pillow and closed his eyes. The pounding in his head seemed to bounce from one side of his head to the other.

"I don't think so. She only does that when she wants you out of the house." Helen wrapped her arms around him and took in a deep breath. "Chris?"

"Huh?" He focused on the sound of her voice.

"I love you."

He ran his fingers through her hair. "I love you, too."

They lay in silence.

Helen lifted her head from his chest. "Chris?"

"Huh?" He blinked several times until his vision cleared. She was staring at him. "What?"

She cocked her head at him.

"Are you going to dump me again? It's because I live with my mother, isn't it?"

"No. I'm just wondering ..." Her voice trailed off. "Why haven't you asked me?"

"Ask you what?"

"About why—"

"What happened back then is back then. It's gone—in the past." He grasped her hand. "I love you. You've always been the one. Whatever happened—"

Helen blinked away the tears that came to her eyes. "The thing is we aren't past it."

"We'll get past it."

"Not until I tell you the truth."

"If you cheated on me—"

"Chris, I couldn't drag you into my life because you meant too much to me. You had so much going for you and I—" she hiccupped.

"I don't understand."

"You and I didn't meet until high school," she said. "By then, my background was a thing of the past. I was settled in with the Lawsons."

Chris cocked his head at her. "You were adopted. I knew that."

"But you didn't know all of it."

"Cause you never talked about it," he said. "I assumed that when you wanted to talk about it, you would. Just because you were adopted doesn't make you damaged goods."

She looked up at the ceiling. "I never talked about my background because it's humiliating. How do you tell a loving, functional family, who have good firm beliefs of right and wrong, that you're a phony?"

"You're not a phony, Helen."

"Come on." She sniffed. "You'd look at me and the Lawsons, and you saw a family just like yours."

Chris squinted his eyes and shook his head. "Maybe it's the blow to the head. I'm not understanding."

"Functional, Chris. Your family is so functional, it's scary. So are the Lawsons. And since I lived with them, you assumed I was, too."

"You broke my heart because my family is functional?"

"How do you tell the man you love and his perfect family that you come from the mother of all dysfunctional families?" She swallowed. "That my mother lives under a bridge somewhere, if she's even still alive?"

"You say it like you've just now said it."

"The Lawsons were good people," she said. "They're my folks. With them, I could almost believe I was normal."

"You are normal, Helen."

"Now," she said. "But we had a long hard way to go to get there."

Unsure if he heard her right, Chris shook his head. "We?"

"I have two younger brothers and a sister who were still in the system when I turned eighteen and moved to Morgantown. They weren't lucky enough to find permanent homes. I had promised them that as soon as I turned eighteen I would become their guardian, they'd come live with me, and go to college."

Chris sat up. "You hid your family from me?"

"Because I knew that you loved me enough to take them all on," she cried. "They were my responsibility—not yours. I couldn't let them down. They had no one except me and for me to turn my back on them. They were my family. Can't you see?"

As she started to slump over the pain she had caused, he took her into a tight hug. "How could you keep that from me?" he whispered into her hair. "Couldn't you see that I'd love them as much as I've loved you, because they were your family?"

"You thought I was this perfect, well-adjusted girl from a good loving functional family, just like yours."

"Have you met my mother?" He chuckled. "She blew a man's brains out today—wearing a red silk robe with a fur collar. We have a female rabbit named Thor."

She giggled into his shoulder as he rocked her in his arms. He took her face into his hands. Their eyes met. He kissed her softly on her lips. With a sigh, they lay back onto the bed, wrapped in each other's arms.

"I love you, Helen Clarke. You and your whole family—functional or not. When do I get to meet them?"

"Soon." She kissed him on the jaw before whispering in his ear, "I promise."

"Hey, Dad, are you awake?" Nikki yelled from the bottom of the stairs.

"We've got your Valentine's dinner for you," Sierra called.

Helen climbed out of the bed and pulled the comforter up to cover Chris. "They cooked dinner all by themselves."

"All of them? Together?"

"Doris spilled the beans about us." She rolled her eyes. "So much for sneaking around."

The pleasant scent of Italian cheese and buffalo wings reached the room before the four girls, three large dogs and a rabbit rushed in. They carried two pizza pans, a huge platter of buffalo wings, and two liters of soda. They set the food on the desk and dresser. Emma passed out paper cups, plates, and napkins to everyone.

"Nonni didn't cook any of this." Chris was suspicious that the food smelled good. Yet, he found it difficult that his daughters could carry off such a feast.

"No, we cooked everything." Nikki filled a paper cup with soda.

"With Elliott's help," Katelyn said while serving up two slices on a plate. "He made the pizza crust from scratch."

"Tossed it in the air and caught it like those guys you see on television." Sierra handed the plate to Chris.

"You need to leave room for dessert," Helen said. "I stopped at the Dairy Queen and picked up an ice cream cake."

"And we're taking you downstairs to watch whatever movie you want, because that's our gift to you." Emma placed Thor on the bed. The bunny was dressed in a bright red dress and cape reminiscent of Little Red Riding Hood.

"Where's Elliott and Mom?" Chris asked between bites of his pizza. "Elliott made a great crust. Shame that he's not getting any."

The girls exchanged wicked grins.

"Elliott and your mother are using your Bavarian Inn reservations," Helen said. "They're meeting another couple. Some guy named Bruce and his wife."

"Leaves more food for us." Chris took a buffalo wing from Emma's plate as she laid down next to him. "They're missing a great Valentine's Day party." He bit into the chicken wing.

"The last thing your mother said on her way out the door was to not wait up."

"That's my mom," Chris said. "Blows a man's brains out in the morning and goes out dancing in the evening."

"Speaking of that …" Pizza slice in hand, Sierra sat at the desk. "In the barn, you told your mom to put down that big huge gun. As soon as she did, I saw you jerk to the side and she shot the one she was hiding in her pocket. So you had to know she had a second gun. How'd you know?"

"Because Harry was my dad's gun," Chris said. "Mom prefers to use Annie when it comes to serious shooting."

"Harry?" Helen asked. "Annie?"

"The forty-four Magnum is Harry," Chris said. "When I saw Mom aiming Harry at Carson, I knew Annie was close by."

"Annie?"

"The pearl handled Smith and Wesson is Annie. That's Mom's gun."

"Your parents name their guns?"

Chris picked up Thor, splendid in her bright red dress and cape. "And you call my family functional."

CHAPTER THIRTY

Chris's mind was clear the next morning. He woke up to find the house strangely quiet and his bed empty. He slipped into his bathrobe and slippers, and made his way downstairs. He found Helen curled up on the sofa in front of the living room fireplace, which had a welcoming fire. She was surrounded by three dogs in various dog beds. Dressed in a pink faux fur vest, Thor was tucked in next to her.

"You're up." Helen closed the lid to her laptop and picked up a mug that was resting on the end table. "Coffee is over an hour old. I can make a fresh pot for you if you'd like." She gave him a hug and a quick kiss.

Chris read the time on the grandfather's clock. "I missed church."

"Your mom said to tell you that she'll teach your Sunday school class."

"The last time Mom taught my Sunday School class, I spent the next month unteaching the kids what she'd taught them."

"She is a trip." With a laugh, Helen tucked her laptop under her arm and led the way into the kitchen, with Sadie and Mocha falling in line behind her. "She offered to take Sierra to church with the girls. She jumped at it—especially when Doris threw in pancakes at iHop."

She placed her laptop on the kitchen counter on the way to the coffeemaker. "Ever since Sierra found out your mother is a sharpshooter—and was a beauty queen—she is now the biggest thing since texting."

"Were you elected, or did you volunteer to babysit me?" Chris climbed onto a stool at the counter.

"Volunteered, of course." With a wink, she lifted the lid of her laptop. "I've watched the gym's security recording of Rodney arriving and leaving the gym the night Felicia got killed a hundred times. He did it. I can tell by the smug look on his face when he looks right up at the camera before he leaves the gym. He thinks we're too stupid to figure out how he did it and it makes me so mad."

While Helen emptied the carafe and prepared a fresh pot of coffee, Chris viewed the recording on her laptop. The overhead angle of the film showed the front entrance, service desk, and juice bar of the athletic club. As gym members walked in, they would hold out their key tabs under the scanner to read their membership bar code. The recording had a date and time stamp across the lower right corner.

With his athletic bag slung over his shoulder, Rodney Bell, dressed in sweats, arrived at six-fifty-six in the evening, and scanned his gym key tag. Greeting the attendant behind the juice bar, he sauntered beyond the front desk and out of view.

The scent of freshly brewed coffee wafted through the kitchen.

"Later on the recording shows Rodney stopping at the juice bar and ordering a green smoothie before leaving," Helen said while slipping onto the stool next to his. "That time is eight-twenty-seven, the same time that the fire trucks arrived at the Bell home."

Chris fast forwarded through the recording to get to the shot of Rodney ordering the green smoothie.

"He orders the smoothie, talks to the trainer while she makes it, and then he leaves," Helen said.

"Did he take his bag into the cardio cinema?" Chris asked while slowing down the recording as he neared the point where Rodney would enter the shot again.

"He says he did. He walked straight back to the cinema and did the treadmill through the whole movie. Then he got a smoothie and headed straight home."

With narrowed eyes, Chris watched Rodney casually enter the screen from the same direction as he had left. As before, he was dressed in a heavy athletic jacket, pants, and shoes. Chatting and smiling at the pretty fitness instructor, Rodney dropped the athletic bag to the floor while taking out his money for the drink. "Did you talk to this trainer?"

"Yes," Helen said with a growl. "No, Rodney had never ordered a smoothie from them ever before. This was his first."

"Because you don't scan the gym's key tag when you leave," Chis said as he watched Rodney hand his money to the trainer. "He wanted to make sure she remembered him being there and leaving."

After paying for his drink, Rodney looked up in the direction of the security camera. A slim grin crossed his face as he drew the straw up to his mouth.

"You son of a bitch," Chris murmured.

"I talked to the arson investigator and you're right," Helen said. "The lamp did have a remote set up with their smart home network. I contacted the server through which the Bells had their network set up and guess what."

"You need a warrant to access their account," Chris said.

"Forensics says that if Rodney turned on that lamp remotely, there would be a footprint in the smart home network. He would have had to have set up the network to give that phone access. Even if he used a burner phone, tossed it afterwards, and deleted the phone from the network, there'd be a record of it and what it did."

"We're talking about a remote command from that phone telling that lamp to turn on."

"Precisely," Helen said. "The downside is—"

"If Rodney used a burner phone, he wouldn't have been so stupid to have bought it with a credit card," Chris said. "And he would have tossed it for sure by now."

"And knowing him," she said, "he'll argue that someone else—Opie—hacked into their network. Once again, it's a good theory, but you have to prove it."

Chris turned back to the security recording, which had looped back to the beginning. "He got out of that athletic club, killed Felicia, burned down the house, and got back inside—all without anyone seeing or there being any record."

"Yet, he says he had spent the whole time in the cardio cinema where it was dark, so no one can confirm he was there," she said.

Chris slowed down the recording to watch as Rodney reached out to scan the key tag on his way into the gym.

The coffee brewed, Helen went around the counter and took a mug out of the cabinet for Chris. As she traveled the length of the counter, she slid a large white envelope containing a picture of a dog and cat snuggling together on the front in his direction. "Doris said this is for you. It's got coupons and you need to pick up dog food today."

"Why does she always wait until the day she runs out of dog food to tell me to pick it up?" Chris paused the recording to study Rodney's image.

She poured the coffee into the mug for him. "I get advertisements like that all the time. I toss them without even opening the envelopes."

"Oh, but you should open them." Chris inserted his finger between the flap and the seal and tore it open. "You know those shoppers bonus cards you have?"

"I only have about a dozen or so." She extracted her keys from the front flap of her purse and shook it for him to see the wide variety of key cards. "If these stores want to give discounts to their shoppers, why don't they just lower their prices? Why do we have to sign up and carry this junk around on our key chains and remember to scan them to get the discount?"

"I say the same thing," Chris said with a shake of his head. "Mom is always giving me those tags and telling me to put them on my key chain." He extracted the coupons from the envelope. "But, you don't just get any discounts or coupons when you use the shopper's card. The bar code tells the store's computer system what you've bought. Based on that, the company's system creates an algorithm to tailor coupons just for you."

He held up a colorful coupon for twenty per cent off a brand of dog food. "We buy grain-free food that's pretty pricy. But since I buy it at this store and use their shopper's card, I get around twenty percent off every bag. That's about fifteen dollars. Now, if I bought a different brand at that store, the store's computer would note that and send me different coupons." He slapped the coupon down on the counter. "That's why I always make sure I use their key tag. The others," he shrugged his shoulders, "not so much."

Picking up his coffee, he rewound the recording again to when Rodney entered and held the key card under the scanner.

Chris paused the recording and narrowed his eyes to peer closely at the keys in Rodney's hand.

Helen watched Chris staring at the image on the screen. "Do you see something?"

"Maybe," he said in a low voice. He slid off the stool and headed for the back stairs. "I need to go to the club."

"Do you know how he left the gym without going in and out the front entrance?"

"No," he called down to her, "but I will. You're going to need a couple of warrants."

"A couple?"

"A couple."

Luckily, the gym's cardio cinema did not view their matinee until early that afternoon. So, Chris and Helen were able to examine the emergency exit, located along the wall opposite the screen, with the lights on.

"Perfect." Chris noted that the treadmills were lined up in the last row. They faced away from the emergency exit that led into the alley behind the club. "Once the movie got going, all he had to do was get off the treadmill, slip out the door, go kill Felicia, and return without anyone noticing that he'd left."

"The movie was an hour and eighteen minutes long," Helen said. "It takes seventeen minutes to drive from here to their house."

"And Rodney was driving a county sheriff's police cruiser, which people would have seen if he had driven that to the crime scene."

"Nobody saw a police cruiser in the neighborhood."

"How about Morgan Park?" Chris asked. "The park is right on the other side of the woods behind their house. The bike path is less than a mile from their back door. Rodney could run that in less than ten minutes—closer to seven."

"Seventeen minutes to drive there. Run in seven. That's twenty-four minutes there. Twenty-four minutes back." She added up the numbers on her phone's calculator. "Forty-eight minutes."

"Leaving about a half hour to rape and murder his wife, clean up any incriminating evidence, douse the house with gasoline, and set up the lamp and match to burn the place down."

"Except for the matter of how did Rodney leave this room." Helen gestured with a wave of her hand at the door. "The door not only sounds an alarm when it's opened, but it also sends a notification to the gym's security company, who then notifies the police and fire service."

Chris looked up at the lit exit sign above the door and examined the doorframe. There was a keypad on the wall next to the door. He rested his fingers on the keypad. "Unless you punch in the code first. Then the alarm won't go off. Who has the code?"

"The gym's manager, and it's on record with the security company."

"If the door is opened, and the alarm goes off, the security company calls the club to see if there's an issue," Chris said. "If it's a false alarm, the manager turns it off by inputting the code. Right?"

Helen nodded her head.

"But what if the manager isn't here?"

"The security company will give the code to the police or fire service at the scene or any employee that the manager deems okay to give it to."

A slow grin crossed Chris's face.

Helen's eyes grew wide. "And Rodney is the deputy sheriff. He's the police. But we still have to prove it."

"Get those two warrants and we will prove it." Checking the statistics on the fitness monitor he wore around his wrist, Chris climbed up onto one of the treadmills. "In the meantime, I'm going for a run."

Days later, Rodney Bell and his lawyer sat across the conference table from Helen and Chris at the state police barracks.

Eyeing Chris with contempt, the defense attorney asked Helen what he was doing there.

"Chris Matheson is a retired federal agent working on contract with the state police on this case," Helen said. "Since Felicia Bell's murder had the same MO as that of a series of murders, which the FBI had been investigating, he was brought onto the case."

"Opie Fletcher is a serial killer?" With a shake of his head, Rodney chomped on a toothpick. "Now I—"

"No, he's not," Chris said. "Opie Fletcher didn't kill anyone."

"Your own father named him as a suspect in Mona Tabler's murder," Rodney said. "Several witnesses heard him brag about it."

"How do you know my father listed Opie Fletcher as a suspect in Mona Tabler's murder?" Chris asked.

"He told me," Rodney said.

"No, he didn't," Chris said. "Because you weren't on the case. Dad only named suspects to those working the case."

"Mona Tabler's murder fell under the jurisdiction of the state police," Helen said. "We share case files with the local department when a request is made for a copy of the case file."

"I'm sure someone told you that Opie Fletcher had been a suspect in Mona's murder," Chris said. "That rumor had been flying around for years. But you didn't know the particulars of the case."

"That's why you requested a copy of the case file." Helen took a form from a folder and slid it across the table.

"I didn't request—"

"You requested it using the sheriff's name and email," Helen said. "But you were the one who used it. I saw it on your desk."

"After learning the specific details of how Mona Tabler was killed, you copied her murder when you killed Felicia," Chris said.

"My client has an airtight alibi for the time of the murder," the lawyer said.

Ignoring him, Chris said, "You set up Opie Fletcher. You recommended him for Felicia to hire to do yard work and odd jobs around the house so that he would have the opportunity to commit the murder."

"My client has never met Opie Fletcher."

"All the better for deniability," Chris said.

"Felicia's mother has stated that her daughter told her that your client gave her Opie Fletcher's phone number, saying he had run a background check on him," Helen said.

"Which is a lie," Rodney said. "Sylvia never did like me."

"For good reason," Helen said.

"Mothers never did like me." Rodney licked his lips. "But their daughters loved me." He winked at Helen. "Something you know about personally, huh, Helen?"

"Anything Felicia told her mother is inadmissible," the lawyer said. "It's hearsay."

Uttering a deep sigh of boredom, Rodney held up his hands. "Listen, Sheriff Bassett is still on sick leave. I have a police department to run. Can you prove that I left the gym and went out to Shepherdstown to kill my wife?"

"Oh yes," Chris said. "You were on the treadmill in the cardio cinema, watching a movie, when Felicia was murdered."

"That's right. Unfortunately, it was dark, so I have no witnesses who can say for certain I was there—"

"If you had gone out through the front door, then the security camera would have captured that," Chris said. "And, if you had gone out through the emergency exit in the cinema, then the alarm would have gone off and everyone would have heard it. The security company would have received a notice and called the gym to see if they needed to contact emergency services."

"And the alarm didn't go off and the security company didn't get any notices," Rodney said.

"Unless," Chris held up his finger, "you typed in the security code on the keypad next to the door. Then you can open the door without the alarm going off. There's a keypad on the inside and outside. Four-digit code. Both the gym manager and the security company have it."

Helen took a sheet of paper from the file resting in front of her and slid it across the table. "The security company keeps a log of who they hand out security codes to and when. One week before Felicia's murder, Sheriff Deputy Roger Williams, badge number 54-678, requested the security code to check out the premises after a 9-1-1 call of suspicious activity in the shopping center. He believed he saw someone entering the gym which was closed." She slid a written statement across the table. "Deputy Williams says he made no such request. No such call was made to 9-1-1. At the time of that request, Williams was on break. But then, as deputy sheriff, you had access to that information, didn't you, Rodney?"

"I seem to recall Williams checking Felicia out every time he saw her," Rodney said while rolling the toothpick between his fingers. "Maybe he made a move on her after we separated and he resented her rejecting him."

"Deputy Williams has an alibi for the night of the murder," Helen said.

"And so do I," Rodney said. "I was on the treadmill at the gym."

"That's right," Chris said. "You were on that treadmill the whole time and you never got off."

"For the entire movie."

"You didn't get off the treadmill for even a couple of minutes?"

"No."

"Are you sure about that?" Chris asked.

"Positive."

Chris shot a glance at Helen out of the corner of his eye. The corner of his mouth curled upward.

For the first time, a flicker of doubt crossed Rodney's face. "Do you have any witnesses saying I wasn't on the treadmill between seven o'clock and eight-thirty that night?"

"No," Chris said, "we have no witnesses saying that."

Helen opened the folder and slid a sheet of paper containing a bar graph over in front of Chris, who placed it in the center of the table for Rodney and his lawyer to see. He held up his arm to show them the fitness monitor he wore on his wrist.

"I noticed you wear a fitness monitor, Rod."

Rodney looked down at his monitor.

Folding his arms in front of him, Chris leaned across the table. "Do you know how they work?"

Rodney looked at him from out of the top of his eyes. His mouth tightened.

"It monitors your heart rate. The more physical you are, the faster your heart beats, the more calories you burn. The faster you run, the faster your heart rate is. The less active you are, the slower your heart rate is."

"And this bar graph proves my client killed his wife?" The lawyer chuckled.

"Actually," Chris said, "this is my chart. You see, the other day, I re-enacted Felicia's murder. To prove your client could do it. As luck would have it, the gym was playing the same movie. Helen got the code from the security company—"

"Because I'm the police," she said. "I gave them my badge number, and they gave it to me."

"I got on the treadmill," Chris continued, "and watched the start of the movie." He pointed to the beginning of the chart. "As you can see, for the first ten minutes, my heart rate is rising. Then, as soon as everyone in the cinema was focused on his or her workout and the movie, I slipped off the tread-mill, went to the door behind me, put in the code, and slipped out."

"What about my cruiser?" Rodney said. "All cruisers, including mine, are outfitted with a GPS so that dispatch can locate it when need be."

"That was a snap to disable," Chris said with a wave of his hand. "Disconnected the wire in less than a minute."

He pointed to the chart. "Now here's the interesting part." His finger followed the flow of the bar chart in which the tall red bars, marking the accelerated heart rate turned to blue and became shorter. "After I got in the car and started driving to Shepherdstown, my heart rate slowed down considerably. By the time I got to Morgan Park, it was a resting heart rate. Then, I parked the cruiser, less than a mile away from your house, Rodney."

The bars once again turned red and rose in height. "This is where I started running. As you can see, my heart rate went up again for seven and a half minutes until I reached the back door of the house." He pointed to where it turned blue and dipped again. "This is when I went into the house. I'm sure when we see your client's chart, his heart rate will accelerate again as he rapes and murders his wife. Then once again my heart rate increased for eight minutes when I ran back to the cruiser." Chris moved his finger along the chart to where the bars turned blue. "Then we have a resting heart rate when I drive back to the gym, used the code to go in through the back door. Then, it went up again when I got on the treadmill and spent the last twenty minutes running until the end of the movie."

The lawyer looked over at Rodney, who had covered up his fitness monitor with his hand. "Good theory. Only proves that he could—"

Helen slapped another chart down on top of Chris's. "Your client's heart rate for the time of the murder is almost identical to Chris's."

When the lawyer opened his mouth to object, she held up her hand. "We got your client's data from his fitness monitor with a warrant."

"His heart rate is slightly higher than mine," Chris said. "Of course, stress does play a factor in one's heart rate. The stress of having just killed your wife. Not knowing if the match is going to light when you turn on the lamp remotely and burn up any evidence you may have inadvertently left. Generally," he leaned over to compare the two charts, "they are identical."

"Okay, I lied." Rodney shoved the two charts back at Chris. "I took a couple of breaks and got off the treadmill. That explains why my heart rate slowed down those times."

"You just told us numerous times that you were running the whole time," Helen said.

"Unless you can prove I was at the house, killed Felicia, and set the fire while I was at the gym, all this chart proves is that I took a couple of breaks at the gym."

Chris said in a casual tone, "We can prove you started the fire while at the gym."

Rodney chuckled. "I started the fire in Shepherdstown while miles away at the gym?"

"Yes, you did," Chris said. "The arson investigator reports that the bedroom lamp was set up in the network so that it could be voice activated using the smart home network. You set it up."

Rodney paused while looking from one of them to the other.

"No point in denying it, Rodney," Chris said. "The server was set up using your email, and the account is in your name."

Rodney took the toothpick out of his mouth. "Yeah. So?"

Chris held up his phone and waved it for Rodney and his lawyer to see. "The lamp could also be turned on and off using an app downloaded onto your smart phone."

"And I assume you requested a copy of my client's cell phone records to show that he sent a remote command to turn on the lamp to start the fire?"

"No, he didn't do that," Chris said.

The lawyer chuckled. "I'm sure he didn't."

"He used a burner phone."

"Do you have any credit card receipts to prove that he purchased the phone that started the fire?"

"Not any receipts. No, no credit card receipts. Your client was much too smart to use his credit card. He knew it'd create a paper trail."

The lawyer stood. "We're done here."

Rodney leaned over to tell Chris. "Better luck next time, Buddy."

"I notice you have a frequent shoppers card for SuperMart," Chris told Rodney as he started to rise from the table.

Rodney and his lawyer stopped.

Chris took his keys out of his pocket and held up the key tag for the major department store. "When you use this key tag you get special discounts on what you buy." He grinned up at the two men. "That means the store keeps track of what you   buy so that they know what coupons would be most useful for you."

Helen opened the case file and slid a print out across the table. "We got a warrant for your client's records from

SuperMart. Less than a week before his wife was murdered, he bought a prepaid phone. No, he did not use his credit card. He paid cash, but he did use his frequent shoppers card."

The lawyer's eyes were wide when he picked up the print out.

Rodney dropped down into his seat. The toothpick dropped from his mouth, tumbled to the floor, and rolled under the table.

"That forty cents you got off on the phone using your frequent shoppers card is going to cost you twenty-five to life, Buddy," Chris said.

"Not only did your client create a paper trail using the shoppers card," Helen said, "but the brand he bought automatically activated the phone when he purchased it. The date and the time the phone was activated matches with the date and time he purchased it using his shoppers card."

"And that phone's serial number was recorded on the server when he connected the device with his smart home network," Chris said. "Even though he deleted the phone from the network and tossed it after the murder, its digital fingerprint is still there. The system has a record of the phone and its serial number, which led us to the store where it was purchased and activated," — He held up the store printout — "which matches the data on his shoppers card."

Chris leaned across the table. "We can connect you to the phone used to remotely send the command to turn on the lamp which lit the match which started the fire after you left Felicia for dead."

"Only she was still alive," Helen said. "When you sent the code, she got trapped in the fire and jumped out a second floor window to escape."

Slowly, the lawyer lowered himself into the chair.

All cockiness dissolved from Rodney Bell's demeanor.

The four of them sat in silence.

"That bitch took everything from me. The house. The boys." He frowned. "Neither of my sons will speak to me."

Chris started to ask, "Have—"

"She stole my dreams!"

"Your dreams?" Helen asked.

"Do you remember our dreams, Chris?" Rodney's eyes were wide with anger. "You and me. Together. We were going to be big bad FBI agents and travel all over chasing down the biggest baddest bad guys." His hand shook when he pointed at Chris. "You got to live your dream. I didn't be—"

"They rejected your application," Chris said in a soft voice. "No one knows why."

"I know!" Rodney brought both hands down on the tabletop with a crash. "Because of her! Felicia got herself knocked up so that I'd have to marry her. That's why the FBI turned me down!"

"You don't know that, Rodney," Chris said.

"Yes, I do!" Rodney's face was red. "I figured it out." His hand was shaking with rage when he pointed at Chris. "They picked you, but they rejected me. We were both in the same stuff in school. We served in the same unit in the Army Rangers. We both had good physicals. Everything was equal. The only difference was that I was married with a kid, and you were free and single with no strings holding you back."

"You murdered Felicia because the FBI turned you down twenty-four years ago?" Helen's eyes were filled with tears.

"Do you know why Felicia left you for me all those years ago?" Rodney asked Chris.

Unable to find his voice, Chris shook his head.

"She told me that you were too good. Too nice."

Chris furrowed his brow in confusion.

Rodney gazed at the two-way mirror behind Chris. "The lies, deception, sneaking around turned her on." His voice was soft. "Little did we know back then that it'd be the bad boy who'd end up killing her. Ain't it ironic?"

Epilogue

"Who's the babe?" Ray rolled his wheelchair back from the table when he saw Helen walk into the next book club meeting with her hand in Chris's.

"That's Helen," Francine said with a knowing grin. "She's Chris's friend." She put a special emphasis on the word 'friend.' She dumped a couple of handfuls of popcorn into a small bowl, which she placed on the floor for Sterling, their K-9 member.

"I don't care who Chris is sleeping with," Ray said. "She's obviously not retired. Way too young. I have cheese in my fridge older than she is."

"Need we remind you, Chris, that you're still on probation." Jacqui held out a goblet to Bruce, who was opening a bottle of white wine. "And what is the number one rule for our book club?"

"Never talk about the Geezer Squad," Helen said.

There was a collective gasp around the room. Obviously, Chris has talked about the Geezer Squad. That was the only way Helen could have known about it.

"This is all Elliott's fault," Bruce said. "He's the one who brought this young scamp into our club. Where is Elliott by the way?"

"He's teaching a concealed carry gun class to our church women's group," Chris said. "It's the only night they could reserve the shooting range."

"A *gun* class to a *church women's* group?" Bruce's eyes grew wide.

"That's one bunch of church ladies who know how to scare the hell out of you," Francine said.

"I like women who know how to take care of themselves." Ray turned to Chris. "Are any of them single?"

"You're all missing the point," Jacqui said. "Elliott ditched us for Doris. Didn't I tell you? As soon as a man falls in love, he becomes worthless for anything."

"Helen offered to come in his place," Chris said.

Helen held up a mystery that she was holding in her hand. "I read the book."

The members of the group exchanged glances filled with uncertainty.

"We can't kill her," Francine said.

"Why not?" Bruce said.

"Because she's a lieutenant with the state police," Francine said. "Besides, she's Chris's girlfriend."

"No problem," Ray said. "We'll kill him, too. He's the big mouth who blabbed about us. Jacqui, have you got any lye in your trunk?"

"But I like Chris," Francine objected. "He's got such pretty eyes and a cute butt."

While the group compared methods of disposing of their bodies, Helen extracted a case file from her bag. She handed it to Chris, who held it up for them all to see.

"Helen brought a cold case that she'd like us to heat up for her."

The Geezer Squad stopped. In silence, they exchanged questioning glances.

With a wide grin, Bruce picked up a glass of burgundy wine and crossed the room to hold it out to Helen.

"Welcome, to the Geezer Squad, my dear."

The End

ABOUT THE AUTHOR

Lauren Carr

Lauren Carr is the international best-selling author of the Mac Faraday, Lovers in Crime, and Thorny Rose Mysteries—over twenty titles across three fast-paced mystery series filled with twists and turns!

Now, Lauren has added one more hit series to her list with the Chris Matheson Cold Case Mysteries. Set in the quaint West Virginia town of Harpers Ferry, *Ice* introduces Chris Matheson, a retired FBI agent, who joins forces with other law enforcement retirees to heat up those cold cases that keep them up at night.

Book reviewers and readers alike rave about how Lauren Carr's seamlessly crosses genres to include mystery, suspense, crime fiction, police procedurals, romance, and humor.

Lauren is a popular speaker who has made appearances at schools, youth groups, and on author panels at conventions. She lives with her husband, and three dogs, including the real Sterling, on a mountain in Harpers Ferry, WV.

Check Out
Lauren Carr's Mysteries!

All of Lauren Carr's books are stand alone. However for those readers wanting to start at the beginning, here is the list of Lauren Carr's mysteries. The number next to the book title is the actual order in which the book was released.

Joshua Thornton Mysteries

Fans of the *Lovers in Crime Mysteries* may wish to read these two books which feature Joshua Thornton years before meeting Detective Cameron Gates. Also in these mysteries, readers will meet Joshua Thornton's five children before they had flown the nest.

1) A Small Case of Murder
2) A Reunion to Die For

Mac Faraday Mysteries

3) It's Murder, My Son
4) Old Loves Die Hard
5) Shades of Murder
     (introduces the Lovers in Crime: Joshua Thornton
     & Cameron Gates)
7) Blast from the Past
8) The Murders at Astaire Castle
9) The Lady Who Cried Murder
     (The Lovers in Crime make a guest appearance
     in this Mac Faraday Mystery)
10) Twelve to Murder
12) A Wedding and a Killing
13) Three Days to Forever

15) Open Season for Murder
!6) Cancelled Vows
17) Candidate for Murder
  (featuring Thorny Rose Mystery detectives
  Murphy Thornton & Jessica Faraday)

Lovers in Crime Mysteries

6) Dead on Ice
11) Real Murder
18) Killer in the Band

Thorny Rose Mysteries

14) Kill and Run
  (featuring the Lovers in Crime in
  Lauren Carr's latest series)
19) A Fine Year for Murder
22) Murder by Perfection

Chris Matheson Cold Case Mysteries

21) ICE

A Lauren Carr Novel

20) Twofer Murder

MURDER BY PERFECTION

A Thorny Rose Mystery

Frustrated with their busy schedules, Murphy Thornton and Jessica Faraday attempt to find togetherness taking a couple's gourmet cooking course at the Stepford Kitchen Studio. Successful Chef Natalie Stepford is the model of today's modern woman—perfect in looks, home, and business.

When Natalie ends up dead, the Thorny Rose detectives peel back the layers of Natalie Stepford's life to discover that the pursuit of perfection can be deadly.

Coming Summer 2018!

Made in the USA
Monee, IL
10 September 2021

77714341R00203